I0577151

Austin Dobson, William Hogarth

William Hogarth

Austin Dobson, William Hogarth

William Hogarth

ISBN/EAN: 9783742813756

Manufactured in Europe, USA, Canada, Australia, Japa

Cover: Foto ©Andreas Hilbeck / pixelio.de

Manufactured and distributed by brebook publishing software
(www.brebook.com)

Austin Dobson, William Hogarth

William Hogarth

WILLIAM HOGARTH

BY

AUSTIN DOBSON

" Vice, if it e'er can be abash'd,
Must be or *Ridicul'd*, or *Lash'd*."
SWIFT.

SAMPSON L

ST. DUNST

F

CHISWICK PRESS:—C. WHITTINGHAM AND CO., TOOKS COURT,
CHANCERY LANE.

TO

COSMO MONKHOUSE

IN TOKEN OF

MANY YEARS OF UNINTERRUPTED FRIENDSHIP

THIS VOLUME IS INSCRIBED

PREFACE.

NE of the first lessons experience teaches to the maker of books is a wholesome distrust of the possible pitfalls of a Preface. If he be wise, he generally contrives to dispense with that decoration altogether. Yet there are occasions when, " by way of precaution, not puff" (as Hogarth would have said), some preliminary explanations are absolutely required. This is the case with the present volume. It is the amplification of a smaller book published, more than ten years since, in the "Great Artists" series. The limits of that series were inexorable; and it was not feasible, in the circumstances, to do more than give a summary or skeleton of Hogarth's life and work. In the re-issue now offered to the reader, an attempt has been made to clothe this skeleton, if not completely, at least sufficiently. With exception of the introductory chapter, which has only been verbally revised, the " Memoir " has been entirely re-written, with the effect of extending it to more than double its original length. To have ex-

*tended it still farther, would not have been difficult,
but since this would simply have increased the already
disproportionate space allotted to the discussion of
Hogarth's work, as compared with that occupied by
the meagre story of his life—it has been thought
better to restrict it to its present form. The Author
desires to add that, in remodelling the book, and
incorporating into it such fresh information as has
come to light during the last decade, he has freely
made use of the fugitive articles on the subject written
by himself during that period. This he has done,
in some cases, without great alteration of the words.*

*The above remarks apply exclusively to the "Memoir,"
now described as "Part I." "Part II.," which
contains the "Bibliography" and "Catalogues," is
virtually new. In the earlier sketch the "Bibliography" occupied little more than a page: it here
occupies thirty-nine pages. The "Catalogue of
Prints," which was previously comprised in eight pages,
at present extends to eighty-eight pages; while the
"Catalogue of Paintings" has been increased from two
pages and a half to twenty-six pages. These figures of
themselves will show that the additions have been considerable. In both the "Bibliography" and "Catalogue
of Prints" the actual books and engravings have as a
rule been consulted; and it is only where direct inspection
has proved impracticable, that the particulars given*

*have been derived from any other source. As respects
the "Catalogue of Paintings," every effort has been
used to render it comprehensive, but the Author does
not pretend to have included in it every picture which
has ever been proclaimed to be Hogarth's by its over
sanguine possessor. The principle upon which the
two Catalogues have been compiled will be found to
be indicated in the introductory notes.*

*It remains to specify the various obligations which
have been incurred in the progress of the work. To
Mr. G. A. Aitken, whose fortunate discovery of an
advertisement in the "Craftsman" gave the first clue
to the curious rectification of the date of "A Harlot's
Progress;" to Mr. Robert Hoe, who sent the Author
a number of valuable books from New York; to Mr.
R. W. Ketton of Felbrigge Park, Norfolk; to Mr.
A. H. Bates of Edgbaston; to Mr. W. Mitchell;
to Mr. F. Locker-Lampson; to Colonel F. Grant;
to the Officials of the Reading and Print Rooms at the
British Museum; and to the Author's friend and
counsellor in this and many previous enterprises, Mr.
R. F. Sketchley of the Dyce and Forster Library,
South Kensington—his most cordial thanks are specially
due. He has also to thank Messrs. Macmillan,
Messrs. Cassell, and Messrs. Harper of New York
for their obliging permission to use certain blocks; and
he desires to record the fact that their rights are in no*

way prejudiced by the appearance in this place of the illustrations in question. Lastly, it is his pleasant duty to express to Messrs. Walker and Boutall, of Clifford s Inn, his grateful sense of the anxious care and invariable skill with which they have selected and employed the different methods of reproducing the pictures and plates. Only those accustomed to Hogarth's manner can fully appreciate the way in which these gentlemen have endeavoured, in spite of the drawbacks of a reduced scale, to give what Hogarth gave, without essential loss of his characteristics as an artist and an engraver.

A USTIN DOBSON.

Ealing, November, 1891.

CONTENTS.

I. MEMOIR.

II. Bibliography and Catalogues.

List of Illustrations.

Photogravures.

Other Illustrations.

[** The above illustrations, when not from the original pictures, are copied from prints in the British Museum or in the collection of the author. This, of course, does not apply to the views of localities, etc. The cut of Hogarth's mulberry-tree, it should be added, is here printed by permission of Messrs. Harper of New York.]

PART I.

MEMOIR.

B

WILLIAM HOGARTH.

CHAPTER I.

INTRODUCTORY.

HOGARTH'S PUNCH-BOWL.

THE greatest of our native pictorial satirists has not wanted for commentators and expounders of all sorts, even of those

> "who view
> In Homer more than Homer
> knew."

The two earliest—Jean Rouquet, the enameller, who described some of Hogarth's plates for the use of foreigners, and the Rev. Dr. Trusler, who "moralized" the majority of them—are more noteworthy for their respective relations with the painter and the painter's widow than for any special merit of their own. Horace Walpole, who followed these, was, on the contrary, a critic of a higher order.

But he reserved his enthusiasm too exclusively for fashionable amateurs like Lady Di. Beauclerk, and the Hon. Mrs. Damer, to do real justice to the plain-spoken artist of Leicester Fields. Georg Christoph Lichtenberg, a German *littérateur* of considerable sagacity, and John Ireland, the Westminster collector, were thoroughly sympathetic, and have written exhaustively of their theme; but both are somewhat too prone to use it as a peg on which to hang fantastic and often irrelevant disquisition. The great body of Hogarth fact is to be found in the successive " Anecdotes " of the antiquary and printer John Nichols, and in the volume issued in 1833 by his son, John Bowyer Nichols. In the case of the former, considerable allowance must be made for the malice of his assistant and adviser, George Steevens, the critic, who, it has been truly said, "seems to have taken pleasure in mingling his own gall with the milk of his coadjutor's narrative." As to the rest, Samuel Ireland, the author of the " Graphic Illustrations," is to be regarded rather as " a snapper-up of unconsidered trifles " than a contributor of genuine information; while the commentaries to Cook's and Clerk's editions are practically worthless. Besides these, there are the lively, but in some respects inaccurate, life by Allan Cunningham (edited not long since by the late Mrs. Charles Heaton); the brief though technically authoritative sketch in Redgrave's " Century of Painters;" the picturesque pages contributed to the " Cornhill " by Mr. Sala; and—not to mention some minor names

and anonyms—the deservedly well-known essays of
Charles Lamb, Hazlitt, Thackeray, and James
Hannay.

At first sight, then, it would appear that enough
has already been said respecting a subject which has
occupied so many pens. And, in truth, were a
"Hogarth Society" to be founded, it may be doubted
whether any substantial addition could now be made
to the slender stock of existing data respecting the
painter's life. It is not likely, for example, that any
new light—if new light be needed—will ever be
thrown on that undignified quarrel with Wilkes and
Churchill. Nor can it be supposed, because we are able
to regard the much-abused *Sigismunda* without the
passion which seems to have animated the partisans
of the "Black Masters," that anything important will
transpire to clear materially that clouded reputation.
Some day, no doubt, a critic, with (or without) the
transfiguring enthusiasm of a Sainte-Beuve, will take
up the "Analysis," and demonstrate once more that
it contains much common-sense and some unregarded
verities; but it will scarcely again enter into general
circulation, or be commended in pompous commonplace by our latter-day Warburtons and Hoadlys.
Nevertheless, if the main circumstances of the
painter's career should still remain unaltered, there
must always be a side of his work which will continue
to need interpretation. (In addition to painting the
faults and follies of his time, he was pre-eminently
the pictorial chronicler of its fashions and its furniture.
The follies endure; but the fashions pass away. In

our day—a day which has witnessed the demolition of Northumberland House, the disappearance of Temple Bar, and the removal of we know not what other time-honoured and venerated landmarks— much in Hogarth's plates must seem as obscure as the cartouches on Cleopatra's Needle. Much more is speedily becoming so; and without some guidance the student will scarcely venture into that dark and doubtful rookery of tortuous streets and unnumbered houses—the London of the Eighteenth Century.

Were it not beyond the reasonable compass of a methodical memoir, it would be a pleasant task to loiter for a while in that vanished London of Hogarth, of Fielding, of Garrick;—that London of Rocque's famous map of 1746, when "cits" had their country-boxes and "gazebos" at Islington and Hackney, and fine gentlemen their villas at *Marybone* and *Chelsey;* when duels were fought in the "fields" behind the British Museum, and there was a windmill at the bottom of Rathbone Place. We should find the Thames swarming with noisy watermen, and the streets with thick-calved Irish chairmen; we should see the old dusky oil-lamps lighted feebly with the oil that dribbled on the Rake when he went to Court; and the great creaking sign-boards that obscured the sky, and occasionally toppled on the heads of his Majesty's lieges beneath. We should note the sluggish kennels and the ill-paved streets; and rejoice in the additional facilities afforded for foot-passengers at the "new buildings near *Hanover* Square." We might watch King George II.

yawning in his Chapel Royal of St. James's, or follow
Queen Caroline of Anspach in her walk on Constitution Hill. Or we might turn into the Mall, which is
filled on summer evenings with a *Beau-Monde* of
cinnamon-coloured coats and pink *négligés*. But the
tour of Covent Garden (with its column and dial in
the centre) would take at least a chapter, and the pilgrimage of Leicester Fields another. We should
certainly assist at the Lord Mayor's Show; and we
might, like better folk before us, be hopelessly
engulfed in that great westward-faring crowd, which,
after due warning from the belfry of St. Sepulchre's, swept down the old Tyburn Road on "Execution Day" to see the last of Laurence Shirley,
Earl Ferrers, or the highwayman James M'Lean.
It is well, perhaps, that our limits are definitely
restricted.

Moreover, much that we could do but imperfectly
with the pen, Hogarth has done imperishably with
the graver. Essentially metropolitan in his tastes,
there is little notable in the London of his day of
which he has not left us some pictorial idea. He
has painted the Green Park, the Mall, and Rosamond's Pond. He has shown us Covent Garden
and St. James's Street; Cheapside and Charing
Cross; Tottenham-Court Road and Hog-Lane, St.
Giles's. He has shown us Bridewell, Bedlam, and
the Fleet Prison. Through a window in one print we
see the houses on Old London Bridge; in another
it is Temple Bar, surmounted by the blackened
and ghastly relics of Jacobite traitors. He takes us

to a cock-fight in Bird Cage Walk, to a dissection in Surgeon's Hall. He gives us reception-rooms in Arlington Street, counting-houses in St. Mary Axe, sky-parlours in Porridge Island, and night-cellars in Blood-Bowl Alley. He reproduces the decorations of the Rose Tavern or of the Turk's Head Bagnio as scrupulously as the monsters at Dr. Misaubin's museum in St. Martin's Lane, or the cobweb over the poor-box in Mary-le-bone Old Church. The pictures on the walls, the Chinese nondescripts on the shelves, the tables and chairs, the pipes and punchbowls, nay, the very tobacco and snuff, have all their distinctive physiognomy and prototypes. (He gives us, unromanced and unidealized, "the form and pressure," the absolute details and accessories, the actual *mise-en-scène*, of the time in which he lived.[1])

But he has done much more than this. He has peopled his canvas with its *dramatis personæ*—with vivid portraits of the more strongly-marked actors in that cynical and sensual, brave and boastful, corrupt and patriotic age. Not, be it understood, with its Wolfes and Johnsons,—he was a humourist and a satirist, and goodness was no game for his pencil,—rather with its Lovats and Chartres, its Sarah Malcolms and its Shebbeares. He was a moralist

[1] "It was reserved to Hogarth to write a scene of furniture. The rake's levee-room, the nobleman's dining-room, the apartments of the husband and wife in *Marriage A-la-Mode*, the alderman's parlour, the poet's bed-chamber, and many others, are the history of the manners of the age." So says Horace Walpole ("Anecdotes," etc. 1771, p. 74), and in this, at least, he was an unimpeachable authority.

after the manner of eighteenth-century morality, not savage like Swift, not ironical like Fielding, not tender-hearted at times like Johnson and Goldsmith ; but unrelenting, uncompromising, uncompassionate. He drew vice and its consequences in a thoroughly literal and business-like way, neither sparing nor extenuating its details, wholly insensible to its seductions, incapable of flattering it even for a moment, preoccupied simply with catching its precise contortion of pleasure or of pain. In all his delineations, as in that famous design of Prud'hon's, we see Justice and Vengeance following hard upon the criminal. He knew, no doubt, as well as we, that not seldom (humanly speaking) the innocent are punished and the guilty go at large. What matter! that message should not be preached—by him at any rate. So he drew his "Bogey" bigger, if possible, and drove his graver deeper in the copper.

What antecedents, what progress of circumstance, what special conditions produced this unique and individual artist in an era of mediocrities like Knapton and Shackleton, Highmore and William Kent?—in an age given over to auctioneers and art charlatans, to adventurers like Heidegger of the "Masquerades," to Italian singers and French ballet-dancers? In the chapters that follow he shall speak for himself; but when all is said and done, the reader will probably find no more satisfactory reply to the question than this :— that he was a great and an exceptional genius, not to be entirely accounted for by any preconceived theory respecting his race, his epoch, or his environment.

CHAPTER II.

BIRTH, EDUCATION, AND EARLY YEARS.

OME time before the year 1796, John Ireland, of 3, Poets' Corner, Westminster, received from Mary Lewis, Mrs. Hogarth's cousin and executrix, then resident in Hogarth's house at Chiswick, a number of documents which had been religiously preserved by his widow. They included the manuscript of the "Analysis of Beauty," corrected by the author, and among the rest a brief sketch of his life. Apart from the story of his engravings it was not an eventful one; but the fragmentary account which he has left of it is thoroughly characteristic, and throws much interesting light_upon his mode of work, and the singular—in some respects the unique —training for his vocation which he adopted. As far as we can, we shall interweave it with the facts of the following memoir.

"The family of *Hoggerd*, ancestors of the celebrated William Hogarth, were tenants of this abbey [*i.e.*, Shap Abbey in Westmoreland] at the time

of the Dissolution, and several members of it still
[1814] continue in the neighbourhood." Thus
the authors of the "Beauties of England and
Wales" at p. 138 of their fifteenth volume. Nichols
and the earlier biographers are not as specific, nor
do they travel so far back. The Hogards, Hogarts,
or Hogarths,[1] they tell us, came originally from
Kirkby Thore, which is not very far from Shap;
and Hogarth's father, Richard Hogarth, was the
third son of a yeoman farmer who lived in the vale
of Bampton, about fifteen miles north of Kendal.
His mother's maiden name, as given in an old
Bible which once formed part of the collection of Mr.
H. P. Standly of St. Neots, was Ann Gibbons. Of
the rest of his relatives little is known; but he had
a quasi-literary uncle in Thomas Hogarth ("Auld"
or "Ald Hogart") of Troutbeck, a rustic dramatist
and satirist, some of whose "Remnants of Rhyme"
were published at Kendal as late as 1853, from manuscripts "preserved by his Descendants." Richard
Hogarth himself was educated at Archbishop

---

[1] As to the derivation of the name, a correspondent of "Notes
and Queries," 27 Sept., 1890, writes,—"If Hoggerd is the original,
the meaning would seem to be Hogherd (= swine-herd); if
Hoggarth or Hoggard, it might be "hog-enclosure;" if Hogarth,
possibly it might be "house enclosure." Nichols ("Anecdotes."
1781, p. 7) affirms that the family name was Hogart, but that
Mrs. Richard Hogarth, before the birth of her son, prevailed
upon her husband to liquefy it into Hogarth. Hartley Coleridge,
however, gives another, and perhaps more plausible explanation.
According to him, Hogart is only the north-country pronunciation
of Hogarth. (See, for the entire passage, the " Bibliography " in
Part II. under " Hogarth, Bewick and Green.")

Grindal's Free School of St. Bees, and subsequently kept a school in his native county. This proving unsuccessful, he came to London, his travelling companion being Dr. Gibson, brother of that Bishop Gibson (the " Codex " of the caricaturists) whose " Pastoral Letter " serves such base uses in Scene III. of *A Harlot's Progress*. In London, according to the register of Births at Great St. Bartholomew's, West Smithfield, "in Barth^w Closte, next doore to Mr. Downinge's the Printer's, November ye 10th, 1697," was born his famous son. William Hogarth was baptized, in the still existent font of the church, "ye 28th Novr. 1697." [1]

Two daughters,—Mary, who was born on the 23rd November, 1699, and also baptized, on the 10th December, at St. Bartholomew's; and Ann, born in October, 1701, and baptized on the 6th November at St. Sepulchre's,—followed their brother William. [2]

[1] Colonel J. L. Chester, in " Notes and Queries," 6th March, 1880.

[2] Little has been preserved with regard to Hogarth's sisters beyond the facts, that he painted one or more portraits of them, hereafter mentioned, and that the younger, Ann, survived him. The following inscription, taken from a shop bill executed by him for them about 1725, shows at least that they were independent of their brother :—" Mary & Ann Hogarth from the old Frock shop the corner of the Long Walk facing the Cloysters, Removed to ye King's Arms joyning to ye Little Britain-gate, near Long Walk. Sells ye best & most Fashionable Ready Made Frocks, sutes of Fustian, Ticken, & Holland, stript Dimmity and Flañel Wastcoats, blue & canvas Frocks, & blue coat Boys Dra^rs. Likewise Fustians, Tickens, Hollands, white stript Dimñitys, white & stript Flañels in ye piece by wholesale or Retale at Reasonable Rates."

When Richard Hogarth's first two children saw the
light, he was evidently living in Bartholomew Close;
but when Ann was baptized, it was from St. John
Street, Clerkenwell. It is also recorded that he kept a
school in Ship Court, Old Bailey, in a house "three
doors from Newgate-street on the west side" (says
Mr. Peter Cunningham), which was pulled down in
1862 to make room for Messrs. Dickinson's paper
warehouse. His London "academy" would not seem
to have been more prosperous than its provincial pre-
decessor, for he is also reported to have been engaged
from the outset as a corrector of the press,—perhaps
by "Mr. Downinge the printer" referred to in the St.
Bartholomew's register; perhaps by another dweller
in this type-loving precinct, the Samuel Palmer who
later had Benjamin Franklin for journeyman. But, by
whomsoever employed, he must have been a man of
exceptional acquirements. He compiled, but never
published, a Latin dictionary in extension of Littleton, of which his son possessed the manuscript.[1] "It
was deposited," says William Hogarth in his autobiographical notes, "in confidence, in the hands of a
certain printer [perhaps Mr. Downinge again], and,
during the time it was left, letters of approbation were
received from the greatest scholars in England, Scotland, and Ireland. But these flattering testimonials

[1] Mary Lewis gave John Ireland one volume of this performance,
a corrected 4to copy of Littleton and Robertson's "Phrases," with
about 400 pages of manuscript additions, and reference is made
to the existence of another volume. On his (Ireland's) copy Hogarth
had written: "The manuscript part of this dictionary was the work
of Mr. Richard Hogarth."

from his acquaintance (who, as appears from their letters, which I have still by me, were of the first class) produced no profit to the author." Besides the dictionary there are some Latin epistles by Richard Hogarth in the British Museum ; and, six years before his death, he printed a little book called *Disputationes Grammaticales*, further described by himself as "an Examination of the Eight Parts of Speech by way of Question and Answer, English and Latin, whereby Children in a very little time will learn, not only the Knowledge of *Grammar*, but likewise to Speak and Write *Latin*, as I have found by good Experience." It was published in 1712,[1] but it must be concluded that its success was not remarkable.

Of his own childhood Hogarth writes,—"My father's pen, like that of many other authors, did not enable him to do more than put me in a way of shifting for myself. As I had naturally a good eye, and a fondness for drawing, *shows* of all sorts gave me uncommon pleasure when an infant ; and mimicry, common to all children, was remarkable in me. An early access to a neighbouring painter drew my attention from play ; and I was, at every possible opportunity, employed in making drawings. I picked up an acquaintance of the same turn, and soon learnt to draw the alphabet with great correctness. My

---

[1] There is a copy in the British Museum. It is a small *octavo* of some 90 pages, published by W. Taylor of the Ship in Paternoster Row (the publisher seven years later of "Robinson Crusoe"). At the end is a laborious "Chronological Index of *Men* and *Things*" which must have given "Ricardus Hogarth, Ludimagister," a considerable amount of trouble.

exercises when at school were more remarkable for the ornaments which adorned them, than for the exercise itself.   In the former, I soon found that blockheads with better memories could much surpass me ; but for the latter I was particularly distinguished." [1]

Neither the "neighbouring painter" nor the "acquaintance of the same turn" has been identified. The foregoing circumstances, however, coupled with the boy's daily experience of "the precarious situation of men of classical education," as exemplified in his father's career, brought his school-days to a premature conclusion.   By his own desire he was apprenticed to a "silver-plate engraver," Mr. Ellis Gamble, at the sign of the "Golden Angel," in Cranbourne Street or Alley, Leicester Fields.[2]   There is still extant a shop card, engraved for his master by the young apprentice, in which the angel of the sign poises a bulky palm branch in a somewhat volatile fashion over an announcement of Mr. Gamble's dealings in "all sorts of Plate, Rings, and Jewells," or as the French version has it, with some superfluity of spelling—" Argenterie, Bagues, & Bijouxs."

But long before the expiration of this apprentice-

[1] "Hogarth Illustrated," iii. 3-5.
[2] Colonel Chester's "London Marriage Licenses, 1521-1869," contains the record of the marriage at All Hallows-in-y^{c}-Wall, on the 12 Augt. 1707, of Edmund Hogarth of St Magnus, London, bachelor, 35, and Sarah Gambell, of St Swithin, spinster, 30. The conjunction of names is curious, and suggests that Ellis Gamble may have been connected by marriage with the family of his apprentice.

ship, the decoration of salvers and tankards with
florid heraldic monsters had been found by young
Hogarth to be far too limited for his ambition. He
felt the consciousness of capacity, and craved for
something better. This "something better" at first
seemed to be "engraving on copper." "Engraving

ELLIS GAMBLE'S SHOP-CARD.

on copper was, at twenty years of age, my utmost
ambition," he says. For this, however, he was not
sufficiently skilled as a draughtsman. How to find
some royal road to this latter attainment, which
should not too much interfere with his pleasure (he
frankly confesses to this), was his first endeavour.
Drawing from the life he regarded as too mechanical;

copying (which he learned to do with tolerable exact-
ness) "little more than pouring water out of one
vessel into another"[1]—in short, he was face to face
with the problem, how to become an artist without
going through the usual course of study ; or, as one
of his colleagues humorously put it,—"how to draw
well without drawing at all."

"For this purpose, I considered what various ways,
and to what different purposes the memory might be
applied ; and fell upon one which I found most suit-
able to my situation and idle disposition—laying it first
down as an axiom, that he who could by any means
acquire and retain in his memory, perfect ideas of
the subjects he meant to draw, would have as clear
a knowledge of the figure, as a man who can write
freely hath of the twenty-four letters of the alphabet
and their infinite combinations (each of these being
composed of lines), and would consequently be an
accurate designer."   To attain the power of making
original designs, as opposed to mere copies, was, he
says, his first and greatest ambition.   " I therefore
endeavoured to habituate myself to the exercise of a
sort of technical memory, and by repeating in my
own mind, the parts of which objects were composed,
I could by degrees combine and put them down with
my pencil.   Thus, with all the drawbacks which re-

---

[1] Probably Hogarth was thinking of "Tristram Shandy," for
vols. ii. and iv. of which he supplied frontispieces. "Shall we
for ever make new books, as apothecaries make new mixtures, by
pouring only out of one vessel into another?" (vol. v., ch. i.).
Sterne, in his turn, had characteristically borrowed this lament
over borrowing from Burton's "Anatomy" (" Introduction," p. 4).

sulted from the circumstances I have mentioned, I had one material advantage over my competitors, viz., the early habit I thus acquired of retaining in my mind's eye, without coldly copying it on the spot, whatever I intended to imitate. Sometimes, but too seldom, I took the life, for correcting the parts I had not perfectly enough remembered, and then I transferred them to my compositions." [1]

As the old French balladist has it, *Il ne faict pas ce tour qui veult.* That this method of study succeeded with William Hogarth, should not recommend it as a model; and even in his case its disadvantages were always more or less apparent. It is quite possible, too, that, looking back with the complacency of old age (he must have written the above account in the last years of his life), he depreciated his skill to magnify his theory. At all events, his silver-plate engraving of the arms of Ermengard de Schulemberg, Duchess of Kendal, which both of the Irelands have copied, shows that even during his bondage to Mr. Gamble he was no mean designer. As to his singular power of seizing expression, there is a well-known story which may be here quoted from its first source :—" During his apprenticeship, he set out one *Sunday*, with two or three companions, on an excursion to *Highgate.* The weather being hot,

---

[1] " Hogarth Illustrated," iii. 10-12. John Ireland, in a note on this passage, refers to a curious habit of Hogarth, the practice of pencilling minute sketches of striking characters, etc., upon his thumb nail. These indications were afterwards transferred to paper. Some of these transferred sketches Ireland had seen.

they went into a public-house, where they had not
been long before a quarrel arose between some
persons in the same room, in which one of the dis-
putants struck the other on the head with a quart
pot, and cut him very much. The blood running
down the man's face, with the agony of the wound,
which had distorted his features into a most hideous

HOGARTH'S SHOP-CARD.

grin, presented *Hogarth*, who showed himself thus
early 'apprised of the mode Nature had intended he
should pursue,' with too laughable a subject to escape
the powerful efforts of his genius. He drew out his
pencil, and produced on the spot one of the most
ludicrous figures that ever was seen. What rendered this piece the more pleasing was, that it exhi-

bited an exact likeness of the man, with the portrait of his antagonist, and the figures in caricature of the principal persons gathered round him. This anecdote was given by one of his fellow apprentices then present, a person of indisputable character, and who continued his intimacy with *Hogarth* long after they grew up to be men."[1]

The autobiographical passages already quoted apparently relate to a period when the apprenticeship referred to in the above anecdote was at an end, as Hogarth states that he was twenty. In May, 1718, succumbing partly to disappointment arising from the non-fulfilment of great men's promises, partly to the hard usage of the Curlls and Osbornes of the day, his father died, and was buried on the 11th, at St. Bartholomew's. As his residence at the time of his death was in Long Lane, it would seem that he still haunted the printers of the Close, from whom he probably drew his surest means of support. His son seems at first to have intended to follow the trade to which he had been educated, for, if we except a gold snuff-box lid engraved with a scene from the "Rape of the Lock," his earliest work was his own business card, decorated with Cupids, and inscribed, "W. Hogarth Engraver Aprill ye 23. 1720." From the fact that John Ireland had seen one of these cards on which Hogarth had written, "Near the *Black Bull, Long Lane,*" it may be assumed that after his father's death, he continued to reside with his mother and sisters. "His first employment,"

[1] Nichols, "Anecdotes," 1781, 8-9.

MASQUERAIDES AND OPERAS.
From Hogarth's Engraving.

says Nichols, "seems to have been the engraving of
arms and shop-bills." From this he passed to
"plates" and satirical designs for booksellers. Two
of the earliest of these latter were *An Emblematic
Print on the South Sea Scheme* and *The Lottery.*
Except for the tradition that the South Sea print contains portraits of Pope and Gay, and for the indications they both afford that the artist had made himself
familiar with the works of Jacques Callot, there is no
necessity to linger over these confused, and—compared with his later work—obscure performances.
After them, in 1723, come eighteen or more illustrations of the tedious travels of Aubry de la Motraye
(in which collectors have done their best, though
without great success, to discover traces of the true
Hogarthian vein); seven plates to "The New
Metamorphosis" (Briscoe's Apuleius); the plate
known as *Masquerades and Operas, Burlington Gate,*
1724, which is notable as being the first he published on his own account; five plates for the third
edition of Sir Charles Cotterel's "Cassandra"; the
Burlesque on Kent's Altar Piece at St. Clement's,
1725; a frontispiece to Amhurst's Oxford Squib of
" Terræ-Filius," 1726; and twelve large and sixteen
small designs for Butler's "Hudibras." Of these
(we have omitted to chronicle some minor and doubtful pieces which will be found in our final catalogue),
only *Masquerades and Operas,* the *Burlesque on Kent,*
and the plates to "Hudibras," need more than a
passing comment.

Masquerades and Operas, which Hogarth in his

autobiographical notes calls the " Taste of the *Town*,"
shows how definitely he had chosen his *rôle* from the
beginning. (Throughout his whole life we shall find
him striking vigorously at foreign favourites and
dubious exotics, at charlatans and shams of all sorts ;
and in this little plate he touches the key-note of his
future work. Crowds are seen flocking eagerly to
the Italian Opera, to Fawkes the Conjuror's " Dexterity of hand," to the Lincoln's Inn Fields Pantomime of " Dr. Faustus," and to Swiss Heidegger's
impure Masquerades ; while the neglected folios of
Shakespeare, Dryden, Otway, and Congreve are
wheeled to the waste-paper shops.) On a show-cloth
above, the Earl of Peterborough (Swift's " Mor-
danto ") is on his knees to that " little siren of the
stage," Francesca Cuzzoni, the singer, who had come
to England in the previous year. At the back rises
the gate of Burlington House, labelled " Accademy
[*sic*] of Arts," and surmounted by the figure of the
fashionable " Jack of all Trades," William Kent, who
has Raphael and Michael Angelo for his supporters.
Kent, a pretender who had recently been recommended to the King by Lord Burlington for the
paintings at Kensington, was not a personage whom
our sturdy satirist could be expected to hold in any
particular reverence. Nor would he be likely to
hear much good of him at the art school just opened
by Kent's far abler rival, Sir James Thornhill, on
the east side of James Street, Covent Garden—an
institution which Hogarth now began to attend,
upon those rare occasions when he " took the life " to

KENT'S ALTAR PIECE.
From Hogarth's Engraving.

correct his memories. Indeed it has been stated, and there is no reason why the statement should not be correct, that this happy pictorial pasquinade secured his admission not only into the ranks of Thornhill's students, but also into their master's good graces.

However this may be, in those good graces he was destined to progress. The blow he struck at Thornhill's *bête noire* in *Masquerades and Operas* was feeble in comparison with that by which he followed it up a year later,—to wit, the " Burlesque" (" faithful copy" is his own description) of the famous Altarpiece with which Kent's evil genius prompted him to decorate St. Clement's Danes. Already, in consequence of the criticisms of the parishioners, who pretended to be unable to decide whether the figures were meant, as contended by some, for St. Cecilia and her harp, or, as maintained by others, for the Princess Sobieski and her son, the Bishop of London, to "preserve peace and unity" had, on his visitation, caused it to be taken down. This was humiliating enough ; but Hogarth covered it with further ridicule by a print purporting to be " exactly engraved" after it. His little satire is a very masterpiece of feeble drawing and inventive incoherence, but is not easily describable in words, and we must refer our readers to the accompanying copy.[1] The original picture,

---

[1] Allan Cunningham implies that Hogarth's print caused the removal of the altar-piece ; and this is doubtless what every staunch Hogarthian would like to be the truth. But—unless we must regard it as a humorous anticipation—the very inscription

after its degradation in September, 1725, was deposited in the old vestry of the church, where it
remained in John Ireland's day; and Nichols adds
that it was occasionally used on concert-nights to
ornament the music room of the Crown and Anchor
Tavern in the Strand. Thirty years ago, it was
said to be still preserved in the new vestry room
in Picket Street, but Picket Street itself is now no
more.

By the small illustrations to " Hudibras," issued in
1726, Hogarth, says John Ireland, "first became known
in his profession," and they are undoubtedly his most
extensive efforts in the direction of book illustration.
It is noticeable, however, that—probably from some
timidity on the part of the " Congers," or associated
booksellers, who employed him—he seems to have
relied in part upon his graphic predecessors. " In
design," says Ireland, " these (i.e., the inferior set
of plates) "are almost direct copies from a series
inserted in a small edition of the same book published sixteen years before." This was certainly

on the print itself contradicts this. It is there called the " celebrated Altar-piece in St. Clement's Church *which has been taken
down* by order of yᵉ Lord Bishop of London."

[Since the above was in type (it may be added), a reference
to the MS. notes, now in the British Museum, which Horace
Walpole bought from Vertue's widow (Add. MSS. 23,076, p. 66),
tends to show that, in the sequel, the laugh did not remain
wholly on Hogarth's side. According to Vertue, Kent was
afterwards successful in preventing Hogarth from executing
certain commissions which depended wholly upon Court favour;
and this, it is stated, was a direct consequence of Hogarth's
caricatures of Kent.]

BURNING OF RUMPS AT TEMPLE BAR.

From Hogarth's Engraving.

not to the advantage of the artist's work, for although
he was far too individual to be ever entirely successful as an interpreter of other men's ideas, he
frequently manifested his own originality by his very
deviations from his text.   This is exactly what he
has done in the infinitely superior series of twelve
large plates, also from " Hudibras," issued separately
in the same year, and dedicated to William Ward,
Esq., of Great Houghton, in Northamptonshire, and
" Mr. Allan Ramsay [the poet] of Edinburgh."
Here, as a very superficial comparison of the two
sets of illustrations will show, he has added a mass
of fresh humorous detail to his presentment of the
text, of which the hay-maker in Plate II., who, in
his burlesque salutation of the hero and his squire, is
upsetting the apple stall, may serve as an example.
Nevertheless, as pictorial characterizations, Hudibras
and Ralpho are, upon the whole, only moderately
successful, and the widow and Trulla are but rela-
tively better.   The designer is at his best in the
concluding plates, the " Procession of the Skimmington "[1] and the " Burning of Rumps at Temple Bar,"
compositions in which he already exhibits something
of the skill which later grouped the guards in front
of the " Adam and Eve " in Tottenham Court Road,

---

[1] The "Skimmington" is defined by Scott, in the notes to the
"Fortunes of Nigel," as "a species of triumphant procession in
honour of female supremacy, when it rose to such a height as to
attract the attention of the neighbourhood." It is a distinction
with which the Jin Vin of that story threatens Dame Ursley
Suddlechop.   See also "Hudibras," Part ii., Canto ii., ll. 585,
et seq.

and built up that wonderful crowd which accompanies Tom Idle to Tyburn. He had always a kindness for these designs from Butler, and never ceased to regret that he had parted with the plates.

To the years 1727-8 belongs one of those rare occurrences which have survived to give incident to Hogarth's biography. Among other commissions, he received one from an upholsterer and tapestry-worker named Joshua Morris to execute a design on canvas for the *Element of Earth*, a subject which, although Hogarth with great intrepidity undertook it, does not suggest anything particularly definite. The price was to be thirty pounds; but Morris, who—as one of the painter's critics has said—must have had a good deal of the "element of earth" in his own composition, having been told that the designer was "an engraver, and no painter," managed to grow dissatisfied with the work beforehand, and finally refused to pay for it. Thereupon the indignant artist, holding that the labourer was worthy of his hire, carried the case, in May, 1728, before Chief Justice Eyre. Morris produced a number of experts to prove that the painting was unfitted for its purpose; but Hogarth's witnesses—Thornhill, King, Jack Laguerre (the scene-painter), and Vanderbank,[1] all testified vigorously to the contrary—the result being that Morris was defeated.[2] As to the fate of the

[1] This was most probably the Vanderbank, "who works in Arras, and makes very good Tapestry Hangings," to whom Steele refers in "Tatler" No. 3. Blackmore wrote a poem recommending him to celebrate Marlborough's campaigns in tissue.

[2] So affirms Nichols the Elder. Allan Cunningham, it is true,

Element of Earth, history is silent. It is not likely, however, that it was more successful than some of Hogarth's subsequent efforts in the "grand style."

Meanwhile he had discovered that working for the booksellers was neither dignified nor lucrative, and that designing on his own account (as he had done in the case of *Masquerades and Operas*) was simply an incentive to plagiarism and piracy. "The first plate I published," he says, "called the Taste of the Town [i.e., the above *Masquerades and Operas*], in which the reigning follies were lashed, had no sooner began to take a run, than I found copies [1] of it in the printshops, vending at half-price, while the original prints were returned to me again ; and I was thus obliged to sell the plates for what-ever these pirates pleased to give me, as there was no place of sale but at their shops." Probably it was owing to these circumstances, coupled with the aspersion thrown by the above-mentioned trial upon his skill as a painter, that he now turned his attention more directly to oil painting, for about this date, as appears from a memorandum among his papers, he

implies the contrary. Probably he had only before him the *second* edition of the "Anecdotes" (1782) which says, p. 21, "it is probable that Hogarth was nonsuited." In the *third* edition of 1785, p. 24, this account is corrected as in the text. The point is not without importance, because the erroneous story has misled other writers into boldly stating that Hogarth had been declared by a court of law to be "no painter."

[1] One of these copies is in the British Museum collection. It has neither artist's name nor publication line, but has two quatrains underneath beginning — "Long has the stage productive been."

began to paint "small conversation pieces, from twelve to fifteen inches high." "This (he says) having novelty, succeeded for a few years." His chief works in oil from 1728[1] (the year of the Morris suit) until 1732 may be briefly enumerated. They are *The Wanstead Assembly*, painted for Lord Castlemaine; *The Committee of the House of Commons examining Bambridge*, an infamous warder of the Fleet Prison, painted for Sir Archibald Grant of Monnymusk; several versions of the Polly and Lucy scene in Gay's "Beggar's Opera," notable for their portraits of the beautiful actress, Lavinia Fenton and her future husband, the Duke of Bolton; *Before* and *After*, painted for a Mr. Thomson; a little picture of *The Politician*, being the likeness of one Tibson, a lace-man in the Strand; *The Wollaston Family*; and lastly, the charming composition, which Leslie praises so warmly, representing the performance by a number of children, at Mr. Conduit's, of Dryden's "Conquest of Mexico." Leslie, who saw this at Holland House, declares it to be beautifully coloured, and ranks it as "one of those early works painted from Nature, the execution of which prepared the way to Hogarth's greater efforts." "Three girls and a boy are on the stage, and seem to be very seriously doing their best; but the attitude of one little girl, on a front seat among the audience, is

---

[1] He had already, if we may trust an often-repeated statement, produced the Hudibras series in oils. Respecting these there is considerable controversy, for which the reader is referred to the "Catalogue of Paintings" in Part II.

matchless. She is so entirely absorbed in the performance, that she sits bolt upright, and will sit, we
are sure, immovably, to the end of the play, enjoying
it as a child only can, and much the more because
the actors are children." [1]

During the greater part of this period we must
assume that he preserved his connection, if not with
the school in Covent Garden, at least with Sir James
Thornhill, who, as we have seen, was one of his witnesses against Morris. His relations with some of
the family, in fact, were of the closest, for he was the
chosen associate of John Thornhill, Sir James's son,
and, in 1729, he ran away with his only daughter
Jane, to whom, as the register of Old Paddington
Church still testifies, he was married privately on the
23rd of March. [2] The lady was between nineteen and
twenty, and, judging from her husband's portrait of
her, now in the possession of Mr. H. B. Mildmay, must
have been extremely handsome. Her father, as may
be gathered from the nature of the match, was wholly
averse from the alliance; but it seems that Lady
Thornhill connived at it. Jane Hogarth made an
admirable wife, and cherished the memory of her

---

[1] "Handbook for Young Painters," 1855, p. 131. The picture
was exhibited at the British Gallery in 1814.

[2] Tradition, by the voice of Mrs. S. C. Hall, asserts that the
lovers took flight from the little "country-box" which afterwards
belonged to Hogarth at Chiswick. This, as will be shown in
Chapter VIII., could scarcely have been the case. It is probable
that, in 1729, Jane Thornhill was domiciled at her father's residence in the Great Piazza, Covent Garden, "the second house
eastward from James Street." In the Paddington register she is
described as "of St. Paul's, Covent Garden."

husband, whom she long survived, with a fidelity only equalled by that of Mrs. Garrick for her David.

"Soon after his marriage," says Nichols, "*Hogarth* had summer-lodgings at *South-Lambeth*." Here he made or improved the acquaintance of Jonathan Tyers, who at that time was preparing to re-open New Spring Gardens, as Vauxhall was then called, with an entertainment styled a *Ridotto al Fresco.* Hogarth is supposed to have rendered him signal service by suggesting the decoration of the place with pictures ; and, upon the venerated precedent of the ingenious M. Josse, nothing could be more natural than that a painter should put forward paintings as an indispensable adornment. But one of the earliest and most trustworthy of the guides, the "Sketch of the Spring Gardens, Vauxhall : In a Letter to a Noble Lord," seems to indicate Hayman as the "only begetter" in this matter. It is certain, however, that Hogarth contributed specimens of his own works to the cause, and that, as time went on, others were copied. According to Nichols, Hayman reproduced the later series of the *Four Times of the Day* for Vauxhall, two of which were still there in 1782, while in the portico of the Rotunda to the left of the entrance, was an unquestionable picture from Hogarth's brush, dating from his marriage year, and representing Henry VIII. and Anne Boleyn. Another work claimed as his, when in 1841, obscured by dirt and slashed by sandwich knives, the relics of the Vauxhall Gallery came to the hammer, was Harper and Miss Raftor (afterwards Mrs. Clive) as Jobson the Cobbler and his wife

Nell in Coffey's farce of " The Devil to Pay ; or, the
Wives Metamorphosed," but this, as well as a *genre*
piece called *The Wapping Landlady*, in which a
short-trowsered tar of the Tom Bowling era is
deliberately executing a nautical *pas-scul* in the parlour of a waterside alehouse with the aid of a whangee,
is plainly attributed to Hayman in Sayer's contemporary print from the painting.   There is a look of
Hogarth's children in *Building Houses with Cards ;*
but, on the whole, it may be concluded that there
was in reality little of his original work among the
sea fights, popular games, and so forth, which decorated the garish old supper boxes in The Grove.
His picture in the Rotunda portico, however, coupled
with his permission to reproduce his other works,
would be ground enough to justify the gold ticket,
designed by himself, and inscribed *In perpetuam
Beneficii memoriam,* with which he was presented by
the grateful Tyers.   This ticket, admitting " a coach-
full," that is, six persons, was, in 1808, in the
possession of Mrs. Hogarth's cousin, the Mary
Lewis mentioned at the beginning of this chapter.
It had passed to other hands in 1825, when (with
five silver passes, all said to have been struck at
different times from Hogarth's designs, and including
among the rest that of George Carey, the author of
many Vauxhall songs) it was engraved by James
Stow for Wilkinson's " Londina Illustrata."

Although, between 1726 and 1732, Hogarth painted
much, he did not entirely relinquish the graver, for
the list of his prints at this time contains several

frontispieces for the booksellers. In the *Large Masquerade Ticket*, 1727, he once more satirized Heidegger and fashionable depravity. Another plate, *Rich's Glory*, is of doubtful authenticity, but it is interesting from its view of Old Covent Garden in the days of the open market and central dial. Besides these, should be noted the frontispiece to Fielding's "Tragedy of Tragedies" (the enlarged edition of "Tom Thumb"), which, it may be, marks the beginning of his friendship for the famous author of "Joseph Andrews;" and *The Man of Taste* or *Burlington Gate*, 1731. In this Kent again figures, supported as before by reclining statues of Raphael and Michael Angelo. On a scaffolding the diminutive figure of Alexander Pope is seen, vigorously whitewashing the gate and bespattering the passers-by, including the Duke of Chandos, while Lord Burlington brings the whitewash. This is a transparent allusion to Pope's attack on the Duke in his epistle to Lord Burlington, "Of Taste," in which under the title of "Timon," his Grace, and his seat of Canons near Edgware, were held up to ridicule. The print gave great offence; and Nichols alleges that the impression was recalled, and the plate suppressed. But as it was reduced in 1732 for the frontispiece to "A Miscellany on Taste; by Mr. Pope, etc.," published by Lawton and others, the suppression could not have been effectual. Pope, who might have been expected to retaliate, made no sign. Perhaps he was too wise.

To Hogarth's first great work, *A Harlot's Pro-*

THE MAN OF TASTE.
From Hogarth's Engraving.

gress, and its successor, *A Rake's Progress*, the
ensuing chapter will be devoted. But the present
may not inappropriately be closed with brief reference
to an amusing holiday jaunt which, a few weeks
after the appearance of the prints of *A Harlot's
Progress*, the artist helped to organize, and to per-
petuate with his pencil. On an evening at the close
of May, 1732, it occurred to certain boon companions
at the Bedford Arms Tavern in Covent Garden to
enter upon an impromptu expedition. The company
consisted of Hogarth, his brother-in-law John Thornhill, Samuel Scott (afterwards to be known as the
" English Canaletto "),[1] a much-experienced draper
of Tavistock Street named William Tothall, and
Ebenezer Forrest, an attorney. They started at
midnight, each with a shirt in his pocket, down the
river in a tilt boat to Gravesend. "At Cuckold's
Point we sung *St. John*, at Deptford *Pishoken ;* and
in Blackwall Reach eat hung beef and biscuit, and
drank right Hollands." And so forth. It is a cheery
record of small jests and much mirth; of songs sung
and flip-cans emptied; of the jovial and not very
admirable fooling of a party of overgrown schoolboys
playing truant, and relieving the tedium of sight-
seeing by friendly exercises such as bolstering
matches, hop-scotch, and "fighting perukes." From

---

[1] A good example of Scott's work—"A View of Westminster
from the River"—has recently been acquired for the National
Gallery, where it hangs in Room XVII. Hogarth sometimes
supplied the figures for his friend's pictures. There is a humorous
group by him in Scott's "View of Bloomsbury Square and Bedford House."

Gravesend they go by the Gadshill cherry-orchards
to Rochester—from Rochester to Chatham, Upnor,
Hoo, and elsewhere. At Stoke they are shaved by a
shock-haired fisherman; at Queenborough they fore-
gather with the local sexton; at Minster they sketch
the tomb of that Lord of Shorland whom Ingoldsby
has immortalized in the "Legend of Sheppey."[1]
Their doings find a faithful chronicler in Forrest,

[1] Forrest's version of this story may be given here as a specimen
of his style :—"The Legend of the Last being remarkable I shall
relate with all it's Circumstances; In the Reign of Queen Elizabeth, This Lord having been to Visit a Friend in this Island And
passing by this Church in his Way home to Shorland ab' Two Miles
off, he saw a Concourse of people gather'd together in the Church
yard, and Inquiring the Reason, was Inform'd that the parson
who stood by there, refused to Bury the Corps: bro' for that purpose, because there was No Money to pay the Burial Fees, His
Lordship being Extreamly Mov'd at y° parson Ordered the people
to Throw him into the Grave and Bury him Quick which they
accordingly Did and He Died; My Lord went home, and there
reflecting on what he had Done and fearing to forfeit his Life for
the Offence, He wrote a petisõn Setting forth the Nature of his Case
and Hearing the Queen was on Board one of the Shipps at the Nore
(to which place she came to take a Veiw of her Fleet (Design'd to
oppose the Spanish Armada) He took a Horse and Rode Directly
into the Sea & Swam to y° Nore above Three Miles off and
coming to the Ship's Side beg'd to See her Majesty who came
Imediately and he presented his petition, The Queen reĉed,
Read, and Granted it, and he without Quitting his Horse Swam
back again to the Island, and Coming upon the Shore, mett an
Old Woman who told him that tho' the Horse had then Saved his
Life, he would be the cause of his Death, His Lordship fearing
(and in order to prevent) the accomplishment of the Old
Woman's Prophecy, Alighted from his Horse, Drew his Sword
and kill'd him and left him there, and his Carcass was by y° force
of the Sea Thrown some Little Way on the Land.

"Some Years after this My Lord Walking with Some of his

who sets them down gravely "as a burlesque on historical writers recording a series of insignificant
events entirely uninteresting to the reader." When,
after five days' wandering, the pilgrims returned
before "a mackarel gale" to Billingsgate, the journal
was promptly bound, gilt-lettered, and read out at the
Bedford Arms Club for the edification of the members assembled. The book thus produced, a thin
oblong volume in brown ink, still exists in the Print
Room of the British Museum, having been purchased in 1847 for about £100. The drawings,
which include a grotesque head- and tail-piece, are by
Hogarth and Scott; the map is by Thornhill. The
title-page, *verbatim, punctatim et literatim*, runs thus :
—" An Account/ of what Seem'd most Remarkable
in the Five Days Peregrination/ of the Five Following Persons viz', Messieurs/ Tothall, Scott,
Hogarth, Thornhill & Forrest./ Begun on Saturday
May the 27th 1732/ and Finish'd/ On the 31" of
the same Month./ *Abi tu et fac Similiter.*—Inscrip-
ton [*sic*] on Dulwich Colledge porch." Some time
after its exhibition to the Club, the journal was lent
to Hogarth's friend, the Rev. William Gostling,
M.A., a Minor Canon of Canterbury Cathedral,
who amused himself by turning it into Hudibrastic
rhyme, in which form more than one of Hogarth's

Friends near the Sea Side, Espied the Skull and Some other Bones
of the Horse Lying there, and relating the foregoing acco' happened
to kick the Skull and Hurt one of his Toes which Mortified and
kill'd him, and he Lyes In Minster Church and a Monument is
Erected over his Grave, On which he is Figur'd, with a Horse's
Head (supposed to be in the Waves) plac'd by him."

biographers, misled, no doubt, by the line, " And
Forrest, who this journal wrote," appear to have
thought that it was at first composed. The title-
page of Gostling's version says that it is " Imitated
. . . with Liberty of some Additions." It is possible that a few minor details may have been inserted
from particulars supplied by one or other of the
travellers ; but, although the couplets are respectable,.
the Canterbury Canon's metrical paraphrase cannot
compete in freshness with Forrest's prose. Here
is its " transversing" of the final lines :—

> " With pleasure I observe, none idle
> Were in our travels, or employ'd ill.
> *Tothall*, our treasurer, was just,
> And worthily discharg'd his trust ;
> (We all sign'd his accounts as fair) :
> *Sam Scott* and *Hogarth*, for their share,
> The prospects of the sea and land did ;
> As *Thornhill* of our tour the plan did ;
> And *Forrest* wrote this true relation
> Of our five days peregrination.
>   This to attest, our names we've wrote all.
>   Viz. *Thornhill*, *Hogarth*, *Scott*, and *Tothall.*"

Until 1781 both versions remained in manuscript.
Then John Nichols struck off twenty copies of Mr.
Gostling's poem " as a literary curiosity,"[1] and in the
year following, Richard Livesay the engraver made
aquatint *facsimiles* of the original drawings. These *facsimiles* he issued, " at Mrs. Hogarth's, Leicester Fields,"

[1] This Nichols subsequently reproduced in the " Biographical
Anecdotes" of 1782, pp. 403-27, having hitherto withheld it "in
compliment to the writer of the prose journey " (p. 327). Gostling's
version was also reprinted in Hone's " Table Book," ii. pp.
290-319.

with a reprint of Forrest's text.[1]   From the aforegoing
account of this last-named performance, it will be
gathered that it can scarcely be regarded as a serious
contribution to literature ; and it is easy to conceive
that its fun was somewhat too highly flavoured for
the fastidious palate of critics like Horace Walpole,
whose favourite, Scott, figures, moreover, as the butt
of the party.   Yet it has its interest as an unvar-
nished record of the frank and hearty, albeit not over-
refined, fashion in which our middle-class ancestors
took their pleasure in the cock-fighting, bull-baiting,
cudgel-playing England of George the Second.   It
helps us, in addition, to comprehend the humour
of those liberal " flicks " and " dowses "—assaults and
batteries—which play so prominent a part in the
fictions of Smollett and Fielding.

[1] Livesay's prose tour is included in Nichols and Steevens's
"Genuine Works," iii. (1817), pp. 113-131.

TAIL-PIECE TO HOGARTH'S TOUR.

40586

CHAPTER III.

The Two Progresses.

OR many years after the expiration of Hogarth's apprenticeship,—when, it is to be presumed, he lived with Mr. Gamble in Cranbourne Alley,—we have no definite data as to his dwelling-place, save and except those stray references of John Ireland and Nichols to Long Lane, and "summer lodgings in South Lambeth." That he had other summer lodgings is not unlikely. When the *Rake's Progress* was painted, it is stated that he was staying at Isleworth ;[1] and according to a recent authority,[2] he sometimes resorted to the "Bull and Bush" Inn at North End, Hampstead, where a yew bower in the garden is still reported to have been planted by his hand. These, however—to use Prior's figure—were but his "visits ;" his "home" was, or was shortly to be, in Leicester Fields. To Leicester Fields, then, he came—as the rate books tell us—in 1733, and here, with occasional

---

[1] Nichols, "Anecdotes," 1781, p. 14.
[2] Baines's "Hampstead," 1890, p. 233. It was then a farm-house.

LEICESTER SQUARE.
From an Old Print.

absences at the "villakin" he bought sixteen years later by the Thames at Chiswick, he lived mainly until his death. The house he occupied (the last but two on the east side) was what was afterwards the northern half of the Sablonière or Jaquier's hotel, which has now given place to Archbishop Tenison's school; and the painter, in that bust of him by Joseph Durham which decorates Mr. Albert Grant's glorified enclosure, must be exactly turning his back upon the site of his ancient habitation. In Hogarth's day this was conspicuous for its brass plate and its gilt sign of the "Golden Head,"—a bust of Van Dyck which he had himself carved from pieces of cork glued together.[1] At Leicester Fields he would be in convenient proximity to his genial friends of the Bedford Arms, when he was minded to a cheerful cup, and "Why should we quarrel for Riches?" or "Drink and agree," or any of the chirrupping ditties comprised in that collection of Richard Leveridge, the singer, for which, in 1727, he had engraved a frontis-

---

[1] J. T. Smith ("Life of Nollekens," 1828, ii. 209) well remembered this sign. It was followed, says Nichols ("Anecdotes," 1782, p. 91), by a head in plaster; and this again, when Nichols wrote, had been superseded by a bust of Sir Isaac Newton. The house, in which Mrs. Hogarth lived for many years after her husband's death, may still be detected in contemporary views of the square (*e.g.* those of Maurer and Bowles, 1753), and must have been a fairly "commodious residence" for those days, as Cunningham says it was rated to the poor in 1756 at £60. As late as 1823 the tradition survived that Hogarth was accustomed to walk of evenings within the enclosure, in a scarlet "rocklow" or *roquelaure*, "with his hat cocked and stuck on one side, much in the manner of the great Frederick of Prussia."

piece. Leveridge, by the way, kept a famous tavern
in Tavistock Street, where, no doubt, he occasionally
obliged his customers with his own admirable setting
of " Black-Eyed Susan"; and not far off, in all
probability, was George Lambert, the scene-painter
of Lincoln's Inn Fields and the future founder of
the "Beef Steak Club"; while burly John Pine, the
engraver, whose " Horace" is still a delight to the
collector, had a print-shop in St. Martin's Lane.
Captain Coram, too, the benevolent originator of the
Foundling Hospital, would perhaps be in the neighbourhood, for that good man and philanthropist
died "at his lodgings near Leicester Square." But
Hogarth, as may be gathered, had not yet attained
to widespread repute with the general public. Joseph
Mitchell, Sir Robert Walpole's poet, for whose "Scot's
Opera" he designed a plate, had indeed apostro-
phized him as "an eminent History and Conversation Painter."

> " Large Families obey your Hand ;
> Assemblies rise at your Command,"—

says this tuneful panegyrist in June, 1730,[1] and in
some other verses, unaccountably neglected by the

---

[1] A year later Mrs. Delany (then Mrs. Pendarves) thus testifies
to Hogarth's skill as a portrait-painter. Writing to Mrs. Anne
Granville, 13 July, 1731, she says :—" I have released Lady
Sunderland from her promise of giving me her picture by Zinck
[*sic*], to have it done by Hogarth. I think he takes a much greater
likeness." . . . . She goes on to say that Hogarth is to teach her
drawing by "some rules of his own that he says will improve me
more in a day than a year's learning in the common way,"—a
thoroughly characteristic utterance (" Autobiography, etc. of Mrs.
Delany," 1861, i. 283).

commentators, he shows that he thoroughly appreciated Hogarth's power of expressing character :—

> " You have the Skill to catch the Grace,
> And secret Meanings of a Face ;
> From the quick Eyes to snatch the Fire,
> And limn th' Ideas they inspire ;
> To picture Passions, and, thro' Skin,
> Call forth the living Soul within."

Yet even in the obituary notice of Sir James Thornhill in the "Gentleman's Magazine" for May, 1734, Hogarth is simply referred to as " admir'd for his curious Miniature Conversation Paintings," although he had at the time put forth the first of that wonderful gallery of " pictur'd Morals," which, it might be imagined, should have stamped him, once and for all, as an artist wholly distinct and separate from his predecessors and contemporaries. In 1732,[1] however, there were but few print-shops in London ; and the circulation of works of art must have been extremely languid.

The oil paintings for *A Harlot's Progress*—the series of "pictur'd Morals" above referred to—are believed to have been begun soon after the artist's marriage, as the date upon the coffin in the last plate, which has been taken to denote the conclusion of the work, is "2ᵈ Sep. 1731". Apart from the supposition that the necessity for devising some connecting link between the figures in his " conversation pieces " had suggested the extension of that connection from one

---

[1] Rouquet (" L'Etat des Arts en Angleterre," 1755, p. 44) limits the *boutiques de marchands d'estampes* in London before the Act of 1735 to two; but this statement would seem to be exaggerated.

canvas to another, it would be of considerable
interest if we could learn what fortunate accident
of inspiration suggested this particular idea to
Hogarth.   The relating of a tale or biography by
means of pictures was, of course, not new, witness
the life of St. Bruno by Le Sueur which Walpole and
Gray saw in the Convent of the Chartreux at Paris.
But Hogarth, unless we misread him greatly, knew
no more of Le Sueur than of St. Bruno. His own
account of the matter, meanwhile, is too general to
be explicit.   Portrait painting, he gives us to understand, was laborious; and to a conscientious man
who scorned to consent (after the manner of your
Hudsons and Knaptons, be it understood!) to de-
grade it into a mere manufacture—" not sufficiently
profitable to pay the expenses my family required.
I therefore turned my thoughts to a still more novel
mode, viz., painting and engraving modern moral
subjects, a field not broken up in any country or any
age." . . . " I wished to compose pictures on canvas,
similar to representations on the stage; and farther
hope, that they will be tried by the same test, and
criticised by the same criterion.   Let it be observed,
that I mean to speak only of those scenes where the
human species are actors, and these I think have
not often been delineated in a way of which they are
worthy and capable.   In these compositions, those
subjects that will both entertain and improve the
mind, bid fair to be of the greatest public utility,
and must therefore be entitled to rank in the highest
class." . . . " I have endeavoured to treat my sub-

ject as a dramatic writer;[1] my picture is my stage, and men and women my players, who by means of certain actions and gestures are to exhibit _a dumb show._" . . . . " This I found was most likely to answer my purpose, provided I could strike the passions, and by small sums from many, by the sale of prints, which I could engrave from my own pictures, thus secure my property to myself."[2]

Here, of course, is his theory, as it presented itself to his memory after thirty years, but it still leaves us in the dark with respect to the special train of suggestion. To a mind so alert to employ surrounding material—so ready to seize the humorous or satiric aspect of the moment, there should surely have been some proximate cause that prompted this picture-chronicle of hapless Mary Hackabout. Major thinks, indeed, that a paper by Steele in the "Spectator" (No. 266), in which a procuress is shown hypocritically catechizing a raw country girl who has come to town in a waggon, may have furnished the first hint. But this, even if it suggested Plate I., need not (although it may) have suggested the entire set.[3] The artist, at all

[1] It is to be noted that in the advertisements of _A Harlot's Progress_, and in more than one of his plates—_e.g._, _The Sleeping Congregation_—he speaks of himself as the "author," not the "artist." And Hazlitt in his lectures classes him with the "comic writers."

[2] "Hogarth Illustrated," iii., pp. 26-8, 29, 31.

[3] From a note at p. 56 of the MSS. already referred to on p. 24 n., it would appear that some of Hogarth's contemporaries ascribed to the series an altogether commonplace origin. According to Vertue, Hogarth first painted Scene III. as an independent

events, takes us further. From that first declension into evil paths, his heroine passes, through a Martin's summer as the mistress of a rich Jew, to " Captain Macheath " and Drury Lane,—to Bridewell and beating hemp,—to Disease and Death,—to a shameful funeral and a forgotten grave. It is all acted out *coram populo*. There is no decorous veiling of the catastrophe, no abatement of the pitiable detail, no Rossetti-like—

> " passing thought
> Of the old days which seem to be
> Much older than any history
> That is written in any book ;
> When she would lie in fields and look
> Along the ground through the blown grass,
> And wonder where the city was
> Far out of sight, whose broil and bale,
> They told her then for a child's tale."

For such retrospective sensibility, such regretful sentiment, Hogarth had neither space nor inclination. He had a plain and straightforward message to deliver. If you do that, this will follow,—and this,—and this. With such accessories, grotesque or terrible, as may be.

Where the narrator is so unflinching and matter-of-fact, it is obvious that, in this century at least, his work, however fundamentally moral and didactic in its

work,—a kind of " *Lever* in Low Life," one may suppose. It attracted so much attention, that he was pressed to execute a companion-piece, and so went on by degrees to complete the six pictures. Vertue further says that, while the plates were engraving, Hogarth lived in Common [Covent] Garden with his father-in-law, Sir James Thornhill. This must be added to the "dwelling-places" specified at the beginning of the chapter.]

intention, is not always quite easy to write about ; and there are—it must frankly be confessed—details here over which, as the prints can be consulted, one may pass without regret. But some of the characters—for some of the characters were real persons—require to be named.) The man at the door and the elderly woman, in Plate I., undoubtedly represented the infamous Colonel Francis Charteris and the equally infamous Mother Needham, the latter of whom died after exposure in the pillory in 1731. The magistrate who enters the room in Plate III. is Sir John Gonson, a well-known " harlot-hunting justice ;" the wig-box in the same plate is that of James Dalton, a highwayman who had been hanged at Tyburn in 1730. The wrangling practitioners in Plate V. are said to be Drs. Misaubin and Ward,[1] two quacks of the day; while the clergyman (!) of Plate VI. is identified with a certain dissolute "chaplain of the Fleet," and the shrieking beldam with a procuress named Bentley. Of the numberless minor details it is here impracticable to speak at length. But the attention of the reader may be briefly directed to the destruction caused by the famished horse in Plate I., the significant pictures on the walls in Plate II.; the degradation of the Bishop's " Pastoral Letter " in Plate III.; the Jew's-bread used as a fly-trap, and the Anodyne necklace advertisement in Plate V.; and finally the sprigs of yew for the prevention of infection in the concluding plate.

[1] See *Marriage A-la-Mode*, p. 98, and *The Company of Undertakers*, p. 67.

By some of the commentators this concluding
plate (*The Funeral*) has been regarded, not only as
involving in its details a certain neglect of probability, but even as in itself an anachronism and a
superfluity.   This was the opinion of Hogarth's own
inspired interpreter, 'Rouquet.   To him the tragedy
finishes with the fifth picture ; the sixth is simply
the farce, or after-piece,—"*une farce dont la defunte
est plutôt l'occasion que le sujet.*"[1]   Dr. Trusler follows
him so closely as almost to quote his words.   The
plate, he says, is "the farce, of which death is oftener
the occasion than the subject."   That, as both
imply, Hogarth intended to satirize the senseless
funeral ceremonial of his day, and that, in doing so
upon the present occasion, he has somewhat strained
consistency, is true.   But it is also true that he was
wiser than his critics, and that all this was merely subordinate to a deeper and sterner lesson, more inti-
mately connected with the subject.   What other
epilogue, indeed, could there be to such a life ! Conventionalism, no doubt, would have stepped in with its
ready tear and faded " Requiescat."   But Hogarth
scorned Conventionalism, and copied human nature,
hard-hearted, frivolous, unrepentant, incorrigible.
In his experience, harlots were harlots to the end of
the chapter—and after.   There were no Magdalens
among them.   Their mourning was a mockery ;
their priest a profligate.   He will not even have the

---

[1] Hartley Coleridge ("Essays and Marginalia," 1851, ii. 212)
has the same idea.   In his view—"The print may be regarded as
the satyricon appended to a fearful tragedy."

poor child impressed ;—how should he be with such a mother ? No, let him wind up his " castle-top " in the foreground,—" the only thing in that assembly (as Lamb says) that is not a hypocrite." This painter painted life as he saw it ; he cared to do no more.

One of the first results of *A Harlot's Progress* was to reinstate him in the good graces of Sir James Thornhill, who had hitherto declined to forgive him for running away with his daughter. By the contrivance of Lady Thornhill and Mrs. Hogarth, some of the pictures were placed in the old man's dining room. He eagerly asked the artist's name, and on learning it said, " Very well; the man who can furnish representations like these, can also maintain a wife without a portion " —a speech which was the herald of reconciliation. This reconciliation may probably be placed at the end of 1731 or the beginning of 1732.[1] Shortly after the paintings, or part of them, were finished, Hogarth began to engrave them, issuing as the subscription ticket the clever little etching entitled *Boys peeping at Nature*. From an advertisement in the "Country Journal ; or, the Craftsman," for January 29, 1731-2, it would seem that he had not at first intended to undertake all the engraving personally.[2] " The

[1] According to the " Somerset House Gazette," ii. 207, Mr. Carpenter of Old Bond Street had, in July, 1824, a picture by Hogarth [?] representing this incident. Besides the principal parties concerned, it contained portraits of Fielding and Justice Welch. It is said to have been well painted.

[2] This is confirmed by an undated note in Vertue's MSS. (p. 51). " For the Harlot's progress Mr Hogarth having now

AUTHOR of the *Six Copper Plates*, representing a
Harlot's Progress," runs the notice; "being disap·
pointed of the Assistance he proposed, is obliged to
engrave them all himself, which will retard the
Delivery of the Prints to the Subscribers about Two
Months; the particular Time when they will be
deliver'd will be advertised in this Paper." "No
more," it was further stated, "will be printed than
are and shall be subscribed for, nor Subscriptions
taken for more than will receive a good Impression."
How many good impressions Hogarth considered
might be obtained is not specified, but it is recorded
that above 1,200 names were entered on his books.
This—supposing all the subscribers to pay—meant
some £1,260, as the price of the set was a guinea.

In conformity with the engagement made in the
advertisement of January, a further advertisement of
March, in the " Daily Journal" and " Daily Post,"
which was subsequently repeated, announced that
the plates were then "printing off," and would be
ready for delivery on Monday, the 10th of April.
At the same time notice was given that subscriptions
would be received until the 3rd; and as an un-
authorized explanation of the series in pamphlet
form was published on the 21st,[1] it must be assumed that they were duly issued on or about the

---

12 hundred Subscribers—he had proposed to get them graved by
the best gravers in Lond. but none that he employed pleasing
him he has set about them himself—to grave or finish the
gravings ".]

[1] " Daily Journal," 21 April, 1732.

date specified.[1] Their success seems to have been instantaneous. As soon as Plate III. appeared, says Nichols, the Lords of the Treasury hastened to the print-shop for Sir John Gonson's portrait. In addition to the prose account above referred to, a Grub Street rhymer set himself to celebrate Moll Hackabout's career in Hudibrastics under the title of "The Harlot's Progress; or, the Humours of Drury Lane," an example which was followed a year later by "The Lure of Venus," a more pretentious description in creaking heroics by "Joseph Gay" (Pope's "empty Joseph"), the *nom de guerre* of a certain Captain John Durant Breval, formerly of Trinity College, Cambridge, who should have been capable of better things. Neither Breval's book nor the other—it need scarcely be observed—is conceived in Hogarth's spirit or animated by his purpose. Besides these metrical efforts, in February, 1733, the story was turned into a ballad opera entitled "The Jew Decoy'd," which, however (according to the "Biographia Dramatica"), was never performed; and in the same year Theophilus Cibber converted it into a pantomime, produced in April at Drury Lane. Another evidence of the popularity of the prints was their transfer to fanmounts[2] and cups and saucers. Lastly, they were freely pirated, and Steevens saw no fewer than

[1] Nichols dates the *Harlot's Progress* 1733-4. But he had evidently never seen the above advertisements, concerning which some further particulars are given in Part II., "Bibliography."

[2] One of these is now in the British Museum. They were sold by M. Gamble at the "Golden Fan" in St Martin's Court, near Leicester Fields ("Daily Journal," Jan. 24, 1733).

E

eight different sets of fraudulent imitations, no doubt
including the illustrations which accompanied " The
Lure of Venus." One of these sets of imitations,
perhaps the best known, was by Elisha Kirkall,
or Kirkhall, of Dockwell-Court, Whitefriars—the
" bounteous Kirkall" of the " Dunciad." The plates,
in green ink, were reversed copies as large as the
originals, and were issued in November, 1732.[1]

Hogarth had before suffered from depredations of
this kind, his first published print, *Masquerades and
Operas*, having, as already stated, been feloniously
reproduced. In 1735, in concert with George Vertue,
Gerard Vandergucht, his friends Pine and Lambert,
and several others, he petitioned Parliament for leave
to bring in a bill to vest in designers and engravers
an exclusive right to their own works, and to restrain
the multiplying of copies without their consent. This
bill was duly introduced, and received the Royal
Assent on the 15th May, 1735, becoming the well-
known Act 8 Geo. II., cap. 13. Although Hogarth's
personal grievance does not seem to have been pro-
minently brought forward on this occasion, he found
the major portion of the funds ; the Act is generally
spoken of as his; and it was drawn by his friend
William Huggins, author of the Oratorio of " Judith."
He commemorated its passing by a long and jubilant
inscription on the plate entitled *Crowns, Mitres,*
etc., afterwards used as a subscription ticket to the
Election series. Yet the measure was only partially
successful in remedying the evil at which it aimed,

[1] "Craftsman," Nov. 18, 1732.

THE LAUGHING AUDIENCE.
From Hogarth's Etching.

and to the mortification of the painter—as reported by Sir John Hawkins—it failed, in a case tried before Lord Hardwicke in Chancery, to secure any benefit to an assignee claiming under assignment from the original inventor.[1]

One of Hogarth's main objects in promoting the above enactment was, no doubt, the protection of the series of paintings depicting *A Rake's Progress*, with which he was preparing to follow up *A Harlot's Progress*. This fresh series, in fact, must have been begun immediately after the earlier pictures were completed, since from an advertisement in "The Country Journal; or, the Craftsman" of December the 29th, 1733, he was, at that date, occupied upon the engravings. They were subscribed for in the same year, the ticket being the capital little etching, *A Pleased Audience at a Play*, afterwards styled *The Laughing Audience*. As in the previous Progress, Hogarth himself christened his chief character. In the first plate "Tom Rakewell" (the name, Mr. Stephens points out, is as appropriate to the miser father as to the prodigal son) has entered suddenly upon his inheritance. In a jumble of leases, bonds, and the miscellaneous hoardings of avarice, he is being measured

---

[1] Writing not long before his death, Hogarth's retrospect, nevertheless, is not ungrateful:—"After having had my plates pirated in almost all sizes, I in 1735 applied to Parliament for redress; and obtained it in so liberal a manner, as hath not only answered my own purpose, but made prints a considerable article in the commerce of this country, there being now more business of this kind done here than in Paris, or anywhere else, and as well" ("Hogarth Illustrated," iii. 35).

for his mourning. Already his knavish attorney
plunders him ; and he himself begins badly by casting
off the poor girl whom he has ruined while at Oxford.

> " Prodigus æris,
> Sublimis, cupidusque, et amata relinquere pernix,"

his fortune is written in his face.

The next plate (*The Levee*) transforms the clumsy
lad into an awkward man-of-fashion. His ante-
chamber is thronged with milliners, wigmakers,
tailors, and hatters. The "dealers in dark pictures"
have equipped him as a connoisseur—witness the
Judgment of Paris on the wall. A much-bewigged
musician is trying over " The Rape of the Sabines "
at a harpsichord ; a French hornplayer preludes
noisily upon his instrument. He dabbles in Bridgeman's landscape gardening, and maintains one poet,
if not two. But the majority of the visitors at his
reception are professors of those sterner arts which
in 1732-5 no gentleman could be without. He must
have his cocks at Newmarket, and his racers at
Epsom, where his horse, " Silly Tom," has won a
cup. Essex must instruct him in dancing ; Dubois
in fencing ; the great Figg himself in quarter-
staff.[1] And lest his proficiency in the two latter
sciences should fail to save his skin, he must enlist
the hireling " man-of-honour" who comes recommended by " Wm. Stab." Roistering " bloods" who
finish their revels at the " Shakespear's Head" or the

---

[1] The figures in the plate are said to be portraits of these
persons. Dubois died in May, 1734, of a wound received in a
duel.

"Rose" by broiling a waiter or "pinking" a chairman, sometimes require the aid of henchmen like the Captain, when their humorous exploits fall flat upon the spectators.

One of these exploits is depicted in Plate III. The Rake is discovered drunk in a tavern in Drury Lane at three in the morning, surrounded by the trophies of a street row, largely supplemented by further contributions from the apartment itself. His companions, mostly recruited from the *simplices nymphæ* of the neighbourhood, are in scarcely better case. One (like Prior's "Kitty") sets the world on fire (in a map). Another spirts brandy in the face of her furious *vis-à-vis*, who threatens her with a knife.[1] A harper is twangling at the door; a tattered beggar-wench sings the "Black Joke." We omit the remaining details of the plate, which may be studied at full in Nichols and John Ireland.

This is the Rake's zenith; in the next scene he enters upon the first stage of his decline. He is ignominiously arrested for debt in St. James's Street, as he is going to Court in a new suit on Queen Caroline's birthday, also St. David's Day, as is indicated by an irascible-looking Welshman with an enormous leek in his hat. Some temporary assistance is rendered to him by the unfortunate girl whom he discarded in Plate I.; but it is only temporary, for in the plate that follows he is repairing

[1] Hogarth had actually witnessed an incident of this kind when in company with his crony Frank Hayman (Smith's "Nollekens," i. 94).

his fortunes by an alliance in old Mary-le-bone Church, then much used for private marriages, with an elderly heiress. The bride is one-eyed, and tremulously exultant; the bridegroom, indifferent, and already engrossed by the good-looking lady's-maid. The church, which had been recently repaired, and was taken down altogether six years later, is depicted, no doubt as a fitting frame to the bride, in an extremely dilapidated condition. The Creed has been destroyed by damp, and a crack runs through the Ninth Commandment. As a further evidence of neglect the slot of the poor-box is covered by a cobweb.

Henceforward Tom Rakewell "progresses" at a headlong rate. Plate VI. shows him in a Covent Garden gaming-house. He has lost all his recently-acquired wealth, and flings himself upon the ground in a paroxysm of fury and execration. In allusion to the burning of White's, in April, 1733, flames are seen bursting from the wainscot, but the absorbed gamblers take no heed. The next scene is in the Fleet; the last in Bedlam. In the one he is a poor distracted wretch, dunned by the gaoler for "garnish," pestered by the unpaid pot-boy, deafened by the rancorous virago, his wife, and overwhelmed by Mr. Manager Rich's letter, returning his manuscript:— "Sᵣ. I have read yᵣ Play & find it will not doe." In the other he is an incurable maniac, fettered and dangerous, who tears at himself with the heartrending laugh of the insane.

Our rapid outline does but scant justice to this

tragical story, and scarcely touches at all upon the affluence of detail with which it is presented.[1] We are told that it did not meet with the success of *A Harlot's Progress*. The causes are not far to seek. It flew at higher social game. It attacked the vices of the man instead of the vices of the woman; and to the vices of the man society is notoriously indulgent. Then it was less probable. To use the words of a critic who compares it with its forerunner, its "catastrophe is one of so rare occurrence in real life, as to produce no more effect than a bugbear would. It is not in the ordinary course of events that profligates and debauchees become the inhabitants of a mad-house." Lastly, it is longer, and more unequal than *A Harlot's Progress*. Although it rises to a higher level in the later scenes, in the fourth plate, which Hogarth tried to improve, it was, for him, weak and hesitating. It is is scarcely likely, to say the least, that a poor

[1] Among minor touches may be noticed:—the shoe-sole cut from the cover of the Bible in the second state of Plate I., and the cap on the mantelpiece which, in the same plate, establishes the identity of the dead miser with the portrait; the Farinelli caricature on the floor in Plate II.; the twelve Cæsars and Pontack's head, in Plate III.; the little fellow with the pipe and "Farthing Post," in Plate IV.; the dogs and the ragged charity boy of Plate V.; the highwayman of Plate VI.; the wings of the inventor and the absorbed alchemist of Plate VII.; and lastly, the two women visitors in the Bedlam scene. Scott knew these prints of Hogarth's, for in his "Journal" (1891, i. 140) he likens himself, when writing on the Currency, to the projector with his scheme for paying the National Debt, in Plate VII.; and in another place he borrows his illustration from the "Better to Work than Stand thus" of Plate IV. of *A Harlot's Progress*.

milliner would carry about with her sufficient money
to relieve a fine gentleman in peril of the tipstaves.
Her presence after Plate I. is an illustration of that
" pathetic fallacy " of which we occasionally hear so
much. Some one, it must be supposed, had remarked
upon the want of tenderness in *A Harlot's Progress*,
and Hogarth met the objection in *A Rake's Progress*
by the introduction of his ruined sweetheart. But her
re-appearances are ill-managed and almost super-
fluous. She adds little to the effect of the scenes in
the prison or the madhouse, and they would scarcely
suffer by her absence. If the above conjecture be
a correct one, this is another of the many instances
in which Hogarth was apparently led astray by his
importunate advisers.

Early in June, 1735, the plates of *A Rake's Progress* were printed off. Their delivery to subscribers
was, however, deferred until the 25th, the date they
bore, in order to give them the full protection of the
new Act, which came into operation on the 24th. Probably the words " According to Act of Parliament,"
now so common on engravings, made their first appearance upon this occasion. But notwithstanding all
these precautions, the painter, as we learn from one of
his many advertisements, could not escape the fraudulent imitator. " Several printsellers," he says in
" The London Daily Post Boy" of June 14, " who have
of late made their chief gain by unjustly pirating the
inventions and designs of ingenious Artists, whereby
they have robbed them of the benefit of their labours,
being now prohibited such scandalous practices from

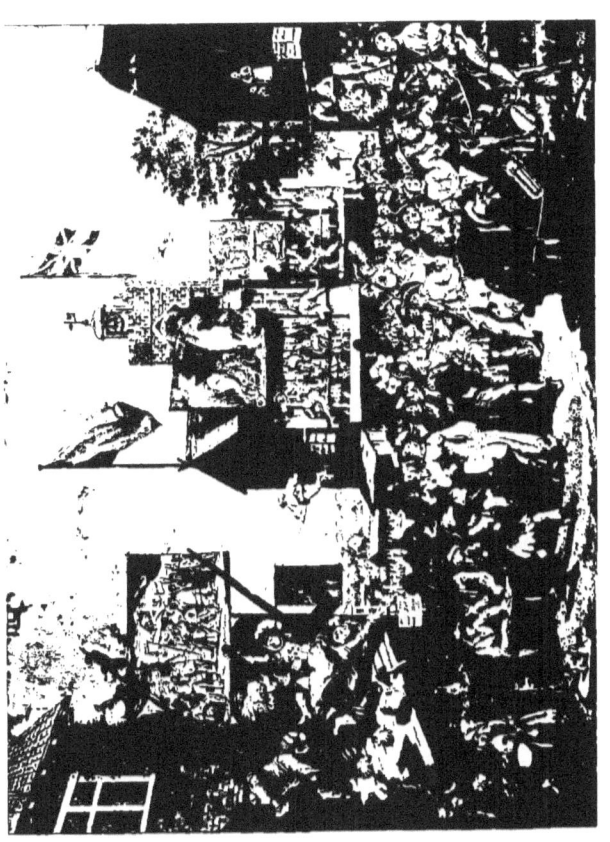

the 24th of June next, by an Act of Parliament
passed the last Session, intituled, ' An Act for the
Encouragement of the Arts of Designing, Engraving,
Etching, &c.,' have resolved notwithstanding to continue their injurious proceedings, at least till that
time; and have, in a clandestine manner, procured
persons to come to Mr. Hogarth's house, under pretence of seeing his Rake's Progress, in order to
pirate the same, and publish base prints thereof
before the Act commences, and even before Mr.
Hogarth himself can publish the true ones. This
behaviour, and men who are capable of a practice
so repugnant to honesty and destructive of property, are humbly submitted to the judgment of
the publick, on whose justice the person injured
relies."[1] According to Nichols, a series of copies by
Boitard, all on one sheet, must have appeared almost
simultaneously with this notice; and the prints were
also plagiarised in another series issued by Overton,
Bowles and others, a few days later. To counteract,
as far as possible, the evil effect upon the sale of
the originals of these cheap piratical reproductions,
Hogarth caused small copies to be prepared, which
were sold at 2s. 6d. the set by " T. Bakewell, print
and mapseller, next Johnson's Court in Fleet Street,
London." These, after some delay, were issued
in August, accompanied by a broadside sheet of
explanations.

With the original engravings of *A Rake's Progress*
was published a print of earlier date, which had been

[1] " Genuine Works," i. 83.

kept back to give it the advantages of protection,
i.e., that known as *The Fair*, or *Southwark Fair*,
one of the liveliest of the separate plates, albeit
somewhat coarse in execution. This festival (or
carnival) was suppressed in 1762; but in 1733,
when Hogarth drew it, it was diligently frequented,
during the fortnight for which it was held, by
"persons of all distinctions of both sexes." Its
notabilities are faithfully depicted. Elkanah Settle's
droll of the "Siege of Troy," as given at Lee
and Harper's booth; the "posture-master" and
"curious Indian birds" of Mr. Fawkes, the conjuror;
the wax-work exhibiting "the whole Court of
France;" Müller, or Miller, the Leipzic giant;
Violante, the tumbler; Cadman, the steeple-flyer—
all these have been carefully set down. The "Fall
of Bajazet," at Cibber and Bullock's, is tragically
illustrated by the collapse of the "parade" in front
of the booth; whilst in the crowd a couple of bailiffs
arrest a buskined hero from the same company who,
with a beautiful drummeress, is beating up for an
audience. But the incident of the plate would take
several pages to describe.

Among the other works which belong to this
chapter, and have not been mentioned hitherto, is
the drinking scene called *A Midnight Modern Conversation*, 1733. Its proper place lies between the
two *Progresses*. In this a party of eleven, whose
degrees of intoxication are admirably characterized,
have finished some two dozen bottles of claret, and,
at four in the morning, are commencing a capacious

1. Midnight Modern Conversation

from Hogarth's engraving

bowl of punch presided over by a rosy-gilled parson, —the

"fortem validumque combibonem
Lætantem super amphora repleta"

of the Westminster Latinist, Vincent Bourne ;[1] but, in real life, identified both with the famous "Orator" Henley and the Rev. Cornelius Ford, a dissolute cousin of Dr. Johnson.[2]   The frontispiece to Henry Carey's "Chrononhotontologos," and one or two minor pieces show—like the list of presents to Farinelli in Plate II. of *A Rake's Progress*—the artist's unconquered antipathy to the foreign favourites upon whom the British public squandered fortunes "for a shrug or a song."   Perhaps it was not natural under the circumstances that Hogarth should do justice to Farinelli ; but the British public of his day were not far wrong in their admiration of that most wonderful of sopranos.

In addition to the passing of the Act against piratical printsellers, no facts of equal importance in Hogarth's life during this period have been recorded. From the presence of Sir James Thornhill at New-

---

[1]   "Poematia," 1734, p. 146.

[2]   From an example in Solon's " Old English Potter," 1883, p. 185, a modelled white ware mug (salt-glaze), it appears that this popular design was transferred to pottery ; and it is often to be found on snuff-boxes.   It was also used as a fan-mount. (See " Daily Journal " for May 24th, 1733, where it is advertised as sold at Mr. Chenevix's and other toy-shops, and having prefixed to it, "for the Entertainment of the Ladies, a Description of each particular Person . . . introduced.")   The ticket for the *Midnight Modern Conversation* was the etching known as *The Oratorio; or, A Chorus of Singers.*

gate, when in March, 1733, Hogarth painted the portrait of Sarah Malcolm the murderess, afterwards executed in Fleet Street,[1] it is plain that the reconciliation already referred to had proved an enduring one. In May, 1734, Thornhill died, his death being followed, a year later, by that of Hogarth's mother, occasioned, says the "Gentleman's Magazine," by a fright arising out of a fire in Cecil Court, St. Martin's Lane. By the decease of his father-in-law the drawing school in Covent Garden practically passed into Hogarth's hands. " I became (he says) possessed of his (Sir James's) neglected apparatus ; and thinking that an academy conducted on proper and moderate principles had some use, proposed that a number of artists should enter into a subscription for the hire of a place large enough to admit thirty or forty people to draw after a naked figure. This was soon agreed to, and a room taken in St. Martin's Lane. To serve the society, I lent them the furniture which had belonged to Sir James Thornhill's academy ; and as I attributed the failure of that and Mr. Vanderbank's[2] to the leading members assuming a superiority which their fellow students could not brook, I proposed that every member should contribute an equal sum to the establishment, and have

[1] "Craftsman," 10th March, 1733.

[2] John Vanderbank, the portrait-painter, had endeavoured to establish a rival school to Thornhill's, with the additional attraction of a living model. He illustrated "Don Quixote" for Lord Carteret, who preferred his designs to those of Hogarth. See Part II., Catalogue of Prints. There is a portrait of Newton by Vanderbank in the National Portrait Gallery.

THE ORATORIO.
From Hogarth's Etching.

an equal right to vote in every question relative to the society. . . . By the regulations I have mentioned, of a general equality, etc., it has now [1762] subsisted near thirty years ; and is, to every useful purpose, equal to that in France, or any other."[1] The exact locality of this art-centre, it may be added, was " in Peter's Court, against Tom's Coffee-house in S. Martin's Lane." Thus it is described in an advertisement of 1710, when it was a Dancing School. Subsequently it became the studio of Roubillac the sculptor, from whom it passed to Hogarth and his coadjutors.   In this institution, most of the artists of the reign of George II., and the early part of the reign of George III., were trained ; and its usefulness only ceased with the establishment of the Royal Academy, to which its "anatomical figures, busts, statues, etc.," were transferred in 1768.   Hogarth painted a picture of the interior, showing the students drawing from the life.   This painting is preserved at Burlington House, having been purchased not many years ago.

From the " Παραινετικόν " of Vincent Bourne quotation has been made.   But, in 1736, a passage in Swift's " Legion Club " showed that Hogarth's fame had reached the terrible Dean at Dublin :—

> " How I want thee, humorous Hogarth !
> Thou, I hear, a pleasant rogue art.
> Were but you and I acquainted,
> Every monster should be painted :

---

[1] " Hogarth Illustrated," iii. 66-7, 68-9.

>   You should try your graving tools
>   On this odious group of fools ;
>   Draw the beasts as I describe them ;
>   Form their features, while I gibe them ;
>   Draw them like, for I assure ye,
>   You will need no *car'catura ;*
>   Draw them so that we may trace
>   All the soul in every face."

Four years later, in February, 1740, Somervile the
poet, claiming kinship as a satirist of vice and folly,
dedicated his "Hobbinol" to Hogarth as "the
greatest master in the burlesque way"; and a few
months subsequently came a tribute from the pen of
a still more eminent writer, Henry Fielding. As it
refers solely to the *Progresses*, it may the more fitly
find place here. "I esteem," says Fielding, in the
"Champion" (June 10), "the ingenious Mr. *Hogarth*
as one of the most useful Satyrists any Age hath
produced. In his excellent Works you see the delu-
sive Scene exposed with all the Force of Humour,
and, on casting your Eyes on another Picture, you
behold the dreadful and fatal Consequence. I almost
dare affirm that those two Works of his, which he
calls the *Rake's* and the *Harlot's Progress*, are calculated more to serve the Cause of Virtue, and for
the Preservation of Mankind, than all the *Folio's* of
Morality which have been ever written; and a sober
Family should be no more without them, than without the *Whole Duty of Man* in their House." In that
admirable "Preface" to "Joseph Andrews," in which
he compares comic writing and burlesque to comic
painting and caricature, he returns to the same theme :

" He who should call the ingenious Hogarth a burlesque painter, would, in my opinion, do him very
little honour : for sure it is much easier, much less
the subject of admiration, to paint a man with a nose,
or any other feature of a preposterous size, or to
expose him in some absurd or monstrous attitude,
than to express the affections of men on canvas. It
hath been thought a vast commendation of a painter,
to say his figures seem to breathe ; but surely it is a
much greater and nobler applause, that they appear
to think." Hogarth acknowledged this compliment
in 1743 by referring to Fielding's " Preface " as a
further explanation of the little etching of *Characters
and Caricaturas.*

HOGARTH'S VAUXHALL TICKET.

CHAPTER IV.

THE welcome which the engravings of Hogarth's picture-comedies had received should—one would think—have convinced him that his best means of permanent success lay in this direction. Yet according to his own account, which, unhappily, it is not possible to date, it would appear that he had other and different ambitions. His desire was to take rank with the Haymans and Thornhills,—to say nothing of artists more ancient and illustrious. " Before I had done anything of much consequence in this walk [*i.e.*, 'painting and engraving modern moral subjects '], I entertained some hopes of succeeding in what the puffers in books call *the great style of history painting;* so that without having had a stroke of this *grand* business before, I quitted small portraits and familiar conversations, and, with a smile at my own temerity, commenced history painter, and on a great staircase at St. Bartholomew's Hospital, painted two Scripture stories, the

Pool of Bethesda, and the *Good Samaritan*, with figures seven feet high.   These I presented to the charity, and thought they might serve as a specimen, to show that were there an inclination in England for encouraging historical pictures, such a first essay might prove the painting them more easily attainable than is generally imagined.   But as religion, the great promoter of this style in other countries, rejected it in England, I was unwilling to sink into a *portrait manufacturer;* and still ambitious of being singular, dropped all expectations of advantage from that source, and returned to the pursuit of my former dealings with the public at large."[1]

This is, in some respects, a singular utterance. If we accept 1736, which is the date painted upon the staircase of the hospital, as the date of the *Good Samaritan* and the *Pool of Bethesda*, then the expression "anything of much consequence" seems a strange under-valuation of the two *Progresses* which had made him a name.   Seeing, however, that the sentence, "I quitted small portraits and familiar conversations," does not cover these series, it may be that the Bartholomew's Hospital pictures were executed before 1736.   But even if we put them back five years, Hogarth would still have painted the *Harlot's Progress*, and the expression "anything of much consequence" would remain inexplicable, except by attributing to the artist a perverse, though not unprecedented, blindness as to his abilities.   Moreover, his "Scripture stories" were

[1] "Hogarth Illustrated," iii. 29-31.

F

a mistake ; and if they were not good in his own
day, they are homelier than ever in ours, when the
realism of artists like Holman Hunt and Gérôme
have imported into our galleries the very types and
atmosphere of the East. With the record that the
pictures made the painter a governor of the hospital,
and the statement that they were not engraved until
after his death, we may pass over the *Pool of
Bethesda* and the *Good Samaritan*.

During the period covered by the present chapter,
that is to say, from 1735 to 1744, Hogarth did not
put forth any series of plates corresponding in importance to the *Rake's* and *Harlot's Progresses*.
Indeed, with the exception of the *Four Times of the
Day*, he did not publish any series at all. Doubtless
he was maturing and elaborating his masterpiece,
Marriage A-la-Mode, which was advertised in April,
1743, and will form the subject of the ensuing
chapter. But in this interval, several separate prints
appeared, which are among the most popular of his
works—*i.e.*, the *Strolling Actresses Dressing in a
Barn*, the *Enraged Musician*, and the *Distressed Poet*.
And here we may observe that it is the defect of
his biography that it lies almost wholly in the
description of his works. To the facts of his life
the account of his works must always bear much the
same relation in bulk as the commentary of Warton
to the " Minor Poems " of Milton, or the notes to
the text in an article by Bayle. Lamb said truly
that we "read" his prints, and "look" at other
pictures. He might have added that the type is of

the smallest, and the page is crammed to the margin.

The earliest plates belonging to the year 1736 are the *Company of Undertakers* or *Consultation of Physicians*; and the *Scholars at a Lecture*. The *Company of Undertakers* is a whimsical coat-of-arms, composed of doctors " poising their gilt-head canes " (as in Tennyson's " Princess "), with the motto, "*Et Plurima Mortis Imago.*" Conspicuous among them in a harlequin suit ("issuant checkie ") is Mrs. Sarah Mapp, a famous bone-setter or "shape-mistress," who enjoyed a brief popularity *circa* 1736-7. Two other figures which support her have been identified, one as a famous quack oculist or " Opthalmiator " known as the "Chevalier" Taylor: the other as the Dr. Joshua Ward, to whose nostrums Fielding had recourse in his last illness, and who figures in Pope's

"Ward try'd on Puppies, and the Poor, his Drop."

But if he was a quack, he was a quack of genius, for he inspired Bolingbroke with confidence, and he attended George II. The *Company of Undertakers* is dated March. The *Scholars at a Lecture*, a number of, for the most part, vulgar academical heads, requires no special notice. To the month of April belongs a ticket for Fielding's benefit in " Pasquin." There is a doubt whether this is really the work of Hogarth ; but the strokes at political morality in that "dramatic Satire on the Times" would have been so much to the taste of the artist who later designed the inimitable Election Prints,

that one is inclined to give him the benefit of any
uncertainty.   Concerning the *Sleeping Congregation,*
which came out in October of the same year, there
is no doubt at all.   The slumbering auditory are
poorly treated ; but the Rev. Dr. John Theophilus
Desaguliers, if he it be, who,

> "In one lazy tone
> Through the long, heavy, painful page drawls on,"

and his pompous clerk, struggling between drowsi-
ness and the ill-guarded attractions of the pretty girl
at his side who has fallen asleep with her prayer-
book open at " Matrimony," are not to be improved
upon.   Whether the preacher, once famous for his
lectures on Experimental Philosophy in what is now
Cannon Row, Westminster, deserved the satire, we
know not.   But, to judge by the design, he will certainly soon be able to say, in the words of Horace
which have been suggested as its motto,—" OMNES
composui." [1]

In 1737 Hogarth was probably at work on the
Four Times of the Day, the engravings of which were

---

[1] *The Sleeping Congregation* would not be an inappropriate
frontispiece to Swift's singular sermon on "Sleeping in Church "
(" Works," by Scott, 1824, viii. pp. 17-27).   It begins—" I have
chosen these words [*i.e.* the story of Eutychus, Acts xx. 9] with
design, if possible, to disturb some part of this audience of half
an hour's sleep, for the convenience and exercise whereof, this
place, at this season of the day, is very much celebrated."   The
epigraph might be borrowed from his "Thoughts on Various
Subjects," 1726,—" Query, Whether churches are not dormitories
of the living as well as of the dead ? "   Goldsmith also touches on
this regrettable infirmity of human nature ("Citizen of the World,"
Letter xli.).

THE SLEEPING CONGREGATION.
From Hogarth's Engraving.

advertised as finished early in 1738. Nothing of any importance is recorded for the previous year, save a very characteristic letter which he addressed, over the signature of " Britophil," to the " St. James's Evening Post," of June 7-9, 1737, in defence of Sir James Thornhill, upon whose paintings at Green- wich certain aspersions had been cast by another journal.[1] We take it from Nichols, who professes to have "correctly transcribed" it ("Genuine Works," i. 97-102). After commenting upon the criticism which condemns an entire work because of some minor and quite subordinate defect (a kind of ap- praisement, by the way, not wholly extinct even in these days), the writer proceeds to a vigorous attack upon his favourite enemies, the "picture-dealers":—

"There is another set of gentry more noxious to the Art than these, and those are your picture- jobbers from abroad,[2] who are always ready to raise a great cry in the prints whenever they think their craft is in danger; and indeed it is their interest to depreciate every English work, as hurtful to their trade, of continually importing ship-loads of dead Christs, Holy Families, Madona's [sic], and other dismal dark subjects, neither entertaining nor orna- mental; on which they scrawl the terrible cramp

---

[1] The authority for attributing this letter to Hogarth is the "London Magazine," which, reprinting it from the "Post," declared it to be "by the first Painter in England, perhaps in the World, in his way."

[2] "An abuse grown to such a height, that the Legislature has endeavoured to put a stop to it, by laying a duty on the importa- tion of foreign pictures."—(Hogarth's note.)

names of some Italian masters, and fix on us poor
Englishmen the character of *universal dupes*. If a
man, naturally a judge of Painting, not bigoted to
those empirics, should cast his eye on one of their
sham virtuoso-pieces, he would be very apt to say,
' Mr. Bubbleman, that grand Venus (as you are
pleased to call it) has not beauty enough for the
character of an English cook-maid.' Upon which
the quack answers with a confident air, 'O Lord,
Sir, I find that you are no connoisseur—that picture,
I assure you, is in Alesso Baldovinetto's second and
best manner, boldly painted, and truely [*sic*] sublime ;
the contour gracious ; the air of the head in the high
Greek taste, and a most divine idea it is.' Then
spitting on an obscure place, and rubbing it with a
dirty handkerchief, takes a skip to the other end of
the room, and screams out in raptures, ' There is an
amazing touch ! a man should have this picture a
twelve-month in his collection before he can discover half its beauties.' The gentleman (though
naturally a judge of what is beautiful, yet ashamed
to be out of the fashion in judging for himself) with
this cant is struck dumb, gives a vast sum for the
picture, very modestly confesses he is indeed quite
ignorant of Painting, and bestows a frame worth
fifty pounds on a frightful thing, without the hard
name on it not worth as many farthings."[1]

[1] " *E g.* A monstrous Venus at Kensington, valued at a thousand pounds, said to be painted by Michael Angelo di Buonarotti
or Jacomo di Pontermo, or Sebastiano del Piambo" (*sic*).—
(Hogarth's note.)

We have quoted this passage because it shows that, notwithstanding the sneers cast at the painter's education, he could write graphically and with vigour when his feelings were aroused. If his sketch be not worthy of the immortal genius who defined connoisseurship as consisting in the assertion that the picture might have been better if the painter had taken more pains, and in praising the works of Pietro Perugino—if it be not worthy of Oliver Goldsmith, it might well have come from the pen of him who drew that painter Pallet whom Peregrine Pickle met in the Palais Royal at Paris. It would do no dishonour to Smollett. No doubt Hogarth's inimical critic, George Steevens, would probably hint that the letter was "corrected" by Hoadly or Ralph ; but, in the absence of any such insinuation, we may at least concede (with John Ireland) that it "carries internal evidence of his mind." It will help us to understand the pictures on the walls in Plate I. of *Marriage A-la-Mode*, and the future story of *Sigismunda*.

The engravings of the *Four Times of the Day* are dated March 25th, 1738. They represent three scenes in London and one at Islington ; and the pictures, as already stated in Chapter II., were originally designed for Mr. Jonathan Tyers of Vauxhall. If only as illustrations of the time, they are extremely interesting. The first plate shows us Covent Garden at early morning on a winter's day, with a disorderly company coming out of "Tom King's Coffee House ;"[1] the second, a congregation issuing at

[1] "What rake is ignorant of King's Coffee-house?"—asks

noon, on Sunday, from the French chapel in Hog
Lane, St. Giles's (now Crown Street); the third, a
citizen and his wife returning from Sadler's Wells on
a sultry summer's evening; and the fourth, the
neighbourhood of Charing Cross at night, on " Restoration Day," with the "Salisbury Flying Coach"
upset in the middle of a bonfire. The last is the
worst of the series, the second is the best; but all
are filled with a multiplicity of detail that deserves
careful study. The uproarious misery of the lad in
Noon, who has broken his pie-dish by resting it too
heavily upon a post, and the delightful coxcombry of
the Frenchman in his *ailes-de-pigeon* and *solitaire*, the
much-enduring dyer and his melting wife in *Evening*,
and the drunken freemason in *Night*, are excellent.
But the cream of the characters represented is certainly the censorious prude in the first scene with
her lank-haired and shivering footboy. She is said
to have been an aunt of the painter, who, like
Churchill, lost a legacy by too inconsiderate a frank-
ness. Fielding borrowed her lineaments for the por-

Fielding in his "Covent Garden Tragedy" of 1732, and he refers
to it again four years later in "Pasquin," where his "comic poet"
is arrested as he leaves this disreputable resort. It stood,
according to J. R. Smith, opposite to Tavistock Row, and not in
front of the church, where, by artistic licence, Hogarth has
placed it. Of Moll King, its proprietor at the date of this
chapter, and a successful rival of the Needhams and Bentleys of
her epoch, Mr. Edward Draper, of Vincent Square, Westminster,
has a remarkable portrait, ascribed on good authority to Hogarth.
In this she appears as a bold, handsome, gipsy-looking woman,
holding a cat in her lap. She died in retirement at Hampstead,
September 17, 1747.

Noon.
from Hogarths Engraving.

trait of Miss Bridget Allworthy, and Thackeray has
copied her wintry figure for one of the initials to
the "Roundabout Papers." To her, too, Cowper,
whose early satires bear unmistakable traces of close
familiarity with Hogarth, has consecrated an entire
passage of "Truth":—

> "Yon ancient prude, whose wither'd features show
> She might be young some forty years ago,
> Her elbows pinioned close upon her hips,
> Her head erect, her fan upon her lips,
> Her eyebrows arched, her eyes both gone astray
> To watch yon amorous couple in their play,
> With bony and unkerchief'd neck defies
> The rude inclemency of wintry skies,
> And sails with lappet head and mincing airs
> Duly at clink of bell to morning prayers.
> To thrift and parsimony much inclined,
> She yet allows herself that boy behind ;
> The shivering urchin, bending as he goes,
> With slipshod heels and dewdrop at his nose,
> His predecessor's coat advanced to wear,
> Which future pages yet are doom'd to share,
> Carries her Bible tuck'd beneath his arm,
> And hides his hands to keep his fingers warm."

One of the results brought about by the bitter per-
sonalities of Fielding's "Pasquin" and of its successor
the "Historical Register," was the passing of that
"Act against Strolling Players," which, among other
things, made it penal to represent plays out of the
city and liberties of Westminster for hire, gain, or
reward. This gave rise to the excellent print which
Hogarth issued with the *Four Times of the Day*, viz.,
Strolling Actresses Dressing in a Barn. The play to
be represented is " The Devil to pay in Heaven," a

piece which will be vainly sought for in the " Play-
House Companions" of the period. It is, however,
aptly enough symbolized by the plate itself—surely
the most laughable assemblage of vaulting preten-
sions and creeping commonplaces that were ever
combined together. In the centre Diana, not much
more closely clad than Shakespeare's "chariest maid,"

> " If she unmask her beauty to the moon,"

recites (and probably rants) her part. Near to her
Flora is tallowing her hair, while Night (a negress)
darns a hole in Juno's stocking.[1] Jupiter, " *rubente
dextra*," is peaceably superintending the removal by
Cupid of some stockings from the pasteboard cloud
upon which they have been hung to dry. Ganymede, a Siren, and Aurora are engaged in mutual
civilities; the eagle is feeding her baby with a
spoon; the Witch clips a cat's tail to get blood for
scenic purposes, and two boy-devils—their foreheads
budding with their first horns—are fighting at an
altar for a pot of beer. The plate is crowded with

---

[1] Leslie specially draws attention to " the exquisite prettiness of
this lady," and cites her—with the handsome drummeress of *Southwark Fair* and the country girl who, in the same plate, is wonder-
ing at the prize-fighter—as an instance of that sense of beauty
which (as Coleridge observes) was never extinguished in Hogarth
by the satirist. " I know not any painter (says Leslie) in whose
works so many extremely pretty female faces are to be found ; and
though they are often given to negative characters, yet he could
combine great beauty and delicacy of feature with utter physiognomical depravity, as in some of the women in the third plate
of *The Rake's Progress*" ("Handbook for Young Painters,"
1855, 123-5). See also Coleridge's " Friend," Dec. 7, 1809,
No. 16.

minute strokes of humour—such as the fowls roost-
ing upon the waves, the crown jewels in a hamper, the
kittens sporting with the orb, the plays in the bishop's
mitre ; but the mere catalogue of them would be
lengthy.   The worst fault of the design is that it
has no definite central interest, although we may
agree with Walpole that " for wit and imagination
without any other end" (the italics are ours) it is " the
best of all his works."   To the original picture,
however, it is now impossible to appeal, as it was
unhappily burnt at Littleton in 1874.

In the establishment of the Foundling Hospital,
for which a Royal Charter was granted in 1739,
Hogarth seems to have taken a genuine interest.
It was the object of Captain Coram, the patient
philanthropist with whom the scheme originated, to
provide some asylum for those deserted infants who,
under the callous Poor Laws of the day, were too
often committed to the tender mercies of the street.
That such refuges are of doubtful expediency, and
are even open to serious abuses, are now recognized
facts ; facts, moreover, that were amply illustrated
by the after history of the Foundling itself, which
has long since judiciously revised its original pro-
gramme.   But when the plan was first ventilated,
charities were in the air, and the plausible benevolence
of its purpose found many enthusiastic supporters,
among the foremost of whom was Hogarth.   He
figures in the Charter as " a Governor and Guardian ;"
he was an active member at the meetings of the
Institution ; and he aided it with his money, his

graver, and his brush. The little print known as *The Foundlings* (the plate of which is still in the custody of the Governors) was prepared by him as a headpiece to a Power of Attorney for collecting subscriptions ; he designed the heraldic shield placed over the door of the hospital's first home in Hatton Garden ; and, lastly, by presenting it, in May, 1740, with an admirable full-length of its brave old founder, he initiated its embellishment by works of art.

He himself considered *Captain Coram* the best of his single portraits, and the judgment of posterity has ratified his opinion. " The portrait which I painted with most pleasure (says he), and in which I particularly wished to excel, was that of Captain Coram, for the Foundling Hospital ; and if I am so wretched an artist as my enemies assert, it is somewhat strange that this, which was one of the first I painted the size of life, should stand the test of twenty years' competition, and be generally thought the best portrait in the place, notwithstanding the first painters in the kingdom exerted all their talents to vie with it." [1] The rivals indicated were Hudson, Shackleton, Reynolds (then plain Mr.), Cotes, Ramsay (the poet's son), Highmore, and Wilson. But the great genius of Sir Joshua had not attained its majority in the portrait of Lord Dartmouth, to which reference is made ; and it must be admitted that the picture of Coram stands a successful comparison with any of the remaining portraits in the Foundling.

[1] " Hogarth Illustrated," iii. 51.

Excellent as is Nutter's copy, it gives no idea of the superb colouring and masterly qualities of the original painting.

As may be gathered from the foregoing reference to rival performances, other artists in due time followed Hogarth's example, by contributing, or promising to contribute, works to the institution. When, in December, 1746, the west wing was completed, all those who had assisted in this manner were, at a general Court of the Hospital, elected Governors, with power to meet once a year for the purpose of considering " what further ornaments could be added to the building without expense to the charity." An immediate, if not an indispensable, consequence of this arrangement was an annual dinner on the 5th November, at which, regarding " Liberty as the Parent and Friend of the Fine Arts," the assembled painters were accustomed to commemorate the landing of William the Third, using for their pious libations a fine old white and blue dragon-china punch-bowl, generally described as Hogarth's, which is still carefully preserved in one of the cases—of the Court-room.[1]   But a more practical result of the appointment of the Artist-Governors, was the ultimate formation of that remarkable collection of works of art which " made a visit to the Foundling the most fashionable lounge of the reign of George II.," and, by a succession of circumstances, the record of which scarcely belongs to these

---

[1] A copy of this punch-bowl is given in the initial to Chapter I.

pages, indirectly, but not the less surely, brought about the establishment of the Royal Academy.[1]

To return to the succession of engravings. In 1738 Hogarth prepared a set of plates for an edition of *Don Quixote*. His Maritornes is better than his Don (who is the grotesque of the old renderings, and not the demented gentleman of the modern versions); but like the bulk of his illustrations to books, none of these efforts has any especial value. The hard frost of 1739-40, which stimulated so many delineations of " Ice-Fairs" and the like, appears to have passed by him unnoticed. But to the years 1740 and 1741 belong two delightful single plates, the *Distressed Poet* and the *Enraged Musician*. The former of these, it is true, had been first issued as far back as 1736, but it was republished with variations in 1740, and was followed a year later by the *Enraged Musician*, with which it is convenient to treat it. From an advertisement in the " London Daily Post," for November 24th, 1740, the artist appears to have contemplated a " third on Painting," but although there is reason to believe that a sketch in oils was completed, it was, for some unexplained reason, never engraved.[2]

[1] To complete the record of Hogarth's connection with the Foundling Hospital, it may here be added that his patronage of the institution took the practical form of maintaining at his own expense some of the children, who, in accordance with custom, were put out to nurse. In a case in the Court-room is still to be seen his discharged account for the keep, etc., at Chiswick, of two little girls, Susan Wyndham and Mary Woolaston, who, at his death, were sent back to the Hospital by his widow.

[2] See " Gazette des Beaux Arts," xxv. 209.

THE DISTRESSED POET.
From Hogarth's Engraving.

Was Oliver Goldsmith thinking of the *Distressed Poet* when, in August, 1758, he described himself to his friend Bob Bryanton as "in a garret writing for bread, and expecting to be dunned for a milk score"? Except that the milkmaid has already arrived, and is angrily exhibiting her tally, this is the precise *status quo* of Hogarth's print. The poor verseman, high in his Drury Lane or "Porridge Island" sky-parlour, has risen by candlelight to finish a poem on "Riches" for some contemporary Curll. He is exactly in the case of Cowper's bard—

> "Who having whelp'd a prologue with much pains,
> Feels himself spent, and fumbles for his brains."

Neither the map of the "Gold Mines of Peru" nor "all his books around"—a magnificent total of three,[1] the "Grub Street Journal" on the floor not included —can help him at his need. Meanwhile his vociferous creditor (with the Michaelmas daisies round her hat) clamours for the score; a dog, which has entered with her, steals the meagre meal; the cupboard is bare, and the wind whistles "through the

---

[1] We are describing the impression of 1740. That of Mar. 3, 1736, has under it the four following lines from Pope's "Dunciad," 1735, i. 111-14, which may have suggested the design :—

> "Studious he sate, with all his books around,
> Sinking, from thought to thought, a vast profund [*sic*]!
> Plung'd for his sense, but found no bottom there,
> Then writ, and flounder'd on, in mere despair."

Instead of a poem on "Riches," he is writing on "Poverty," and instead of the "Mines of Peru," there is a print of Pope thrashing Curll. There are also two more books.

broken pane." [1] He has a consolation, however, that poor Goldsmith lacked through life, one of the sweetest female companions that Hogarth ever drew. She is the ancestress of Thackeray's "Mrs. Shandon," this patient, conciliatory lady, who gazes so mildly and so helplessly at the long array of chalk-marks. And (O bathos! O "most lame and impotent conclusion!") she is darning her shivering spouse's small-clothes, while the cat and kittens nestle familiarly on his bardship's coat. [2]

More crowded with incident, but not nearly so suggestive, is the *Enraged Musician*. It is simply a *ne plus ultra* of discord. Cats wrangle on the tiles, a dog howls dismally, bells ring in St. Martin's steeple, a farrier winds his horn, and a sweep shrills eerily from a chimney-pot. Below, a handsome milkmaid cries her ware, a dustman bawls "Dust ho!" a costermonger yells "Flound-a-a-rs;" while a knife-grinder, a ballad-woman singing the "Lady's Fall," a wretched oboe-player, well known to the Londoners of that day, an amateur drummer, and an escaped parrot swell the orchestra. And all this cacophony for the benefit of the befrogged, and

[1] The shield-like object over the mantle-shelf is one of the *cruces* of the commentator. We are inclined to think with Mr. F. G. Stephens ("Satirical Prints," iii. 213) that it is a group of circular mirrors. These were made of watch glasses, and are still to be found occasionally in old furniture shops.

[2] "The poet's wife is perhaps the most loveable figure that ever Hogarth drew; while the milk-woman has as little milkiness about her as if she had been suckled on blue ruin and brimstone" (Hartley Coleridge, "Essays and Marginalia," 1851, ii. 217).

of course foreign, violinist, who glares infuriate, and
with stopped ears, from his (or, rather, Hogarth's
friend Huggins's) open window. The picture, as
Fielding said in his "Voyage to Lisbon," is "enough
to make a man deaf to look at."

Besides the *Enraged Musician* and the *Distrest
Poet*, the only other works of this period which need
be chronicled are a painting and a pair of portraits.
Of the latter, one was the likeness of Martin Folkes,
a mathematician, an antiquary, and a vice-president
of the Foundling. The other was a moderately
successful likeness of that full-blown and prosperous
prelate, Dr. Benjamin Hoadly, Bishop of Winchester,
whose copious paragraphs Pope, mindful of His
Grace's Hanoverian propensities, had satirized in the

> "Swift, for closer style,
> And Hoadly for a period of a mile,"

of the second imitation of Donne. Hogarth was
intimate with the Bishop's family, and often visited
at the old two-storeyed Palace at Chelsea, which
once stood at the bottom of Oakley Street; and
here, when the building was demolished in 1825,
was found a mural drawing of nine figures, affirmed
by enthusiasts to be unmistakably Hogarthian.[1]
Benjamin Hoadly, M.D., the Bishop's eldest son,
and the author of the clever comedy of "The
Suspicious Husband," is said to have been one of the
numerous editors of the "Analysis of Beauty;"[2] and

[1] They were copied in 1826 by Miss E. Gulston, and afterwards,
on two plates, by W. J. Smith.

[2] Hogarth painted his portrait. See Part II., "Catalogue of
Paintings," 1740.

John, a clergyman, supplied the verses to the *Rake's Progress*. John Ireland ("Hogarth Illustrated," iii. 61) prints a letter from this latter about the retouching of his father's portrait. "My love to him [the Bishop]," he writes, "and desire him, when his wife says he looks charmingly, to drive immediately to Leicester Fields (Square, I mean, I beg your pardon), and sit an hour or two, or three, in your painting-room." The letter is not dated, but the extract indicates that, at all events before the Bishop's death in 1761, Leicester Fields was still a little nervously insecure in its status as a square.

Taste in High Life, the painting, is one of the most popular of Hogarth's occasional pieces, although with himself it was never a favourite, no doubt because it was executed to order. A certain opulent and eccentric Miss Edwardes, of Kensington, designing to revenge herself upon the unfriendly critics of her own emphatically original costume, commissioned Hogarth, for sixty guineas, to ridicule the reigning fashions in 1742. This he did by exhibiting an elderly lady wearing a sacque covered by monstrous full-blown roses and expanded by a huge hoop, in a transport of affected admiration with an equally fantastic old beau (Lord Portmore) over a tiny cup and saucer. Another lady, a black boy, and a monkey make up the group, and the furniture and other accessories minutely satirize the contemporary craze for gimcracks, exotics, dancers, pets, and so forth. These can scarcely be enumerated here, and the same note is, moreover, struck with equal skill in *Marriage*

TASTE IN HIGH LIFE.
From the Engraving by Phillips.

A-la-Mode. A surreptitious print from the picture was published in May, 1746, by Jarvis of Bedford-court ;[1] but it was not elaborately engraved until long after Hogarth's death.

Although by this time popular with the public through the medium of the print-shops, Hogarth had not yet succeeded in conquering the prejudices of the picture-buyers. The majority of his more important paintings still remained on his hands. At the beginning of 1745—to stray a few months beyond the limits of this chapter—he advertised several of them for sale by a species of auction. As usual, his mode of procedure was entirely original.

" The biddings" [we quote from Nichols, "Genuine Works," i. 117] "were to remain open from the first to the last day of February, on these conditions : ' 1. That every bidder shall have an entire leaf numbered in the book of sale, on the top of which will be entered the name and place of abode, the sum paid by him, the time when, and for which picture. 2. That, on the last day of sale, a clock (striking every five minutes) shall be placed in the room ; and when it hath struck five minutes after twelve, the first picture mentioned in the sale-book will be deemed as sold ; the second picture when the clock hath struck the next five minutes after twelve ; and so on successively till the whole nineteen pictures are sold. 3. That none advance less than gold at each bidding. 4. No person to bid on the last day, except those whose names were before

---

[1] " General Advertiser," 24 May, 1746.

entered in the book.—As Mr. Hogarth's room is but small, he begs the favour that no persons, except those whose names are entered in the book, will come to view his Paintings on the last day of sale.' The pictures were sold for the following prices :—

	£	s.	d.
Six *Harlot's Progress*, at 14 gs. each	88	4	0
Eight *Rake's Progress*, at 22 gs. each	184	16	0
Morning, 20 gs.	21	0	0
Noon, 37 gs.	38	17	0
Evening, 38 gs.	39	18	0
Night, 26 gs.	27	6	0
Strolling Players, 26 gs. . . .	27	6	0
	£427	7	0 "

The ticket of admission to this auction was the etching, probably suggested by Swift's "Battle of the Books," entitled the *Battle of the Pictures*. It depicts a spirited, though unequal, contest between the forces of the Black Masters on the one hand and the canvasses of Hogarth on the other. Under a standard emblazoned with an auctioneer's hammer, long ranks of spurious *replicas* of the *Rape of Europa*, *Apollo flaying Marsyas*, and the like, are drawn up in front of a sale-room, the weathercock of which is ornamented, in place of the usual signs, with the letters P, V, F, S (puffs). In the air the champions are already engaging. Sallying forth from Hogarth's studio to the right, the Tavern Scene in the *Rake's Progress* cleaves its way gaily through Titian's *Feast of Olympus*, while the *Midnight Modern Conversation* makes a breach in a bacchanalian procession by Rubens. Below, a kneeling Magdalen gives a vicious downward dig to the *Harlot's Progress* (Picture III.), and a St. Francis, also absorbed in his devotions, contrives not less irreparably to injure the starched Prude of the *Four Times of the Day*. Even in the inscription on this ticket, there is a touch of that half-ironic, half defiant tone which is never entirely absent from the painter's public utterances :—" *The Bearer hereof is entitled* (if he thinks proper,) *to be a Bidder for Mr. Hogarth's Pictures, which are to be sold on the Last Day of this Month.*" The prices realized were of course wholly inadequate ; but it must be borne in mind that the method of sale was peculiar, and little calculated to attract or conciliate the limited public of purchasers.

HOGARTH'S INVITATION TO DR. KING.

CHAPTER V.

MARRIAGE A-LA-MODE.

THE auction with which the last chapter concluded took place at the "Golden Head" in February, 1745, when the six paintings of *Marriage A-la-Mode* were also announced for sale, "as soon as the Plates then taking from them should be completed." A hint of the new series had already been given in the *Battle of the Pictures*, where the second scene, still inoffensively reposing upon the easel, is wantonly assaulted by a copy of the *Aldobrandini Marriage*. In April following the set of engravings was issued, the subscription ticket being the etching of heads known as *Characters and Caricaturas*. Plates I. and VI. were engraved by Scotin, Plates II. and III. by Baron, and Plates IV. and V. by Ravenet. Exactly two years earlier, Hogarth had heralded them by the following notification in the "London Daily Post, and General Advertiser" of April 2nd, 1743: —" Mr. HOGARTH intends to publish by Subscription,

SIX PRINTS from Copper-Plates, engrav'd by the best Masters in Paris, after his own Paintings; representing a Variety of *Modern Occurrences* in *High-Life*, and called MARRIAGE A-LA-MODE. Particular Care will be taken, that there may not be the least Objection to the Decency or Elegancy of the whole Work, and that none of the Characters represented shall be personal."[1] Then follow the terms of subscription. The last quoted lines were probably a bark at some forgotten detraction, and if not actually ironical, doubtless about as sincere as Fielding's promise, in the Prologue to his first comedy, not to offend the ladies. Those who had found inelegancy and indecency in the previous productions of the painter, would still discover the same defects in the masterpiece he now submitted to the public. And although it may be said that the "characters" represented are not "personal" in a satirical sense, his precautions, as he himself tells us, "did not prevent a likeness being found for each head, for a general character will always bear some resemblance to a particular one."[2]

But what, no doubt, interested his critical contemporaries even more than these preliminary protesta-

---

[1] To the advertisement of April 4th and subsequent issues was added :—"The Heads for the better Preservation of the Characters and Expressions to be done by the Author ;" and John Ireland accordingly finds traces of Hogarth's burin in the faces of the Citizen and Peer, Plate I. second state ("Hogarth Illustrated," iii. 343).

[2] "Hogarth Illustrated," iii. 343. See also *Characters and Caricaturas* in Part II., Catalogue of Prints.

tions, was the painter's promise to represent, in his new work, "a variety of modern occurrences in high-life." Here, it may be admitted, was a proposition which certainly savoured of temerity. What could one whose pencil had scarcely travelled beyond the limits of St. Giles's, know of the inner secrets of St. James's? A Hervey or a Beauclerk, or even a Fielding, might have sufficed; but a Hogarth of Leicester Fields, whose only pretence to distinction (as High Life conceives it) was that he had run away with Thornhill's handsome daughter,—what special title had he to depict that charmed region of cards and folly, ringed with its long-resounding knockers, and flambeau-carrying footmen! This was, however, to reckon without genius, which over-leaps loftier barriers than these. It is true that the English Novel of Manners, which has since stimulated so many artists, had only just made its appearance; and "Pamela" and "Joseph Andrews" but falteringly foreshadowed "Clarissa" and "Tom Jones." Yet there is nothing in the story of *Marriage A-la-Mode* which was beyond the powers of a *spectator ab extra*, always provided he were fairly acquainted with the Modelys and Wildairs of the stage, and the satires of Johnson and Pope. The plot, like that of all masterpieces, is extremely simple. An impoverished nobleman who marries his son to a rich citizen's daughter; a husband who, pursuing his own equivocal pleasures, resigns his wife to the temptations of op-portunity; a foregone sequel and a tragic issue:— this material is of the oldest, and could make but

slender claim to originality.[1] Submitted to Colman or
Garrick as the *scenario* of a play for Yates and Mrs.
Woffington, it would probably have been rejected as
pitifully threadbare. Yet combined and developed
under the brush of Hogarth, set in an atmosphere
that makes it as vivid as nature itself, decorated with
surprising fidelity, and enlivened by all the resources
of the keenest humour, it passes out of the line of
mere transcripts of life, and retaining the merits of
the specific and particular, becomes a representative
and typical work, as articulate to-day, as direct and
unhesitating in its teaching, as it was when it was
first offered to the world.

How well-preserved, even now, these wonderful
pictures are! It would almost seem as if Time, un-
reasoning in his anger, had determined to ignore in
every way the audacious artist who treated him with
such persistent indignity. Look at them in the
National Gallery. Look, too, at the cracks and
fissures in the Wilkies—the soiled rainbows of
Turner,—the bituminous riding-habit of Lady Douro
in Sir Edwin's *Story of Waterloo*. But these paintings of William Hogarth are well nigh as fresh to-

---

[1] Mr. John Forster ("Life of Swift," i. 453) asserts that Hogarth
had in mind the case of Mr. John Sayer, who, in January, 1713,
was stabbed by one Noble, an attorney, whom he had surprised
in company with Mrs. Sayer at a house in the Mint. Noble, who
is referred to in Swift's "Journal to Stella," was subsequently
hanged. This story, which is to be found in Howell's "State
Trials," xv. 731-62, has been examined by the present writer in
"Notes and Queries" for Ap. 3, 1880, with a view to show that
there is little reason for supposing that Hogarth was indebted to
it. Mr. Forster gives no authority for his statement.

day as when, new from the easel, they found their
fortunate purchaser in Mr. Lane of Hillingdon.
They are not worked like a Denner, it is true, and
the artist is often less solicitous about his method
than about the result of it; yet they are soundly,
straightforwardly, and skilfully executed. Lady
Bingley's red hair, Carestini's nostril, are shown in
the simplest and directest manner. Everywhere
the desired effect is exactly produced, and without
effort. Take, as an illustration, the inkstand in the first
scene, with its bell and sand-caster. In these days
it would be a patient *trompe-l'œil*, probably better
done than the figures using it. Here it is merely
indicated, not elaborated; it holds its exact place as
a piece of furniture, and nothing more. And at this
point it may be observed that if in the ensuing descriptions we should speak of colour, the reader will
remember we are describing, not the performances
of Messrs. Ravenet and the rest, but Hogarth's
original pictures at Trafalgar Square. It is the more
necessary to bear this in mind, because, besides
being reversed, the paintings frequently differ in
detail from the engravings.[1]

The first of the series represents the signing of the
marriage contract. The scene, as the artist is careful
to signify by the ostentatious coronets on the furni-

---

[1] The coronet on the flank of the dog in Plate I., for example,
is confined to the print. Excellent photogravures of the six
paintings (and the superiority of the paintings to the engravings
in this case is incontestable) are to be found in Ward's " English
Art in the Public Galleries," 1887, Part I.

ture and accessories (they are to be discerned even
on the crutches), is laid in the house of an earl, who,
with his gouty foot swathed in flannels, seems with a
superb—if somewhat stiff-jointed—dignity to be
addressing certain pompous observations respecting
himself and his pedigree (dating from William the
Conqueror) to a sober-looking personage opposite,
who, horn-spectacles on nose, is peering at the
endorsement of the "Marriage Settlem^t of the R^t
Honble. Lord Viscount ['Squanderfield]." This
second figure, which is that of a London merchant,
with its turned-in toes, the point of the sword-sheath
between the legs, and the awkward constraint of its
attitude, forms an admirable contrast to the other. A
massive gold chain denotes the wearer to be an
alderman. Between the two is a third person, perhaps the merchant's confidential clerk or cashier,
who holds out a "Mortgage" to the Earl. Gold and
notes lie upon the table, where are also an inkstand,
sealing-wax, and a lighted candle in which a "thief"
is conspicuous. At the back of this trio is the be-
trothed couple—the earl's son and the alderman's
daughter. It is in fact an alliance of *sacs et parche-
mins*, in which the young people are rather involved
than interested. The lady, who looks young and
pretty in her bridal-dress, wears a mingled expression
of *mauvaise honte* and distaste for her position, and
trifles with the ring, which she has strung upon her
handkerchief, while a brisk and well-built young
lawyer, who trims a pen, bends towards her with a

¹ The name is added in the print.

whispered compliment. Meantime the Viscount—a
frail, effeminate-looking figure, holding an open snuff-
box, from which he affectedly lifts a pinch—turns
from his *fiancée* with a smirk of complacent foppery
towards a pier-glass at his side. His wide-cuffed coat
is light-blue, his vest is loaded with embroidery. He
wears an enormous *solitaire*, and has high red heels
to his shoes. Before him, in happy parody of the
ill-matched pair, are two dogs in coupling-links :—the
bitch sits up, alert and curious, her companion is
lying down. The only other figure is that of an old
lawyer, who, with a plan in his hand, and a gesture
of contempt or wonder, looks through an open
window at an ill-designed and partly-erected building,
in front of which several idle servants are lounging or
sitting. Like Pope's "Visto," the Earl has "a taste,"
and his taste, interrupted for the moment by lack of
funds, is the ruinous one of bricks and mortar.

The pictures on the wall exemplify and satirize the
fashion of the time. The largest is a portrait in the
French style of one of the earl's ancestors, who tra-
verses the canvas triumphantly. A cannon explodes
below him, a comet is seen above; and in his right
hand, notwithstanding his cuirass and voluminous
Queen-Anne peruke, he brandishes the thunderbolt
of Jupiter. *Judith and Holofernes, St. Sebastian, The
Murder of Abel, David and Goliath, The Martyrdom
of St. Laurence*, are some of the rest, all of which, it
is perhaps needless to note, belong to those "dismal
dark subjects, neither entertaining nor ornamental,"
against which we have already heard the painter

inveigh. Upon the ceiling, with a nice sense of decorative fitness, is *Pharaoh in the Red Sea*. From a sconce at the side, a Gorgon surveys the proceedings with astonishment. Hogarth has used a similar idea in the *Strolling Actresses*, where the same mask seems horrified at the airy freedom of the lightly-clad lady who there enacts the part of Diana.

In the picture of the *Contract*, the young couple and "Counsellor Silvertongue," as he has been christened by the artist,[1] are placed in close proximity. These are the real actors in the drama. Building *immemor sepulcri*, the old earl had but few years to live. Henceforth he is seen no more; and the alderman reappears only at the end of the story. The next scene is laid in a handsome saloon.[2] A clock shows the time to be twenty minutes past twelve; but lights are still smouldering in the heavy chandelier, and a yawning footman in curl-papers is languidly arranging the furniture in the background. From the cards and "Hoyle" on the floor, the two violins and the music-book, it must be inferred that the establishment is but now awakening from the fatigues of a prolonged entertainment. At a round table by the fire, with a teapot and one cup upon it, sits, in a coquettish night-cap and morning jacket, the lady of the house, holding a pocket mirror in her right hand. She stretches her arms wearily, with a sidelong glance

[1] See this name prefixed to his "Last Dying Speech" on the floor in the final picture.

[2] This room, it is said, was copied from the drawing-room of a house in Arlington Street.

at her husband, who reclines upon, or rather is supported by, a chair at the opposite side of the fire-
place. Nothing in Hogarth is finer than this latter
figure, for which, it is stated, Hayman the painter
served as model. Worn out and nauseated, Lord
Squanderfield has returned from some independent
nocturnal expedition. His rich black velvet coat
and his waistcoat are thrown open, his disordered
hair has lost its ribbon, his hands are plunged deeply
into his small-clothes. In undisguised disregard for
the presence of his plebeian partner, he still wears
his laced hat. His sword, which he has unbuckled
and thrown upon the floor, is broken ignominiously
in its sheath ; and a lap-dog snuffs at a woman's cap
half-thrust into his pocket. His whole appearance,
the physical prostration of his posture, the tired and
cynical disgust upon his features, bear witness to
the reaction after excess in a constitution already
enfeebled. Hazlitt, in his review of these pictures at
the Exhibition of 1814, points out how skilfully his
pallid unhealthy face is contrasted with the yellow-
whitish colour of the mantelpiece behind. He seems
in a stupor of lassitude ; and neither he nor his wife
takes any notice of the Methodist steward (the only
other personage in the picture) who, after vainly
attempting to attract attention to his accounts, quits
the room with uplifted eyes and a single paid bill on
his file. From his pocket peeps a book labelled
" Regeneration."

The splendid apartment in which this scene takes
place affords a further illustration of the interiors of

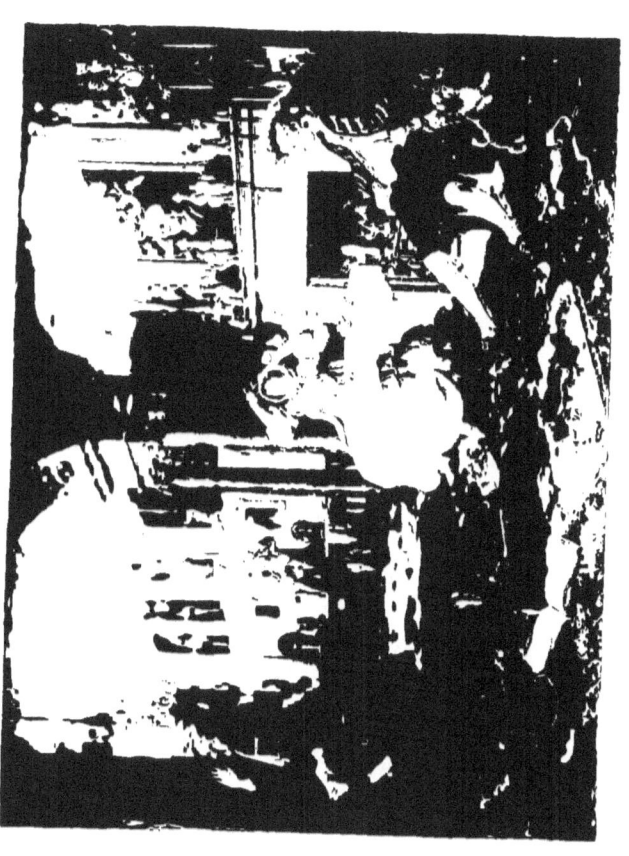

the Georgian era. It is divided into two by an arch supported on dark blue marble columns. The pictures visible on the walls, one of which is partially veiled by a curtain, disclosing only a naked human foot, are less striking than the decorations in Scene I. Indeed, those in the background appear to be figures of the Apostles. Over the mantelpiece is Cupid playing upon the bagpipes in the midst of ruins; immediately below him is a bust with mended nose, which Lichtenberg conjectures to represent "Faustina." On either side, the shelf is crowded with Indian pagods and auction monstrosities,— toads, and the "fat squabs" so well described in Cowper's couplet :—

> " Gorgonius sits, abdominous and wan,
>   Like a fat squab upon a Chinese fan."

On the right hand of the mantelpiece hangs a nondescript trophy of leafage in brass surrounding a clock, and surmounted by a cat in china, life-size. Fishes appear among the leaves below. The whole, like the jumble of bad architecture in Scene I., is probably a supplemental satire on William Kent, who designed everything, from picture-frames to petticoats.[1]

---

[1] Kent, who really deserved credit as a landscape-gardener, was a mediocrity in everything else. An excellent epigram by Lord Chesterfield upon his efforts as a portrait-painter has recently come to light among the Windham Collection at Felbrigge Park, Norfolk (Mr. R. W. Ketton's). We print it as it appears in the "Twelfth Report of the Historical Manuscripts Commission," Appendix, Part IX. 1891, p. 191 :—

> " As, to Apelles, Ammon's son
>   Would only deign to sit;

That the viscount and his lady have elected to take their pleasures apart, is evident. What those pleasures are, is indicated specifically in the third and fourth pictures. Over that relating to those of the husband we shall not linger long, both by reason of its subject and the obscurity of its story. None of the commentators, not even of those whose inspiration is said to be derived direct from Hogarth, has given a satisfactory explanation of it. Churchill, in the after-days of his enmity, affirmed that the artist himself did not know what he meant, but had worked from the imperfectly apprehended suggestion of some friend. This, in a man of Hogarth's type, is improbable. It is far more likely that he did not choose to be entirely explicit. The design may be thus briefly described. The reader will remember a woman's cap (in the painting it has a blue ribbon), which peeped from the viscount's pocket in the saloon scene. In the present picture, a similar blue-ribboned cap is worn by a slight girlish figure in a laced "manteel" and brocaded skirt, who has been brought by the nobleman to consult a quack doctor, one of that worshipful fraternity whose electuaries and catholicons gene-rally formed the tailpiece to the eighteenth cen-tury newspaper. The girl's health, and the quack's

> So, to thy pencil, Kent! alone
> Will Brunswick's form submit :
>
> "Equal your envied wonders ! save
> This difference we see,
> One would no other painter have—
> No other would have thee."

treatment of it, is certainly the question under discussion; and the viscount, who is seated, with lifted cane threatens a fierce-looking and masculine woman (who may be the quack's wife, or a procuress, or both), to whom he sarcastically holds out a box of pills. She, in return, is preparing to retort with a formidable clasp-knife. The bow-legged practitioner, an admirable figure, whose face, Hazlitt says happily, "seems as if it were composed of salve," stands near her; and is apparently addressing some snarling query to the unfortunate patient, who listens in a mute, impassive attitude, with a handkerchief to her mouth.[1] But if the meaning of the figures is not clear, there is no doubt about the objects by which they are surrounded. These are the stock-in-trade of an empiric of the first water. Skulls, stuffed crocodiles, retorts, mummies, and the like, decorate the apartment.[2] To the left of the canvas, in obvious

[1] Rouquet's interpretation, said by Steevens to be derived from the artist, is not inconsistent with the above. "*Il falloit* (he says) *indiquer la mauvaise conduite du héros de la pièce. L'auteur pour cet effet l'introduit dans l'appartement d'un empirique, où il ne peut guères se trouver qu'en conséquence de ses débauches; il fait en même tems rencontrer chez cet empirique une de ces femmes qui perdues depuis long-tems, font enfin leur métier de la perte des autres. Il suppose un démêlé entre cette femme & son héros, dont le sujet paroit être la mauvaise santé d'une petite fille, du commerce de laquelle il ne s'est pas bien trouvé*" (p. 34). Unfortunately, Trusler's account, which has the sanction of Mrs. Hogarth, differs entirely from this; and, though other explanations have been suggested, the subject is not one upon which detailed discussion is possible.

[2] One of the rare rays of illumination vouchsafed to Trusler relates to certain of these accessories. In a case at the back is the

ridicule of the futile ingenuities of science, is a cumbrous apparatus of levers and cog-wheels for setting collar-bones ; near this is a smaller one devoted to the humbler office of drawing corks. Both are invented by " Mons. de la Pillule" (presumably the quack himself), and have been " seen and approved by the Royal Academy of Sciences at Paris." The room, according to Smith's life of Nollekens, was copied from one at 96, St. Martin's Lane, once the residence of Dr. John Misaubin, the lean physician of the *Harlot's Progress* and Fielding's " Mock Doctor," who died there in April, 1734. He was the proprietor of a famous pill; and if, as Smith further says, he had an " Irish wife," it may well be that Hogarth, though he did not reproduce the actual individuals, was really thinking of the Misaubin *ménage*.[1]

In the next picture (the *Toilet Scene*) we pass to the bedroom of the countess, a lofty chamber, with the state bed standing, after the manner of the eighteenth century, in its alcove, and surmounted by a coronet. There is another over the mirror ; by this time the old Earl is certainly dead. The pic-

quack's wig on its block, in company with a skeleton and an *écorché*. According to Hogarth's " moraliser," the bones are supposed to be warning the flesh of what it may come to, if it trusts to the intervention of quack doctors.

[1] Much material for conjecture respecting the meaning of this picture is contained in Mr. F. G. Stephens' " Catalogue" under *Prenez des Pilules*, No. 1,987 ; *Quackery Unmask'd; Or, Empiricism Display'd*, No. 3,019 ; and in the account of Plate V. of *A Harlot's Progress*.

Harrum à la Mode. N°11

— in Common courses

tures on the wall are *Jupiter and Io, Lot and his Daughters,* the *Rape of Ganymede,* and the portrait of . . . Counsellor Silvertongue! That gentleman himself,

"*Gros et gras, le teint frais, et la bouche vermeille*"

(like Molière's " Tartuffe "), is lounging upon a sofa in the posture of a privileged visitor, and talking with easy familiarity to the countess, who, in a *peignoir* and yellow dressing-gown, sits at her toilet table under the hands of a Swiss valet, engaged in curling her hair. That she is now a mother is shown by the child's coral hanging from her chair. She listens with a compliant expression to her admirer's conversation, which, from his indication of the figures (a nun and a friar) on the screen at his back, and the fluttered masquerade-ticket in his hand, plainly relates to that entertainment; but we fail to discern in her look "the heightened glow, the forward intelligence, and loosened soul of love," which Hazlitt found in it. It is possible to be over sympathetic as a critic.

These two are absorbed in their own affairs. The rest of the company, with exception of one stout and slumbering gentleman in the background, are listening intently to the performances of an Italian singer and a German flute-player. Into the portrait of the former, alleged to be intended for the famous contralto, Giovanni Carestini, Hogarth has infused all his spleen against exotic artists. The unwieldy, awkward form : the gross, almost swinish, physiognomy, the pampered look and posture, the profusion of

jewels, and the splendid costume of the popular
idol, are all expressed with the closest fidelity.
The wooden-featured flute-player is a certain Weide-
man.   The chief listener is a red-haired lady in
a Pamela hat and white dress, Mrs. Fox Lane,
afterwards Lady Bingley.[1]   She rocks herself to the
notes in an ecstasy, regardless of her black servant,
who hands her some chocolate, and is amazed
at his mistress's enthusiasm.   Sitting near her, a
gentleman, with a fan dangling from his wrist, screws
his face into an affected simper of delight; next to
him a slim macaroni with his hair in curl papers,
and his *queue* loose like a woman's tresses, sips at his
cup with a fixed look of resigned connoisseurship.
Both of these last are fantastic and ridiculous : what
other men, according to Hogarth, would listen, or
pretend to listen, to Italian song—that "*Dagon* of
the Nobility and Gentry which had so long seduced
them to Idolatry."   The foreground is littered with
invitation and other cards, while in the right-hand
corner is a pile of recent purchases from the sale,
perhaps at Mr. Cock's in the Piazza, of the "collection of the late Sir Tim' Babyhouse."   Beside these
kneels a second black boy, who significantly touches
the horns of an Actæon.

---

[1] It was Mrs. Fox Lane who, from a side-box at the Opera,
uttered the profane exclamation on the caricature in Plate II. of
the *Rake's Progress*.   The enthusiasm for exotic minstrelsy sometimes took whimsical forms.   In the "Gentleman's Magazine"
is recorded the case of another lady who justified a breach of
promise in a Court of Equity upon the ground among other
things that her lover was no admirer of Farinelli.

The succeeding pictures pass swiftly to the tragic
termination of the story. The fifth scene, as appears
from the paper on the floor, is laid in the "Turk's
Head Bagnio." Quitting the Masquerade, separate chairs, swinging away speedily between their
trotting Irish bearers, have conveyed the Countess
and the Counsellor to the place of assignation.
Upon the pair the Earl, following in brief space, has
come suddenly, bursting open the lock, of which the
hasp lies upon the ground. A table has been hastily
pushed aside; a stool with its litter of feminine
apparel overturned; and the quarrel between the
husband and the seducer has been fought out, briefly
and fatally, in the dying firelight. The Counsellor,
naked, escapes through the window into the darkness;
the Earl, run through the body, sways vaguely with
filmy eyes and falling sword in the centre of the
room. His wife, in an agony of terror and remorse,
has flung herself on her knees at his feet, while the
frightened keeper of the place, a constable, and a
watchman are entering at the door.

The last scene shifts to the old home in the city,
to which, in her dishonour, the Countess has returned.
Through the window we see London Bridge, with
the tottering houses upon it which were taken down
in 1758. Counsellor Silvertongue has been hung at
Tyburn for murder; his "Last Dying Speech" is on
the floor. The Countess has poisoned herself with
laudanum fetched by a half-witted serving-man, and
a whimpering nurse, with puckered anile face, holds
up a rickety child to kiss the yet warm cheek of its

mother.[1] Meanwhile the hastily-summoned physician, powerless in the circumstances, majestically
quits the apartment; the baulked apothecary rates
the imbecile messenger, and the alderman (careful
soul!) with prudent forethought draws a valuable
ring from his daughter's finger before it stiffens
with the *rigor mortis.*

We have only dealt briefly with these concluding
pictures, the decorations and accessories of which
are to the full as minute and effective as those of the
ones that precede them. The furniture of the
bagnio, with its portrait of Moll Flanders humorously
continued by the sturdy legs of a Jewish soldier in
the tapestry *Judgment of Solomon* behind, the half-
burned candle flaring in the draught of the open
door and window, the reflection of the lantern on the
ceiling and the shadow of the tongs on the floor, the
horror-stricken look on the mask of the lady and the
satanic grin on that of her paramour, all deserve
notice. So do the gross Dutch pictures in the
alderman's house, the sordid pewter plates and the
sumptuous silver goblet, the stained table-cloth, the
egg in rice, and the pig's head which the half-starved
and ravenous dog is stealing. There is no defect of
invention, no superfluity of detail, no purposeless
stroke in this "owre true tale." From first to last it
progresses steadily to its catastrophe by a forward

[1] Mr. Sala, in an interesting paper in the "Gentleman's Magazine" on George Cruikshank, notes that the poor child is a girl.
The Earl is the last of his race in the male line, and the title is
therefore extinct. This is one of those subtle touches which,
except in Hogarth, we may seek for in vain.

march of skilfully linked and fully developed incidents. It is like a novel of Fielding on canvas ;
and it seems inconceivable that, with this magnificent
work *en évidence*, the critics of that age should have
been contented to re-echo the opinion of Walpole
that "as a painter Hogarth had but slender merit,"
and to cackle the foot-rule criticisms of the Rev.
William Gilpin as to his ignorance of composition.
But so it was. Not until that exhibition of his works
at the British Institution in 1814, to which reference
has been made, was it thoroughly understood how
excellent and individual both as a designer and a
colourist was this native artist, whom "Picture-
dealers, Picture-cleaners, Picture-frame-makers, and
other Connoisseurs"—to use his own graphically
ironical words—had been allowed to rank below the
third-rate copyists of third-rate foreigners.

Beyond the remark that the "jaded morning
countenance" of the Viscount in Scene II. "lectures
on the vanity of pleasure as audibly as anything in
Ecclesiastes," Lamb's incomparable essay in "The
Reflector" makes no material reference to *Marriage
A-la-Mode*. His comments, besides, are confined to
the engravings. But Hazlitt, who saw the pictures
in the above-mentioned exhibition of 1814, devotes
much of his criticism to the tragedy of the Squanderfields, chiefly, it would seem, because Lamb had left
the subject untouched. Hazlitt's own studies as an
artist, his keen insight and his quick enthusiasm,
make him a memorable critic of Hogarth, whose
general characteristics he defines with admirable

exactitude. ⹁ Much quotation has made his description of the young Lord and Counsellor Silvertongue sufficiently familiar. But he is equally good in his vignette of the younger woman in the episode at the Quack Doctor's, a creation which he rightly regards as one of Hogarth's most successful efforts. "Nothing," he says, "can be more striking than the contrast between the extreme softness of her person and the hardened indifference of her character. The vacant stillness, the docility to vice, the premature suppression of youthful sensibility, the doll-like mechanism of the whole figure, which seems to have no other feeling but a sickly sense of pain,—show the deepest insight into human nature, and into the effects of those refinements in depravity, by which it has been good-naturedly asserted, that 'vice loses half its evil in losing all its grossness.'" In the death of the Countess again, he speaks thus of two of the subordinate characters :—"We would particularly refer to the captious, petulant self-sufficiency of the apothecary, whose face and figure are constructed on exact physiognomical principles, and to the fine example of passive obedience, and non-resistance in the servant, whom he is taking to task, and whose coat of green and yellow livery is as long and melancholy as his face.[1] The disconsolate look, the

---

[1] Long as it is, the coat is alleged to have been longer. "A close observer," says a note in Timbs's "Anecdote Biography," 1860, p. 40, "will perceive, that the servant lad is clothed in one of his master's old coats, which has been shortened, and that the cloth cut off is turned, and made into new cuffs; this is more plainly seen in the picture, by the contrast of the colour of them

haggard eyes, the open mouth, the comb sticking in
the hair, the broken, gapped teeth, which, as it were,
hitch in an answer—everything about him denotes
the utmost perplexity and dismay." Some other of
Hazlitt's comments are more fanciful, as, for example,
when he compares Lady Squanderfield's curl papers
(in the " Toilet Scene") to "a wreath of half-blown
flowers," and those of the macaroni-amateur to "a
chevaux-de-frise of horns, which adorn and fortify the
lack-lustre expression and mild resignation of the face
beneath." With his condemnation of the attitude of
the husband, in the scene at the "Turk's Head
Bagnio," as "one in which it would be impossible for
him to stand, or even to fall," it is difficult to coin-
cide; and it is an illustration of the contradictions of
criticism that this very figure should have been
selected for especial praise, with particular reference
to the charges made against the painter of defective
drawing, by another critic who was not only as keenly
sympathetic as Hazlitt, but was probably a better
anatomist—the author of "Rab and his Friends."[1]

with the faded hue of the coat." The suggestion is ingenious;
but would the alderman wear green and yellow? Is it not, rather,
an inherited livery!

[1] Here is the entire passage, from the notes which Dr. John
Brown wrote in 1846 for Hugh Miller's "Witness:"—"If Hogarth
did not know the naked human figure (and we deny that he did
not), he knew the human face and the naked human heart—he
knew what of infinite good and evil, joy and sorrow, life and death,
proceeded out of it. Look at the second last of the series of
Marriage A-la-Mode. If you would see what are the wages of
sin, and how, after being earned, they are beginning to be paid,
look on that dying man—his body dissolving, falling not like his

To Hazlitt's general estimate of Hogarth we shall
not now refer.[1]   But his comparison of Hogarth and
Wilkie may fairly be summarized in this place, because it contains so much excellent discrimination
of the former.   Wilkie, Hazlitt contends, is a simple
realist; Hogarth is a comic painter. ⌈While one is a
" serious, prosaic, literal narrator of facts," the other
is a moral satirist, " exposing vice and folly in their
most ludicrous points of view, and, with a profound
insight into the weak sides of character and manners
in all their tendencies, combinations, and contrasts.
. . . He is carried away by a passion for the *ridiculous*.   His object is not so much ' to hold the mirror
up to nature ' as ' to show vice her own feature,
scorn her own image.'   He is so far from contenting

sword, firm and entire, but as nothing but a dying thing could
fall, his eyes dim with the shadow of death, in his ears the waters
of that tremendous river, all its billows going over him, the life of
his comely body flowing out like water, the life of his soul !—who
knows what it is doing ?   Fleeing through the open window,
undressed, see the murderer and adulterer vanish into the outer
darkness of night, anywhere rather than remain ; and that guilty,
beautiful, utterly miserable creature on her knee, her whole soul,
her whole life, in her eyes, fixed on her dying husband, dying for
and by her !   What is in that poor desperate brain, who can
tell !   Mad desires for life, for death,—prayers, affections, infinite
tears,—the past, the future,—her maiden innocence, her marriage,
his love, her guilt,—the grim end of it all,—the night-watch with
their professional faces,—the weary wind blowing through the room,
the prelude, as it were, of that whirlwind in which that lost soul is
soon to pass away.   The man who could paint so as to suggest all
this, is a great man and a great painter " (" Horæ Subsecivæ,"
1862, 244-45).

[1] A passage from it is quoted in the " Bibliography," under
Hazlitt's article.

himself with still-life that he is always on the verge
of caricature, though without ever falling into it.
He does not represent folly or vice in its incipient,
or dormant, or *grub* state ; but full-grown, with
wings, pampered into all sorts of affectation, airy,
ostentatious, and extravagant. . . . There is a perpetual collision of eccentricities—a tilt and tourna-
ment of absurdities ; the prejudices and caprices of
mankind are let loose, and set together by the ears,
as in a bear-garden. Hogarth paints nothing but
comedy or tragi-comedy. Wilkie paints neither one
nor the other. Hogarth never looks at any object
but to find out a moral or a ludicrous effect. Wilkie
never looks at any object but to see that it is
there. . . . In looking at Hogarth, you are ready to
burst your sides with laughing at the unaccountable
jumble of odd things which are brought together ;
you look at Wilkie's pictures with a mingled feeling
of curiosity and admiration at the accuracy of the
representation." The distinction thus drawn is, in
the main, a just one. Yet, at certain points, Wilkie
comes nearer to Hogarth than any other English
artist ; and that elegant amateur, Sir George How-
land Beaumont, reasoned rightly when he judged the
painter of the *Village Politicians* to be, in his day,
the only fit recipient of Hogarth's mahl-stick.

To return to *Marriage A-la-Mode*. Notwithstanding that the pictures were, as stated at the
beginning of this chapter, announced for sale in
1745, it was five years before they actually found a
purchaser, although, in the interval, they seem to

have been freely exhibited both at the "Golden Head" and at Cock's Auction Rooms. In 1750, however, they were at last disposed of by another of those unfortunate schemes devised by Hogarth for disposing of his works. The bidding, said the announcement in the "Daily Advertiser," was to be by written notes; no dealers in pictures were to be admitted as bidders; and the highest bidder at noon on the 6th June was to be the purchaser.

Whether this mode of sale, coupled with the characteristic manner of its notification, "disobliged the Town" or not, it is impossible to say; but it is certain that when Mr. Lane, "of Hillingdon, near Uxbridge," who was to become the lucky proprietor of the pictures, arrived on the date appointed at the "Golden Head," he found he was the only bidder who had put in an appearance.[1] In fact, there was no one in the room but the painter himself and his friend Dr. Parsons, Secretary to the Royal Society. The highest written offer having been declared to be £120, Mr. Lane, shortly before twelve, said he

[1] Not the "sole bidder," as Allan Cunningham and others have inferred. If this were so, in "making the pounds guineas," Mr. Lane would be bidding against himself, a thing which occasionally occurs at auctions, but is not recommended. We have failed to find any other account of this transaction than that supplied to Nichols for his second edition of 1782, pp. 225-7, by Mr. Lane himself, which is summarized above. Cunningham seems to have derived his information from the same source; but he strangely transforms it. We can but surmise that he followed Ireland's transcript, in which the highest bid is given at £110, instead of £120—a rather unfortunate mistake, for it appears to have misled a good many people.

would " make the pounds guineas," but subsequently, and much to his credit, offered the artist a delay of some hours to find a better purchaser. An hour passed, and as, up to that time, no one had appeared, Hogarth, much mortified, surrendered the pictures to Mr. Lane, who thus became the owner of the artist's best work, and the finest pictorial satire of the century, for the modest sum of £126, which included Carlo Maratti frames that had cost Hogarth four guineas a-piece. Mr. Lane, who readily promised not to sell or clean the pictures without the knowledge of the painter, left them at his death to his nephew, Colonel J. F. Cawthorne, by whom they were put up to auction in March, 1792, but were bought in again for 910 guineas. In 1797 they were sold at Christie's for £1,381 to Mr. John Julius Angerstein, with the rest of whose collection they were acquired in 1824 for the National Gallery.

In 1746 a description of the prints in Hudibrastic verse was published under the title of " Marriage-A-la-Mode; an Humourous Tale, in Six Canto's," &c. It appeared without Hogarth's sanction, and has no especial value. In 1754 the series furnished the ground-work of Dr. John Shebbeare's political novel of " The Marriage Act;" and, twelve years later, the authors of the capital comedy of " The Clandestine Marriage " (Colman and Garrick) acknowledged their not very manifest obligations to the same source. " To-night," says Garrick in his " Prologue "—

> " To-night, your matchless Hogarth gives the Thought,
> Which from his Canvas to the Stage is brought.

> And who so fit to warm the Poet's Mind
> As he who pictur'd Morals and Mankind?
> But not the same their Characters and Scenes ;
> Both labour for one End, by different Means :
> Each, as it suits him, takes a separate Road,
> Their one great Object, MARRIAGE-A-LA-MODE!
> Where Titles deign with Cits to have and hold,
> And change rich Blood for more substantial Gold !
> And honour'd Trade from Interest turns aside,
> To hazard Happiness for titled Pride.
> The Painter dead, yet still he charms the Eye ;
> While England lives, his Fame can never die ;
> But he who *struts his Hour upon the Stage*,
> Can scarce extend his Fame for Half an Age ;
> Nor Pen nor Pencil can the Actor save,
> The Art, and Artist, share one common Grave."

The idea in the last couplet, which the author of the Prologue is thought to have borrowed from " The Actor " of Robert Lloyd (who, in turn, had "conveyed" it from Cibber's " Apology"), afterwards found its way into Sheridan's " Monody on Garrick." Sheridan, says Steevens (discreetly mindful of the fact that the author of the " Rivals " was still living), " condescended to borrow it, only because it spared him the labour of unlocking the richer storehouse of his own imagination."

To conclude this account of *Marriage A-la-Mode*, it should be added that Hogarth projected a companion series, to be entitled the *Happy Marriage*, some designs for which have been preserved.[1] The

---

[1] See S. Ireland's "Graphic Illustrations," ii. 125 *et seq.*, and "Genuine Works," iii. 158 (*The Parson's Head*). The Country Dance in Plate I. of the " Analysis of Beauty " is also said to have been intended for *The Happy Marriage*.

idea was abandoned, not, as Wilkes obligingly informs us, because "the rancour and malevolence" of the artist's mind "made him very soon turn with envy and disgust from objects of so pleasing contemplation," but no doubt because the unruffled features of contented matrimony did not, upon consideration, afford the requisite variety to his pencil. As to John Major's suggestion—with which we may close the chapter—that there is a relationship between *Marriage A-la-Mode* and Dryden's play of the same name, we have only to say, after reading Dryden, that it appears to have no greater weight than the Welsh captain's comparison of Monmouth and Macedon. There are a husband and wife in the one and a husband and wife in the other, and there are seducers in both.

OLD LONDON BRIDGE. *From Marriage A-la-Mode.*

CHAPTER VI.

Contemporaries.   March to Finchley.
Minor Prints.

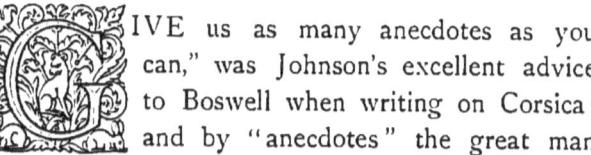

IVE us as many anecdotes as you can," was Johnson's excellent advice to Boswell when writing on Corsica; and by "anecdotes" the great man was understood to mean what would now be styled "information hitherto unpublished." In the narrative of Hogarth's life nothing is more tantalizing than the absence of particulars, not only respecting his domestic life, but also respecting his contemporaries and friends. His social qualities and his established reputation should, one would think, have brought him into frequent contact with personages eminent or notable. At places like Old Slaughter's coffee-house in St. Martin's Lane or "The Feathers" in Leicester Fields, at the annual dinner in the Foundling Hospital and at the "Turk's Head" in Gerard Street, in the Green Room of Drury Lane or at the Beef Steak Club in Covent Garden, he must often have met many of the artistic and literary

celebrities of his time. But the record of such encounters is, in the main, conspicuous for its absence.
With the Hoadly family, indeed, as already related,
he was familiar. He knew Dr. Morell, of Chiswick

("Sive tu mavis Morĕlus vocari,
Sive Morĕllus"),

and the Rev. Mr. Townley of "High Life Below
Stairs ;" he knew Dr. Arnold King, to whom he
sent his ingenious "Eta Beta Py" invitation;[1] he knew
Fielding's friend Ralph, the Ralph of "The Champion" and "The Dunciad ;" and in John Ireland's
"Illustrations" is printed a letter—which implies a
certain measure of intimacy—written to him by
Bishop Warburton. Horace Walpole, too, collected
his prints, and patronized him with the grudging
generosity which that aristocratic critic extended
to Genius born out of the purple. If we are to
believe George Steevens, the Abbot of Strawberry
once invited the artist to meet Gray at dinner. But
the author of the "Long Story"—strange to say—
was anything but garrulous, and Hogarth was glum
and ill at ease, so that the entertainment scarcely
got beyond the "uncommunicating muteness" of a
Quakers' meeting. With Richardson Hogarth had
some acquaintance, and, says Boswell, was "a pretty
frequent visitor" at the novelist's house in Salisbury
Court. Here, for the first time, he saw—although
he was not then made known to—the "great Cham"
himself. Talking one day to the author of "Pamela"

[1] See p. 85, and Part II., Catalogue of Prints, 1782.

I

about the execution of the Jacobite Dr. Cameron,
he observed a gentleman "standing at a window in
the room, shaking his head and rolling himself
about in a strange ridiculous manner." He concluded that he was some person of defective intelligence, placed by his friends under Richardson's
care. But presently the figure came forward, and
plunged into an animated invective against George
the Second (whose clemency had been under discussion), displaying such an unexpected power of
eloquence that Hogarth stared at him with astonishment, and "actually imagined that this idiot had
been at the moment inspired." He had afterwards
many opportunities of hearing and admiring that
wonderful oratory. But he was also fully alive to
the Doctor's peculiarities, and especially to his
ingrained and radical incredulity. "Johnson," he
told Mr. Salusbury, "though so wise a fellow, is
more like king David than king Solomon ; for he
says in his haste that all men are liars."[1]

With Johnson and Johnson's name was to be
inseparably connected that of another of Hogarth's
friends. He was on terms of great familiarity with
Miss Hester Lynch Salusbury, afterwards Hester
Thrale, who calls him "dear Mr. Hogarth," and
refers to the "odd particular directions about dress,
dancing, and many other matters" that he was
accustomed to give her as a girl.[2] He used fre-

---

[1] "Anecdotes," etc., by Hester Lynch Piozzi, 1786, p. 137.
[2] Mainly for its reference to Goldsmith's "Royal Game of
Goose," the following may be quoted from a letter in Hayward's

quently, she says in her "Anecdotes," to talk to her about Johnson, and exhort her to obtain, if possible, his acquaintance and friendship, which, nevertheless, did not come about until Hogarth was in his grave. In his later years, he had some intercourse with Goldsmith, of whom, according to Mr. Forster, he made a sketch. This (which is engraved in the more modern editions of Forster's "Life," and belonged to Mr. Studley Martin of Liverpool) shows "Goldy" hard at work in his Islington lodgings, not forgetting the ruffles and rings in which his soul delighted. Hogarth was also at one time on friendly terms with Wilkes and his boon-companion Churchill, although but for his unfortunate quarrel with them we might never have heard of the fact, and he had been the guest of Sir Francis Dashwood (Lord Despencer), whom he painted in his Medmenham Abbey costume, engaged in the adoration of Venus. But the connection of which we find the most certain traces is that with David Garrick and Henry Fielding. Fielding, as we have seen, had written of him admiringly in the "Champion" and "Joseph Andrews," and he refers to Hogarth's designs for the prototypes

"Autobiography, etc., of Mrs. Piozzi (Thrale)," 1861, ii. 130:— "My father and he [Hogarth] were very intimate, and he often dined with us. . . . I had got a then new thing, I suppose, which was called Game of the Goose, and felt earnest that we children might be allowed a round table to play at it, but was half afraid of my uncle's and my father's grave looks. Hogarth said, good-humouredly, 'I will come, my dears, and play at it with you.' Our joy was great, and the sport began under my management and direction. The pool rose to five shillings, a fortune to us monkeys, and when I won it, I capered for delight."

of more than one of his minor characters. Both
Parson Thwackum and Mrs. Partridge have their
admitted originals in *A Harlot's Progress*. Hogarth,
on his side, etched at least one benefit ticket for the
author of "Tom Jones," and we shall find him in this
chapter assisting him with a headpiece for one of
his journalistic ventures. With Garrick his connection probably began not long after the actor's
first appearance at Goodman's Fields, and it continued until his (Hogarth's) death. Among the
letters in the "Garrick Correspondence" is a graceful apology to the painter for remissness in visiting him; and later, when Churchill had announced
that he was meditating his unjustifiable "Epistle,"
Garrick lost no time in expostulating :—"I must
intreat of you," says an autograph note in the
Forster collection, "by the Regard you profess to
me, that you dont tilt at my Friend Hogarth before
you see me. . . . He is a great and original Genius,
I love him as a Man, and reverence him as an
Artist. I would not for all the Politicks and
Politicians in the Universe that you two should
have the least Cause of Ill-will to each other. I am
sure you will not publish against him if you think
twice." Unhappily "The Bruiser" was not to be
so persuaded. But this extract pleasantly illustrates
the relations of Hogarth and "Little Davy," of
whom he left several portraits, the most important
of which, the *Garrick as Richard III.*, was engraved in 1746—the year with which this chapter
opens.

THE FARMER'S RETURN.
From Basire's Engraving.

"For the portrait of Mr. Garrick in Richard III.," says Hogarth, "I was paid two hundred pounds (which was more than any English artist ever received for a single portrait), and that too by the sanction of several painters who had been previously consulted about the price, which was not given without mature consideration."[1] The purchaser was Mr. Duncombe, of Duncombe Park, Yorkshire; and when one remembers that *Marriage A-la-Mode* only realized £126, it must be admitted that the price paid for the *Garrick* was munificent. The picture itself, which was exhibited at the Grosvenor Gallery in 1888, is striking and effective; but unless much is allowed for the exaggeration of acting, the resemblance to Garrick's face and figure is not great.[2] Hogarth has left a better likeness in the combined portraits of *Garrick and his Wife*, which belonged to Mr. Locker of Greenwich Hospital, who sold it to George IV. Here Garrick is represented writing the prologue to Foote's comedy of "Taste," while his wife behind him takes the pen from his hand, a conceit which, as Steevens is careful to acquaint us, is borrowed from Vanloo's portrait of *Colley Cibber and his Daughter.* This work, a canvas

---

[1] "Hogarth Illustrated," iii. 56.

[2] Grignion the engraver, Hogarth's colleague in the plate, told John Ireland the following anecdote. "*Hogarth* (he said) etched the head and hand, but finding the head too large, he erased it, and etched it a second time, when seeing it wrong placed upon the shoulders, he again rubbed it out, and replaced it as it now stands, remarking—'*I never was right, until I had been wrong'*" ("Hogarth Illustrated," iii. 346.)

of 50 × 40 inches, in unimpaired condition, was exhibited at the recent Guelph Exhibition (1891). Of
the two the portrait of the lady, although some critics
have unaccountably pronounced it vulgar, was the
more beautifully painted; but the work unfortunately
suffered the fate of some other of the artist's efforts.
An obscure dispute arose between Garrick and
Hogarth on the subject, and the latter in a fit of
irritation drew his brush across the face.[1] The
picture remained unpaid for at his death, when
his widow sent it to Garrick without any demand.
Another presentment of Garrick is contained in the
frontispiece to the "Farmer's Return from London"
(an interlude by the actor which was very popular
in 1762), where an honest rustic pays a visit to the
"fine hugeous City," sees the coronation of George III.,
goes to Laureate Whitehead's "School for Lovers,"
and sits up with the Cock Lane Ghost. Garrick
dedicates it to Hogarth, whose sketch is most admirably facsimiled by Basire, "as a faint Testimony
of the sincere Esteem which the Writer bears him."
Finally, to complete the sum of Hogarth's relations
with the "English Roscius," at the time of the
Shakespeare Jubilee he designed him a chair, for
which he carved a medallion from a piece of the
Stratford mulberry-tree. It is a cumbrous and over-
decorated piece of furniture, which reflects but

---

[1] "The eyes of Garrick being coarsely painted, ill-drawn, and
evidently by another hand than Hogarth's, attest the truth of
this story" (F. G. Stephens in "Grosvenor Gallery Catalogue,"
1888).

SIMON LORD LOVAT.
From Hogarth's Etching.

slender credit upon its "author" as a rival of
Sheraton and Chippendale.[1]

In the August of 1746, however, Hogarth produced a portrait in which his characteristic powers
are far more evident than in any picture he ever
made of Garrick. In that month the notorious Simon
Fraser, Lord Lovat, was brought in a litter to St.
Albans on his way to London, where he was tried,
and subsequently executed on Tower Hill. Upon
the invitation of a local physician (Samuel Ireland's
friend, Dr. J. Webster) Hogarth went to St. Albans to
meet him. He found him on the 14th at the "White
Hart Inn" under the hands of a barber. The old
lord (he was over seventy) rose at his approach, and
"bussing" him demonstratively after the French
fashion on the cheek, contrived to transfer no small
portion of the soapsuds on his own face to that of
the painter. The short squat figure, the crouching
attitude, the crafty eyes, and the "pawky" expression of Lovat as he counts over the various Highland
Clans on his fingers, are admirably rendered; and it
is no wonder that this most effective sketch, having
besides its own merit all that of an à-propos, should
have been widely popular. The rolling press could
not supply impressions enough ; and though they
were sold at a shilling each, for several weeks
Hogarth received payment at the rate of twelve

---

[1] There is a copy of it by Jane Ireland in vol. ii. p. 147 of her
father's "Graphic Illustrations." In the "Illustrated London
News" for 20th July, 1861, it is said to have been bought by
Lady Burdett-Coutts.

pounds a day. Whether he was also the author of
the mezzotint which appeared nearly ten months
afterwards, entitled *Lovat's Ghost on Pilgrimage* [*i.e.*
to Scotland], is not certain from the evidence of that
work itself. But if the Dr. Webster above-mentioned really told Samuel Ireland that he had received
it from the artist " with an assurance of it's being his
own design," the historical testimony must be regarded as unimpeachable.

To the year 1747 belongs *The Stage Coach ; or,
Country Inn Yard*, and the series called *Industry and
Idleness. The Stage Coach* is more interesting as a
little piece of everyday eighteenth-century life than
for any dramatic element which it contains, although
there is an election procession in the background.
From the wooden-galleried courtyard of the *Old
Angel Inn, Tom Bates from London*, the creaking
and lumbering Ilford Stage (?) prepares (God willing)
to run its snail-like course of so many—or so few—
miles *per diem*. In the foreground may be seen
" T. B." himself, justifying his lengthy score to a
hard-featured lawyer (with the " Act against Bribery "
in his pocket) who discharges it reluctantly. Mrs.
Landlady, from her sanctum among the lemons and
Barbadoes water, is bawling vociferously for Susan
Chambermaid, detained for the moment by the too
demonstrative farewells of a gentleman in a bag-wig.
A stout woman is being squeezed in at the door of the
vehicle by a diminutive man, perhaps her husband,
who hands up a dram-bottle after her. Behind come
a vinegar-faced spinster and a squalling child. To

THE STAGE COACH.

From Hogarth's Engraving.

the right a portly personage, with a sword and cane, disregarding an appeal from the hunchbacked postilion, is waiting to follow the stout woman. Among the baggage in the "basket" an old crone is smoking; and on the roof an English sailor (see "Centurion" on the bundle) and a dejected French-man have taken their perilous places.[1] To put the finishing touch to the bustle of departure, a man blows a post horn out of a window. The whole scene might serve as an illustration to "Peregrine Pickle" or "Tom Jones."

Industry and Idleness, says Hogarth himself, ex-hibited "the conduct of two Fellow-prentices; where the one, by taking good courses, and pursuing

---

[1] Both of these modes of travelling, the basket and the roof, are illustrated by Charles P. Moritz, whose "Travels, chiefly on Foot, through several parts of England," was translated from the German in 1795. Taking coach to Northampton, he mounts the top, in company with a farmer, a young man, and "a black-a-moor." This eminence proving as dangerous as it looked, he creeps into the basket, in spite of the warnings of the black. "As long as we went up hill (he says) it was easy and pleasant. And, having had little or no sleep the night before, I was almost asleep among the trunks and packages; but how was the case altered when we came to go down hill; then all the trunks and parcels began, as it were, to dance around me, and everything in the basket seemed to be alive; and I every moment received from them such violent blows, that I thought my last hour was come. . . . I was obliged to suffer this torture nearly an hour, till we came to another hill again, when quite shaken to pieces and sadly bruised, I again crept to the top of the coach, and took possession of my former seat." His conclusion is, that it is safest to take inside places in English post coaches, though it may be added that, from his account, travellers on the top seem to have had the assistance of handles which are not shown in Hogarth's plate.

those points for which he was put apprentice, becomes
a valuable man, and an ornament to his country:
whilst the other, giving way to idleness, naturally
falls into poverty, and most commonly ends fatally,
as is expressed in the last Print."[1] The intention,
as Leigh Hunt says, was "an avowed commonplace" . . . "while the execution of it was full
of much higher things and profounder humanities."
There is no more eloquent stroke in the whole of
Hogarth than that by which the miserable player
at "halfpenny-under-the-hat" in Plate III. is shown
to have but a plank between him and the grave;
nor is there anything more vivid in its squalid
realism than the episode in Thomas Idle's career
to which Dr. King subjoined for epigraph—"The
sound of a shaken leaf shall chase him." Very touching, too, is the grief of the widowed mother when her
reprobate son is being sculled past Cuckold's Point
to the ship which is to carry his graceless fortunes
to a foreign land. The whole series of prints is full
of contemporary detail of the most interesting description. In Plate VI. we see the newly married
couple greeted by the old discordant hymenean (a
"kind of wild Janizary music," Lichtenberg calls it)
of the marrow-bone and cleaver men.[2] Plate VIII.
displays a civic feast; and the last two plates, a

[1] Genuine Works," i. 134.

[2] "When, therefore, properly struck," says Lichtenberg of these
instruments, "they produce no despicable clang; at least certainly a better one than logs of wood emit when thrown to the
ground; and yet the latter are said to have occasioned the invention of the rebeck."

The IDLE PRENTICE at Play in the Church Yard during Divine Service.

Proverbs. Chap. XIX. v. 29.
Judgments are prepared for scorners,
& stripes for the back of fools.

INDUSTRY AND IDLENESS.   (Plate III.)
From Hogarth's Engraving.

Lord Mayor's Show, and an execution at Tyburn.
The first idea for this series is said to have been
suggested by the *Eastward Hoe* of Chapman, Jon-
son, and Marston, with which it has some affinities.
Although of set purpose executed coarsely, it was
extremely popular, was dramatized, and gave rise to
several publications graphic and otherwise. One of
these was the imitation of Northcote, *Diligence and
Dissipation*, a picture-history, in ten plates, of two
housemaids, patched together from Hogarth and
Richardson's " Pamela." " There could not be a
more lamentable failure," say the biographers of
Reynolds ; "and Northcote never forgave Hogarth."

In 1747 Hogarth executed a rude headpiece for
the " Jacobite's Journal," a newspaper begun by
Henry Fielding in December of that year, with the
double object of supporting the Government and
ridiculing the rebel cause. Hogarth's contribution
to it—if his indeed it be—does not require any
further notice. But in the next year took place that
memorable journey to France which, in the lean
record of his life, looms so large, and the narrative
of which has afforded so much gratification to the
more malicious of his biographers. According to
these, Hogarth, when in France, behaved himself
with a plentiful lack of *savoir-faire*. Nothing satis-
fied him. He pooh-poohed the houses, the furniture, the ornaments, or spoke of them openly with
scornful opprobrium. " In the streets he was often
clamorously rude. A tatter'd bag, or a pair of silk
stockings with holes in them, drew a torrent of

imprudent language from him." His travelling companions, among whom were his crony, Frank Hayman, and Cheere the sculptor (afterwards Sir Henry),
strove in vain to induce him to be more guarded in
his language, especially as there were plenty of Irish
and Scotch within hearing, who would have rejoiced
to mob the sturdy little Englishman. But admonition of this kind was only thrown away. Hogarth
merely laughed at it; "and treated the offerer of it
as a pusillanimous wretch, unworthy of a residence
in a free country, making him the butt of his ridicule
for several evenings afterwards." At last matters
culminated when he was amusing himself with a
slight sketch of the gate of Calais. He was forthwith
haled before the Commandant, and, though the
drawings found upon him established the innocence
of his purpose, was informed that, had not the Peace
of Aix la Chapelle been actually signed, he would
assuredly have been hanged upon the ramparts.
"Two guards," says Steevens, "were then provided
to convey him on shipboard; nor did they quit him
till he was three miles from the shore. They then
spun him round like a top, on the deck; and told
him he was at liberty to proceed on his voyage
without further attendance or molestation. With the
slightest allusion to the ludicrous particulars of this
affair, poor Hogarth was by no means pleased.
The leading circumstance in it his own pencil has
recorded." [1]

It is quite possible that this account loses nothing

[1] Nichols, "Anecdotes," 1782, p. 42-4.

The IDLE PRENTICE turned away, and sent to Sea.

Proverbs Chap XV, v 1
A foolish Son is the heaviness of his Mother

INDUSTRY AND IDLENESS. (Plate V.)

From Hogarth's Engraving.

under the malicious pen of George Steevens, who,
from whatever source he derived his information,
doubtless heightened it *more suo*. Horace Walpole's
version, written at the time in a letter to Mann
of December 15, 1748, is far less "picturesque."
" Hogarth has run a great risk since the peace ; he
went to France, and was so imprudent as to be
taking a sketch of the drawbridge at Calais. He
was seized and carried to the Governor, where he
was forced to prove his vocation by producing
several *caricaturas* of the French ; particularly a
scene of the shore, with an immense piece of beef
landing for the Lion-d'Argent, the English inn at
Calais, and several hungry friars following it. They
were much diverted with his drawings, and dismissed
him."

After this we may fairly give the story as Hogarth, who probably himself told it to Walpole,
relates it in the Ireland MSS. " The next print I
engraved," says he, " was the *Roast Beef of Old
England* [published March 6, 1749], which took its
rise from a visit I paid to France the preceding year.
The first time an Englishman goes from *Dover* to
Calais, he must be struck with the different face
of things at so little a distance. A farcical pomp of
war, pompous parade of religion, and much bustle
with very little business. To sum up all, poverty,
slavery, and innate insolence, covered with an affectation of politeness, give you even here a true picture
of the manners of the whole nation : nor are the
priests less opposite to those of Dover than the two

shores. The friars are dirty, sleek, and solemn; the soldiery are lean, ragged, and tawdry; and as to the fish-women—their faces are absolute leather.

"As I was sauntering about and observing them, near the gate which it seems was built by the English, when the place was in our possession, I remarked some appearance of the arms of *England* on the front.[1] By this and idle curiosity, I was prompted to make a sketch of it, which being observed, I was taken into custody; but not attempting to cancel any of my sketches or memorandums, which were found to be merely those of a painter for his private use, without any relation to fortification, it was not thought necessary to send me back [?] to Paris. I was only closely confined to my own lodgings, till the wind changed *for England*: where I no sooner arrived, than I set about the picture; made the gate my back-ground; and in one corner introduced my own portrait, which has generally been thought a correct likeness, with the soldier's hand upon my shoulder. By the fat friar, who stops the lean cook that is sinking under the weight of a vast sirloin of beef, and two of *the military* bearing off a great kettle of *soup[c] maigre*, I meant to display to

---

[1] It was announced in 1884 that Calais Gate was doomed. But according to recent advices, the sentence has not yet been carried out. "Hogarth's gate, with its drawbridge, indeed, still hobbles on, but sadly mauled and defaced. As can be seen from the picture, it was in his day handsomely decorated with sculptures; and at one period could be made out the traces of the English Royal arms on one side, which had been but partially erased." ("Saturday Review," 2 May, 1891.)

INDUSTRY AND IDLENESS. (Plate X.)

From Hogarth's Engraving.

my own countrymen the striking difference between the food, priests, soldiers, etc., of two nations so contiguous, that in a clear day one coast may be seen from the other. The melancholy and miserable Highlander, browzing on his scanty fare, consisting of a bit of bread and an onion, is intended for one of the many that fled from this country after the rebellion."[1]

Besides the figures Hogarth mentions, there are, to the left of the picture, a pair of basket-women, who are making merry over the resemblance to a human face which a sufficiently "leathern" fishwife has discovered in a skate she holds in her lap. But the artist has cleverly suggested a fact of which they themselves are ignorant, and that is the strong similarity between this face and their own weather-beaten features. In the representation of the two sentinels he has given full value to the "ragged and tawdry" element in the French soldiers. One has paper ruffles, on which the words "Grand Monarch, P" are plainly legible; his smallclothes are fastened by a skewer, and he has a large hole in his gaiter. Opposite, his equally famished and tattered companion spills his skillet of *soupe maigre* from sheer astonishment at the goodly English fare. Next to this personage is the squinting and stunted figure of an Irish mercenary, to whose national bravery the painter has paid a compliment by giving him a bullet-hole through his hat. In the background, through the gate, a priest is carrying the Host

[1] "Hogarth Illustrated," iii. 349-50.

to a sick person, and the people fall on their knees
as it passes. The fat Franciscan was a portrait of
Pine, of St. Martin's Lane, who was only moderately
gratified with the compliment, as it procured him
the nickname of " Friar Pine." He endeavoured to
induce the artist to modify the likeness, but this
Hogarth resolutely refused.

Though not one of Hogarth's capital works,
Calais Gate, in its engraved form, at once became
popular on account of its subject. The starved
French sentinel was speedily appropriated as a
heading for recruiting advertisements, where he
figured in humiliating contrast to a well-fed British
volunteer. Besides this, Theodosius Forrest, son
of the Forrest who had been Hogarth's companion
in the " Five Days' Tour," turned the whole into
a cantata, which was headed by a reduced copy of
the print.[1] These are the initial lines of this patriotic
performance :—

> " 'Twas at the Gates of *Calais*, HOGARTH tells,
> Where sad Despair and Famine always dwells ;
> A meagre Frenchman, *Madam Gransire's* Cook,
> As home he steer'd his Carcase, that Way took,
> Bending beneath the Weight of fam'd *Sir-Loin*,
> On whom he often wish'd in vain to dine.
> Good Father *Dominick* by Chance came by,
> With rosy Gills, round Paunch, and greedy Eye,
> Who, when he first beheld the greasy Load,
> His Benediction on it he bestowed," &c.

[1] Theodosius Forrest, of George Street, York Buildings, was the
solicitor to Covent Garden Theatre, and the friend of Colman and
Garrick. He was a good amateur painter, a song-writer, and a
kind of notability in his day. In a mezzotint by Nathaniel Hone,

From the second edition of this, which is dated 1759, it would appear that Forrest's cantata was "performed at the Theatre in the Haymarket." [1]

The *Gate of Calais* was a subject which might well be expected to awaken all the insular prejudices of Hogarth, to say nothing of the "least little touch of spleen" on his own account at the ignominious treatment he had received in France. But although he was so keenly alive to the dilapidated and un-dignified appearance of the French soldiery, he was not the less sensible of the weak points of the British Grenadier. In the *March of the Guards towards Scotland in the Year* 1745, commonly called the *March to Finchley*, he has exhibited all the disorders of a military dislodgment. While the vanguard are winding away to the horizon, the fore-ground, between the "King's Head" inn and the "Adam and Eve," at Tottenham Court Turnpike, is filled with a confusion of departure that defies description. Sutlers, soldiers, spies, spectators and camp-followers are all blended inextricably in one of those wonderful crowds of which he had already given notable example in the Execution scene of the

dated 1772, he and Francis Grose, the antiquary, appear as a pair of monks. He committed suicide in 1784, at the age of fifty-six.

[1] In 1851, Mr. W. P. Frith, R.A., exhibited a *Hogarth Brought before the Governor of Calais as a Spy* at the Royal Academy, borrowing for his epigraph in the catalogue the above-quoted pas-sage from Walpole. It is curious to note that in 1818, Wilkie, too, was taken before the mayor for sketching Calais Gate, although he was politely dismissed by that functionary.

Apprentice series. The most prominent figure is that of a stalwart young Guardsman, "like Paris handsome, and like Hector brave," hopelessly embarrassed by the rival adieux of "his twa Dèborahs," one violent, the other pathetic. Near him is a drummer, who is endeavouring, with an inimitable screw of the face, to drown his own grief and that of his wife and child by a thundering "point of war." Elsewhere an officer kisses a milkmaid, while a soldier pours the milk into his hat; another soldier directs the attention of a grinning pieman to this diverting incident, and at the same time takes the opportunity of purloining some of his wares. Not far off, a barrel of spirit is tapped with a gimlet upon its unconscious owner's shoulder; and in the right foreground a number of chickens are running wildly in search of their vanished mother, pouched safely in a predatory pocket. Beside the gutter a drunken fellow turns with disgust from a malicious proffer of water, and holds out his hand to a female gin-seller for more gin, while the wizened infant at her back imitates his gesture. In the crowd the soft unfurrowed face of another child is happily contrasted with the plotting eagerness of a couple of Jacobite intriguers. At the back, in the extreme left, a fight is going on, watched by excited spectators. But here, as in many other cases, we must resign ourselves to a mere indication of the chief riches of the plate. It has, moreover, been excellently described in Christopher Smart's "Student," ii. 162, by Hogarth's and Fielding's friend, Justice Welch. The artist at

BEER STREET.
[From the Original Engraving.

first intended to dedicate the picture to George II., but that monarch had, as Walpole says, "little propensity to refined pleasures," and he is reported to have received the intended homage with anything but enthusiasm, even hinting that the designer deserved to be picketed for burlesquing the "gentlemen of the army." Thereupon Hogarth, in a fume, inscribed the print to the King of Prussia, as "an Encourager of *Arts* and *Sciences*," and his majesty made fitting acknowledgment of the honour done him. Like others of the painter's works, it was sold by lottery, and thus, by good fortune, became the property of the Foundling Hospital, where it remains to this day, having of late years been glazed for additional security.[1]

The plate of the *March to Finchley* was published in December, 1750. It was engraved by Luke Sullivan.[2] The only other prints which concern

[1] Rouquet (see "Bibliography, Part II.) wrote with reference to this picture a special letter which, *inter alia*, serves to show how completely Hogarth had inspired his friends with his hatred of the "Black Masters." Rouquet begins by apologising ironically for the newness of the work,—"*cette ignoble fraicheur, qu'on découvre dans la nature, & qu'on ne voit jamais dans les Cabinets bien célèbres. Le tems ne l'a point encore obscurci de cette docte fumée, de ce nuage sacré, qui le cachera quelque jour aux yeux profanes du vulgaire, pour ne laisser voir ses beautés qu'aux initiés.*" But he also takes opportunity to comment incidentally upon the inveterate Gallomania both of Hogarth and Fielding. Rouquet's letter was translated in the "Old Woman's Magazine," i. 182.

[2] Sullivan is the angel in *Paul before Felix*. The *March to Finchley* is his masterpiece as an engraver. He was a man of extremely irregular and dissolute habits ; and Hogarth is said to have

this chapter are *Beer Street* and *Gin Lane*, 1751 ; the *Four Stages of Cruelty*, 1751 ; the plates of *Paul before Felix*, 1751 and 1752, and *Moses brought to Pharaoh's Daughter*, 1752. The first pair, which were prompted by the agitation connected with the Act for restricting the sale of spirituous liquors, are among the best known of Hogarth's minor works, although Sir Wilfred Lawson and the total abstainers of to-day would probably regard the bloated prosperity of *Beer Street* as scarcely less dangerous than the starved emaciation of *Gin Lane*. With the lusty beer-drinkers everything prospers but the pawn-broking business ; with the consumers of "Bung-your-eye" and "Strip-me-naked" everything is the reverse, and the gentleman at the sign of the "three balls" is driving a roaring trade. We cannot linger on these plates further than to call attention to the inimitable professional complacency of the ragged sign-painter in *Beer Street* (in those days there was a regular sign-market in Harp Alley, Shoe Lane), and to the appalling figures of the itinerant gin-seller and the maudlin mother in the companion print. Charles Lamb has left an enthusiastic description of *Gin Lane*.[1] The *Four Stages of Cruelty* are a set of

experienced considerable difficulty in keeping him under his eye during the progress of the plate. He had a habit of disappearing mysteriously for weeks at a time ("Hogarth Illustrated," iii. 353).

[1] It is too well known to quote. But the characteristic, and equally sympathetic comments of Dickens upon Hogarth and Lamb are not so familiar but that they may find place here :—" I have always myself thought the purpose of this fine piece [*Gin Lane*] to be not adequately stated even by Charles Lamb. 'The very

GIN LANE.
From the Original Engraving.

plates exhibiting the "progress" of one Thomas
Nero, who, from torturing dogs and horses, advances
by rapid stages to seduction and murder, and finishes
his career on the dissecting table at Surgeons' Hall.
They have all the downright power of Hogarth's
best manner; but they are unrelieved by humour of
any kind, and are consequently painful and even
repulsive. "The leading points in these as well
as the two preceding prints," says Hogarth, "were
made as obvious as possible, in the hope that their
tendency might be seen by men of the lowest rank.
Neither minute accuracy of design, nor fine engraving was deemed necessary, as the latter would

houses seem absolutely reeling' it is true; but beside that wonderful picture of what follows intoxication, we have indication
quite as powerful of what leads to it among the neglected classes.
There is no evidence that any of the actors in the dreary scene
have ever been much better than we see them there. The best
are pawning the commonest necessaries, and tools of their trades;
and the worst are homeless vagrants who give us no clue to their
having been otherwise in bygone days. All are living and dying
miserably. Nobody is interfering for prevention or for cure, in
the generation going out before us, or the generation coming in.
The beadle is the only sober man in the composition except the
pawnbroker, and he is mightily indifferent to the orphan-child
crying beside its parent's coffin. The little charity-girls are not
so well tanght or looked after, but that they can take to dram-
drinking already. The church indeed is very prominent and
handsome; but as, quite passive in the picture, it coldly surveys
these things in progress under shadow of its tower, I cannot but
bethink me that it was not until this year of grace 1848 that a
Bishop of London first came out respecting something wrong in
poor men's social accommodations, and I am confirmed in my
suspicion that Hogarth had many meanings which have not grown
obsolete in a century" (Forster's "Life," Bk. vi. Ch. 3.)

render them too expensive for the persons to whom
they were intended to be useful."[1] These words
should be borne in mind in considering them, especially the *Four Stages of Cruelty*. The price of the
ordinary impressions was a shilling the plate, and an
unsuccessful attempt was made to sell them even
more cheaply by cutting them in wood.[2]

Paul before Felix and *Moses brought to Pharaoh's
Daughter* were essays in that historical style to which
Hogarth now and then returned like the moth to
the flame. *Paul before Felix* was painted for Lincoln's
Inn Hall, to decorate which Lord Wyndham had
left a legacy of £200 :[3] the other the painter pre-

[1] "Hogarth Illustrated," iii. 355.

[2] Stages 3 and 4 only were executed in this way. A reduced
facsimile of the former is given in the "Catalogue of Prints." The
size of the original block is 14½ × 17½ in. ; but even the reduction shows that the drawing on the wood, doubtless by Hogarth
himself, was infinitely more vigorous than the copper-plate, which
is also copied on the opposite page.

[3] Hogarth obtained the commission through the instrumentality
of Lord Mansfield. A search among the archives of the Society
of Lincoln's Inn not long since brought to light the following
letter and receipt with reference to this subject. We make no
apology for inserting them here, as they establish the date of the
painting :—

"S[r]   "June 28, 1748.

"According to your order, I have consider'd of a place for the
Picture, and cannot think of any better than that over the sound
board, in the hall, all the advantages to be gain'd for Light, can
only be by setting the bottom near the wall, and Inclining the
Top forward as much as possible, it being thus Inclin'd will make
ornaments on the sides improper, so that a frame only is necessary. I have enquired of Mr. Gosset, a Frame maker in Berwick
Street about the price of one somewhat in the manner of the

THE FOUR STAGES OF CRUELTY. (Plate III.)
From the Original Engraving.

sented to the Foundling Hospital. Neither of them
can be said to have been thoroughly successful,
though Haydon certainly goes too far when he says
that the painter merited a strait-waistcoat if he really
thought the *Moses* a serious painting. But if they
were not successful, they were at all events the cause
of a success. As a subscription ticket to the engravings of these two pictures, Hogarth issued a
burlesque *Paul before Felix*, " design'd and scratch'd
in the true Dutch taste." Everything that he chose
to see in Rembrandt and his school—the imputed
vulgarity—the absence of beauty—the anachronisms
in costume—is carefully ridiculed. This etching was
at first merely given away to the artist's acquaintance,
etc., but it became so popular that it ultimately sold

Sketch below [see facsimile], he believes it may come to about
30 pound Guilt, to about half as much unguilt and about five pounds
less if my Lord Windham's armes are omitted. Frames may be
carried up to a great expense, but he thinks one cannot be made
in proportion to the picture for less.

"I am Sir your
"Most obed^t Humble
"Ser^t to com^d
"WM. HOGARTH.

"I have removed the picture home again in hopes of making
some improvements whilst the Frame is making."

"July the 8th, 1748.

"Reced of Jn° Wood Esqr Treasurer of the Honble Society of
Lincoln's Inn by the hands of Richd Farshall Chief Butler to the
Said Society the Sum of two hundred pounds being the Legacy
given by the late Lord Wyndham to the Said Society laid out in
a picture drawn by M^r. Hogarth According to order of Council
Dated the 27th day of June last."

"£200." "WM. HOGARTH."

for nearly as much as the larger prints. This chapter may be concluded with the very characteristic finish of the notice in the " Daily Advertiser" announcing the appearance of the prints, as well as the auction of the *Marriage A-la-Mode*, of which we have already given an account in Chapter V. " As (according to the standard of judgment, so righteously and laudably established by Picture-dealers, Picture-cleaners, Picture-frame-makers, and other Connoisseurs) the works of a Painter are to be esteemed more or less valuable as they are more or less scarce, and as the living Painter is most of all affected by the inferences resulting from this and other considerations equally uncandid and edifying; Mr. Hogarth, by way of precaution, not puff, begs leave to urge, that, probably, this[1] will be the last suit[e] or series of Pictures he may ever exhibit, because of the difficulty of vending such a number at once to any tolerable advantage, and that the whole number he has already exhibited of the historical or humorous kind does not exceed fifty, of which the three sets called *The Harlot's Progress*, *The Rake's Progress*, and that now to be sold, make twenty; so that whoever has a taste of his own to rely on, not too squeamish for the production of a Modern, and courage enough to own it, by daring to give them a place in his collection (till Time, the supposed finisher, but real designer of Paintings, has rendered them fit for those more sacred repositories where

[1] That is, the series of *Marriage A-la-Mode*.

June 28 1748

W.m Hogarth

I have removed the picture
home again in hopes of making
some improvements whilst the
Frame is making

with carving
at the corner
and in that
Middle

S.r   June 28 1748

According to your order, I have consider'd of a place
for the Picture and cannot think of any better than
that over the sound board, in the hall, all the advantage to be gain'd for Light, can only be by fitting
the bottom near the wall and Inclining the Top
forward as much as possible, it being thus Inclin'd will
make ornaments on the sides improper, so that a
Frame only is necessary. I have enquired of Mr
Goffs, a Frame maker in Barwick for w.t labour
the price of one some what in the manner of the
sketch below, he believes it may come to about
30 pound Guilt, to about half as much unguilt
and about five pounds less if my Lord Winthams
arms are omitted. Frames may be carried up to a
great expence—but he thinks one cannot be made
in proportion to the picture for less.

my Lord Windhams   arms if judg'd proper

                                   I am S.r yours
a Moulding   most obed.t Humble
of 11 or 12   serv.t to com.d
Inches broad
with carving   W.m Hogarth
at the corners
and in the
Middis

                     I have removed the picture
                     home again in hopes of making
                     some improvements whilst the
                     Frame is making

Schools, Names, Heads, Masters, etc., attain their last stage of preferment), may from hence be convinced that multiplicity at least of his (Mr. Hogarth's) pieces will be no diminution of their value." [1]

It is humiliating to reflect that, notwithstanding the persuasive ingenuity of this appeal, the tragedy of the Squanderfields brought no more to its Author than what, in his "Rhymes on Art," Sir Martin Archer Shee rightly describes as "a sum too contemptible to be named."

[1] Genuine Works," i. 181-2.

SUBSCRIPTION TICKET TO THE "MARCH TO FINCHLEY."

CHAPTER VII.

The Analysis, Election Prints, and Sigismunda.

N 1753 Hogarth was fifty-six years of age. He had done his best work ; and, with the exception of the *Four Prints of an Election*, produced nothing after this date worthy of the brain which contrived *Marriage A-la-Mode.* Horace Walpole, indeed, regards *Credulity, Superstition, and Fanaticism* as, "for useful and deep satire," the "most sublime" of his efforts. But no doubt the note—in the followers of Wesley and Whitefield—of what the late Matthew Arnold termed "provinciality," was distasteful to refined Mr. Walpole ; and in common with many of his contemporaries, he would probably have welcomed any effective satire on Methodism as "useful and deep."[1] In this instance, as in others, we do not share his opinion. It is to be observed, however, that if Hogarth in these last years of his life

[1] Cf. his account of Wesley and his preaching at Bath ("Letter to Chute," 10 October, 1766).

gave birth to nothing which could add to his fame, on the other hand he issued one or two productions which, though they now affect his reputation but little, had a remarkable influence upon his credit at the time. Those which concern this chapter are the book called the "Analysis of Beauty" and the picture of *Sigismunda*. These two ill-starred performances gave just that opportunity to his detractors, which, as long as he confined himself to the delineation of vices and follies, was lost in the general applause. And he had many enemies. With all picture-mongery and sham-connoisseurship he was at war. His success had alienated some of his colleagues; his plain-spoken opinions some of his friends. Added to this, he was an older, perhaps a weaker man. Yet it was precisely at this period that he set himself to compose in the "Analysis" a treatise "fixing the fluctuating Ideas of Taste," and sought in *Sigismunda* "to rival the ancients on their own ground." He was not in any sense a literary man (he speaks of himself as "one who never took up the pen before"); yet he selected a subject which above all requires the utmost resources of style and verbal *finesse*, of orderly arrangement and untroubled exposition,—the subject of Æsthetics : he had won his spurs in the unworked field of pictorial satire ; yet with that strange fatality which so often betrays the wisest to their discomfiture, he dreamed of competing successfully with the magic colouring and the voluptuous imagination of the Italians. In either case his failures were more than respectable ; and they were the failures of genius; but they were failures all the same. Their worst result was, that they embittered his remaining days; and involved him in acrimonious disputes at a time of life when he might reasonably have expected a peaceful close to his prolonged and laborious career.

The "Analysis of Beauty" had the following origin. In the picture of himself which Hogarth had painted in 1745—that excellent portrait in which his shrewd, sensible, blue-eyed head in its Montero cap looks out at us from the canvas in the National Gallery—he had drawn on a palette in the corner a serpentine curve with these words under it—"The Line of Beauty and Grace." "No Egyptian hiero-glyphic ever amused more than it did for a time," he says; and so numerous were the requests which he received for a solution of the enigma, that, after applying without success to several of his friends to take up the pen in his behalf, he finally made shift to explain his symbol in print himself. That he was fully alive to the perils of such an enterprise, is humorously expressed in an epigram he wrote :—

> "What! a book, and by Hogarth!—then twenty to ten,
> All he's gain'd by the *pencil*, he'll *lose* by the pen.
> Perhaps it may be so—howe'er, miss or hit,
> He will publish—*here goes—it is double or quit*."

In the correcting of both the manuscript and the proofs he seems to have had the assistance—more or less intermittent and occasional—of certain of his literary acquaintance; but this was not sufficient to save the "Analysis" from a fair proportion of those

errors of spelling and expression which afforded so
much delight to the petty pedantry of the day. For
the book itself, it was just such an one as might have
been expected under similar conditions. In parts it
was shrewd and sensible like its author; it contained
many practical hints and ingenious ideas; but as a
whole it was wanting in method, development, precision of language—perhaps of idea. This makes it
difficult to describe except as a desultory pamphlet
having for its text (or rather pretext) the not-very-
definite axiom attributed in Lomazzo's "Trattata della
Pittura"[1] to Michael Angelo, namely,—that a figure
should be always "pyramidal, serpent-like, and multi-
plied by one, two, and three"—an axiom concerning
which it may be observed that if it contains some
obvious artistic truth, it does not of necessity include
all. The fate of the volume was exactly what might
have been anticipated. The world of professional
scoffers and virtuosi fell joyously upon its obscurities
and incoherences,[2] while the caricaturists diverted
themselves hugely with fancy representations of
"Painter Pugg" and his ungainly "Graces." It is not

---

[1] Hogarth employed Richard Haydocke's folio translation of
1598, which he had purchased from Dr. Kennedy, the antiquary
and connoisseur.

[2]   *Hogarth*, thy Fate is fix'd; the Critic Crew,
        The Connoisseurs and Dabblers in *Vertû*,
        Club their united Wit, in ev'ry Look,
        Hint, Shrug, and Whisper, they condemn thy Book:
        Their guiltless Minds will ne'er forgive the Deed;
        What Devil prompted thee to write and read?"—
                        Gray's Inn Journal, 15th Dec., 1753.

worth while to attempt any serious enumeration of
these pictorial efforts, a number of which are fully
described in Mr. F. G. Stephens's Catalogue of "Satirical Prints and Drawings in the British Museum."
But it may be asserted generally that there is the same
difference between their involved brutalities and the
direct onslaught of Hogarth that Corporal Trim distinguished between one honest "home-thrust of a
bayonet" and the obscure and complicated manœuvres
of Messieurs Gymnast and Tripet. On the other hand,
friendly advocacy did all it could to secure a *succès
d'estime*. Mr. Richard Owen Cambridge, of Twicken-
ham, referring to the author as "the nicest observer
of our times," spoke of the book in the "World" for
December 13, 1753, as a "most rational" one; Mr.
Townley, of Merchant Taylors', wound up a com-
plimentary poem to the author by declaring that

> "Our sons, in time to come, shall strive
> Where the chief honour they shall give,
> Or to your pencil, or your pen";

and Mr. Ralph, of Chiswick, in prose, went even farther still. "Composition," he declared, "is at last
become a science; the student knows what he is in
search of; the connoisseur what to praise; and fancy
and fashion, or prescription, will usurp the hacknied
name of taste no more." As both Mr. Ralph and
Mr. Townley are reported to have been among the
number of the artist's volunteer assistants, neither of
these latter verdicts can be regarded as wholly disin-
terested. But "Sylvanus Urban" was scarcely less
kind. In the regulation "copy of verses" prefixed

to his twenty-fourth volume (1754), he refers to the
" Analysis " as follows :—

> " The *Proteus* BEAUTY, that illusive pow'r,
> Who changing still, was all things in an hour,
> Now, fix'd and bound, is just what Reason wills,
> Nor wayward Fancy's wild decrees fulfils ";

and he gave, besides, a lengthy summary of the book,
which he did not shrink from describing as "written
with that precision and perspicuity, which can only
result from a perfect knowledge of the subject in all its
extent." " The player and the dancing master," he
went on, "whom others consider as patterns of just
action and genteel deportment, are not less instructed
than the statuary and the painter ; nor is there any
species of beauty or elegance that is not here inves-
tigated and analyzed." Others, as sympathetic,
followed suit ; and even the great Mr. Burke, when
he came to write his famous treatise " On the Sublime
and Beautiful," admitted that " the very ingenious
Mr. Hogarth's" idea was in general " extremely
just." Under the author's supervision, a rendering
of the " Analysis" into German was made by one
Christlob Mylius in 1754; and in 1761 an Italian
version appeared at Leghorn. It was not translated
in France until 1805, when it was taken in hand by
Jansen, Talleyrand's librarian ; but it was evidently
known to French criticism long before this date.[1]

---

[1] Diderot, for example, must have been familiar with it. Commenting in his "Salon de 1765 " on Hogarth's statement at p. 121
that " France hath not produced one remarkable good colourist,"
he gives him the lie direct. *" Vous en avez menti, monsieur
Hogarth,"* he says. *" C'est, de votre part, ignorance ou platitude* . . .

The "two explanatory prints" by which the *Analysis of Beauty* is illustrated deserve a passing word. They represent a *Country Dance* and a *Statuary's Yard*, and each is set in a framework of smaller illustrations. To make these latter perfectly intelligible, the book itself must be consulted; but the dance, which occupies the centre of the former, requires no lengthy explanation. It is said to be intended for the Wanstead Assembly, and to include the figures of Earl Tylney, his countess and their children, tenants, etc. It is also stated that the principal male dancer represents George the Third, when young, or the Duke of Kingston. In any case, the performers exhibit almost every eccentricity which it is possible for the poetry of motion to assume. Hogarth's own comment on the plate—a comment which, it will be seen, anticipates some of the revelations of modern instantaneous photography —is this :—" The best representation in a picture, of even the most elegant dancing, as every figure is

Peignez, peignez mieux, si vous pouvez. Apprenez à dessiner et n'ecrivez point." Both contradiction and admonition were a little belated, as Hogarth had been dead for some months. But Chardin, of whom Diderot was speaking, was certainly a "remarkable good colourist"; and, moreover, is not unfrequently compared with Hogarth himself. What is even more curious is, that, a few pages further on, in speaking of Loutherbourg, Diderot seems to be remembering the "Analysis." *"La pyramide* (he says) *est plus belle que le cône qui est simple, mais sans variété. La statue équestre plait plus que le statue pédestre ; la ligne droite brisée, que la ligne droite ; la ligne circulaire, que la ligne droite brisée ; l'ovale, que la circulaire ; la serpentante, que l'ovale"* ("Œuvres," x. (1876) pp. 303, 368).

rather a suspended action in it than an attitude, must
be always somewhat unnatural and ridiculous; for
were it possible in a real dance to fix every person at
one instant of time, as in a picture, not one in twenty
would appear to be graceful, tho' each were ever so
much so in their movements; nor could the figure
of the dance itself be at all understood."[1]   The sub-

COLUMBUS BREAKING THE EGG.   *From Hogarth's Etching.*

scription ticket to the "Analysis" was *Columbus
breaking the Egg,* in order to make it, according to
the well-worn anecdote, stand on end.   Hogarth's
object here was to direct attention to the fact that,
although his theory of the line of Beauty (symbolized
in the design by two eels upon a plate) was old and

[1] "Analysis of Beauty," 1753, 137.

simple, at least he was the first who had definitely announced it.

At the bottom of page 141 was quoted an epigram on the *Analysis* which appeared in the "Gray's Inn Journal" for Dec. 15, 1753. Not many weeks afterwards followed in the same periodical another passage on Hogarth which, more especially because it seems to anticipate Walpole's "writer of Comedy with a pencil," deserves something better than the depressed distinction of a foot-note. The writer, no doubt, is Arthur Murphy, the author of the paper. He is replying to Voltaire, who has been accusing the English of a lack of genius for Painting and Music, and he adduces Hogarth among his proofs to the contrary, as far as pictures are concerned : — "*Hogarth*," he says, "like a true Genius, has formed a new School of Painting for himself. He may be truly stiled the *Cervantes* of his Art, as he has exhibited with such a masterly Hand the ridiculous Follies of human Nature. In many of his Pieces there is such a grave and couched Kind of Humour, that it requires a discerning Eye to perceive the several latent Beauties ; and he may be said to be the first, who has wrote Comedy with his Pencil. His *Harlot's Progress*, and *Marriage A-la-Mode* are in my Opinion, as well drawn as any Thing in *Molière*, and the Unity of Character, which is the Perfection of Dramatic Poetry, is so skilfully preserved, that we are surprised to see the same Personage thinking agreeably to his complexional Habits in the many different Situations, in which we afterwards perceive him. The Fribble, the Bully, the Politician, the Lawyer, the Miser, and in short all the Foibles of the human Mind are, by this Gentleman, so admirably depicted upon Canvas, that I am convinced *Voltaire* would be at a loss to show where he has been excelled."[1] Murphy, although he was Fielding's biographer, does not write like Fielding, nor is his opinion of equal weight; but it is worth quoting for the double reason that it has not been often quoted before, and that it represents, accurately enough, the view taken by those of the painter's educated contemporaries who were not politicians or connoisseurs.

The only other prints which belong to the interval between the "Analysis" and the Election series in 1755-8 are a whimsical frontispiece to Kirby's "Perspective," embodying almost every error in that science of which ignorance could possibly be guilty (it has been said that even ignorance would have escaped one or two of them); and the plate of *Crowns, Mitres*, etc., already referred to in Chap. III. as prompted by the Act of 1735. This was employed as a subscription ticket to the *Four Prints of an Election*.

The first of this set—*An Election Entertainment* —was issued in February, 1755. The general elections of the preceding year, and perhaps those at Oxford in particular, probably suggested the original paintings. This supposition is sustained by the reference in the plate to the "Jew Bill" and "Mar-

[1] "Gray's Inn Journal," February 9, 1754.

riage Act" of 1753, and to the change in the calendar
of 1752 ("Give us our Eleven Days"). At a couple
of tables in the large wainscoted room of a country
inn, the "yellows" or Court party are feasting their
constituents—"Speak and Have" (according to the
escutcheon) being the profuse motto of the festivities.
Outside is passing the procession of the rival party.
One candidate, a young well-dressed man, submits
unwillingly to the fulsome caresses of a stout lady,
perhaps the hostess. This "fair conjunction" is
assisted by a man behind, the ashes from whose pipe
drop into the gentleman's neat bagwig. The other
candidate ("Sir Commodity Taxem"), between the
delighted fraternity of a cobbler with a glass of
champagne, and the reeking confidences of a maudlin
barber, who has been terribly scratched in some
domestic altercation, is equally embarrassed. A
heavy-jowled parson mopping his bald pate over a
steaming chafing-dish; a long-chinned nobleman
hob-a-nobbing with a longer-chinned fiddler; a wag,
with a face smeared on his knuckles, who is singing
"An Old Woman clothed in Gray" to a couple of
grinning yokels; an alderman in a fit from a surfeit
of oysters; and an agent stunned by a brickbat from
without while he is registering the "sure" and
"doubtful votes"—are some of the principal guests.
At the back of the insensible oyster-eater, an incor-
ruptible, but squinting, Methodist tailor is plied at
once by agent, wife and son. In the foreground a
butcher, with "For Our Country" bound on his
broken head, pours Geneva into the green wound of

a wincing bludgeon man, who takes a dram of the
same remedy internally ; a frightened boy brews rack
punch in a tub ; and a squat Quaker pedlar distrust-
fully eyes a promissory note, appropriately dated
April 1st, which he has received from " Richard
Slim "—presumably the younger Candidate—in payment for his wares. Finally, a sword is seen quitting
the room at the head of a posse of cudgels. These
are only a few of the incidents in this "matchless"
picture, as Charles Lamb calls it.[1]

The second scene exhibits the *Canvassing for
Votes*. Upon an election show-cloth which hangs
before the " Royal Oak " inn, a stream of secret
service money is seen issuing from the Treasury
(with which the artist has maliciously contrasted
Kent's stunted Horse Guards) ; and in the lower

---

[1] Hogarth told George Steevens that the singing gentleman was
the only portrait in the picture. It represented Sir John Parnell,
a nephew of the poet, and was inserted by request of the sitter.
Concerning the butcher and bludgeon-man, John Ireland found
the following among the painter's memoranda :—" These two
patriots, who, let what party will prevail, can be no gainers, yet
spend their time, which is *their* fortune, for what they suppose
right, and for a glass of gin lose their blood, and sometimes their
lives, in support of *the cause*, are, as far as I can see, entitled to an
equal portion of fame with many of the emblazoned heroes of
ancient Rome : but such is the effect of prejudice, that though
the picture of an antique wrestler is admired as a grand character,
we necessarily annex an idea of vulgarity to the portrait of a
modern boxer. An old blacksmith in his tattered garb is a coarse
and low Being ;—strip him naked, tie his leathern apron round
his loins,—chisel out his figure in free-stone or marble, precisely as
it appears,—he becomes elevated, and may pass for a philosopher,
or a deity." (" Hogarth Illustrated " iii. 361.)

compartment, Punch, ministerial "candidate for Guzzledown," scatters the golden shower among eager electors. Yet, notwithstanding this pictorial deprecation of the corrupt practices of the "yellows," the "blue" landlord may be seen below contending with his rival of the "Crown" for the vote of a newly-arrived farmer, who, as a preliminary, is taking the bribes of both.[1]   Behind, an electioneering agent ("Mr. Tim Partytool"), by judicious gifts from a Jew pedlar's tray, is insuring the suffrages of some girls in the balcony.   Those of the landlady, whose counted gains are watched by a covetous grenadier, have been already bespoken.   The same may be inferred of a dumpy cobbler on the left of the picture, who, with a finger on his newly-acquired guineas, listens unconvinced to the noisy narrative which a barber, aided by sundry bits of tobacco-pipe, is giving of Vernon's popular capture of Porto Bello (figured for the nonce by a quart pot) "with six ships only." In the background, before the "Crown," also the Excise Office, a riotous crowd are tugging at the

---

[1] John Ireland says that the idea of Reynolds's *Garrick between Tragedy and Comedy* [1761] was indisputably taken from this impartial personage, whose mental attitude is very much that of "Mr. Mayor" in Fielding's comedy :—"I never gave a Vote contrary to my Conscience. I have very earnestly recommended the Country-Interest to all my Brethren: But before that, I recommended the Town-Interest, that is, the interest of this Corporation ; and first of all I recommended to every particular Man to take a particular Care of himself. And it is with a certain way of Reasoning, That he who serves me best, will serve the Town best ; and he that serves the Town best, will serve the Country best " ("Don Quixote in England," act i., sc. ix.).

THE INVASION: FRANCE.
From Hogarth's Etching.

sign, which a man is sawing through in blissful ignorance that its fall involves his own destruction. An old ship's figure-head of a Lion swallowing a Fleur-de-lis, which stands in front of the " Royal Oak," alludes to the war with France which broke out in 1755, and was greatly fomented by the country-party.

To the *Canvassing* follows the *Polling*, and the set finishes with the *Chairing of the Members*. In the *Polling*, matters are nearing their termination, as the reserve voters are being brought up to the hustings, and the worn-out constable is dozing. Fortune, whether "blue" or "yellow," is clearly in favour of one of the candidates, whose complacent attitude is being sketched. The other, in manifest discomfiture, scratches his head, while a ballad-woman in front retails an uncomplimentary broadside. The foremost voter at the polling-place is a battered pensioner who has lost a leg, an arm, and a hand in Queen Anne's wars. He lays his iron hook on the Bible. The lawyers wrangle as to the validity of the oath ; the clerk explodes with merriment. Next to the soldier, an idiot with a bib, restrained in his chair by a wooden bar, votes at the prompting of a man in fetters, the infamous Dr. Shebbeare, who was imprisoned and pilloried for libelling George II., and whose sixth " Letter to the People of England " peeps from his pocket. Behind, a half-dead hospital patient with "true blue" in his cap is borne up the steps between a nurse and a noseless wretch, the fumes of whose pipe curl in the face of his ghastly burden. A blind man, carelessly guided by a gaping boy, follows, and a cripple on crutches brings up the rear. In the background, under a bridge occupied by an uproarious electioneering procession, Britannia's coach breaks down, while the unheeding coachman and footman play cards upon the box. Probably most people will agree with Horace Walpole that the introduction of this allegorical incident, although clever enough in itself, is out of keeping with the rest of the composition.

Chairing the Members, the last of the series, would appear at first sight to be a misnomer, as one member only is shown. But the shadow of the other appears upon a wall at the back. The gentleman whose triumph is depicted clearly belongs to the "blue" or "Country" party (see "True Blue" on the banner). Hogarth afterwards held a Court appointment; but, although he has distributed his satire pretty equally, his sympathies in this case were probably with the "blues," whose procession is in temporary disorder. A frightened sow, preceded by her litter, one of which is drowning, has broken the ranks. The back stroke of a flail wielded by a thresher in front strikes one of the chair-bearers, who, tottering, increases the confusion. The unhappy member (said to be intended for the borough-monger, Bubb Dodington, afterwards Lord Melcombe) clings desperately to the arms of his wavering seat; a lady who watches him from the church faints with terror, and the "yellows" in the window, among whom is the old Duke of Newcastle, vastly enjoy his misery. In imitation of the

THE INVASION: ENGLAND.
From Hogarth's Etching.

eagle above Alexander in Le Brun's *Battle of the Granicus*, a goose flies over his head. In front the thresher whose combativeness has already caused so much mischief is engaged in a conflict with a sailor leading a bear. The bear seizes the opportunity of plundering the barrels of offal borne by an ass, whose master retaliates with a cudgel. Further complications are caused by the fact that the terrified wriggling of a monkey on the bear's back discharges a toy-gun in the face of a grinning sweep, who, perched on the churchyard wall, is fitting a pair of gingerbread spectacles on a stone skull.

Much has still been left undescribed in this excellent series ; but the original pictures are luckily still in existence. They are among the best examples of Hogarth's work, broadly and freshly painted. Garrick purchased them for 200 guineas. From him they passed in 1823 for £1,732 10s. to Sir John Soane, in whose museum in Lincoln's Inn Fields they are at present. The last of the prints appeared in January, 1758. In March of the year following was published a "poetical description" of some thirty pages, "written under Mr. Hogarth's Sanction and Inspection." In the "Advertisement" it is stated upon his authority, that no other explanation of his work had given him equal satisfaction—an utterance which implies unusual merit. Nevertheless there is nothing remarkable in the verses, nor do they readily lend themselves to quotation.[1]

[1] Some interesting variations between the pictures and the prints are given in Grego's "History of Parliamentary Elections

In 1756 Hogarth made a final essay in historical painting, and as far as money is concerned, the effort was wholly successful. For the altar-piece of St. Mary Redcliffe at Bristol he received £500. The compartments represented the *Sealing of the Sepulchre*, the *Ascension*, and the *Three Marys*, and are now in the Fine Arts Academy at Clifton. Large mezzo-tints of the side pieces were issued by Isaac Jenner; but the *Ascension* has never been engraved.[1]

One or two minor prints require to be noticed before we come to the *Sigismunda*. In 1756, when people were much exercised by rumours of the threatened invasion of England by France, and its concomitant inroad of Popery and wooden shoes,— when a camp was formed in Surrey, and a "Great Personage" at Kensington, according to the "Gentleman's Magazine," went so far as to say that 10,000 French were actually embarking in their flat-bottomed boats—Hogarth, doubtless still sorely conscious of his Calais mishap, put forth his version of the "present posture of affairs" in a couple of prints entitled *The Invasion; or, France and England.* The subjects might almost be guessed. The French,

and Electioneering," 1886, pp. 138-150. Cf. also the above-named Bubb Dodington's "Diary" from 1749 to 1761, published by H. P. Wyndham in 1785.

[1] "As specimens of colouring"—says Britton in his "Historical and Architectural Essay on Redcliffe Church," 1813,—"they [the pictures] possess much merit, and may be viewed with advantage by the young artist; but in the forms and expressions of the figures, and in their attitudes and grouping, we seek in vain for propriety, dignity, or elegance."

THE BENCH.
From Hogarth's Engraving.

assembling in front of the *Sabot Royal*, are shown as
half-starved frog-eaters, forced unwillingly to depart
from their depopulated land, the only really cheerful
person in the picture being a sanguinary monk, who,
with an ineffable grin, presides over the shipment
of various engines of torture to be employed at a
proposed monastery "*dans Black Friars a Londre.*"
The English, on the contrary, are jubilant at the
prospect of the arrival of their visitors. Hodge,
for whose portrait it is alleged that Garrick stood,
strains valiantly along the sergeant's halberd to
reach the regulation height, while a brawny grenadier is decorating the wall of the " Duke of Cum-
berland" Inn with a fine fresco of Louis the
Well-Beloved, from whose lips, in allusion to the gas-
conading memorial of M. Rouille to Fox, issues a
label,—" You take a my fine ships, you be de Pirate,
you be de Teef, me send you my grand Armies, and
hang you all, Morblu." In earnest of which he
impotently flourishes a gibbet. Garrick wrote some
special verses for these prints ; but, though they are
livelier than those of Dr. John Hoadly to *A Harlot's Progress*, their patriotic note is more conspicuous than their poetical quality.

The print called *The Bench* (Sep. 4th, 1758) requires no lengthy notice. It is said to contain portraits of the Honourable William Noel, Sir Edward
Clive, Lord Chief Justice Willes, and the Honourable Mr. (afterwards Earl) Bathurst, and was designed to show the difference between " Character,"
" Caricatura," and " Outré." Another print, dated

Nov. 5th, 1759, exhibits the old Cock Pit in St.
James's Park with all the "celestial anarchy and
confusion" which, according to Sherlock, characterized the pastime of which it was the theatre.
Jockeys and cock-breeders, sweeps and Quakers,
English Dukes and French Marquises, blind men
and deaf men—are absorbed in this exciting sport.
A defaulter, whose shadow only is seen, has, in
compliance with cockpit law, been drawn up to the
ceiling in a basket, whence he vainly tenders his
watch to satisfy his creditors.[1] This is one of the
best of Hogarth's later prints.

On the 6th of June, 1757, Hogarth was appointed
Serjeant Painter of all his Majesty's Works, "as
well belonging to his Royal Palaces or houses as to
his great Wardrobe, or otherwise." He succeeded
his brother-in-law, the John Thornhill of the "Five
Days' Tour;" and from an autograph note in the
Forster Collection, entered upon his duties on the
16th of July. The salary by the warrant was £10
per annum, payable quarterly; but there were certain "fees, liveries, profits, commodities and advantages" which made it rather more. In one of the

---

[1] Cf. "Another Occasional Letter from Mr. Cibber to Mr.
Pope ":—"Who knows, then, but the second Thought of thy
Readers may humourously mount thee into it [*i.e.* the throne of
the Laureate]; *as the merry mob at a Cock-match hoist up a Cheat
into the Basket, for having lost a Bet he was not able to pay,*" (p. 49).
The old Cockpit, taken down in 1816, stood at some steps leading
from Birdcage Walk into Dartmouth Street, near the top of Queen
Street, Westminster. There is a print of it with figures by
T. Rowlandson, in Ackermann's "Microscosm of London," 1808,
No. 18.

memoranda printed by John Ireland, Hogarth says that it "might not have exceeded one hundred a year to me for trouble and attendance; but, by two portraits, at more than eighty pounds each, the last occasioned by his present Majesty's accession, and some other things, it has for these last five years been, one way or other, worth two hundred pounds *per ann.*"[1]

Although in 1757 he had, in a fit of irritation, announced that he should in future "employ the rest of his time in portrait painting," he appears about 1759-60 to have rather inconsistently "determined to quit the pencil for the graver." "In this humble walk," he says, "I had one advantage; the perpetual fluctuations in the manners of the times enabled me to introduce new characters, which being drawn from the passing day, had a chance of more originality, and less insipidity, than those which are repeated again and again, and again, from old stories. Added to this, the prints which I had previously engraved were now become a voluminous work, and circulated not only through England, but over Europe. These being secured to me by an Act which I had previously got passed, were a kind of an estate; and as they wore, I could repair and re-touch them; so that in some particulars they became better than when first engraved.

"While I was making arrangements to confine myself entirely to my graver, an amiable nobleman (Lord Charlemont) requested that before I bade a

---

[1] "Hogarth Illustrated," iii., 141-2.

final adieu to the pencil, I would paint him one picture. The subject [was] to be my own choice, and the reward,—whatever I demanded. The story I pitched upon, was a young and virtuous married lady, who, by playing at cards with an officer, loses her money, watch and jewels ; the moment when he offers them back in return for her honour, and she is wavering at his suit, was my point of time." [1]

The picture thus indicated is that known indifferently as the *Lady's Last Stake ;* or, *Picquet ;* or, *Virtue in Danger.* In 1825 it was engraved by Cheesman. Lord Charlemont, who paid the painter £100, was greatly delighted with it ; and John Ireland has printed a couple of letters on the subject, which show this nobleman in a very favourable light.[2] To Hogarth's description of the design, it is only necessary to add that Miss Hester Lynch Salusbury (better known as Mrs. Thrale or Mrs. Piozzi) was wont to allege that she sat for the portrait of the heroine.[3]

---

[1] "Hogarth Illustrated,'" iii., 196-7. It is possible that this subject was suggested by an anecdote in a paper by Edward Moore (No. 154 of "The World" for 11th Dec., 1755), where the lady only saves her jeopardized reputation by a fortunate repique. Hogarth's first title is, however, identical with that of a comedy by Colley Cibber.

[2] "Hogarth Illustrated," iii., 198-200. See also the Charlemont Papers in the Appendix (Part x.) to the Twelfth Report of the Historical Manuscripts Commission, 1891, for some further letters on this subject.

[3] For this reason, the *Lady's Last Stake* was engraved, at Lord Macaulay's suggestion, for vol. ii. of Mr. Hayward's edition of Mrs. Piozzi's "Autobiography," etc., 1861. At the Grosvenor

During the process of painting, the *Lady's Last Stake* had found other admirers; and by one of these, Sir Richard (afterwards Lord) Grosvenor, Hogarth was pressed to undertake a second picture "upon the same terms." He selected Dryden's (or rather Boccaccio's) "Sigismunda," weeping over the heart of her murdered lover Guiscardo—the choice of subject having been apparently determined by the large price given for a composition having the same theme, ascribed to Correggio, but really by Francesco Furini, which had been sold in 1758, with Sir Luke Schaub's collection, and had realized £400. Hogarth valued his picture at the same

Gallery exhibition of 1888 it was exhibited with Sir Joshua's portrait of Mrs. Thrale and her daughter "Queenie"; and it must be admitted that the resemblance was by no means obvious. Nor is Mrs. Piozzi's own account of the circumstances, as embodied in a letter to Sir James Fellowes, of 30 Oct., 1815, free from inconsistencies. "The next time we went to Leicester Fields (she says), Mr. Hogarth was painting, and bid me sit to him; 'And now look here,' said he, 'I am doing this for you. You are not fourteen years old yet, I think, but you will be twenty-four, and this portrait will then be like you. 'Tis the lady's last stake; see how she hesitates between her money and her honour. Take you care; I see an ardour for play in your eyes and in your heart: don't indulge it. I shall give you this picture as a warning, because I love you now, you are so good a girl'" (p. 130). If, as is now believed, Mrs. Piozzi was born in January, 1741, N. S., she must have been eighteen, not fourteen, when the picture was painted in 1759. And Hogarth could hardly promise her a work he was painting on commission. Moreover, she told an entirely different story to a correspondent of the "Gentleman's Magazine," in which she affirmed that Hogarth made a sketch of her one evening in the house of an uncle. It is impossible to decide how much truth there is in the tradition.

sum. He took immense pains with it, touching and retouching it repeatedly in obedience to the suggestions of his friends. By the time it was finished, Sir Richard had either, as the painter surmises, got into the hands of the picture-dealers, or, perhaps expecting something of a different kind, had repented of his commission. At all events he took advantage of the artist's conventional offer to release him from his bargain, and rather meanly withdrew from it upon the specious ground that "the constantly having it [the picture] before one's eyes, would be too often occasioning melancholy ideas to arise in one's mind."[1]

[1] Hogarth relieved his excusable irritation by humorously paraphrasing Sir Richard's excuse in some verses addressed to Dr. Hay, and "turned," he says, "into English by my friend Whitehead," i.e., Paul Whitehead, the author of " Manners." Here are the particular lines in question :—

> " Nay ; 'tis so moving, that the Knight
> Can't bear the figure in his sight ;
> And who would tears so dearly buy,
> As give four hundred pounds to cry ?
> I own, he chose the prudent part,
> Rather to break his word than heart ;
> And yet, methinks, 'tis ticklish dealing,
> With one so delicate—in feeling."

There are two versions of this poem, one of forty-two lines which appears in Nichols's " Anecdotes" of 1781-5, and a longer one of seventy-three, which, without explanation, is substituted for it in the " Genuine" Works of 1808, i., 322, and this second version is reproduced in J. B. Nichols's " Anecdotes" of 1833, p. 281. Hogarth also found a partizan in Churchill's friend, Robert Lloyd, who addressed to him a mediocre fable in verse entitled " Genius, Envy, and Time " (" Works," 1774, i., 47).

TIME SMOKING A PICTURE.

From Hogarth's Etching.

Sigismunda, therefore, greatly to the artist's mortification, was left upon his hands. This unfortunate
transaction of course gave rise to much contemporary
criticism, sadly envenomed by party-feeling and
professional antagonism. One result was that, not
being sold to Sir Richard Grosvenor, it was not sold
to any one else. At Hogarth's death, it passed into
the possession of his widow (who is said to have
served as her husband's model[1]) with an injunction
that she was not to part with it during her lifetime
for less than £500. When she died, in 1789, it
became the property of Messrs. Boydell, who bought
it at her sale for 56 guineas. At that time it had
not been engraved, although Hogarth had made
several fruitless attempts to secure an adequate
interpreter, and had even issued as a subscription
ticket the admirable little plate of *Time Smoking
a Picture*, 1761. In 1793 it was reproduced in
mezzotint by Dunkarton, and subsequently, in 1795,
by Bartolozzi's pupil, Benjamin Smith.

At the present day there is no doubt that *Sigismunda* was not fairly treated in the painter's lifetime. The mob of dealers heaped it with obloquy,

---

[1] Ireland says ("Hogarth Illustrated," i. xciv.) that she was at the
time "weeping over the corse of her mother," and a certain confirmation of this statement was supplied by a little housemaid at
Chiswick, who as Mrs. Chappell, of Great Smith Street, Westminster, survived far into the present century, and was accustomed
to assert that a sketch made by Hogarth of her mistress in her
grief was subsequently elaborated into *Sigismunda*. But *Sigismunda*, by the painter's own account, was painted in 1759, and
Lady Thornhill died in 1757, aged 84.

and the caricaturists rejoiced in a new opportunity
for reviling the unpopular author of the "Analysis."
Then Mr. Horace Walpole, summing up in his
"Anecdotes of Painting," declared that it was no
more "like Sigismunda than he to Hercules"—and
it may be cheerfully conceded that there was not
the faintest resemblance between Mr. Walpole and
Alcmena's son. Worse than this, he wrote of it in
terms which were, if not absolutely untrue, at least
exaggerated and unjustifiable;[1] and the "common
cry" of critics followed the example of the illustrious
virtuoso of Strawberry Hill. But those who care to
form an opinion of their own, and who, as Hogarth
recommends,

> "To Nature and Themselves appeal,
> Nor learn of others what to feel,"

can decide the point on visiting the National Gallery,
where, by bequest of the late Mr. James Hughes

---

[1] Walpole's words are an illustration of the coarseness which
sometimes overtakes refined persons who wish to be forcible against
nature. "Not to mention the wretchedness of the colouring (he
says), it was the representation of a maudlin strumpet just turned
out of keeping, and with eyes red with rage and usquebaugh,
tearing off the ornaments her keeper had given her." There is
no tearing off of ornaments in the picture; but as regards a further
statement, namely, that Sigismunda's fingers were stained with
blood, it would seem that this was at one time correct. At all
events in a very clever letter written by Walpole to George
Montagu in May, 1761, describing a recent interview with the
painter, he speaks of *Sigismunda* as being then in the room.
"She has her father's picture in a bracelet on her arm, and her
fingers are bloody with the heart." The evidence of a letter
written almost immediately after the interview must be regarded as
practically conclusive.

FRONTISPIECE TO ARTISTS' CATALOGUE.
From Grignion's Engraving.

Anderdon, this much abused picture has found that final resting-stage, at which, "beyond all auctions, there is peace." They may not be inclined to rank it with Correggio, as its designer intended ; but they will probably admit that it is finely coloured, sound in painting, and full of technical skill. Considering that the attempt was made in a direction so unfavourable to the peculiar cast of the artist's talent, it is wonderful that he succeeded so well. Nevertheless, since the enterprize was achieved with so little profit to his peace and reputation, it is permissible to regret that he ever engaged in it.

Both *Sigismunda* and the *Lady's Last Stake*, together with the *Election Entertainment*, the *Gate of Calais*, and some other of Hogarth's pictures, were shown at Spring Gardens in 1761 by the "Society of Artists of Great Britain." For the catalogue of this exhibition—the story of which is too lengthy to tell in this place, and may, moreover, be read in most histories of the Royal Academy—Hogarth executed a "head" and "tailpiece," which were engraved by Charles Grignion. The former represents Britannia watering the three saplings of "Painting," "Sculpture," and "Architecture," from a fountain surmounted by a bust of George III., "emblematical of the confident hope entertained that native talent in art would be cherished by royal patronage." "*Et spes et ratio studiorum in Cæsare tantum*,"—was its motto. The tail-piece, directed at wealthy collectors, is an admirable figure of a travelled monkey with a magnifying-glass, water-

ing the stumps of three dead trees in pots labelled
" Exotics." These plates made the catalogue, which
also contained an allegorical design by Samuel Wale,
very popular, and not less than thirteen thousand
copies were sold.

TAILPIECE TO ARTISTS' CATALOGUE.

CHAPTER VIII.

WILKES AND CHURCHILL.   DEATH.   CONCLUSION.

N March, 1762, Hogarth issued the
plate known as *Credulity, Superstition,
and Fanaticism: A Medley*. It was
an extension, or—to speak more ex-
actly—an adaptation, of a previous design entitled
Enthusiasm Delineated, of which only two impressions exist.[1] *Credulity, Superstition, and Fanaticism*
is, in fact, simply *Enthusiasm Delineated* re-engraved
upon the same copper ; but the alterations were so
numerous as to make the former an almost entirely
new design.   As this is the one which Hogarth chose
to give to the world, it is with this alone that we have
to do ; but it is never unprofitable to trace the progress of invention in an artist's mind ; and, therefore,
following the majority of our predecessors, we shall
begin by describing *Enthusiasm Delineated*.   The
artist intended, he says, to give in this plate " a

[1] One of these is in the British Museum Print Room; the
other, long in the possession of Mr. White of Brownlow Street,
was sold some years since at Christie's.

lineal representation of the strange effects of literal
and low conceptions of Sacred Beings, as also of the
Idolatrous tendency of Pictures in Churches and
Prints in religious books." Accordingly, from a
pulpit decorated with dangling puppets of Moses
and Aaron, Peter, Paul, and Adam and Eve, an
energetic elocutionist (who, by the scale of vocife-
ration at his side, has reached "Bull Roar") is
declaiming to a motley assembly, whose extra-
ordinary proceedings are watched through the
window by an astounded Mahometan. Under the
preacher's gown is a harlequin suit; under his wig,
which flies off in his gesticulation (carrying away
its attendant "glory" with it) is the tonsure of a
Jesuit. In one hand, to give force to his de-
nunciations, he holds forth a figure with the
symbol of the Trinity; in the other is a devil with
a gridiron. In the pew below, a minute ghostly
personage is collecting the tears of a repentant
thief in a bottle. The other occupants of the pew,
a nobleman and a girl, have apparently discarded
their celestial model for a more earthly teacher.
Under the reading-desk, a dog, with "Whitfield"
on his collar, howls melodiously to the psalmody of
a cherub-flanked clerk above, in whom some have
recognized Whitefield himself. A convulsed woman
in the corner is said to be intended for Mother
Douglas of the Piazza (Foote's "Mrs. Cole"[1]), who

---

[1] In "The Minor," 1760, which also attacks Whitefield.
Methodism, though it was viewed moderately by men like Johnson,
had, at the outset, many assailants, who, with Hogarth, saw in

ended her life in those pious exercises which Fate
and the pillory denied to Mother Needham of *A
Harlot's Progress.* Behind, a sweep is embracing
an image, while a Jew, in a rapture of exaltation,
mechanically sacrifices an importunate insect. There
are other details, but they may be better studied
in the engraving.

This was Hogarth's "first thought," and his language was unmistakable enough. In the second
version, *Credulity, Superstition, and Fanaticism,*
most of the chief features of *Enthusiasm Delineated*
are altered to suit the changed purpose indicated in
the title, and scarcely ever strengthened or improved.
For the symbolical figure of the Trinity is substituted
a witch on a broomstick, while the apparition of
Cæsar, the shade of Sir George Villiers, and Defoe's
"Mrs. Veal" take the places of the scriptural
puppets round the pulpit. The fervid couple in the
pew beneath are metamorphosed into two commonplace personages, and in lieu of the penitent thief
we have a pair of figures, to one of whom a diminutive devil is whispering. As instances of credulity,
the Bilston nail-spouter and the Godalming rabbit-
breeder (Mary Tofts, a notorious impostor in
1726-7) are put instead of Mother Douglas and the
sweep, while King James's "Demonology" and

it nothing but cant, hypocrisy, and "very ugly enthusiasm." As
instances may be cited the "New Bath Guide" of Anstey, 1766,
the "Hypocrite" of Bickerstaffe, 1768, Smollett's "Humphrey
Clinker," 1771, the "Spiritual Quixote" of Graves, 1772, and
even Goldsmith's "She Stoops to Conquer," 1773. (*See* Tony
Lumpkin's song of "The Three Pigeons" in Act i.).

Whitefield's "Journal" appear on the hassock formerly occupied by the dog. There are other alterations which it is needless to enumerate. Probably
the painter's advisers, fearing lest his good intentions
should be misconstrued, recommended him to ex-
punge some of the irreverences of his first design,
and this may have given rise to the modification of the whole idea, a modification so substantial
as to change what was a compact satire into a
desultory work which the artist very properly
denominated "a Medley"—a work of genius for
a lesser man, but scarcely worthy of Hogarth, for
all that Walpole regards it as the "most sublime"
of his works "for useful and deep satire." The
praise would have been more fitly—though still
quite inappropriately—applied to *Enthusiasm Delineated*, which the critic does not appear to have
seen.[1]

We come now to the last notable events in
Hogarth's life :—the publication of the pictorial satire
called *The Times*, and the quarrel with Wilkes and
Churchill. Long before the death of George II.
Hogarth is supposed to have enjoyed the favour of
Lord Bute. Up to this date, however, he had
avoided politics;[2] but shortly before Bute's accession

---

[1] Hartley Coleridge, who is very severe upon this print, supplies,
at the same time, what is in some degree its apology. "His
[Hogarth's] aversion to religious pictures, however, often leads
him to the brink of profaneness; but, in extenuation, it must be
remembered that he lived in a very gross and a very irreligious
age" ("Essays and Marginalia," 1851, ii. 237).

[2] After the publication of *A Rake's Progress*, he had been

THE TIMES. (Plate I.)
From Hogarth's Engraving.

to the Premiership in 1762 the general stagnation
of art, coupled with an unhappy impulse, prompted
him to project some "timed thing" in the ministerial
interest. The announcement of his purpose at once
brought him into collision with the demagogue John
Wilkes, then editor of the opposition "North Briton"
and with Wilkes's "led-captain," Churchill the satirist,
both of whom had previously been his friends.[1]
Wilkes endeavoured to prevent the appearance of
the print by threatening reprisals; Hogarth refused
to desist; and—to use John Ireland's words—"the
black flag was hoisted on both sides." In these cir-

pressed, says Sir John Hawkins ("Life of Johnson," 2nd edit.,
1787, p. 500 n.), to design another series against Sir Robert Walpole,
to be entitled *The Statesman's Progress;* but he had refused. This
must have been the "very lucrative offer," to which Horace
Walpole vaguely refers, "that was made to engage him in a set of
prints against the head of a court party."

[1] M. Augustin Filon ("Revue des Deux Mondes," 15 January,
1885) is virtuously incredulous as to this "friendship" with
Wilkes. "*Qu'y avait-il de commun,*" says he, with a fine indigna-
tion, "*entre le consciencieux négociant de Leicester-Fields, et Wilkes,
le banqueroutier? Entre le dévoué mari de Jane Thornhill et
l'homme qui avait essayé de spolier sa femme? Entre l'honnête
auteur du Rake's Progress, et l'impur auteur de l'Essay on
Woman?*" . . . "*Hogarth et Wilkes se voyaient, cela est clair: on
ne prouvera jamais qu'ils fussent amis*" (p. 420). Unfortunately
there is plenty of testimony to the contrary, not to mention
Hogarth's own among the rest. In his account of this very affair,
he says that Wilkes had up to this time been "rather his friend
and flatterer" ("Hogarth Illustrated," iii. 221). Humour—like
misery—acquaints people with strange company, and we can
scarcely censure Hogarth for being captivated by the witty and
profligate man of the world who had skill enough to disarm even
the hostility of Johnson. (*See* Boswell's account of the dinner
at Dilly's, May 15, 1776).

cumstances, on September 7, 1762, *The Times* (Pl. I.) was published.

The "World" public-house is on fire. Pitt on stilts, as the tyrant Henry VIII., and having, in allusion to his pension, a millstone inscribed with £3,000 hanging from his neck, is exciting the flames; while Bute, played upon with a syringe by a featureless man (Lord Temple), and a brace of garreteers (Wilkes and Churchill), is directing the hose of an engine worked by Highlanders, soldiers, and sailors. A Grub Street hack, with a barrowful of " Monitors " and " North Britons," endeavours to cut the supply pipe. The sign of the " Newcastle Inn " is falling down (the Duke had gone out in May), and an incendiary, with a knife in his pocket, is hoisting in its stead the " Patriot Arms "—four fists clenched and opposed. To the right Frederick of Prussia fiddles among his weeping subjects, while to the left a Dutchman, behind whom a fox peeps out of a kennel, sits on a bale watching the proceedings. There are other allusions, many of them pointed, to contemporary events; but the composition as a whole is laboured, and the leading idea is scarcely novel.

Wilkes kept his word as to reprisals. On the Saturday following the issue of the above satire, the seventeenth number of the " North Briton " appeared, containing a violent attack upon Hogarth's character, both as a man and an artist. The alleged decay of his powers, the miscarriage of *Sigismunda*, the cobbled composition of the

JOHN WILKES, ESQ.
From Hogarth's Etching.

"Analysis," were all discussed with unscrupulous malignity by one who had known his domestic life and learned his weaknesses.[1] There can be little doubt that Hogarth was deeply wounded. "Being," he says, "at that time very weak, and in a kind of slow fever, it could not but seize on a feeling mind." His assailant believed that he had killed him, and wrote to Lord Temple that Hogarth was dying of a broken heart.

The painter, however, was far from dead, although he appears to have deferred his retaliation till he could make it more directly personal. When, in the May of the following year (1763), Wilkes was brought to Westminster Hall upon his trial for libel, Hogarth found opportunity to sketch him. Nature had not favoured the patriotic colonel of the Bucking-

---

[1] As a sample, the following may be cited from Wilkes's diatribe. Speaking of Hogarth's desertion of "his own peculiar walk," he goes on—" I need only make my appeal to any one of his *historical* or *portrait* pieces, which are now considered as almost beneath all criticism. The favourite *Sigismunda*, the labour of so many years [?], the boasted effort of his art, was not *human*. If the figure had a resemblance of any thing ever on earth, or had the least pretence to meaning or expression, it was what he had seen, or perhaps made, in real life, his own wife in an agony of passion ; but of what passion no connoisseur could guess" [Cf. note to Ch. VII., p. 161]. A touching instance of the effect upon Hogarth of this vindictive attack was supplied by one of the items which came into the market at the sale of the collection of Mr. H. P. Standly of Paxton Place, St. Neot's, Hunts. It was a worn copy of No. 17 of the "North Briton," which had been given to Ireland by Mrs. Hogarth in August, 1782, and which had been carried by the painter "in his pocket many days to show his friends."

hamshire militia, and it has been gravely argued that
this squinting semblance of him was, like the sketch
of Lord Lovat, only intended as a portrait.   But the
reference in it to the attack upon himself, and the
inscription under the subsequent plate of Churchill,
show clearly that Hogarth intended also to exhibit
the worthless character of the man through his
features.   If this really resembled Wilkes (and
Wilkes himself allowed it did [1]) he must have carried
in his face a confirmation of some of the worst vices
that have been laid to his charge.

It would have been well for Hogarth if the matter
could have ended here.   But Churchill, who, as
appears from a letter to Garrick printed by Mr.
Forster,[2] had, ever since the appearance of " The
Times," been planning an " Epistle to William
Hogarth," now published *his* contribution to the
quarrel.   It was a slashing and savage performance,

---

[1] " Mr. Wilkes " (says Nichols, " Genuine Works," ii., 255) " has
frequently observed, with his usual good humour, 'that he was
every day growing more and more like his Portrait by Hogarth.'"

[2] Looking to the letter from Garrick to Churchill quoted at
p. 116, the actor's fidgetty curiosity about the poet's onslaught is a
little unexpected, though perhaps not uncharacteristic.   " Pray let
me know "—he writes to Colman from Chatsworth—" how the
town speaks of our friend Churchill's ' Epistle.'   It is the most
bloody performance that has been published in my time.   I am
very desirous to know the opinion of people, for I am really much,
very much hurt at it.   His description of his age and infirmities
is surely too shocking and barbarous.   Is Hogarth really ill, or
does he meditate revenge?   Every article of news about these
matters will be most agreeable to me.   Pray write me a heap of
stuff, for I cannot be easy till I know all about Churchill and
Hogarth " [to both of whom he sends his love].

unequal, like most of the writer's work, and, seeing
that it fell hardest upon Hogarth's advanced years
and failing powers, scarcely worthy of Churchill's
vigorous yet not often unmanly pen. It contains,
however, a well-known tribute to Hogarth's genius
which has out-lived its hostile invective :—

> " In walks of Humor, in that cast of Style,
> Which, probing to the quick, yet makes us smile ;
> In Comedy, thy nat'ral road to fame,
> Nor let me call it by a meaner name,
> Where a beginning, middle, and an end
> Are aptly joined ; where parts on parts depend,
> Each made for each, as bodies for their soul,
> So as to form one true and perfect whole,
> Where a plain story to the eye is told,
> Which we conceive the moment we behold,
> HOGARTH unrivall'd stands, and shall engage
> Unrivall'd praise to the most distant age."

To Churchill's " Epistle " of July the 2nd Hogarth
rejoined, on the 1st of August following,[1] by a print
entitled *The Bruiser, C. Churchill (once the Reverend!)
in the Character of a Russian Hercules, regaling
himself after having kill'd the Monster* Caricatura
that so sorely galled his virtuous *friend, the Heaven-
born Wilkes.* The poet appears as a bear, with
torn bands and ruffles, hugging a club, the knots of
which are inscribed " Lye 1, Lye 2," etc., and
" regaling himself" with a quart pot of his favourite

---

[1] His promptness is the more remarkable because he must (if
the following be not a *canard*) have lain seriously ill when
Churchill's satire appeared. " We hear that Mr. Hogarth is much
indisposed with a Paralytic Disorder, at his House in Leicester
Fields " (" St. James's Chronicle," July 2-5, 1763).

beverage, " British Burgundy." The portrait is propped on Massinger's " New Way to Pay Old Debts," and " A list of the Subscribers to the ' North Britons.' " To intimate the indigence of those who wrote these latter, the pile is crowned by such a padlocked begging-box as was used for poor debtors.

In a subsequent issue of the print the painter added a tablet, on which he is represented with a whip, teaching Wilkes and Churchill to dance while Temple fiddles. Pitt, flanked by Gog and Magog (his City supporters), and having the millstone of *The Times* (Plate I.) suspended above his head by a string, fires a mortar at the dove of peace, but the ball drops short. " The pleasure, and pecuniary advantage," says Hogarth stoutly, " which I derived from these two engravings [of Wilkes and Churchill], together with occasionally riding on horseback, restored me to as much health as can be expected at my time of life." [1]

" Thus" (and here conclude the autobiographical notes so often cited in these pages) "have I gone through the principal circumstances of a life which, till lately, past pretty much to my own satisfaction, and, I hope, in no respect injurious[ly] to any other man. This I can safely assert, I have invariably

---

[1] The original pen-and-ink sketch of Wilkes, and a little blue memorandum book containing, among other things, a rough pencil drawing of a bear for the *Bruiser* are now in the possession of Mr. Frederick Locker-Lampson. The book once belonged to John Ireland, at whose death in 1808 it passed to other hands, being afterwards owned by Mr. George Baker and Mr. H. P. Standly.

A VIEW OF CHISWICK.
From an Old Print.

endeavoured to make those about me tolerably happy, and my greatest enemy cannot say I ever did an intentional injury; though, without ostentation, I could produce many instances of men that have been essentially benefited by me. What may follow, God knows.

FINIS."[1]

There is not much more to tell of Hogarth's life. A print entitled *The Times* (Plate II.) was prepared in 1762; but its publication was abandoned for unknown reasons. It appeared after Mrs. Hogarth's

[1] Into Ireland's reprint of these notes ("Hogarth Illustrated," iii.), he incorporated sundry documents which Hogarth had drawn up as a Supplement to the "Analysis," and which are described as "comprising a succinct history of the Arts in his own time, his account of the institution of the Royal Academy, etc." Some of these are in the MSS. department of the British Museum; and the following characteristic dedication, which the author intended to prefix to the whole, was included amongst the autographs lent to the Guelph Exhibition (1891) by Mr. Alfred Morrison:—

"The no Dedication.

Not Dedicated to any Prince in Christendom for fear it might be thought an Idle piece of Arrogance.

Not Dedicated to any man of quality for fear it might be thought too assuming.

Not Dedicated to any learned body of Men, as either of the Universityes, or the Royal Society, for fear it might be thought an uncommon piece of Vanity.

Nor Dedicated to any one particular Friend for fear of offending another.

Therefore Dedicated to nobody.

But if for once we may suppose Nobody to be every body, as Every body is often said to be nobody, then is this work Dedicated to every body.

By their most humble
and devoted W : Hogarth."

death, when the Boydells issued it.   By that time
its allusions had grown obscure, and no good end
would now be served by describing in this place a
design which enters into the list of Hogarth's works
merely as a curiosity.[1]   In the same year (1762) he
produced a portrait of his friend Dr. Morell; and
that pen-and-ink sketch from memory which, with
the exception of a miniature copied in Nichols's
"Literary Anecdotes of the Eighteenth Century,"
and the doubtful portrait included recently (1891) in
the Guelph Exhibition, is all that we possess in the
way of a likeness of Henry Fielding.   These, with
the frontispiece to Clubbe's "Physiognomy," entitled
the *Weighing House* (1763), bring us to the print of
Finis; or, the Bathos.

A few months before he died, Hogarth set to
work to prepare a "tailpiece" to his works, then
numerous enough to form a bulky volume.   With a
presentiment that his life was nearing its close, he
informed his friends that he had chosen for his subject the *End of all Things*, and, true to his creed,
his last work (to which, in imitation of the "Art
of Sinking in Poetry," he gave the title of *The
Bathos, or Manner of Sinking in Sublime Painting*),
is a blow at his sworn foes, the old masters, whose
occasional pettinesses and incongruities he ridicules
in this tumbled assemblage of fag-ends.   Supported
by the fragment of a column, Time, *moriturus*, with
shattered scythe and glass, exhales the final puff
from his pipe, which breaks as it falls from his

[1] See "Catalogue of Prints," for further particulars.

nerveless hand. By the will at his side he has devised his worldly goods to Chaos, his "sole Executor," and the Fates are witness. Nature is bankrupt; Apollo lies dead in his chariot; the sign of the "World's End" is falling, the ship founders, the trees are withered, and the moon is dark. A play-book open at *Exeunt omnes;* an empty money-bag; a shoe-

FINIS ; OR, THE BATHOS. *After Hogarth's Engraving.*

maker's last and a cobbler's end ; the remnants of a crown ; a halter and a stringless bow ; a cracked bell and a broken bottle ; a broom-stump and a gunstock without a barrel—litter the foreground. *The Times* (Plate I.), the cause of so much heart-burning, crackles and parches in the flames of a candle-end, and the shattered palette of the painter has done its work.

N

Beneath this print to left and right are two sym-
bolic figures in medallions. One represents the
"conic Form" under which Venus was worshipped
at Paphos; the other the cone and "line of Beauty"
from the "Analysis" (Plate I., Fig. 26). The identity of these two figures, we learn from an inscription, "did not occur to the author till two or three
years after the publication of the "Analysis" in
1754[3]." It must have been about this time that
he made use of the former for the crest, of which
we possess the sketch, designed by him for Catton
the coach-painter;[1] and, if we may infer that he then
first set up his carriage, it is clear that he could not
have done so much before 1756 or 1757.

The Bathos was Hogarth's last published work.
During the few months of life that remained to him
he continued, with some assistance, to re-touch and
repair his plates, upon one of which, *The Bench*, he
was working on the day before his death. On the 25th
of October, 1764, he was conveyed from his house

---

[1] The crest in question was engraved by Livesay in 1782. It
consists of a scroll-work design enclosing the word *Cyprus*, and
surmounted by the Cyprian cone. Beneath, on a ribbon, is the
word *Variety*. A lengthy account of it by the late Mr. William
Bates, of Birmingham, will be found in "Notes and Queries" for
February 22, 1879. It may be added that from an entry in the
little blue memorandum book referred to on p. 174 n., it would
appear that, in January, 1763, Hogarth's stables were in the yard
of the Old Nag's Head in Orange Street, Leicester Fields. In the
Crace Collection at the British Museum, there is a water-colour
drawing by Shepherd of this ancient and wooden-galleried inn-
yard, a copy of which, from the "English Illustrated Magazine"
for August, 1886, is here given.

THE NAG'S HEAD YARD.
From the Water Colour by Shepherd.

at Chiswick to Leicester Fields, very weak, but remarkably cheerful, and (says Nichols) "receiving an agreeable letter from the *American* Dr. *Franklin*, drew up a rough draft of an answer to it; but going to bed, he was seized with a vomiting, upon which he rung his bell with such violence that he broke it, and expired about two hours afterwards in the arms of Mrs. *Mary Lewis*, who was called up on his being taken suddenly ill."[1] He was buried in Chiswick Churchyard, where a monument was erected to him by his friends in 1771, on one side of which, under a design representing a mask, laurel wreath, mahlstick, palette, pencils, and a book inscribed "Analysis of Beauty," is an epitaph by Garrick, of which the following is an accurate copy :—

> "Farewel, great Painter of Mankind!
> Who reach'd the noblest point of Art,
> Whose *pictur'd Morals* charm the Mind,
> And through the Eye correct the Heart.
>
> If *Genius* fire thee, Reader, stay:
> If *Nature* touch thee, drop a Tear;
> If neither move thee, turn away,
> For Hogarth's honour'd dust lies here."

From a passage in Mrs. Piozzi's "Anecdotes" it

---

[1] Nichols's "Anecdotes," 1782, p. 84. It is noticeable that Churchill, who, the month before, had heartlessly written of his adversary in "Independence" as already dead—

> ("Hogarth would draw him (Envy must allow)
> E'en to the life, was Hogarth living now"),

only survived him nine days. Horace Walpole devoted to the painter the *inane munus* of precisely three words—"Hogarth is dead, and Mrs. Spence, who lived with the Duchess of Newcastle."—(*Letter to Lord Hertford*, 3rd November, 1764).

has been supposed that the well-known but generally misquoted quatrain by Johnson—

> "The Hand of Art here torpid lies
> That traced the essential form of Grace :
> Here Death has closed the curious eyes
> That saw the manners in the face ;"

was also an attempt at an epitaph by the "great Cham of Literature" which was rejected in favour of Garrick's.   But it is clear from a letter from Johnson to Garrick, dated 12th December, 1771,[1] that Johnson's lines were only a suggested emendation of the first form of the verses submitted to him by Garrick for criticism.

By Hogarth's will, which was dated the 16th August, 1764, he left all his property to his wife. It seems to have consisted principally of his "engraved copper-plates ;" and it was moreover chargeable with an annuity of £80 to his surviving sister Ann, who died in August, 1771, and (besides minor legacies), with one of £100 to the afore-mentioned Mary Lewis.   His estate, however, included the house at Chiswick,[2] for we find Mrs. Hogarth sub-

---

[1] Croker's "Boswell," ed. 1860, p. 225.

[2] According to Cary's "Memoir," 1847, this house was at one time the residence of Sir James Thornhill, who died in 1734. As, at a later date, it belonged to Cary himself, the statement has generally been accepted, and it is of course not impossible that Thornhill may have rented it.   But reference to the Court Roll of the Prebendal Manor of Chiswick shows that one G. A. Ruperty, clerk, was "admitted" copyholder as far back as the 15th July, 1721, and that he held the premises until, on the 13th September, 1749, "William Hogarth of Leicester Fields in the parish of St. Martin in the Fields" was admitted in his stead.   At Hogarth's

HOGARTH'S TOMB IN CHISWICK CHURCHYARD.

sequently bequeathing "all that my copyhold estate, lying and being at Chiswick in Middlesex" to her "cousin Mary Lewis." She appears to have continued to rent the "Golden Head" after her husband's death, since in Nichols's editions of 1781, 1782, and 1785 he speaks of the same Mary Lewis as continuing to dispose of the prints "at Mrs. Hogarth's house in Leicester Square."[1] Mrs. Hogarth certainly let lodgings there, for Richard Livesay, the portrait-painter and engraver was one of her tenants in 1781-82; Thomas Cheesman of the *Lady's Last Stake* was another; and Mr. Dutton Cook, in a pleasant paper in "Once a Week" for December 29, 1860, gave an account of yet a third inmate who in 1772 exhibited from this address, the strange Ossianic enthusiast and friend of Fuseli, Alexander Runciman. It is probable, however, that in her last years Mrs. Hogarth lived principally at Chiswick, where Sir Richard Phillips saw her in his boyhood, and long afterwards drew a vivid

death the house passed to his widow, and then to Mary Lewis, as stated in the text. Nichols says that Hogarth lived there every year during the greater part of the summer season. The present owner is Mr. Alfred Dawson, of Chiswick.

[1] Having regard to the large sums paid by collectors for Hogarth trifles, it may be interesting to note the prices at which the prints were sold to the artist's contemporaries. From a list given by John Nichols in the "Anecdotes" of 1781, it appears that *A Rake's Progress* could be bought for £2 2s. This was the highest amount, *Marriage A-la-Mode* being £1 11s. 6d., *A Harlot's Progress* £1 1s., the *Apprentices* 12s., and the *March to Finchley* 10s. 6d. The rest varied from 7s. 6d. to 1s., and the entire collection was to be obtained bound up for thirteen guineas.

picture of the stately old lady sailing up the nave
of the parish church, with her silk sacque, raised
head-dress, black calash, and crutched cane, accompanied by a relative (Mary Lewis) and preceded by
her grey-haired man-servant Samuel, who, after
wheeling his mistress to the building in her Bath
chair, carried in the prayer-books and shut the pew-
door. In these days, though her dignity remained,
her means must have considerably fallen off. Notwithstanding that, by a special clause of 7 Geo. III.,
cap. 38, the copyright in her husband's prints had
been secured to her personally for twenty years,[1]
their sale had gradually declined ; and she was glad
to accept a pension of £40 from the Royal Academy.
When she died in November, 1789, being then
eighty years of age, she left all she had to Mary
Lewis, who, in consideration of a life-annuity of
£250, transferred her right in the engraved "coppers"
to Alderman Boydell. The Chiswick house reverted
at Mary Lewis's death in 1808 to other persons
named by Mrs. Hogarth in her will. From 1814
to 1826 it was inhabited, though not continuously,
by Charles Lamb's friend, the Rev. H. F. Cary,
the translator of Dante, who for some time held the
curacy and afternoon lectureship of Chiswick.[2] A
subsequent resident was Mr. N. T. (or " Brayvo ")

---

[1] " Genuine Works," i. 81.

[2] According to the Court Roll, Cary held the copyhold from
May, 1814, to December 17th, 1833, but he ceased to live at
Chiswick when he removed to the British Museum in November,
1826.

HOGARTH'S HOUSE AT CHISWICK.

Hicks, a once well-known transpontine actor, not—
as those affirmed who had seen him in Nat. Lee's
" Alexander the Great"—without gifts for better
things. For the last few years the house has been
occupied by a very humble tenantry, and has become
much dilapidated. Little now remains to remind
one of the well-ordered garden which, in Mary
Lewis's time, was "laid out in a good style," and
filled with old-fashioned flower-beds. Of the five
large trees, including a hawthorn, the favoured haunt
of the nightingale (when there were nightingales at
Chiswick!), nothing now survives but an ancient
mulberry, once braced and girdled by Hogarth's
fostering care. This still drags on an amputated
existence, and in good seasons, continues to produce
the fruit which, of yore, was the occasion of an
annual festival to the village children ; but the tombs
of Pompey the dog and Dick the Bullfinch—the
latter said to have been scratched with a nail by the
artist himself—have disappeared, and it is no longer
possible to trace the site of the filbert avenue where
he was wont to play at nine-pins. Nevertheless, on
Hogarth's account, the spot is well worth a pilgrimage ; and those Londoners who, for an afternoon,
care to shake

> " to all the liberal air,
> The dust and din and steam of town,"

may do worse than spend their time in visiting the
tumble-down red-brick villa with the over-hanging
bay-window on the road to Chiswick Gardens, and
the tea-caddy-like tomb in Chiswick Churchyard,

piously restored in 1856 by "William Hogarth of
Aberdeen." Of late the tomb has once more been
renovated in connection with the enlargement and
restoration of the church; and it is consolatory to
think that Mr. Dawson, the present proprietor of
the house, proposes to take every precaution for
its future preservation.[1]

There are numerous portraits of Hogarth, several
of them being from his own hand. The best is that
in the National Gallery, in which he is shown as
a blue-eyed, intelligent little man, with a scar over
his right eye, and wearing a fur cap. Leigh Hunt
says he has " a sort of knowing jockey look," and
the phrase is not inappropriate. The canvas rests
upon three volumes labelled respectively " Shakespeare," " Milton," and " Swift," and his favourite
pug-dog Trump sits at the right of it. In the left
corner is a palette inscribed " The Line of Beauty
and Grace,"—the famous inscription which gave
rise to the " Analysis ;" and it was an " old plate " of

[1] Sketches of both house and tomb appeared in the " Pictorial
World " for September 26th, 1874. There were also some illustrations in the "Graphic" for November 14th in the same year.
Besides these, an interesting drawing by Mr. Charles J. Staniland,
showing the garden before (by the cutting down of trees, etc.) it
was subjected to modern "improvement," was published in the
"Illustrated London News" for October, 18th, 1873; and an admirable sketch of the mulberry by Mr. C. Graham, is contained in
" Harper's Magazine " for August, 1888. The only record of the
now non-existent tablets to the dog and bird occurs in the " Art
Union" for August 1, 1848. That of the bird was dated 1760;
the other—which, in parody of Churchill's epitaph at Dover, bore
the inscription " Life to the last enjoyed, here Pompey lies "—
must have been erected by Mary Lewis, as it was dated 1791.

this portrait with a "background and a dog ready" which Hogarth made use of in 1763 for his design of " Master Churchill in the character of a Bear." Another portrait is that of *Hogarth painting the Comic Muse*, now in the National Portrait Gallery, in which he sits before his easel in profile. It was engraved in 1758. Others are the head in a hat from *The Gate of Calais*, which forms the frontispiece to the pamphlet on "Gin Lane," etc. ; the head begun by Weltdon and finished by Hogarth himself, which was afterwards engraved by C. Townley ; the head in a tie-wig, of which one copy is prefixed to vol. i. of Samuel Ireland's "Graphic Illustrations;" the "shade" or silhouette (with Garrick) in vol. ii. of the same work; and the woodcut with a pipe by Branston in Major's Walpole's "Anecdotes."[1] Roubillac the sculptor also executed a bust of him, which is now in the National Portrait Gallery, and he modelled Trump the dog. To conclude the list it may be added that Hogarth painted an excellent likeness of his wife, which was exhibited at the Grosvenor Gallery in 1888, portraits of Sir James and Lady Thornhill and their son John, of his own sisters Mary and Ann, of Mrs. Mary Lewis, and of his six servants.

[1] This was also lithographed in 1825 by G. P. Harding. The drawing by Worlidge prefixed to the "Clavis Hogarthiana" and reproduced in "Genuine Works," iii., is said by J. B. Nichols ("Anecdotes," 335) to be in reality the portrait of one Ashley, the keeper of the punch-house on Ludgate Hill. It does not resemble the painter.

There is no need in this place to attempt any elaborate " appreciation " of William Hogarth. Numerous anecdotes respecting him have been retained ; but most of them come to us, if not from a tainted source, at least through a tainted channel.[1] It has been thought indispensable to catalogue his errors in spelling ; and to collect examples of coarseness from his various productions. We shall not scruple to neglect this branch of the subject. But as a matter of fact, there is no special difficulty about his character. Anybody who had been in his company an hour was probably as well informed of his peculiarities as his oldest friends. He was—it is easy to believe—a sturdy, outspoken, honest, obstinate, pugnacious little man who, as one is glad to think, once pummelled a fellow soundly for maltreating the beautiful Drummeress whom he drew in *Southwark Fair*. As a companion he was witty and genial, and to those he cared for, thoroughly faithful and generous. He liked good clothes, good living, good order in his household ; and he was proud of the rewards of industry and respectability. As a master

---

[1] We refer to George Steevens. It is only necessary to read this writer's unmanly and indefensible attack on poor Mary Lewis, whose only error appears to have been an over-sensitive fidelity to Hogarth's memory, to judge of the value of records transmitted through such a distorting medium. (See Nichols's " Anecdotes " *passim*, and for the special passage above referred to, pp. 113-14 of the edition of 1785.) In the " Genuine Works " of 1808-17, the contributions of Steevens are indicated by inverted commas— a course which at once identifies him with the majority of the more splenetic comments.

he was exacting in his demands, but punctual in his payments ; as a servant he did a full day's work, and insisted upon his wage. His prejudices, like those of most self-educated men, were strong ; and he fought doggedly in defence of them without any attempt to conciliate his adversary. That he was not proof against flattery seems to have been true : it is equally true of Garrick and Richardson, and of a hundred others who console themselves for their enemies by their parasites. In his own walk he had succeeded by a course of training which would have failed with nineteen men out of twenty ; and he consequently undervalued the teaching of all academies whatsoever. With the art-patronage and connoisseurship of his day he was hopelessly at war ; he saw in it only the fostering of foreign rubbish at the expense of native talent. But a great deal that has been said on the subject of his attitude to the continental schools of painting has been manifestly exaggerated, and in any circumstances, something must be allowed for the warmth of controversy. An artist of Hogarth's parts could not be wholly insensible to the merits of the Great Masters, as some have pretended. Yet it may well be conceived that such a downright and quick-tongued disputant, in his impatience at the parrot raptures of pretentious and incompetent persons, might easily come to utter "blasphemous expressions against the divinity even of Raphael Urbino, Correggio, and Michael Angelo." His true feelings on the subject are, we think, disclosed in his words to Mrs. Piozzi. He was talking

to her, late in life, of Dr. Johnson, whose conversation, he said, was to that of other men like Titian's
painting compared with Hudson's,—" but don't you
tell people now, that I say so (continued he), for
the connoisseurs and I are at war you know ; and
because I hate *them*, they think I hate *Titian*—and
let them ! " [1]

To Mrs. Piozzi's opportune memories may here
be added one or two characteristic anecdotes which,
in a measure, serve to illustrate Hogarth's personality
as above attempted.   Upon one occasion he painted
a deformed nobleman, and drew his likeness with
that unshrinking fidelity which Mrs. Delany commended.   His sitter, who had expected flattery,
declined the picture, and withheld payment.   After
several ineffectual applications for the money, Hogarth
dispatched the following ultimatum :—" Mr. Hogarth's
dutiful respects to Lord ——.   Finding that he does
not mean to have the picture which was drawn for
him, is informed again of Mr. Hogarth's necessity
for the money.   If, therefore, his Lordship does not
send for it in three days, it will be disposed of, with
the addition of a tail, and some other little ap-
pendages, to Mr. Hare, the famous wild-beast man ;
Mr. Hogarth having given that gentleman a con-
ditional promise of it for an exhibition-picture, on his
Lordship's refusal."   This brought about a settle-
ment of the claim, and the picture was at once
destroyed by its owner.[2]   Another story is related

---

[1] " Anecdotes," etc., by Hester Lynch Piozzi, 1786, p. 136.
[2] " Genuine Works," i. 25.   To give a story against Hogarth,

by Nichols on the authority of a surgeon named
Belchier. "Hogarth (says the narrator) being at
dinner with the great Cheselden, and some other
company, was told that Mr. John Freke, Surgeon of
St. Bartholomew's Hospital, a few evenings before,
at Dick's Coffee-house, had asserted that Greene was
as eminent in composition as Handel. 'That fellow
Freke,' replied Hogarth, 'is always shooting his bolt
absurdly one way or another ! Handel is a giant in
music ; Greene only a light Florimel kind of a com-
poser.'—'Ay,' says our Artist's informant, 'but at
the same time Mr. Freke declared you were as good
a portrait-painter as Vandyck.'—'*There* he was in
the right;' adds Hogarth; "and so by G—— I am,
give me my time, and let me choose my subject!"[1]
A third story illustrates his extreme absence of
mind. "Soon after he set up his carriage, he had
occasion to pay a visit to the Lord Mayor. When
he went the weather was fine; but business detained
him till a violent shower of rain came on. He was
let out of the Mansion House by a different door
from that at which he entered ; and, seeing the rain,
began immediately to call for a hackney coach. Not
one was to be met with on any of the neighbouring
stands ; and our Artist sallied forth to brave the
storm, and actually reached Leicester-fields without

it may be added that he once painted a noted miser and sheriff
(Sir Isaac Shard) trying a Mastiff that had robbed his kitchen.
Thereupon Shard's son went to the studio, and slashed the canvas
to pieces (*Ib.*, i. 147, 412-3.)

[1] "Genuine Works," i. 237.

bestowing a thought on his own carriage, till Mrs. Hogarth (surprised to see him so wet and splashed) asked where he had left it." [1]

The list of *ana* might be extended indefinitely. But of stories more malicious than interpretative, " a small harvest is enough." It remains to supplement what has already been said dispersedly in these pages by a few general observations upon Hogarth's position as a painter, a draughtsman, and an engraver. As a painter, there can now be little doubt that his life-long contest with the connoisseurs, coupled with the slender facilities that then existed for exhibiting works of art, tended greatly to obscure his merits in this respect. Since the first exhibition of his collected works at the British Institution in 1814, his reputation as a mere layer of colours has been steadily increasing, and the reaction thus initiated has been enforced of late years by the appearance in successive exhibitions at Burlington House and elsewhere of numerous portraits and pictures long buried in private galleries. If it be not possible to place him in the highest rank—to class him with those in whose work the gift of colour is pre-eminent—it must at the same time be admitted that his merits as a painter are unquestionable, that his tints are pure and harmonious, his composition perspicuous, and his manner, without being minute or finely finished, singularly easy, dexterous, and direct.[2]

---

[1] "Genuine Works," i. 216-7.
[2] In his fourteenth lecture on Gainsborough, Reynolds, it will

In speaking of his "drawing" a very necessary distinction has, it seems to us, been neglected. That, as certain critics have pointed out, he was not a "fine" draughtsman—in the sense in which that qualification is held to denote the reproducer of the beautiful and elevated in form as opposed to the merely conscientious imitator of a given object—may perhaps be conceded. But apart from this, his equipment in this respect has been too often decided by reference to those of his performances in which his skill is either not conspicuous or entirely suppressed. In his work of caricature or pure grotesque, we obviously cannot expect faultless drawing, and from the remarks which he himself makes in his Memoranda on the *Four Stages of Cruelty*, as to "minute accuracy of design," it is plain that he did not intend that any of his cheaper and more popular

be remembered, depreciated Hogarth. But "even Reynolds and Gainsborough (says an accomplished living critic), colourists often of an inexpressible loveliness, tenderness, and charm, were fumblers in their method as compared with Hogarth. Hogarth, in his best works, catches with a perfect subtlety the colour of rich or poor apparel, indoor furniture and outdoor litter, the satin, bows, jewels, ribbons of the bride, the fur coat and hose and waistcoat of the beau, lace, silk, velvet, broadcloth, spangles, and brocade, rich carpets, rich wall hangings, the look of pictures on the wall; or, on the other hand, the coarse appurtenances of the market place or the street crossing : he catches them, and their tone and relations in the indoor or outdoor atmosphere with a perfect subtlety and sense of natural harmony. And not only so, but without a school, and without a precedent (for he is no imitator of the Dutchmen) he has found a way of expressing what he sees with the clearest simplicity richness and directness" (Sidney Colvin in " Portfolio," iii. p. 152).

works should be advanced as models in this respect.[1] Indeed, it would not be difficult to find in them evidence both of haste and negligence. That they should tell their story clearly as to action and expression was, in short, all that he desired. But if, on the other hand, he is studied in his best work, say, in the *March to Finchley* or *Marriage A-la-Mode*, it will be found, not only that he rises easily to the occasion,— that he is thoroughly capable, expert and accurate,— but also that he exhibits an executive mastery of his subject which the exceptional character of his artistic education would scarcely lead one to anticipate. The wonderful figure of Viscount Squanderfield in the second picture of *Marriage A-la-Mode* is a case in point.

The same remarks apply to his engraving. His work in this way is so well known—so much better known even now than his paintings—that it sounds paradoxical to say that his efforts with the burin are less remarkable than his efforts with the brush. And yet this is in reality a natural consequence of his peculiar qualities. His unequivocal manner, his detestation of the indirect and the redundant, his very energy and veracity—all disqualified him from competing with the slow proficiency of the Grignions and Basires. Beauty and elegance of execution, he plainly gives us to understand, required far more patience than he was

---

[1] In some of his " Advertisements," he speaks of them expressly as "furniture,"—*i.e.*, as intended for decorative purposes rather than for the magnifying-glass of the collector.

disposed to exercise, and he regarded the mere
making of fine lines "as a barren and unprofitable
study." " The fact is," he declares, " that the passions may be more forcibly expressed by a strong
bold stroke, than by the most delicate engraving.
To expressing them as I felt them, I have paid the
utmost attention, and as they were addressed to *hard
hearts*, have rather preferred leaving them *hard*, and
giving the effect, by a quick touch, to rendering them
languid and feeble by fine strokes and soft engraving, which require more care and practice than can
often be attained, except by a man of a very quiet
turn of mind."[1] This is a transparent apology for
what he knew to be the assailable side of his work,
its haste and lack of finish, while at the same time
it invites attention to what were undoubtedly its
special merits—its unflagging spirit, its unvarying
vigour, its straightforward intelligibility. And it
must not be forgotten that the majority of his prints
have one inalienable advantage,—they are autographs. Hogarth engraved by Hogarth must always claim precedence over Hogarth engraved by
any one else.

But it is neither by his achievements as an engraver,
nor by his merits as a painter, that he retains his
unique position among English artists. It is as a
pictorial chronicler of life and manners, as a satirist
and humourist upon canvas, that he makes his chief
claim upon posterity. His skill in seizing upon the

---

[1] " Hogarth Illustrated," iii., 11, 355.

O

ridiculous and the fantastic was only equalled by his power of rendering the tragic and the terrible. And it was not only given to him to see unerringly and to select unfalteringly, but to this was added a rare and special faculty for narrative by action. Other artists have succeeded in single scenes of humorous *genre*, or in isolated effects of passion and horror; but none has combined both with such signal ability, and carried them from one canvas to another with such assured dexterity, as this dramatist of the brush. To take some social blot, some burning fashionable vice, and hold it up sternly to "hard hearts"; to imagine it vividly, and body it forth with all the resources of unshrinking realism; to tear away its conventional trappings; to probe it to the quick, and lay bare its secret shameful workings to their inevitable end; to play upon it with inexhaustible ingenuity; with the keenest and happiest humour; to decorate it with the utmost profuseness of fanciful accessory and suggestive detail; to be conscious at the gravest how the grotesque in life elbows the pathetic, and the strange grating laugh of Mephistopheles is heard through the sorriest story:—these were his gifts, and this was his vocation, a vocation in which he has never yet been rivalled. Let the reader recall for a moment—not indeed such halting competitors as Bunbury and Zoffany, Northcote and the "ingenious" Mr. Penny but—any names of note, which during the last fifty years have been hastily dignified by indulgent criticism with the epithet " Hogarthian," and then consider if he honestly believes them to be in any way on a level with the painter of *Marriage A-la-Mode*. In his own line he stands supreme and unapproached :—

"*Nec viget quidquam simile aut secundum.*"

HOGARTH'S MULBERRY TREE.

Part II.

A Bibliography of Books, Pamphlets, etc. relating to Hogarth and his Works.

A Catalogue of Prints by, or after, Hogarth.

A Catalogue of Pictures by, or attributed to, Hogarth.

HOGARTH'S BOOK-PLATE.

PART II.

A BIBLIOGRAPHY OF BOOKS, PAMPHLETS, ETC.

RELATING TO HOGARTH AND HIS WORKS.

HREE Poetical Epistles. To Mr. Hogarth, Mr. Dandridge, and Mr. Lambert, Masters in the Art of Painting. Written by Mr. Mitchell. *Dabimus, capimusque vicissim.* London : Printed for John Watts, etc., 1731. Price Six Pence.

The epistle to Hogarth occupies pp. 1-5, and is dated "June 12th, 1730." A passage from it is quoted on p. 41. The following, from that to Dandridge, gives the names of Hogarth's artistic contemporaries :—

"Nor wou'd I, partial or audacious strive,
To shew what Artists most excel alive ; . . .
How *Thornhill, Jervas, Richardson,* and *Kent,*
Lambert and *Hogarth, Zinks* [Zincke] and *Aikman* paint ;
What Semblance in the *Vanderbanks* I see,
And wherein *Dall* [Dahl] and *Highmore* disagree ;
How *Wooten, Harvey, Tilliman,* and *Wright,*
To one great End, in diff'rent Roads delight," etc.

The Progress of a Harlot. As she is described in Six Prints, by the Ingenious Mr. Hogarth. . . . Printed for E. Rayner, at the Pamphlet-Shop next the George Tavern, Charing Cross. [1732.] Price One Shilling.

> Advertised in the *Daily Journal* as published April 21, 1732, before which date Hogarth's prints must consequently have appeared.

The Harlot's Progress: or, The Humours of Drury-lane. In Six Canto's. Being the Tale of the noted Moll Hackabout, in Hudibrastick Verse, containing her whole Life; which is a Key to the Six Prints already publish'd by Mr. Hogarth. London : Printed for B. Dickinson and others. [1732.] Price 1s.

> 8vo. "M. Hackabout" is Hogarth's name for his heroine (See Plate I., Plate III., and the coffin-lid in Plate VI.). There was a real Kate Hackabout whose brother was hanged at Tyburn in April, 1730. This poem appeared very soon after the preceding pamphlet, *i.e.*, in April, 1732. A second edition, enlarged, and with "an Epistle to the Ingenious Mr. *Hogarth*," followed early in May (*Daily Post*, May 4, 1732). To the fourth edition, also issued in May, illustrations in " Chiaro Obscuro " were added, raising the price to two shillings (*Daily Journal*, May 11, 1732).

The Progress of a Rake. . . . To which is prefixed, by way of Introduction, a Poem, call'd, The Rakes Night. London : Printed for N. Cox, Book-seller under the Middle-Piazza, " near Mr. Hogarth's, Covent Garden ; " and others. [1732.]

> Advertised in the *Daily Journal* as published May 5, 1732.

*The Progress of a Rake : or, The Templar's Exit.
In Ten Cantos, in Hudibrastick Verse. . . . .*
By the Author of *The Harlot's Progress.* [With
a "Curious Frontispiece."]   London : Printed
for B. Dickinson and others, 1732.

> 8vo. Title ; Text, 3-61. Advertised in the *Daily Journal*
> as published May 11, 1732. Neither this pamphlet nor its
> predecessor has anything to do with Hogarth's *Rake's
> Progress* of three years later ; but both owe their origin
> to the popularity of his *Harlot's Progress.*

*The Jew Decoy'd : or, The Progress of a Harlot, a
New Ballad Opera of Three Acts.*   With a
curious Frontispiece.   London : Printed for E.
Nutt, price 1*s*. [1733.]

> "This piece was never performed"—says the *Biographia
> Dramatica.* It was published in February, 1733. There
> is a copy at the British Museum dated 1735 (Title ; *Dra-
> matis Personæ* ; pp. 3-48).

The Harlot's Progress : or, The Ridotto Al' Fresco.
[By Theophilus Cibber.]   1733.

> 4to. This, which is advertised as "a New Grotesque
> Pantomime Entertainment," was acted in April 1733 at
> Drury Lane. Although to be obtained at the Theatre in
> book-form, copies are extremely rare, and one which was
> sold at Isaac Reed's sale in 1807 (N°. 7758) fetched
> £8,—the purchaser being M^r. Kemble.

*The Lure of Venus ; or, a Harlot's Progress.   An
Heroi-comical Poem.   In Six Canto's.*   By Mr.
Joseph Gay [Capt. John Durant Breval].   Lon-
don : Sold by J. Wilford behind the Chapter-
House, near St. Pauls.   Price 1*s*. 6*d*. [1733.]

> 8vo. Title ; pp. i-iii, 1-56. "Illustrated with Six Prints,

neatly engraved from Mr. Hogarth's Designs." The Preface is dated "S^t. James's *Nov.* 30, 1732." Breval, the
"empty Joseph" of Dunciad, ii. 128, was the author of
The Hoop Petticoat, 1716, *The Art of Dress*, 1717, *The
Confederates*, a Farce, 1717 (which earned him the notice
of Pope), and various other works. He died at Paris in
1738. This poem was published in May (*Daily Journal*,
May 1, 1733). There is a Dublin reprint dated 1739 in
the British Museum.

*The Rake's Progress; or, The Humours of Drury-
Lane. A Poem. In Eight Canto's. In Hudi-
brastick Verse. Being the Ramble of a Modern
Oxonian; which is a Compleat Key to the Eight
Prints lately published by the Celebrated Mr.
Hogarth . . . .* London, Printed for J. Chett-
wood, etc. (Price 1s.) 1735.

> Title; pp. 1-54. Published in July, 1735. Of late years
> this has been reprinted in a limited edition, but not on
> account of its literary merits or its moral tone.

*An Explanation of the Eight Prints of The Rake's
Progress. . . . Copied from the Originals of
Mr. William Hogarth, according to Act of
Parliament, by Thomas Bakewell, Printseller,
next Johnson's Court in Fleet-Street, London,
August 1735 . . .*

> A double-column sheet or broadside which, as Hogarth
> allowed Bakewell to sell copies of the prints, may be looked
> upon as an authorized commentary. It says that the girl
> and her mother in Pl. I are the Rake's "bedmaker and
> her daughter" who have followed him from Oxford; and
> it adds that they reappear in the background of Pl. V.

*Marriage A-la-Mode: an Humorous Tale, in Six
Canto's, in Hudibrastic Verse; being an Ex-*

planation of the Six Prints lately published by the Ingenious Mr. Hogarth. London: Printed for *Weaver Bickerton,* in *Temple-Exchange Passage,* in *Fleet-Street.* 1746. (Price One Shilling.)

Title and "Preface," i-iv; Text, 1-59. Published in February, 1746.

*Lettres de Monsieur * * à un de ses Amis à Paris, pour lui expliquer les Estampes de Monsieur Hogarth.* [By Jean Rouquet.] Imprimé à Londres : et se vend chez R. Dodsley, dans Pall-Mall ; & chez M. Cooper, dans Paternoster-Row. MDCCXLVI. (Le prix est de douze sols.)

Title ; pp. 1-44. 8vo. Describes the two *Progresses* and *Marriage A-la-Mode,* and refers to nine other plates. "This pamphlet (says Steevens) was designed, and continues to be employed, as a constant companion to all such sets of his [Hogarth's] prints as go abroad" (*Biographical Anecdotes,* 1782, p. 93). He says, moreover, that "it was certainly suggested by *Hogarth,* and drawn up at his immediate request" (p. 92). Published in April, 1746. It is reprinted in Tome 3 of the *Bibliothèque Choisie et Amusante,* Amsterdam, 1748, pp. 371-400.

Description du Tableau de M. Hogarth, qui represente la Marche des Gardes à leur rendez-vous de-Finchley, dans leur Route en Ecosse. [By Jean Rouquet. 1746 ?]

Pp. 1-7. 8vo. At the head of the description is :—"*Cette Lettre de Mr. Rouquet, connu par ses Ouvrages d'Email, à été écrite à un de ses amis à Paris, pour l'amusement & peut-être par les ordres d'une personne très-distinguée* [Marshal Belleisle ?], *qui se trouvoit à Londres lorsqu'il commença d'écrire celles qui ont déja paru sur les autres Ouvrages de Mr. Hogarth.*" "The letter descriptive of the *March to Finchley* (says Steevens) was particularly meant for the instruction of Marshal *Belleisle*" (*Biographical Anecdotes*, etc. 1782, p. 93). It was written, as appears from the opening lines, before the picture had been engraved. Steevens also says (p. 94) that Hogarth, "in compliance with the repeated solicitations of his customers," had determined to have Rouquet's work translated and enlarged by additional descriptions.

The Effects of Industry and Idleness, illustrated in the Life, Adventures, and various Fortunes of Two Fellow 'Prentices of the City of London, etc. Printed by Charles Corbett, at Addison's Head in Fleet-street. [1748.] Price 1s.

8vo. It is further described as "being an Explanation of the Moral of Twelve celebrated Prints lately published, and designed by the ingenious Mr. Hogarth." It was published in March, 1748. Several little books were prompted by this series, among which may be mentioned Murray's "Two City Apprentices," 1846, which contains some useful notes. A pantomime was also based upon it.

A Dissertation on Mr. Hogarth's Six Prints lately publish'd, viz. Gin-Lane, Beer-Street, and the Four Stages of Cruelty. . . . Humbly inscrib'd to the Right Honourable Francis Cokayne, Esq.; Lord Mayor of the City of London, etc. London, Printed for B. Dickinson, on *Ludgate-Hill*, 1751. Price One Shilling.

Title; pp. 3-59. 8vo. Portrait of Hogarth from "Calais Gate." Contains little information respecting the prints named in the title, but much upon Gin Drinking.

Low-Life: or, One Half of the World, knows not how

*the Other Half lives. Being a Critical Account
of what is transacted by People of almost all
Religions, Nations, and Circumstances, in the
Twenty-four Hours between Saturday-Night
and Monday-Morning, in a true Description of
a Sunday, as it is usually spent within the Bills
of Mortality. Calculated for the Tenth of June.
With an Address to the ingenious Mr. Hogarth.
—Let Fancy guess the rest. Buckingham.*
London: Printed for the Author; and sold by
T. Legg, at the *Parrot* and *Crown* in *Green-
Arbour-Court* in the *Little-Old-Baily*, etc.   N.D.
[Price One Shilling.]

Title; "To Mr. Hogarth," pp. iii-viii.; Text, 1-52.   8vo.
From a reference to *Calais Gate* in the "Address," it
must have been written subsequent to March, 1749.   It
was published in May, 1752.   The author thus admits his
obligations to the painter:—" I say, that this Essay owes
its Existence partly to Your Works.   And who will not
believe me, when I direct them to those four Pieces of
Yours, called *Morning, Noon, Evening*, and *Night?* where
are many Things made visible to the Eye in the most
elegant Colours, which are here only recorded."   To the
third edition of 1764 is added a frontispiece representing
" St. Monday."   The book, which is full of minute eighteenth-century details, was highly valued both by Thackeray and Dickens, and suggested his " Twice Round the
Clock " to Mr. G. A. Sala.

*The Analysis of Beauty. Written with a view of
fixing the fluctuating Ideas of Taste.* By William
Hogarth. [Motto from Milton, and Pyramidal
Design subscribed " Variety."]   London :
Printed by J. Reeves for the Author, and sold

by him at his House in Leicester-Fields.
MDCCLIII.

> Title; "Preface," pp. iii-xxii.; " Contents " and "Errata;"
> "Introduction," 1-12; Text, 13-153; " Prints Publish'd,"
> etc. and " Figures referr'd to in the Book."   4to. There
> are "two explanatory prints." The book was published
> in December, 1753. It is reprinted in Cook's *Anecdotes*,
> and also by Clerk and Nichols. There is besides an undated
> issue by Bagster, with which is printed Grose's *Rules for
> Drawing Caricaturas*, etc. A German translation by
> Christlob Mylius, made in this country "under the
> author's inspection," was published at London, Hanover,
> Berlin and Potsdam in 1754; an Italian translation at
> Leghorn, 1761 ; and a French translation by Talleyrand's
> librarian, H. Jansen, at Paris, An xiii. (1805).

*A Poetical Description of Mr. Hogarth's Election
Prints: in Four Cantos.   Written under Mr.
Hogarth's Sanction and Inspection.   Things un-
attempted yet in Prose or Rhime.   Milton.*
London: Printed for T. Caslon, opposite Sta-
tioners-Hall :   And sold by J.   Smith, at
Hogarth's Head, in Cheapside, etc.   1759.

> Title ; Advertisement; and pp. 1-30.   4to.   It was pub-
> lished in March, 1759.   The Advertisement, which is
> signed " John Smith," and dated "Cheapside, March 1,
> 1759," professes to quote *verbatim* Hogarth's opinion—
> " That the Thoughts intirely coincide with his own ; that
> there is a well-adapted Vein of Humour preserved through
> the Whole ; and that, though some of his Works have been
> formerly explained by other Hands, yet none ever gave
> him so much Satisfaction as the present Performance."

*The Roast Beef of Old England.   A Cantata.   Taken
from a celebrated Print of the Ingenious Mr.
Hogarth . . . As it is Performed at the Theatre*

in the Hay-Market. The Words by a Man of
Taste, and set to Musick by Signior Carbonado.
The Second Edition. . . . London : Printed
for R. Withy, etc. MDCCCLIX. (Price Six-
Pence.)

Title; pp. 3-8, and title again at end. The "Man of
Taste" was Theodosius Forrest (see p. 128).

The North Briton. Numb. xvii. Saturday, Sep-
tember the 25th, 1762. [By John Wilkes.]
Printed for G. Kearsly, in Ludgate Street.

Pp. 97-102. The motto is from Pope [Sat. i. 85-6] :—

> "Its proper pow'r to hurt, each creature feels,
> Bulls aim their horns, and Asses lift their heels."

In the Steevens collection at Felbrigge Park, Norfolk, is a
reprint of this dated "May the 21st, 1763" (*i.e.* five days
after the issue of Wilkes's portrait), which has, in addition
to the motto, a rude wood-engraving of the artist with the
words "William Hogarth, Engraver, Cut in Wood from the
Life." The greater part of the paper is printed at pp.
72-78 n. of the *Biographical Anecdotes*, 1782.

An Epistle to William Hogarth. By C. Churchill.
Ut Pictura, Poesis. Hor. London : Printed for
the Author, and sold by J. Coote, at the King's
Arms in Pater-Noster-Row. MDCCLXIII.

Half-title; title; pp. 1-31. 4to. It was published on
Saturday, July 2, 1763—a second edition following on
the 7th.

Hogarth Moralized. Being a complete Edition of
Hogarth's Works. Containing near Fourscore
Copper-Plates, most elegantly engraved. With
an Explanation, pointing out the many Beauties

that may have hitherto escaped Notice; and a
Comment on their Moral Tendency. Calculated
to improve the Minds of Youth, and, convey In-
struction, under the Mask of Entertainment.
Now First published, with the Approbation of
Jane Hogarth, Widow of the late Mr. Hogarth.
[With 78 plates.] London: Sold by S. Hooper,
the East Corner of the New Church in the
Strand; and, Mrs. Hogarth, at her House in
Leicester-Fields. MDCCLXVIII.

> Engraved Title,—*The Works of Mr. Hogarth Moralized,*
> *London.* Second title as above; "Dedication" and "Ad-
> vertisement"; "Preface," pp. i-viii; Text, pp. 1-212;
> "Index," i-v. 8vo. It was originally published in 14
> numbers or parts. There were subsequent editions in
> 1821, fol.; 1831, 8vo; and 1833, 4to, 2 vols. with "Anec-
> dotes . . . by J. Hogarth and J. Nichols." The best
> modern issue is John Major's "revised, corrected, and
> somewhat enlarged" edition of 1841, to which there is
> an introductory Essay. "The history of the work," says
> Steevens, "is as follows: The Rev. *John Trusler* engaged
> with some engravers in this design, after *Hogarth's* death,
> when they could carry it into execution with impunity.
> Mrs. *Hogarth*, finding her property would be much
> affected by it, was glad to accept an offer they made
> her, of entering into partnership with them; and they
> were very glad to receive her, knowing her name would
> give credit to the publication, and that she could certainly
> supply many anecdotes to explain the plates. Such
> as are found in the work are probably all hers" (*Bio-*
> *graphical Anecdotes*, etc., 1781, p. 62, n). Mrs. Hogarth's
> own Advertisement of the first Number in the *London*
> *Chronicle* for August, 16-19, 1766, says that she has
> "engaged a Gentleman to explain each Print, and moralize
> on it in such a Manner as to make them instructive as
> well as entertaining." The first Number contained *The*

Harlot's Progress; the second, which followed in September,—*The Rake's Progress.* After this the parts continued to appear until the volume was completed in July, 1768. Dent and Corbould were the engravers of the plates.

Les Satyres de Guillaume Hogarth, Œuvre moral et Comique en LXIX [LXXIX] *Sujets. Ridiculum Acri.* A Londres, chez Robert Sayer, Marchand de Cartes et d'Estampes dans Fleet-Street, No. 53. MDCCLXVIII.

Title (French); "Index" of two pages, with brief descriptions in English. *Folio.* Some of the copies are stated to be published with "y⁰ consent of Mrs. Hogarth."

An Essay upon Prints, etc. [By the Rev. W. Gilpin.] Second Edition. London: Printed by G. Scott, for J. Robson, etc. MDCCLXVIII.

8vo. Pp. 164-173 relate to Hogarth generally; pp. 212-229 describe the *Rake's Progress.*

Die Werke des Hrn Willm Hogarth in Kupferstichen Moralisch und Satyrisch erlautert. Hamburg, 1769.

Sm. 4to. With Twenty copperplate engravings.

Anecdotes of Painting in England . . . By Mr. Horace Walpole . . . Volume the fourth and last. Strawberry Hill: Printed by Thomas Kirgate, MDCCLXXI.

4to. Pp. 68-89 relate to Hogarth, of whose works Walpole had an extensive collection. There is also an Appendix of one leaf, "Prints by or after Hogarth discovered since the Catalogue was finished." The volume had been in type as far back as 1770, but was not published until

October, 1780. "I have left with Lord Harcourt for you my new old last volume of 'Painters' (*Walpole to Mason,* 13 Oct. 1780)." The ostensible reason for the deferred issue is stated in the "Advertisement." "The publication (it says), though a debt to the purchasers of the preceding volumes, was delayed from motives of tenderness." The author was "unwilling to utter even gentle censures, which might wound the affections, or offend the prejudices of those related to the persons whom truth forbad him to commend beyond their merits." If these were the real motives, they were not effectual, for Mrs. Hogarth, who is said to have been her husband's model for *Sigismunda,* was justly incensed at the coarse contempt which Walpole lavished upon that work (see *ante,* p. 162 n.) "It is whispered," says a note by George Steevens in the *Biographical Anecdotes* of 1781, pp. 43-4, ("we know not with how much truth) that Mrs. *H.* was hurt by this description of the picture, and that she returned no thanks for the volume that contains it, when it was sent to her as a present by its author." Walpole confirms the fact of her displeasure in a letter to Cole of 16 June, 1781. "She was not pleased with my account of her husband." It is difficult to imagine how she could have been pleased, or how he reconciled his account of *Sigismunda* with his professions of consideration for the representatives of those criticised. In the second edition of vol. iv. (8vo. 1782), Walpole refers to Nichols's *Anecdotes,* and says he has made use of them to correct and extend his own account.

Biographical Anecdotes of William Hogarth ; and a Catalogue of his Works chronologically arranged ; with [1] *occasional Remarks.* London, Printed by and for J. Nichols. MDCCLXXXI.

———— *The Second Edition, enlarged and corrected.* London : Printed by and for J. Nichols.

[1] This is "and" in eds. 2 and 3.

MDCCLXXXII. With second engraved Title— *Biographical Anecdotes of William Hogarth,* and knife, fork, and plate vignette—" Published as the Act directs, August 1st, 1872."

Biographical Anecdotes of William Hogarth ; and a Catalogue of his Works chronologically arranged ; with occasional Remarks. The Third Edition, enlarged and corrected. London : Printed by and for J. Nichols, in Red-Lion-Passage, Fleet-Street. MDCCLXXXV. With second engraved Title (as in second edition)—"Published as the Act directs, Nov'. 10th, 1785."

First Edition : Title ; pp. 3-157. Second Edition : Titles ; pp. iii-v ; 1-474. Third Edition : Titles ; pp. iii-xx ; 1-529. These Anecdotes, according to the "Memorandum" prefixed to the third edition, dated "Nov. 10, 1785," grew out of "a note of about a page's length" which the writer, John Nichols, the bookseller and printer of Red-Lion-Passage, Fleet-Street, allotted to Hogarth in his Memoir of Bowyer. The fourth volume of Walpole's *Anecdotes of Painting,* 1780, gave such an impetus to the collection of Hogarth's works, that this brief account was speedily expanded into a pamphlet, afterwards enlarged as above in the editions that followed. Nichols's chief collaborator was George Steevens, the Critic. The first edition was at once translated into German in 1783 by "the ingenious Mr. Crayen of *Leipzig.*" Prefixed to this translation was a head of the artist copied by Edner from his portrait when painting the Comic Muse.

An Explanation of Several of Mr. Hogarth's Prints. [Mottoes from Garrick, Churchill, Walpole and Smart's *Hilliad.*] London : Printed for the

Author [Mr. Felton] ; and sold by J. Walter, Charing-Cross. MDCCLXXXV.

> Title ; "Preface," pp. iii-iv ; "Contents," v-vi ; Text, 1-117 ; "Errata." 8vo. Mr. Felton, according to Nichols's *Genuine Works*, iii. (1817), p. 317, was the "Author of 'Imperfect Hints towards a new Edition of Shakespeare,' and of some elegant 'Testimonies to the Genius and Memory of Sir Joshua Reynolds.'" His Preface explains his book to be simply an "addition, or supplement" to Walpole, Nichols, Gilpin and Trusler. It "points out some minutiæ," and deals only with the "most considerable of Mr. *Hogarth's* prints"—i.e. the two Progresses, a Midnight Modern Conversation, the Sleeping Congregation, the Distrest Poet, the Four Times of the Day, the Strolling Actresses, the Enraged Musician, Marriage A-la-Mode, a Stage Coach, Industry and Idleness, the March to Finchley, Beer Street and Gin Lane, the Stages of Cruelty, the Election series, the Cockpit and Southwark Fair. The "Appendix" (pp. 92-117) contains a collection of valuable extracts from contemporary sources bearing upon Hogarth and his work.

Rules for Drawing Caricaturas : with an Essay on Comic Painting. [By Francis Grose, Esq., F.A.S.]. London : Printed by A. Grant, Wardour-Street, for S. Hooper, No. 212, High-Holborn, MDCCLXXXVIII.

> Title ; pp. 3-38. 8vo. With four plates.

Ut Pictura Poesis ! or, the Enraged Musician. A Musical Entertainment. Founded on Hogarth. Performed at the Theatre Royal in the Haymarket. Written by George Colman. Composed by D^r. Arnold. London : Printed by T. Cadell, in the Strand. MDCCLXXXIX.

> 8vo. Title ; "Characters" ; Text, pp. 5-17. The copy in the British Museum has a MS. Prologue.

A Catalogue of the Pictures and Prints ; the Pro-
perty of the late Mrs. Hogarth, Dec⁴. Amongst
which is the Sigismunda, several Portraits,
Sketches and Prints by Hogarth, framed and
glazed, choice ancient Impressions ; the Bust of
Hogarth, by Roubilliac [*sic.*] ; *Twelve Plates,*
painted at Delft, by Sir James Thornill [*sic.*] ;
and other Matters.   Which will be sold by
Auction, by Mr. Greenwood, by Order of the
Executrix, (*on the Premises*) *The Golden Head,*
Leicester-Square, on Saturday the 24*th of April,*
1790, *at Twelve o'Clock.* . . . Printed by H.
Reynell, No. 21, Piccadilly.

The Executrix was Mary Lewis (see p. 181). *Sigismunda*
was bought by Alderman Boydell for £58 16s. ; Rou-
biliac's bust, £7 7s. ; cast of Trump and of Hogarth's
hand, £2 16s. ; the *Shrimp Girl,* £4. 10s. ; Hogarth's
six servants, £5 15s. 6d. ; his sisters, £2. The entire sale
realised £255 10s. The copy of the Catalogue in the
British Museum belonged to George Steevens.

William Hogarth.   Original Works, mostly engraved
by Himself.   London : Boydell, 1790.

Atlas folio.   108 plates, 2 portraits.

Hogarth Illustrated.   By John Ireland.   [In Two
Volumes].   Pub. June 1, 1791, by J. & J.
Boydell, Cheapside, & at the Shakespeare
Gallery, Pall Mall.

Vol. i. Engraved Title, with vignette portrait of Hogarth,
engraved by J. Barlow; "Introduction ;" "Errata," "Index to the Plates ;" "Anecdotes," i-cxxii ; Text, 1-311.
8vo.
Vol. ii. Engraved Title, with vignette "Nature ;" Index

to the Plates; Text, 311-607 and List of Hogarth's works sold by Boydell. 8vo. A second ·edition, "corrected," was published in August, 1793. To this was added a supplement of 8 pp., containing a description of *Marriage A-la-Mode* found among the papers of Mr. Lane of Hillingdon, and translated from Rouquet. The majority of the plates in these volumes are from Trusler (*Genuine Works*, i. 453).

A Supplement to Hogarth Illustrated; compiled from his Original Manuscripts, in the Possession of John Ireland, etc. [Motto from Walpole.] London: Published, March, 1798, for the Author, No. 3, Poets' Corner, and others.

Engraved Title as in Vols. i. and ii., with vignette of the Serpentine Candlestick; second title as above; "Advertisement," pp. iii-viii; "Introduction," ix-xxi; "Index to the Prints," xxii-xxiii; "Contents;" "Anecdotes," 1-227; "Description of the Prints, etc.," 229-330; "Appendix," 331-377; "Index to the Variations, etc." 8vo. Ireland's "proposals" for this volume are dated July 7ᵗʰ, 1796. There were further editions of *Hogarth Illustrated* in 1806 and 1812.

Graphic Illustrations of Hogarth, from Pictures, Drawings, and Scarce Prints[1] *in the Possession of Samuel Ireland, Author of this work, etc.* [In Two Volumes.] London: Published by R. Faulder, New Bond Street; and others. MDCCXCIV-IX.

Vol. i. (1794). Half-Title; Title; "Preface," pp. v-xii; "Prints," etc. xiii-xvi; Text, 1-183. Vol. ii. (1799). Half-Title; Title; "Preface" (dated May), pp. v-xi; "Prints," etc. xiii-xix. Text, 1-150. 8vo.

[1] In vol. ii. it is "from Pictures and Drawings" only.

G. C. Lichtenberg's ausführliche Erklärung der Hogarthischen Kupferstiche, mit verkleinerten aber vollständigen Copien derselben von E. Riepenhausen. [Fourteen vols.] Göttingen im Verlag von Joh. Christ. Dieterich. 1794-1834 (?)

8vo. Lichtenberg visited England in 1770, and again in 1774 when he stayed for four years. He died 24th February, 1799. The "Introduction" to the fifth volume is dated after his death; and thenceforward the commentary is derived mainly from the English authorities. A thirteenth part (preface dated October, 1832) was added by J. P. Lyser; a fourteenth (preface dated December, 1834), by Dr. le Petit and Karl Gutzkow. A "*Neue verbesserte Ausgabe*" (including parts 13 and 14) was issued in 1850-4. The completion of Lichtenberg was also undertaken separately *circa* 1839-40 by Dr. Franz Kottenkamp, a third edition of whose work appeared at Stuttgard in 1873. Lichtenberg's descriptions of Plate I. of the *Harlot's Progress*, and Plates I., II. and III. of the *Rake's Progress* were translated in the *London Magazine* for September and October, 1820, pp. 277-284, and pp. 388-402. A French translation by M. M. Lamy appeared at Gottingen in 1797. See also *infra*, "Lichtenberg and Hogarth."

Hogarth Restored. The whole works of the Celebrated William Hogarth, as originally published, with a Supplement, consisting of such of his Prints as were not published in a collected Form. Now re-engraved by Thomas Cook. Accompanied with Anedotes of Mr. Hogarth, and explanatory Descriptions of his Designs. London : 1801-3.

Atlas *folio*. The "Anecdotes," first issued in 1803, in royal 8vo. are frequently found apart from the plates. The 4to. issue of 1811 has a rude woodcut portrait of the painter. There is also an 8vo. edition of 1813.

The Genuine Works of William Hogarth ; illustrated
with Biographical Anecdotes, a Chronological
Catalogue, and Commentary. By John Nichols,
F.A.S. Edinb. & Perth; and the late George
Steevens, Esq., F.R.S. and F.S.A. In Two
Volumes. London: Printed for Longman,
Hurst, Rees, and Orme, Paternoster Row.
1808-1810.

> Vol. i. Title; "Preface," pp. iii-vii; Text, 1-524. Vol. ii.
> Title; "Advertisement" and "List of Plates," pp. iii-viii;
> 1-444, and Index. There are 160 plates, engraved by T.
> Cook from the original pictures or proof impressions. In
> this edition the contributions of Steevens, who died in
> 1800, "are in general pointed out." Another coadjutor,
> "in the theatrical part more particularly," was Isaac Reed.

The Genuine Works of William Hogarth ; with
Biographical Anecdotes. By John Nichols,
F.S.A. Lond. Edinb. and Perth; and the late
George Steevens, Esq., F.R.S. and F.S.A. In
Three Volumes. Volume III. Containing
Clavis Hogarthiana, and other Illustrative Es-
says: with fifty additional Plates. London :
Printed by and for Nichols, Son, and Bentley,
etc. 1817.

> Title; "Advertisement," "Contents," "Plates," etc. pp.
> iii-xxxii; Text and Index, 1-358. Reprints *inter alia* the
> *Prose Tour* (see p. 35) with Livesay's Etchings. There are
> also many "Additions and Corrections" to vols. i. and ii.

The Works of William Hogarth, (including the
' Analysis of Beauty,') elucidated by Descriptions,
Critical, Moral, and Historical ; (founded on the
most approved Authorities.) To which is pre-

fixed some Account of his Life. By Thomas
Clerk. In Two Volumes [each having an
engraved title page,—"The Works of Wm.
Hogarth," and vignette]. London. Printed for
R. Scholey, 46, Paternoster Row. 1810.

Volume I.: Title; "Preface," pp. iii-v; "Contents";
"Some Account of William Hogarth" 1-32; Text, 33-203.
Volume II.: "Contents"; Text, 1-96; *Analysis of Beauty*
unpaged. 8vo. The editor is said to have been T. H.
Horne. Another edition followed in 1812.

*On the Genius and Character of Hogarth; with some
Remarks on a Passage in the Writings of the
late Mr. Barry.* By "L" [i.e. Charles Lamb].
Article in No. iii. of *The Reflector.*

Pp. 61-77 of vol. ii. (1811). 8vo. "I contend," says Lamb
in this famous paper, speaking of Hogarth's subjects, "that
there is in most of them that sprinkling of the better nature,
which, like holy-water, chases away and disperses the con-
tagion of the bad. They have this in them besides, that
they bring us acquainted with the every-day human face,
—they give us skill to detect those gradations of sense and
virtue (which escape the careless or fastidious observer) in
the countenances of the world about us; and prevent that
disgust at common life, that *tædium quotidianarum for-
marum,* which an unrestricted passion for ideal forms and
beauties is in danger of producing. In this, as in many
other things, they are analogous to the best novels of
Smollett and Fielding" (p. 77).

*A Descriptive Catalogue of the Works of Hogarth,
placed in the Gallery of the British Institution
for Exhibition* .... By Mr. Young, Keeper
of the British Gallery. London : Printed by
William Bulmer, and Co., Cleveland Row, St.
James's. 1814.

Title; pp. 3-30. 4to.

On Hogarth's Marriage A-la-Mode. On Hogarth.
Two articles in the *Examiner*, No. 336, June 5,
and No. 338, June 19, 1814. By "W. H." [i.e.
William Hazlitt].

Pp. 366-7 and pp. 398-9 of the volume for 1814.   4to.
These papers were reprinted in the *Round Table ;* and also
as No. vii. of Hazlitt's *Lectures on the English Comic
Writers*, 3rd edn., 1841, pp. 274-311. Quotations from
them already appear in the foregoing " Memoir "; but the
following may be added here :—" Everything in his
[Hogarth's] Pictures has life and motion in it. Not only
does the business of the scene never stand still, but every
feature and muscle is put into full play ; the exact feeling of
the moment is brought out, and carried to its utmost height,
and then instantly seized and stamped on the canvass for
ever . . . Besides the excellence of each individual face,
the reflection of the expression from face to face, the
contrast and struggle of particular motives and feelings in
the different actors in the scene, as of anger, contempt,
laughter, compassion, are conveyed in the happiest and
most lively manner." (P. 398.)

Illustrations of Hogarth : i.e. *Hogarth Illustrated
from Passages in Authors he never read, and
could not understand.* [By the Rev. E. Ferrers.]
London : Printed by and for Nichols, Son, and
Bentley, Red Lion Passage, Fleet Street.
1816.

Title ; " Introduction," pp. 3-8 ; " Postscript " [dated Nov.
13, 1815], 9-10; Text, 11-55. Frontispiece-Portrait of
Hogarth after drawing by Worlidge (see p. 185 n.). 8vo. A
second edition, " enlarged and corrected," with the additional title of *Clavis Hogarthiana*, was issued in 1817.
The book was also reprinted in Vol. iii. of Nichols's *Genuine
Works*, 1817.

The Works of William Hogarth, from the Original

*Plates restored by James Heath, Esq., R.A.;
with the Addition of many Subjects not before
collected: to which are prefixed, a Biographical
Essay on the Genius and Productions of Hogarth,
and Explanations of the Subjects of the Plates,
by John Nichols, Esq., F.S.A.* London : Printed
for Baldwin, Cradock, and Joy, Paternoster
Row, by J. Nichols and Son, Parliament Street.
1822.

Title; "Biographical Essay" and "Contents," pp. iii-xi;
"Explanation of Plates," 1-52. Atlas *folio*. There is a
portrait of Hogarth for frontispiece, and 119 pages of plates,
the original coppers of which in 1822 were in possession of
Messrs. Baldwin and Cradock.

*Nollekens and his Times: comprehending a Life of
that celebrated Sculptor ; and Memoirs of several
contemporary Artists, from the Time of Rou-
biliac, Hogarth, and Reynolds, to that of Fuseli,
Flaxman, and Blake.* By John Thomas Smith,
Keeper of the Prints and Drawings in the
British Museum. In Two Volumes. London :
Henry Colburn, New Burlington Street, 1828.

8vo. There are anecdotes of Hogarth at pp. 46-8; 94;
193-4, and 266-8 of vol. i ; in vol. ii, pp. 224-5 and 340-5
are devoted to him.

*Garrick in the Green Room! a Biographical and
Critical Analysis of a Picture, painted by Wil-
liam Hogarth, and engraved by William Ward.*
By George Daniel. [Motto from the *Modern
Dunciad.*] London : James Webb Southgate,
22, Fleet Street. 1829.

Title; pp. 3-33. 4to.

The Lives of the Most Eminent British Painters, etc. By Allan Cunningham. London [In Six Volumes]. 1829-1833.

> Pp. 54-186 of vol. i (1829) relate to Hogarth. Cunningham's *Lives* were edited in 1879-80 by the late Mrs. Charles Heaton. Hogarth occupies pp. 44-151 of vol. i.

Hogarth, Bewick and Green. [By Hartley Coleridge.] Article in *Blackwood's Magazine*, No. 186, October, 1831.

> Pp. 655-668 of vol. xxx. The paper is No. III. in a series entitled " Ignoramus on the Fine Arts," and the Green is William Green the landscape-painter of the lakes. The pages on Hogarth are sympathetic but desultory. Of his name the writer says—" An early print inscribed William Hogart, and a couplet in Swift's Legion Club,
>
> > How I want thee, humorous Hogart,
> > Thou, I hear, a pleasant rogue art,
>
> are brought to prove that the final H was an unwarrantable innovation. Now, it so happens that the name is common in the north at this day [1831], and is always spelt Hogarth, but pronounced Hogart. Any one passing by the shop of Mr. Hogarth of Keswick, druggist, and sub-distributor of stamps, may resolve his doubts on this important subject (p. 667)." See also same paper in Hartley Coleridge's *Essays and Marginalia*, 1851, i. 250-86. In vol. ii (pp. 201-42), are some characteristic notes on Allan Cunningham's "Life of Hogarth."

Anecdotes of William Hogarth, written by Himself: with Essays on his Life and Genius, and Criticisms on his Works, selected from Walpole, Gilpin, J. Ireland, Lamb, Phillips, and others. To which are added a Catalogue of his Prints; Account of their Variations, and principal copies;

Lists of Paintings, Drawings, etc. [With 48 plates.] London: J. B. Nichols and Son, 25 Parliament Street. 1833.

Title, "Preface," "Contents" and "List of Plates," iii to xii; Text, 1-416. 8vo. John Bowyer Nichols, who compiled the volume, was the son of John Nichols, the antiquary, the collaborator of George Steevens. It was printed in the same manner as John Major's Trusler, 1831, which it was intended to supplement.

Hogarth and his Works. Articles in the *Penny Magazine* for 1834 and 1835.

Pp. 121-8, 209-16, 249-56, 287-8, 329-30, 377-84, 401-2, and 481-2 of Vol. iii ; and pp. 12-13, 29-30, 81-88, 113-14, 145-6, 172-5, 193-5, and 209-216 of vol. iv. There are numerous illustrations drawn on the wood after Hogarth by F. W. Fairholt and engraved by John Jackson. In the concluding paper, it was stated that the series would be republished "with about half as many more additional cuts, and the text enlarged." They were abridged and re-arranged for vol. xii. of the *Cabinet Portrait Gallery of British Worthies,* 1847.

Lichtenberg and Hogarth. Article in the *Foreign Quarterly Review,* No. xxxii (1836).

Pp. 279-303 of vol. xvi. 8vo. "His [Lichtenberg's] 'descriptions'" says the writer, "may in fact be considered his *chef-d'œuvre* among his humorous writings ; it cannot, however, be said that he adheres very strictly to the duties of a commentator, since he not unfrequently allows himself to be carried away by his sportiveness much farther than is necessary, and is moreover apt to put a different construction upon many things, from what Hogarth himself appears to have intended. Often does it happen, again, that he makes what is subordinate in the subject principal in his description of it. . . ." (p. 290). Neither of these criticisms can be gainsaid.

*Patronage of British Art, an Historical Sketch: . . .
illustrated with Notes, Historical, Biographical,
and Explanatory.* By John Pye, Landscape-
Engraver, etc. [Motto from Barry.] London :
Longman, Brown, Green, and Longmans, Paternoster Row. 1845.

> 8vo. Contains many valuable particulars respecting Ho-
> garth and his contemporaries. At p. 89 is a beautiful little
> wood-cut, engraved by John Thompson, of the blue and
> white dragon-china punch-bowl used by the painter and his
> friends when they held their annual dinners at the Foundling
> Hospital (See chapter iv).

*Memoranda ; or, Chronicles of the Foundling Hos-
pital, including Memoirs of Captain Coram, etc.,
etc.* By John Brownlow. London : Sampson
Low, Lamb's Conduit Street. 1847.

> Large 8vo. Title ; "Contents," pp. iii-iv ; text, pp. 1-231.
> The book contains plates of Hogarth's head-piece to a
> Power of Attorney (1739), of the Arms of the Hospital,
> supposed to have been designed by him, and an autograph
> receipt for the maintenance at Chiswick of two of the
> Foundlings during 1761-2 (see chapter iv). It also in-
> cludes portraits of Coram by Hogarth (p. 76 of this book)
> and B. Nebot, autographs of Coram and Wilkes, and
> various particulars respecting the painters and other nota-
> bilities connected with the Institution.

England under the House of Hanover, etc. By
Thomas Wright. With numerous Illustrations,
executed by F. W. Fairholt, F.S.A. In Two
Volumes. London : Bentley, 1848.

> Vol. i., which extends to the beginning of the reign of
> George III., contains much information respecting Ho-
> garth. A revised edition, under the new title of *Caricature
> History of the Georges,* was issued in 1868.

The Tomb of William Hogarth. By Mrs. S. C. Hall. With Notes and Illustrations by F. W. Fairholt, F.S.A. Article in the *Art-Union* for August 1, 1848.

Pp. 252-256 of vol. x. Afterwards reprinted in *Pilgrimages to English Shrines*, 2 vols., 8vo., 1850-3, 1st Series, pp. 274-294. In the *Art Journal* for May, 1851, p. 148, appeared an article on "Hogarth's Tomb at Chiswick," in which attention was drawn to its dilapidated condition.

William Hogarth und Seine Zeit, oder London in 18 *Jahrhundert. Eine Sammlung von Stahlst: nach Hogarth's Originalen, mit Erzahlungen von Adolph Görling.* Leipzig: Payne, 1851-2.

4to. In ten Parts.

The English Humourists of the Eighteenth Century. A Series of Lectures, delivered in England, Scotland, and the United States of America. By W. M. Thackeray. London: Smith, Elder and and Co. 1853.

8vo. Pp. 219-241 are the beginning of the lecture on "Hogarth, Smollett and Fielding," and relate to the painter. The notes are by James Hannay, in whose hands Mr. Thackeray placed the MS. of the Lectures for annotation in October, 1852, before he started for America (*Brief Memoir of the late Mr. Thackeray*, by Hannay, 1864, p. 25 *n*).

La Caricature en Angleterre. By E. D. F. [? E. D. Forgues]. Articles in the *Revue Britannique* for November and December, 1854.

Pp. 201-216 and pp. 321-352 of vol. xxiv.

A Hand-Book for Young Painters. By C. R.

Leslie, R.A. . . . With Illustrations. London : John Murray, Albemarle Street. 1855.

> 8vo. Contains, chiefly in the Chapters on "Invention and Expression" and "Composition," much valuable criticism of Hogarth.

Hogarth in London Streets. By G. Walter Thornbury. Article in *Art Journal,* 1859.

> Pp. 1-4 of vol. v. New Series. Reprinted in Thornbury's *British Artists,* 1861, vol. i. pp. 286-329 as "The Day after Hogarth's Death."

Londres il y a cent Ans. Par Francis Wey. Paris : Michel Lévy Frères, Libraires-Editeurs Rue Vivienne, 2 Bis. 1859.

> Title ; "*Introduction (William Hogarth en France),*" pp. 1-15 ; Text, pp. 17-233. 8vo. A French novel of Hogarth's time by the author of *Les Anglais chez eux.*

William Hogarth : Painter, Engraver, and Philosopher. Essays on the Man, the Work, and the Time. [By George Augustus Sala.] Articles in the *Cornhill Magazine,* from February to October, 1860 (vols. i. and ii.).

> These papers, which were partially illustrated, were republished by Messrs. Smith, Elder and Co., in 1866 (Title, "Contents," "List of Illustrations," and pp. 1-318). They are nine in number, the last ("Tail-Piece") bringing the whole to a somewhat precipitate conclusion, as it deals with nineteen years of the painter's life. From the final lines it would appear that Mr. Sala intended to return to the subject. This, as far as we are aware, he has never done, although it is no doubt to these studies in Hogarth that we owe the remarkable *pastiche* entitled the *Strange Adventures of Captain Dangerous* which followed them not long afterwards in *Temple Bar.*

An English Painter's Tomb. By Charles Allston Collins. Article in *Macmillan's Magazine* for April, 1860.

Pp. 489-94 of vol. i. Records a visit to Hogarth's house and tomb while the painting loft over the stable was still in existence. The writer says the house was Sir James Thornhill's. But see p. 180 n. of this book.

Widow Hogarth and Her Lodger [Alexander Runciman]. By Dutton Cook. Article in *Once a Week* for December 29th, 1860.

Pp. 10-13 of vol. iv. The paper was reprinted in *Art in England*, 1869, pp. 104-122.

Hogarth and his Pictures. A Lecture delivered before the Young Men's Christian Association in Exeter Hall. By the Rev. Hugh Stowell Brown. London : 1860.

8vo. Pp. 321-57 of the volume of Lectures from November, 1859, to February, 1860.

Anecdote Biography. William Hogarth, etc. By John Timbs, F.S.A. [Vignette of " Hogarth's House at Chiswick."] London : Richard Bentley, New Burlington Street. 1860.

8vo. Pp. 1 to 94, and p. 370 relate to Hogarth, of whom there is a portrait on steel from his own picture in the National Gallery.

The Complete Works of William Hogarth: in a Series of One Hundred and Fifty Steel Engravings, from the Original Pictures [?]. With an Introductory Essay, by James Hannay ; and

Q

descriptive Letterpress, by the Rev. J. Trusler,
and E. F. Roberts. [Quotation from Sala.]
London: Richard Griffin and Company, 10,
Stationers'-Hall Court. [1860?]

> Title; "Contents"; "Hogarth as a Satirist" [Hannay's
> Essay], pp. i-xiv; "Biography of Hogarth," xv-xviii; Text,
> 1-201. There is also an engraved title, "Hogarth's Works,"
> with vignette of the Milkmaid from the *Enraged Musician*.
> 4to. Mr. Hannay's Essay, it may be added, although
> restricted to a single aspect of Hogarth's genius, viz., his
> relation to the severer masters of satire, is a most scholarly
> and vigorous contribution to the literature of the subject.

*Histoire des Peintres de Toutes les Écoles. École
Anglaise par M. W. Bürger.* Paris: Vve. Jules
Renouard, MDCCCLXIII.

> Folio. Contains an article of 16 pp. by Philarète Chasles,
> with Portrait and seven illustrations.

Life and Times of Sir Joshua Reynolds . . . Commenced by Charles Robert Leslie, R.A. Continued and concluded by Tom Taylor, M.A.
In Two Volumes. London: John Murray,
1865.

> 8vo. Contains many references to Hogarth (See "Index,"
> ii. 501-2).

*A Century of Painters of the English School; with
Critical Notices of their Works, and an Account
of the Progress of the Art in England.* By
Richard Redgrave, R.A., and Samuel Redgrave.
[Motto from Locke.] In Two Volumes.
London: Smith, Elder and Co., 65, Cornhill,
1866.

8vo. Chap. ii. pp. 44-61 of vol. i. relates to Hogarth. A second edition in one volume of viii, 479 pp., "abridged and continued," was issued in 1890.

William Hogarth. Roman. Von A. E. Brachvogel. [In three vols.] Berlin : Janke, 1866.

8vo. Pp. 987. Brachvogel is also the author of *Hogarth*, a Drama in five Acts, Berlin, 1870, the scene of which is laid in London in September, 1733. Among the characters are Bolingbroke, Sir Robert Walpole, Lord Chesterfield, Sir John Gonson, Richard (!) Thornhill, "Hofmaler," his daughter Mary (!), and "Twakum," gaoler of Newgate, where the piece finishes.

William Hogarth. By Théophile Gautier. Article in *L'Artiste* for August, 1868.

Pp. 155-172. This is reprinted at pp. 315-344 of Gautier's *Guide de l'Amateur au Musée du Louvre*, etc., Paris : Charpentier, 1882. Under the title of "English Art from a French Point of View," M. Gautier's notes in the *Moniteur* on Hogarth at the International Exhibition of 1862 were translated by Mr. Sala in *Temple Bar*, for June and September, 1862, being pp. 320-326 of vol. v. and pp. 258-272 of vol. vi.

William Hogarth. Par M. F. Feuillet de Conches. Article in the *Gazette des Beaux-Arts, Livraison* 147, 1er *Septembre*, 1868.

Pp. 185-214 of Tome xxv. M. de Conches is stronger on the critical than the biographical side. He confounds Vanloo's portraits of Cibber and his daughter with Hogarth; he confuses Colley and his son; and he supposes that, in 1757, Hogarth succeeded his father-in-law as Serjeant Painter, whereas Sir James Thornhill died in 1734. But he speaks of several of the pictures as if he had seen them, and his characterization of Hogarth's painting is well worth quoting—" La peinture d'Hogarth est généralement libre, brutale de touche, un peu terne, molle et lâchée, parce que, pressée d'exprimer ce qu'elle a à exprimer, elle court droit au fait et ne se soucie pas plus que celle de Goya des régles banales. Hogarth savait et beaucoup, mais avant tout c'était un diseur familier qui ne cherchait point les effets de style et qui cependant les trouvait au besoin, toujours vif, saisissant, à force d'émotions intimes, de vie et de vérité. Il n'avait ni le dessein ni le temps de se mettre devant son chevalet pour se montrer peintre, pour lutter de parti pris avec la lumière, se jouer avec un effet de coloris et chercher un triomphe de palette. Ce n'est pas absolument que chez lui l'habitude du burin eut nui à la peinture : sous ce burin était un pinceau ; mais la pensée est sa préoccupation première : le pittoresque vient s'il le peut. L'exécution, toujours suffisante, est parfois énergique ; mais, pour tout exprimer en un mot, elle n'est pas toujours égale en profondeur à la pensée" . . . (p. 212).

Historical Sketches of the Reign of George II. No. xii.—*The Painter* [By Mrs. Oliphant.] Article in *Blackwood's Magazine* for August, 1869 (No. 646).

Pp. 140-168 of vol. cvi. These sketches were afterwards published in two vols. in 1869.

Hogarth's Five Days Peregrination by Land and Water, 1732. Abi tu et fac Similiter. [Sepia Design.] *Hogarth's Frolic. The Five Days' Peregrination around the Isle of Sheppey of William Hogarth and his Fellow Pilgrims, Scott, Tothall, Thornhill and Forrest.* [Small woodcut.] With Sketches in Sepia from the Original Drawings illustrating the Tour by W.

Hogarth and Sam. Scott [and several Wood-
cuts]. London : John Camden Hotten, 74 and
75 Piccadilly, W. [1871.]

Two titles; "Introduction," pp. i-xiv; "Title;" Text,
pp. 1-42. 4to. A Reprint of E. Forrest's prose version
of the Tour, and of W. Gostling's rhymed paraphrase.
Plate i. ("Hogarth painting the Comic Muse"), ii. iii. and
xiii. form no part of the illustrations to the Tour. On the
other hand, the book does not include a copy of Thornhill's map.

The Works of William Hogarth reproduced from the
Original Engravings in permanent Photographs
and newly described with an Essay on the Genius
and Character of Hogarth by Charles Lamb.
[In Two Volumes.] London : Bell and Daldy,
York Street, Covent Garden. 1872.

Volume I. Title; "Preface;" "List of Plates," vii-xi;
"A Few Words about Hogarth," by W[illiam] C[osmo]
M[onkhouse], xiii-xviii; Lamb's Essay, 1-22; Text and
Plates unpaged. Volume II. Title; Text and Plates unpaged. 4to. The descriptions are by Mr. Monkhouse
and the author of the present Memoir. The volumes
include all the prints in Baldwin and Cradock's collection
of 1822, two only excepted ; and they also include one plate
never before reproduced in a volume of Hogarth prints, viz.
a copy of Cheesman's engraving of *The Lady's Last Stake;*
or Picquet, or Virtue in Danger (see p. 158).

William Hogarth. By Carl Justi. Articles in
Lützow's *Zeitschrift für Bildende Kunst*, 1872.

Pp. 1-8, and pp. 44-54 of vol. vii. 4to.

William Hogarth. By Sidney Colvin. Article in
a series "From Rigaud to Reynolds" in the

Portfolio for 1872-3.   With Autotype of *Time Smoking a Picture.*

Pp. 146-155 of vol. iii.   *Folio.*   Mr. Colvin's closely-woven style does not lend itself readily to quotation ; but every student of Hogarth will do well to read his remarks upon the painter's intellectual and moral qualities, as well as upon his colouring, execution, and design,—points too much disregarded by those who regard him almost exclusively as a mirth-maker and caricaturist (see p. 190 n.).

Catalogue of Prints and Drawings in the British Museum. Division I. Political and Personal Satires. Vols. ii. to iv. [June, 1689 to *c.* 1770 :— Nos. 1236 to 4838]. Prepared by Frederic George Stephens, and containing many Descriptions by Edward Hawkins, late Keeper of the Antiquities, F.R.S. Printed by Order of the Trustees, 1873-83.

Four Volumes, volume iii. being in two parts. "In no respect was the Cataloguer more fortunate than in being able in some cases to cast new light, and in a much greater number of instances, a stronger light than time had permitted to remain on the masterpieces of Hogarth, their satiric force, their multitudinous allusions to individuals, their pathetic and moral applications, and even their historical significance (*Introduction* to vol. iii. part i. p. xvii.)" These volumes are in truth, as far as the subject comes within their scope, a vast storehouse of Hogarthiana, not to be safely neglected by any student of his work and epoch. The basis of the work is the Hawkins Collection in the Department of Prints and Drawings ; but it also includes many other Satires both in the Print Room, and contained in works in the Library.

Leicester Square; its Associations and its Worthies. By Tom Taylor, . . . With Illustrations. Lon-

don : Bickers and Son, 1, Leicester Square, W.
1874.

8vo. Chapter xii. (pp. 281-340) is entitled "Hogarth at
the Golden Head." There is a photograph of his picture
in the National Gallery, and a cut of the Chiswick House
from Timbs. Hogarth is also referred to in Appendix C,
pp. 493-5, which relates to the murderer, Theodore
Gardelle.

The East Haddon Hogarths. By "Video." Article
in the *Art Journal* for September, 1874 (No.
cliii. New Series).

Pp. 265-268 of vol. xiii, New Series. An account of
"Twelve oil paintings by Hogarth, illustrative of 'Hudibras'," at East Haddon Hall, an old Northamptonshire
manor-house.

English Graphic Satire, etc. By Robert William
Buss. Printed for the Author by Virtue and
Co. *For Private Circulation only.* 1874.

"Folios" ix and x, pp. 73-90, relate mainly to Hogarth.

William Hogarth. By A. Genevay. Articles in
L'Art for 1875.

Pp. 122-126 and pp. 177-181 of vol. i. Folio. With a
woodcut of *Garrick as Richard III.*

Hogarth as an Historian. By W. J. Morgan.
Article in the *St. James's Magazine* for 1878.

Vol. xliv. p. 206.

*Die Werke von W. Hogarth. Nach den Original-
Platten auf* 118 *Blättern photo-lithographirt.* . . .
nebst einem biographischen Essay über den Genius

*und die Schöpfungen Hogarth's, sowie Erklä-
rungen der einzelnen Bilder von John Nichols.
. . . Bearbeitet von E. C. Barschall,* Brünn
[printed] und Wien, 1878.

Title; "Essay" iii-x; Text, pp. 1-48; "Register." Folio.

Hogarth. By Austin Dobson. London : Sampson
Low, Marston and Co., 1879.

Title ; "Preface," pp. v-vi ; "Contents," vii-viii ; "List of
Illustrations ;" "Bibliography," xi-xii ; Text, "Chrono-
logy," "List of Engravings," etc., "List of Paintings,"
etc., etc., 1-128. 8vo. One of the series of the "Illustrated Biographies of the Great Artists," of which this
volume is an expansion.

Hogarth and Landseer. By W. C. Monkhouse.
Three Articles in the *Art Journal* for September, October and November, 1879. With 14
illustrations.

Pp. 178-9; 201-4; and 245-9 of vol. xviii. 4to. The first
paper is introductory ; the second treats of Hogarth as an
animal painter in relation to Landseer ; the third, of Landseer as a humourist in relation to Hogarth. The key to
the writer's argument is contained in the following :—"The
moral as well as the physical resemblances between man
and brute were caught and utilized by both artists : the
one [Landseer] mainly for the exaltation of the brute, the
other [Hogarth] mainly for the depreciation of man (p.
204)."

The Masters of Genre Painting, etc. By Frederick
Wedmore. With Sixteen Illustrations. Lon-
don : C. Kegan Paul and Co., 1, Paternoster
Square, 1880.

8vo. Pp. 221-7 relate to Hogarth, from whose *Marriage
A-la-Mode* there is an illustration.

Kunst und Künstler. Von Dr. Robert Dohme.
Dritte Abtheilung. Leipzig. Verlag von E.
A. Seeman, 1880.

Part ciii. pp. 3-22, is "William Hogarth, von J. Beaving-
ton-Atkinson." 8vo.

The Normanton Hogarth. By Austin Dobson.
Article in the *Magazine of Art*, for September,
1882.

Pp. 441-43 of vol. v. A description of the "Graham
Family" exhibited at Burlington House in 1882.

William Hogarth. By Feuillet de Conches. Articles in *L'Artiste* for November and December,
1882.

Pp. 365-383, and pp. 463-482 of vol. xvii. (*Nouvelle Période*).
8vo. With copies of the *Oratorio, Scholars at a Lecture,*
the *Strolling Actresses,* the *Cockpit,* and *A Sleeping Congre-*
gation. An editorial note (p. 365) says that these papers
are part of a *Histoire de l'École Anglaise,* etc., by M. de
Conches, published by Ernest Leroux, Paris.

La Peinture Anglaise. Par Ernest Chesneau. Paris:
A. Quantin. [1882.]

Pp. 9-26 and 319-20 relate to Hogarth, whom M. Chesneau
defines as "avant tout un peintre moraliste." His account
has some errors of fact and description for which the
following atones :—"Malgré la lourdeur et l'incorrection
de son dessin, il a poussé plus loin que pas un artiste au
monde l'éloquence, sous le crayon, du geste, de l'attitude,
de l'expression, c'est-à-dire rendu la physiognomie du
visage, la physiognomie du mouvement, et dans un tel et
si parfait accord qu'on lit clairement les pensées de con-
voitise, de haine, de bassesse, de souffrance, d'abêtisse-
ment, de douleur, de folie, de concupiscence, de terreur,
de joie, de misère morale, de misère sociale qui s'agitent

en ces âmes falotes, en ces crânes aplatis ou pointus, en
ces visages bouffis ou émaciés, exsangues ou apoplectiques,
en ces corps gonflés comme une outre ou fendus comme
des pincettes, difformes, tordus, contrefaits par toutes les
maladies qui peuvent, dans l'homme, atteindre l'esprit et
la bête " (p. 320). *La Peinture Anglaise* has been translated by L. N. Etherington, with an Introduction by Prof.
Ruskin, for Cassell's " Fine Art Library."

Hogarth and the Pirates.   By F. G. Stephens.
Article in the *Portfolio* for 1884.   With four
Illustrations.

Pp. 2-10 of vol. xv.

Some Portraits by Hogarth.   By Austin Dobson.
Article in the *Magazine of Art* for November,
1884.

Pp. 40-4 of vol. viii.   With woodcuts of " Dr. Arnold,"
" Miss Arnold " and " Ashby Lodge " from the Fitzwilliam
Museum ; and of " Lavinia Fenton " from the National
Gallery.

La Caricature en Angleterre.   William Hogarth.
Par M. Augustin Filon.   Article in the *Revue
des Deux Mondes*, 15 Janvier, 1885.

Pp. 385-423 of tome lxvii.   M. Filon's paper is rather a
brilliant sequence of descriptions of Hogarth's prints than
an examination of his merits as a painter.   Naturally, he
falls into some minor errors.   Because Mr. Sala speaks of
" Dominie " Hogarth, M. Filon concludes that Richard
Hogarth's christian name was Dominique ; and Counsellor
Silvertongue figures repeatedly as " Silvertong."   He does
full justice, however, to the moral purpose which even
Walpole recognized :—" Deux choses, d'ailleurs, peuvent
ennoblir le réalisme : la pureté des intentions morales, qui
tient lieu de goût, et la précision des peintures, qui donne
à une toile de genre, à mesure qu'elle vieillit, la valeur et
l'autorité d'un tableau d'histoire.   Ni l'une ni l'autre de

ces justifications n'a manqué à l'œuvre réaliste de William Hogarth" (p. 394). Genius he denies to him,—he is a "compilateur de faits psychologiques." "Il est, et doit rester pour nous un homme de talent, au second rang parmi les moralistes, au troisième parmi les dessinateurs. Comme peintre, il ne peut être classé " (p. 423).

The London of Hogarth. By W. E. Milliken. Article in *London Society* for March 1886.

Pp. 235-40 of vol. xlix.

Hogarth's Frolic. The Five Days' Peregrination, 1732. [By "J. G." i.e. Joseph Grego.] Article in the *Graphic* for September 17, 1887. With seven illustrations by Charles Green, R.I.

Pp. 313-6 of vol. xxxvi. Folio. Five of the original drawings for the illustrations were exhibited in 1889 at the Royal Institute of Painters in Water Colours (" English Humourists in Art " Catalogue, p. 34). They are at present in the possession of Mr. Grego and Mr. T. C. Venables.

Old London Picture Exhibitions. By F. G. Stephens. Articles in the *Art Journal* for February, March, September, and December, 1887.

Pp. 44-8, 85-8, 309-12, and 397-401 of vol. for 1887. Contain many particulars respecting Hogarth in connection with the earlier picture-exhibitions.

English Art in the Public Galleries. Published under the direction of T. H. Ward. London : Goupil and Co. [1887.]

Pp. 1-12 (Part I.) contains an article on Hogarth by Austin Dobson, with photogravures of Hogarth's two portraits of himself, of *Sigismunda,* and of the *Marriage A-la-Mode,* all taken from the original pictures. Large *folio.*

A Popular Handbook to the National Gallery . . .
Compiled by Edward T. Cook. London, Macmillan and Co., and New York. 1888.

> 8vo. Pp. 424-27, 429, 430, 433, 435-440, and 444 refer to
> Hogarth and his pictures in the National Gallery.

*Thackeray's Lectures on the English Humourists of
the Eighteenth Century. Mit Bibliographischem
Material, Litterarischer Einleitung, und Sach-
lichen Anmerkungen für Studierende.* Heraus-
gegeben von Ernst Regel. V. *Hogarth, Smollett,
and Fielding.* Halle. Max Niemeyer. 1889.

> 8vo. Pp. 1-33, and pp. 86-7 relate to Hogarth,—pp. 17-33
> being Thackeray's lecture with James Hannay's notes.
> The *Einleitung* (*Bibliographie, Hogarth's Leben und Cha-
> racter, Hogarth in seinen Werken*) is excellently done.

The Royal Academy in the Last Century. By J. E.
Hodgson and Fred. A. Eaton. Article I. in a
series beginning in the *Art Journal* for May,
1889.

> Pp. 129-134 of the volume for 1889, 4to. The paper has
> four illustrations, one being from a picture by Hogarth
> representing the Life School at the Academy in Peter's
> Court, St. Martin's Lane, and another the entrance to the
> same.

William Hogarth. Mit 58 *Illustrationen.* Leipzig.
Verlag von Bruno Lemme. [188 ?]

> Title: pp. 3-128. Nᵒˢ. 16-20 of the *Universal-Bibliothek
> den bildenden Künste.* Sm. 4to.

*William Hogarth. Vortrag von Prof. Emil Soffé,
gehalten in Mährischen Gewerbe-Museum am* 11

November, 1889. Separat-Abdrücke der Mit-theilungen des Mährischen Gewerbe-Museums. Brünn 1890. Druck von W. Burkart.

Title ; pp. iii-xiii. Folio.

Hogarth's Tour. By Austin Dobson. Article in the *Fortnightly Review* for August, 1890 (N°. cclxxxiv.)

8vo. Pp. 218-23 of vol. xlviii. New Series.

Chiswick, Past and Present. By C. J. Hamilton. With Illustrations by Mrs. L. Jopling Rowe. Article in the *English Illustrated Magazine* for September, 1891 (No. 96).

Pp. 874-85 of vol. viii. There are illustrations of Hogarth's house and tomb which should be added to those on p. 184 n.

THE BATTLE OF THE PICTURES. *From Hogarth's Etching.*

A CATALOGUE OF PRINTS

BY, OR AFTER,

HOGARTH.

[*⁎* This Catalogue is intended to include every known print by, or after, Hogarth, excepting a few doubtful or unimportant ones, which are, for the most part, specified in the final note. It does *not* comprise the copies by Riepenhausen, Cook, and others, contained in the ordinary collections. Concerning these, particulars will be found in the preceding "Bibliography." The first dimension given is always the *horizontal* one ; and the space measured is that occupied by the design, exclusive of the writing.[1] When the print has been strained or mounted, the measurements sometimes vary, more or less ; but those here indicated will be found sufficient for purposes of identification. As regards the different "states," it has not been thought necessary to give *all* the variations, but only those more obvious ones which serve to distinguish the earlier from the later impressions. The titles and inscriptions in inverted commas are the titles and inscriptions given on the plates themselves.]

The Rape of the Lock.
[Hogarth.]   [1717 ?]
   Impression from a gold snuff-box lid. An outline copy of
   one of these was made by Samuel Ireland, and published

---

[1] In some cases the writing is inseparable from the design.

1 March, 1786, by W. Dickinson, 158, New Bond Street ; another, more finished, in March, 1798, by F. Legat for John Ireland (*Hogarth Illustrated*, iii. 21). Very few of the original impressions exist. That in the British Museum was bought 23 June, 1842, at the Strawberry Hill Sale, for £21. The same impression (J. B. Nichols, 1833, 318) had fetched £33 at Gulston's sale, 7 February, 1786. John Ireland also had a first state. Samuel Ireland's out-line, which he reprinted in *Graphic Illustrations*, i. 8*, was copied from Lord Orford's. In its first form, this copy was dedicated to the Prince of Wales ; in its second, "To the Admirers of Hogarth."

$3\frac{1}{8} \times 2\frac{1}{4}$ in. (oval).

Hogarth's Shop-card.
" W Hogarth Engraver "   " Aprill yᵉ 23. 1720 "

1720.

J. Ireland had seen an impression inscribed in Hogarth's hand—"Near the *Black Bull, Long Lane*" (*Hogarth Illustrated*, iii. 331). £25, according to S. Ireland (who copied the card in April, 1786, and afterwards included it in *Graphic Illustrations*, i. 21) was paid for an impression. Lord Orford's sold in 1842 for £17 6s. 6d. The day of the month differs in some examples ; we follow that in the British Museum. Nichols's copy (*Genuine Works*, ii. 20) has the inscription—"at yᵉ Golden Ball yᵉ Corner of Cranbone Alley little Newport Street. Aprill yᵉ 29, 1720 ".

4×3 in.

" *The Lottery* "
" Willᵐ Hogarth Invᵗ et Sculpᵗ."   " Price One Shilling."   [1721.]

Below the design is "The Explanation." The *first* state (as above) has no publication line. The *second* has "Sold by Mʳˢ Chilcot in Westminster Hall" and "R. Caldwell Printseller in Newgate Street." The *third* has Mʳˢ Chilcot's

address. The *fourth*, S. Sympson. The *fifth*, Bowles of
the Black Horse. The *sixth*, "Printed for John Bowles,
N° 13, in Cornhill." The *seventh*, price and address
obliterated.

12⅝ × 8¼ in.

An Emblematical Print on the South Sea Scheme.
" W. Hogarth Invenᵗ et Sculpᵗ " " price 1 Shilling " [1721.]

There are twenty doggerel lines engraved below the print
beginning, "See here yᵉ Causes why in London." The
first state (as above) has no publication line. The *second*
has "Sold by Mʳˢ Chilcot in Westminster Hall" and " R.
Caldwell Printseller in Newgate Street." The *third* has
S. Sympson. The *fourth*, John Bowles, N° 13 Cornhill,
and no price. The *fifth*, no publisher's name or price.
From a Notice in the *General Advertiser*, 10 Dec. 1751, it
would appear that Bowles republished this print during
Hogarth's lifetime.

12¼ × 8¼ in.

Plates to the Travels of Aubry de la Motraye.
" W Hogarth sculp", etc.   1723.

These plates are as follow :

1. Tome 1. N° V. " *Vas mirabile ex integro Smaragdo,
   Genoæ,*" etc. The Vase, without the ornaments, and
   with " W. Hogarth scup." is in the British Museum.
2. Tome 1. N° IX. " *Tiara Patriarchalis Græca.*"
3. Tome 1. N° X. A Lady and Black Woman in a Bath-
   Room.
4. Tome 1. N° XI. A Dance of Women. This is copied
   by W. Skelton for Ireland's *Hogarth Illustrated*, iii.
   167.
5. Tome 1. N° XV. A Procession.
6. Tome 1. N° XVII. B. A Group of Figures in Turbans.
7. Tome 1. N° XVIII. A Scene in the Seraglio.
8. Tome 2. N° III. [XXVIB.] Park of the Artillery.

R

9. Tome 2. N° V. [XXX.] "Bender." Portrait of Charles XII.

10. Tome 2. N° VIII. [XXXII.] Head of Charles XII. etc.

11. Tome 2. N° IX. Pl. I. [XXXIII. N° 1.] "*Fodina Argentea Sahlensis.*"

12. Tome 2. N° IX. Pl. II. [XXXIII. N° 2.]   ditto.

13. Tome 2. N° XI. [XXXV.] "*Fodina Ferrea Danmorensis.*"

14. Tome 2. N° XIV. [XXXVIII.] A Lapland Hut, with Rein-Deer, etc.

To these John Ireland adds conjecturally Tome 1, N⁰ˢ XIII. and XVI., as well as the figures at the Corners of Tome 2, N° XXVI. A. (*The Five Muscovites*), and those in Tome 2. C (of which there is a modern copy), while J. B. Nichols would include "two dromedaries with a man feeding them" in the corner of the map marked T. I. B.

Royalty, Episcopacy, and Law.
[Hogarth.]   [1724.]
Under this design is—"Some of the Principal Inhabitants of yᵉ Moon, as they Were Perfectly Discover'd by a Telescope brought to yᵉ Greatest Perfection since yᵉ last Eclipse ; Exactly Engraved from the Objects, whereby yᵉ Curious may Guess at their Religion, Manners, &c.   Price Six Pence." "This print (says J. B. Nichols, *Anecdotes*, 1833, p. 164) was first published 2 Dec. 1724."

7⅛ × 9½ in.

Seven Plates to " The New Metamorphosis."
"W Hogarth fec."   "W Hogarth Invᵗ et sculp."
"W Hogarth Invᵗ et fecᵗ." etc.   [1724.]
Four plates in vol. i.; three plates in vol. ii.,—with signatures varied as above.   Plate 2 in vol ii. in *first* state has no lettering at all.   Two of the plates in vol. i. says J. B. Nichols (*Anecdotes*, 1833, p. 318) are copied from a Translation of Apuleius in 2 vols. 1708.

v. s.

Masquerades and Operas. Burlington Gate.
" W^m. Hogarth Inv^t et Sculp^t."   " Price 1 Shilling.
1724 "   1724.

Under the design come two quatrains, beginning " *Could now dumb* Faustus," engraved on a separate plate. In the *second* state, " Pasquin N° XCV.," which is one of the books in a wheelbarrow in the foreground of the *first* state becomes " Ben John[son]," and the publication line is " To be sold at y° Golden Ball in Little Newport Street Price 1 shill. 1724". The two quatrains are also different; they begin " O how refin'd," etc. J. Ireland thinks this is the plate which Hogarth calls *The Taste of the Town* (*Hogarth Illustrated*, iii. 15). There is a contemporary copy, with the same title and date, and a third set of verses (" Long has the Stage productive been "), but without artist's name and publication line.
6¼ × 4⅞ in.

Frontispiece to " The Happy Ascetick."
[Hogarth.]   1724.

Underneath the design is—" St Matthew Ch. 21. Verse 28. Son, go Work to day in my Vineyard." It forms the Frontispiece to the *sixth* edition of Dr Anthony Horneck's *Happy Ascetick*, London : S. Chapman and others, 1724. The print (says J. B. Nichols) is sometimes known as " The Master of the Vineyard."
3¼ × 6 in.

A Burlesque on Kent's Altarpiece at St. Clement's Dane's Church, Westminster.
[Hogarth.]   [1725.]

There is an inscription under the design, the last word of which, *i.e.* " wings," ends in the *first* state with a long " s." The earlier impressions are generally on *blue* paper, but there are also reproductions on *blue* paper. (See p. 23.)
7 × 11⅛ in.

Five Plates for " Cassandra."

"W Hogarth inv' et sculp." 1725.

These form the frontispieces to the five 12mo volumes of the *third* edition of Sir Charles Cotterel's *Cassandra, a Romance*, London, John Darby and others, 1725.

3 × 5⅛ in.

Fifteen Headpieces for Beaver's " Roman Military Punishments."

"W H"; "W. Hogarth Inv' et sculp." etc.

1725.

These are headpieces to *Roman Military Punishments*, by John Beaver, London, 1725, 4to., and are engraved in the manner of Jacques Callot. "A little figure of a Roman General in the title-page may possibly be by Hogarth, though his name is not to it." (*Hogarth Illustrated*, iii. 333.)

2¹¹⁄₁₆ × 1¼ in.

" A Just View of the British Stage, or three Heads are better than one. Scene Newgate, by MD— V—to."

[Hogarth ?] [1725.]

Represents Booth, Wilks and Cibber, the patentees of Drury Lane Theatre, contriving a Pantomime. There is an explanatory inscription under the design ending " Vivat Rex. price six pence." There are two states. " Mr. Devoto was scene-painter at Drury Lane or Lincoln's Inn Fields Theatre, and also to Goodman's Fields" (J. B. Nichols, *Anecdotes*, 1833, 166).

8⅛ × 7 in.

Berenstat, Cuzzoni, and Senesino.

[Hogarth ?] [1725.]

A scene from the opera of *Julius Cæsar*, the characters.

being Julius Cæsar (Berenstat), Cleopatra (Cuzzoni), and Mark Antony (Senesino). It is also said to represent Ptolemy, Cleopatra, and Julius Cæsar in Handel's *Ptolomeo*, the tall male figure being identified with Farinelli. There are three states of this plate; but it is probably by the younger Vanderbank.

10 × 7¼ in.

Frontispiece to " Terræ-Filius."
" W. Hogarth fec "   1726.

This is the frontispiece to vol. i. of Nicholas Amhurst's *Terræ-Filius : or, The Secret History of the University of Oxford*, 2 vols., London, R. Francklin, 1726. Francklin was the printer of Amhurst's paper, the *Craftsman*.

3⅛ × 5¼ in.

Twenty-six figures to Blackwell's " Compendium of Military Discipline."
[Hogarth.]   [1726.]

On two Sheets. A cartouche in the first is inscribed— " The several Postures of yᵉ Salute wᵗʰ yᵉ half-Pike," etc. " By Jnº Blackwell Adjutant and Clerk."

Sixteen Small Prints for Hudibras, and Butler's Head.
" W Hogarth. Invᵗ et sculp."   1726.

Prepared for an edition of *Hudibras* printed for D. Browne and others in 1726. The alleged head of Butler is in reality Jean-Baptiste Monnoyer, copied from White's mezzotint. These plates were enlarged, and slightly varied by J. Mynde for Zachary Grey's *Hudibras*, 2 vols. 1744. Copies were also inserted in John Towneley's translation into French, 1757 ; and Plate II. was borrowed by I. Ross for Nash's *Hudibras*, 1795.

V. S.

Twelve Large Prints for Hudibras.
"W. Hogarth Inven. et sculp," etc.   1726.

Issued stitched, with the following Title-page :—*Twelve Excellent and most Diverting Prints ; taken from the Celebrated Poem of Hudibras, wrote by Mr. Samuel Butler. Exposing the Villany and Hypocrisy of those Times. Invented and Engraved on Twelve Copper-Plates by William Hogarth* . . . . "Printed, and sold by Philip Overton, Print and Map-Seller, at the Golden Buck near St Dunstan's Church in Fleetstreet ; and John Cooper, in James-Street, Covent-Garden. 1726." There are many minute variations in the later impressions, of which the following may be particularized :—

Plate I. "Frontispiece and its Explanation." The *first* state has Overton and Cooper ; *second* state Overton only ; the *third* Sayer instead of Overton.

Plate II. "Hudibras sallying forth." The later impressions have " Wm Hogarth Inven. et Sculp."

Plate III. "Hudibras's First Adventure." Butcher's waistcoat without stripes in first impressions.

Plate IV. "Hudibras Catechis'd."

Plate V. "Hudibras Vanquish'd by Trulla."

Plate VI. "Hudibras in Tribulation." The later impressions have ",Wm Hogarth Inven. et Sculp."

Plate VII. "Hudibras and the Lawyer." *First* state not numbered.

Plate VIII. "Hudibras beats Sidrophel, and his Man Whacum." The later impressions have " Wm Hogarth inven. et sculp."

Plate IX. "The Committee." The later impressions have " Wm Hogarth Inven. et Sculp."

Plate X. "Hudibras Triumphant." The later impressions have " Wm Hogarth inven. et sculp."

Plate XI. "Burning the Rumps at Temple Bar." The earliest impressions want " Down with the Rumps," on the scroll.

Plate XII. "Hudibras encounters the Skimmington."

Mr. H. P. Standly, says J. B. Nichols (*Anecdotes*, 1833, p.

320) had some apparently unique states of Plates II., IV.,
V., VI., and VII.

v. s.

"*Cunicularii or The Wise men of Godliman in Con-sultation.*"

[Hogarth ?]   [1726.]

A satire on the Godalming Rabbit Breeder, Mary Tofts.
The motto is—

> " They held their Talents most Adroit
> For any Mystical Exploit. Hudib."

There are also explanatory references to the letters on the
plate.

9⅛ × 6¼ in.

"*The Punishment inflicted on Lemuel Gulliver*, etc."

[Hogarth ?]   [1726.]

Under the design to the left is "Nahtanoi Tfiws" (*i.e.*
Jonathan Swift) ; to the right "Hogearth sculp." In the
second state (1757), the title is altered to *The Political
Clyster*, and the Engraver's name is given as " Dʳ O'Gearth
sculp." The publication line is—" Publish'd according to
Act of Parliament, Jan. 1ˢᵗ 1757." There is a third state
without any publication line.

12⅛ × 7¼ in.

"*Musick Introduc'd to Apollo by Minerva.*"

" Hogarth Fecit."   1727.

The publication line is "Sold by J. Clark Engraver &
Printseller in Greys Inn." Nichols (*Anecdotes*, 1782, 133)
affirms this to be a copy from an earlier book of music.

6¼ × 9½ in.

Large " *Masquerade Ticket.*"

[Hogarth.]   " price one Shilling "   [1727.]

There are explanatory references to the letters A and B on
the plate. In the *first* state the word " Provocatives " on

the wall to the left is spelled "Prouocatives"; in the *second*
the "*u*" is altered to a "*v*."

10 × 7¼ in.

Frontispiece to " Collection of Songs."
[Hogarth.]   1727.

The title of this book, which is also engraved, and probably by Hogarth, is *A Collection of Songs, with the
Musick, by Mr. Leveridge* . . . London Engrav'd and
Printed for the Author in Tavistock-street, Covent-Garden.
1727.

3¹¹⁄₁₆ × 6¼ in.

Head of Hesiod for Cooke's Translation.
" W. Hogarth Sculpᵗ."   [1728.]

In the corner of the plate is "Ex musæo Pembrokiano."
J. B. Nichols (*Anecdotes*, 1833, p. 172) says it is copied
"from the bust at Wilton."

4⁷⁄₈ × 6¼ in.

The Beggar's Opera Burlesqued.
[Hogarth.]   [1728.]

Under the design (*first* state) are engraved four lines
beginning — "Brittons attend. — view this harmonious
Stage." There are four other states,—the *second* with a
large lettered title, *The Beggars Opera*, at top ; the *third*,
title erased, and printed from a separate plate ; the *fourth*
with the publication line, "Sold at the Print-shop in the
Strand, near Catherine Street"; and the *fifth* with the
publication line, "Printed for John Bowles at the Black
horse in Cornhill."

9¼ × 7½ in.

King Henry the Eighth and Anne Boleyn.
" Hogarth design. & sculp."   1729.

The original picture hung in the portico of the Rotunda at
Vauxhall Gardens (see *ante*, p. 30). The *first* state

(B. M.) has no title, but under the plate is a printed slip headed, "King Henry VIII. bringing to Court Anna Bullen, who was afterwards his Royal Consort." Then come four quatrains beginning "See here the Great, the daring Harry stands," etc., signed "Allan Ramsay scrip.," with the publication line, "Printed and Sold by Phil· Overton near St Dunstan's Church, Fleetstreet; and Allan Ramsay in Edinburgh. MDCCXXIX." The *second* state has seven couplets beginning "Here struts old pious Harry," etc. The *third* state has the title, "King Henry the Eigth [*sic*] & Anna Bullen," the publication line, "London printed for John Bowles at the Black Horse in Cornhil, Carington Bowles in St Paul's Church Yard & R. Sayer in Fleet Street." "Price 3^s," and in the right corner under the plate, "Design'd, and Engrav'd by W. Hogarth." The *fourth* has the same title as the third; but the price is 5s., and the publication line is "London. Printed for Robert Wilkinson, Cornhil, Carington Bowles in St Paul's Churchyard and R. Sayer, in Fleet Street."

14$\frac{1}{4}$ × 17$\frac{1}{4}$ in.

Frontispiece to " *The Humours of Oxford.*"
"W. Hogarth inv^t" "G. Vander Gucht sculp."
[1729.]

This is a frontispiece illustrating act iv. sc. 1 of *The Humours of Oxford. A Comedy.* "By a Gentleman of *Wadham*-College" [Rev. James Miller]. Second Edition, London, J. Watts, 1730.

4$\frac{1}{8}$ × 6$\frac{1}{4}$ in.

Two Plates to "*Perseus and Andromeda.*"
"W H Fecit" 1730.

These are two plates to Lewis Theobald's [?] *Perseus and Andromeda*, 4to., London, T. Wood, 1730. The first is the frontispiece; the second (Perseus Descending) faces "The Argument."

4$\frac{1}{8}$ × 6 in.

" Gulliver presented to the Queen of Babilary."
" W. Hogarth inv'."   " Ger. Vandergucht sculp."

1731.

This is the frontispiece to vol. i. of J. Lockman's *Travels of Mr. John Gulliver, Son to Cap'. Lemuel Gulliver* (London : Harding, 1731), a translation from the French of the Abbé de S'. Fontaine.

2$\frac{13}{16}$ × 5$\frac{1}{4}$ in.

Frontispiece to " The Tragedy of Tragedies."
" W. Hogarth inv'."   " Ger VanderGucht sculp."

1731.

This is a frontispiece to *The Tragedy of Tragedies ; or, the Life and Death of Tom Thumb the Great* . . . . . *With the Annotations of H. Scriblerus Secundus* [Henry Fielding], London, J. Roberts, 1731, being an enlarged version of the same writer's *Tom Thumb* of the previous year.

3$\frac{1}{4}$ × 6$\frac{1}{4}$ in.

" A Scots Opera."
" W. Hogarth inv'."   " Ger. VanderGucht sculp."

1731.

Underneath the plate is " *Forsan et hæc olim meminisse juvabit.* Virg. " Frontispiece to *The Highland Fair ; or, the Union of the Clans. An Opera.* " Written by Mr Mitchell " [*i.e.* Joseph Mitchell]. London: J. Watts, 1731. It was played at Drury-Lane in March of that year.

3$\frac{11}{16}$ × 6 in.

" Taste."
[Hogarth.]   " Price 6^d "   1731.

There is a reference table below the design. This was Hogarth's reply to Pope's attack on the Duke of Chandos in *Of Taste : an Epistle to the Right Hon. Richard, Earl of Burlington*, London, L. Gilliver, 1731. It is said to have been suppressed (*Genuine Works*, ii. p. 78). It was reduced as the Frontispiece to *A Miscellany on Taste. By Mr. Pope*, etc., London, G. Lawton and others, 1732. In this, the tie-wig, Pope's dress of ceremony, which he wears in the larger plate, is changed into a cap.

$6\frac{1}{4} \times 8\frac{1}{4}$ in.

Boys Peeping at Nature.

[Hogarth.] [1731 ?]

Subscription Ticket for *A Harlot's Progress*. Along a wall on the plate itself is " Antiquam exquirite Matrem. Vir."; below the design :—

"necesse est
Indiciis monstrare recentibus abdita rerum,
—— dabiturque Licentia Sumpta pudenter. Hor."

Below these lines again comes the following form of receipt :—" Rec^d of half a Guinea being ye first Payment for Six Prints of a Harlot" Progress which I Promise to Deliver when Finish'd on Receiving one half Guinea more." It was afterwards used in 1737, with an altered form of Receipt, for the *Four Times of the Day* and the *Strolling Actresses ;* and again in 1751, with variations, for *Moses brought to Pharaoh's Daughter* and *Paul before Felix*. There is a copy in aquatint of the *first* state by Livesay, 1782 (*Genuine Works*, iii. 132).

$4\frac{5}{8} \times 3\frac{1}{4}$ in.

Two Plates to Molière.

" Hogarth Inv." " J Vander Gucht sculp."

1732.

These were frontispieces to the plays of " *L'Avare*" and " *Le Cocû Imaginaire*," in vol. i. of a selection of Molière's comedies published (French and English) in eight volumes in 1732. The *second* states have references to the play engraved below: in the case of " *L'Avare*," " .Act 5. Scene. 5 "; in the case of the other, " .Scene. 6." only. A facsimile of the original washed drawing for *L'Avare* faces p. 76 of *Graphic Illustrations*, ii.

$3\frac{1}{8} \times 5\frac{1}{8}$ in.

" Rich's Glory or his Triumphant Entry into Covent-Garden."
[Hogarth ?]   [1732.]

Over the print is the title given above; below are thirty doggerel lines beginning, "Not with more glory through the streets of Rome." To the left below the verse is "W H I E SULP";[1] and to the right "Price 6^d." In the *second* state the price is omitted.

12 × 6¼ in.

A Harlot's Progress.
" Wm Hogarth inv^t pinx^t et sculp^t "   1732.

See pp. 47-50. The *first* state (*i.e.* that issued to the subscribers), is distinguished by the absence of a black Latin cross which, in the *second* state, appears below the design.[2] There are also many variations in the *second* state, which was much worked upon by the artist. Of these the following may be specified as sufficiently distinctive :—

PLATE I. [Her Arrival in London]. Feet added to the elder woman; "London" added to the address of the clergyman's letter.

PLATE II. [Quarrels with her Protector]. Shadow of the raised leg of the table greatly extended.

PLATE III. [Apprehended by a Magistrate]. Covered or "sugar" dish near the punch-bowl turned into a bottle.

PLATE IV. [Beating Hemp in Bridewell]. Holes in roof filled in.

PLATE V. [Her Death]. Dr. Rock's name added to the paper near the fire.

PLATE VI. [Her Funeral]. Shadow thrown by the bottle of "Nants" on the apron of the woman in the right-hand corner.

---

[1] The same words with "Sculp" instead of "sulp" are traceable on the ground to the left.

[2] Copies of the *first* state are sometimes found *with* the cross. Such a set is in the possession of the writer.

Pirated copies of this set of prints in "chiaro oscuro" (mezzotint) and green ink were published by E. Kirkall or Kirkhall in November, 1732. By Hogarth's permission, copies were also engraved and issued in April "with Ornaments and Explanations" by G. King at the "Golden Head" Brownlow-Street, Drury-Lane. From these were prepared the illustrations to the book called *The Lure of Venus*, 1733. Sayer and Bowles also published copies; and Lavater reproduced some of the heads in his *Physionomie*, 1807. At Mr. H. P. Standly's expense, W. J. Smith engraved in 1829 the first design for the doctors in Plate V. J. B. Nichols, *Anecdotes*, 1733, p. 292, says it had previously been copied by S. Ireland, under the name of "Dr Ward and Dr Misaubin." There is a separate plate of Elizabeth Adams, the woman next the clergyman in Plate VI.; and the whole series were copied on wood in Cruikshank's manner for *Bell's Life (Gallery of Comicalities)*.

14¼ × 11¼ in.

A Chorus of Singers; or, The Oratorio.

[Hogarth.]   [1732.]

This was the Subscription Ticket for *A Midnight Modern Conversation;* and represents the Rehearsal of the Oratorio of *Judith*. Below the design in the *first* state is engraved the following receipt form:—"Rec^d of   Five Shillings being the whole Payment for a Print Call'd the Midnight Moddern Conversation which I Promise to Deliver on ye 1st of March next [i.e. 1733] at farthest, But Provoided the Number Already Printed shall be Sooner Subscribed for, then ye Prints shall be sooner Delivered & time of Delivery will be Advertiz'd." In the *second* state "Provoided" is corrected. It was afterwards issued as an etched print, and described as *A Chorus of Singers*. G. Cruikshank copied this plate in 1831 for Major's edition of Trusler.

6 × 6½ in.

" A Midnight Moddern Conucrsation."

"Wm Hogarth Inv^t Pinxt & Sculpt."   1733.

Some of the impressions of the *first* state are in red. There are four lines under the design beginning—"Think not to find," etc. In the *second* state, "Moddern" is corrected. In the later impressions, among other variations, a shadow thrown by the tobacco paper on the front of the table cloth, is added; and the contents of the vessel in the right hand corner, as well as the vessel itself, are cross hatched. There are various copies, viz' by G. Bickham ($3\frac{1}{2}$ × $2\frac{3}{4}$ in.) in Bancks's *Poems*, 1738, i. 87; by Geo. Bickham Jun' ($17\frac{1}{4}$ × $12\frac{3}{4}$ in.) ; by R. Cooper ($12\frac{5}{8}$ × $17\frac{3}{4}$ in.); by Kirkall (mezzotint); and by a French engraver, Creite ($16\frac{1}{4}$ × $10\frac{1}{4}$ in.). Copies without engravers' names were sold by Sayer and Bowles. A copy was also prepared by Bickham Jun' for his *Musical Entertainer* (1737?) where it appears in a cartouche at the head of a song entitled "The Releif; or Pow'r of Drinking." Some of the heads and figures were reproduced by E. Riepenhausen in a *Manuel contenant diverses Connaissances curieuses*, etc. Gottingen, 1786.

18 × $12\frac{7}{8}$ in.

Sarah Malcolm.
"W. Hogarth (ad Vivum) pinxit & sculpsit."

1733.

At the top of the plate, which was published March 10, is "Price 6ᵈ." The inscription below is, "Sarah Malcolm Executed in Fleet street, March yᵉ 7ᵗʰ 1732 [1733] for Robbing the Chambers of Mᵛˢ Lydia Duncomb in yᵉ Temple, and Murdering Her, Eliz: Harrison & Ann Price" There is an engraved copy with "W. Hogarth ad vivum Pinxit," and there are reversed mezzotint copies. There is also a woodcut in the *Gentleman's Magazine* for March 1733, p. 153. In addition to these, there is a curious print ($4\frac{1}{4}$ × $6\frac{1}{4}$) copied and reversed from Hogarth with the title " Sarah Malcom Ætat. XXII." " No Recompence but Love." At the woman's back, to the right, is a figure in a wig and bands holding a ring ; and through a window to the left is seen the execution. In *Hogarth Illustrated*, ii. 295, John Ireland gives a full-length from a

picture belonging to Josiah Boydell, said to be copied from
Horace Walpole's original oil-sketch at Strawberry Hill.
Ireland's copy is dated May 31, 1791, and engraved by
J. Barlow.

$6\frac{1}{8} \times 6\frac{7}{8}$ in.

Frontispiece to the Oratorio of "Judith."
"W. Hogarth Inv." "G. V^{dr} Gucht sc." 1733.

Underneath the plate is "Per Vulnera Servor Morte tuâ
Vivens. Virg. Æneid." *Judith* was an opera by William
Huggins, set to music by William Defesch. It was pub-
lished in *octavo*, 1733. See *A Chorus of Singers*.

$5\frac{1}{4} \times 3\frac{3}{16}$ in.

"*Sancho's Feast.*"
[Hogarth] [1733.]

There is a "proof before all letters" at the British Museum.
The *second* state has the following title and publication
line :—"Sancho at the Magnificent Feast prepared at his
government of Barataria, is Starved in the midst of Plenty,
Pedro Rezzio his Phisician, out of great Care for his health
ordering every Dish from the Table before the Governour
Tasts it." "Printed for H. Overton & J. Hoole at the
White Horse without Newgate." "W. Hogarth Inv^t et
Sculpsit." The *third* state has above the design,—"This
Original Print was invented and engraved by Willm
Hogarth."

$11\frac{7}{8} \times 10\frac{1}{8}$ in.

The Laughing Audience.
[W. Hogarth.] [1733.]

This was the Subscription Ticket to the *Rake's Progress*
and *Southwark Fair.* Below the design in the *first* state
was engraved, "Rec^d   of   Half a Guinea
being the first Payment for Nine Prints, 8 of Which Represent a Rakes Progress & the 9th a Fair, Which I
Promise to Deliver at Michaelmass next, on Receiving one

Guinea more, the Print of the Fair being Deliver'd at the
time of Subscribing." In the *second* state, "when finish'd"
is substituted for "at Michaelmass next;" and a line is
added "NB: the Rakes alone will be two Guineas after
the time of Subscribing." Many of these receipts have
Hogarth's seal—a palette and pencils. This was set in a
ring which Mary Lewis gave to John Ireland (*Hogarth
Illustrated*, iii. 356). The later impressions of the *Laughing Audience* have no inscription, and were probably issued
as etched prints, and described as *A pleased Audience at a
Play*. Cruikshank copied it for Major's Trusler, 1831.

$6\frac{1}{4} \times 7$ in.

A Satire on Cuzzoni, Farinelli, and Heidegger.
[Hogarth ?]   [1734.]

This satire is also ascribed to Dorothy, Countess of Burlington, who is said to have designed it, and had it etched
by Goupy.

$8 \times 9\frac{1}{4}$ in.

Frontispiece to " Chrononhotonthologos."
[Hogarth ?]   [1734.]

This is a frontispiece to *The Tragedy of Chrononhoton-
thologos* . . . Written by Benjamin Bounce, Esq.; [Henry
Carey]. London : Printed for J. Suckburgh, etc. *n. d.*
There is a copy by Mr. White of Brownlow Street in
which a figure (a page who holds the Queen's train) is
omitted.

$4\frac{1}{4} \times 5\frac{1}{4}$ in.

" *A Rake's Progress.*"
" Invented Painted & Engrav'd by Wm Hogarth, June y^e 25 1735. According to Act of Parliament."   1735.

The inscriptions vary slightly in the arrangement of the
words; and to Plate VI. is added "Sold at y^e Golden
Head in Leicester Fields, Lon^{don}." As to the publication

of this series, see pp. 56-7. The verses below the designs were by Dr. John Hoadly. In the *first* state, the publication line differs from that which appears above, and marks the *second* state.

PLATE I. [He takes possession]. In the *third* state the woollen draper's shop-bill is omitted ; the Bible substituted for the memorandum book, which is moved to the tailor's foot; and the girl is made much older.

PLATE II. [His Levee]. The word "Horlot's" in the *first* state altered to " Harlot's."

PLATE III. [He revels]. "June y* 24ᵗʰ, 1735 " in the *first* state altered to "June y* 25ᵗʰ, 1735 " in the *second*. The Rake's companion has a hat instead of a cap in later impressions, and Pontac's portrait is substituted for the headless Cæsar near the looking-glass.

PLATE IV. [Goes to Court]. In the *second* state, a group of gambling boys takes the place of the shoe-black who steals the Rake's cane.

PLATE V. [He marries]. In the *second* state the Bridegroom's right foot is omitted.

PLATE VI. [He gambles]. "*Second* state : Rays round the candle stronger " (*Hogarth Illustrated*, iii. 339).

PLATE VII. [In the Fleet Prison]. " In the very earliest impressions, 'Plate 7' is not inserted in the margin." (*ibid.*) In the *second* state the wings over the tester are much darker than in the *first* state.

PLATE VIII. [In Bedlam]. The *second* state has " Retouched by the author, 1763," and a halfpenny with a figure of Britannia, and the date 1763, is fixed against the wall to show what the artist thought of the state of the nation.

These plates were copied with Hogarth's consent and sold in August 1735 by Thomas Bakewell, next Johnson's Court in Fleet Street, London. They were also copied by Sayer; and they were plagiarized (see p. 57). An alleged *First Design for the Rake's Progress*, from which Livesay copied the *Matchmaker* and *Old Maid*, faces p. 91 of *Graphic Illustrations*, ii. ; and in the *Newgate Calendar* a print called *Betty Ireland's Dexterity* is borrowed from the woman

S

stealing the watch in Plate III. Besides these, there is a
private etching, *The Fencer*, derived from Plate II.

15¼ × 12¼ in.

Southwark Fair.

"Invented Painted and Engrav'ᵈ by Wᵐ Hogarth.
1733." [1735.]

Also known as *A Fair*, *The Humours of a Fair*. Although
dated 1733, from advertisements in the *London Evening
Post* it was not printed and issued until June 1735.
Copies were sold by Overton and Hoole (34 × 22 in.),
and by Carington and John Bowles engraved by R. Parr
(17¾ × 13½ in.). There is also a smaller copy (13⅞ × 9½ in.)
with French and English titles.

17¼ × 13½ in.

Woman Swearing a Child to a grave Citizen.

"W. Hogarth pinx."   "J. Sympson Junʳ sculp."

[1735 ?]

"Sold by J. Sympson Engraver and Print-seller
at the Dove in Russell Court Drury Lane."

According to John Ireland (*Hogarth Illustrated*, iii. 263),
the design has affinities with a humorous print after Heems-
kirk, under the title of *The Village Magistrate*, engraved by
Dickinson in March 1772 in mezzotint. Hogarth's print
was reproduced as "*Le Serment de la Fille qui se trouve
enceinte*" by J. V. Schley in Picart's *Cérémonies et Coutumes
Religieuses*, etc. 1738; and by Basire in vol. i., p. 248, of
Bancks's *Works*, 1738, where it figures as the illustration
to "The Substitute Father," a tale in verse. John Bowles
also issued a large copy; and there is a mezzotint, dated
June, 1816, by James Young.

13¼ × 10⅛ in.

The Distressed Poet.

"Invented Painted Engraved & Publish'd by Wᵐ

Hogarth March the 3rd 1736. According to Act
of Parliament.   Price 3 Shillings "   1736.

Below the *first* state are four lines from Book I. of
the *Dunciad*, beginning "Studious he sate, with all his
books around." On the wall is an engraving of Pope
thrashing Curll. In the *second* state, the lines from the
Dunciad have disappeared; and for Pope and Curll is substituted, "A View of the Gold Mines of Peru." The date
of publication is also altered to "Decem^{ber} the 15, 1740."
Steevens thought the poet was meant for Lewis Theobald,
the editor of Shakespeare and the original hero of the
Dunciad ; and in January, 1794, the figure was issued by W.
Richardson of Castle Street, Leicester Fields, as Theobald's
portrait. There is an impression of this without letters in
the British Museum. It has also been said to represent
Thomas Rymer, the critic and antiquary.

15$\frac{1}{8}$ × 12$\frac{1}{8}$ in.

A Consultation of Physicians.

" Publish'd by W. Hogarth March the 3^d 1736 "
" Price Sixpence."   1736.

At the base of the design is " *Et Plurima Mortis Imago* " ;
below it "The Company of Undertakers", and a description of their arms. In the *first* state, this description has
" One Compleat Docter " ; in the *second*, the error is
corrected. G. Cruikshank copied this plate in 1831 for
Major's edition of Trusler.

7 × 8$\frac{1}{4}$ in.

The Author's Benefit Pasquin.

[W. Hogarth ?]   [1736.]

" At y^e Theatre in y^e Haymarket." A ticket for the benefit
of Henry Fielding, which, according to an inscription upon
a copy facsimiled by A. W. Ireland in *Graphic Illustrations*,
i. 130, must have been on Tuesday, April 25, 1736.

5$\frac{1}{4}$ × 4$\frac{1}{4}$ in.

The Sleeping Congregation.

"Invented Engraved & Published October 26:
1736 by Wm Hogarth Pursuant to an Act of
Parliament." " Price One Shilling."   1736.

> In the *first* state there is no motto under the royal arms,
> and the angel over the window to the right smokes a
> tobacco pipe ; the *second* is the same with darkened
> shadows ; the *third* has the motto, and the pipe is removed ;
> the *fourth* has engraved along the bottom of the left margin
> " Retouched & Improved April 21 1762 by the Author."
> A copy in mezzotint (9⅞ × 12⅜) was issued by Bowles and
> Carver, of No. 69, St. Paul's Church Yard.   Perhaps this
> is the pirated impression to which Mrs. Hogarth refers in a
> cautionary advertisement in the *London Chronicle* of
> February 2, 1765, where she says that several copies of
> it " have been bought in the Print Shops by her own
> servants."
>
> ' 7¼ × 10 in.

Before and *After* (two prints).

" Invented Engraved & Published Dec^{br} ye 15th
1736 by Wm Hogarth Pursuant to an Act of
Parliament." " Price two Shillings & 6 pence "
1736.

> In the *first* state of "Before," the girl has a light necklace ;
> in the *second* state, this is made much heavier, and the
> back of the bed is darkened.   In " After," " Dec^{br}" in the
> publication line is " Decm^{br}."   There are other variations.
>
> 11⅞ × 14½, and 12⅛ × 14½ in.

" *Tartuffs Banquet.*"
[Hogarth ?]   1736.

> The publication line of this plate is " Publish'd &
> Sold According to Act of Parliament by L : Gilliver at
> Homers head in Fleet street, 1736."   The design only is
> ascribed to Hogarth ; the engraving is by G. Vandergucht.

There is a motto at the sides from Horace; and 14 lines
below from the poetical satire called *Seasonable Reproof*,
1735. The original drawing in bistre was sold in April,
1845, at Mr. H. P. Standly's sale. It had been facsimiled
by W. J. Smith.

8¼ × 7¼ in.

" The Right Honble. Frances Lady Byron."

" W. Hogarth pinx^t " " I. Faber fecit 1736."

1736.

The *first* state is a whole length. The best impressions
are usually in brown ink. The *second* state is cut down to
a three-quarters size, and has the inscription, " Sold by
Faber at the Golden Head in Bloomsbury Square."

12¼ × 17 in. and 9¼ × 12¼ in.

Frontispiece to " The Lawyer's Fortune."

[Hogarth.] 1736.

The Lawyer's Fortune; or, Love in a Hollow Tree, a
Comedy, London : Underhill, 1736, was by Lord Viscount
Grimston.

3 × 5⅛ in.

Scholars at a Lecture.

" Publish'd by W Hogarth January 20th, 173⁶⁄₇ "

1737.

In the *first* state, *Datur Vacuum* is omitted from the book
in the lecturer's hand ; in the *second*, it appears, and the
publication line is " Publish'd by W Hogarth March 3^d
1736 [1737]." G. Cruikshank copied this plate for Major's
edition of Trusler, 1831.

6⅞ × 8 in.

" Æneas in a Storm."

[Hogarth ?] 1737.

Below the plate is :—

" Tanta hæc Mulier *potuit Suadere* Malorum."

The publication line is, " Publish'd pursuant to an Act of

Parliament, 1737." "Price 6ᵈ" This plate, though ascribed to Hogarth, is probably by G. Vandergucht.

9 × 6 in.

The Four Times of the Day.
[Hogarth and B. Baron (*v. infra*).]   1738.

PLATE I. ["Morning"]. "Invented Painted Engrav'd & Publish'd by Wᵐ Hogarth March 25. 1738 according to Act of Parliament." In the *second* state, the carrots are darkened, and the foreground cross-hatched.

PLATE II. ["Noon"]. "Invented Painted & Engraved by Wᵐ Hogarth & Publish'd March 25. 1738 according to Act of Parliament." In the *second* state, the coat of the little boy is darkened, etc.

PLATE III. ["Evening"]. "Invented Painted & Publish'd by Wᵐ Hogarth March 25ᵗʰ 1738, according to Act of Parliament." "Engraved by B. Baron" "Price 5 Shillings." In the earlier impressions the man's hands were printed in *blue*, to indicate his trade, that of a dyer; the woman's neck is *red*, to denote heat. There is a rare *first* state, without the girl, afterwards added on the plate by Hogarth himself to account for the crying of the little boy. The *second* state has the girl; in the *third* state, "the rail post is crossed with intersecting lines, and the clearness of the water is much injured."

PLATE IV. ["Night"]. "Invented Painted Engraved & Published by Wᵐ Hogarth March 25, 1738. According to Act of Parⁿᵗ." In the *second* state the ground on which the watchman and freemason stand is much darkened.

Carver and Bowles copied these plates in their "Artistic Caricatures" and they were mezzotinted by Spooner, "Morning" being, as it should be, reversed so as to bring Lord Archer's house (at present a Sporting Club) to the right instead of the left of the picture. In 1730 [1739 ?], the boy in "Morning" was copied by F. Sykes in a print known by collectors as "The Half-Starved Boy."

14⅞ × 18 in.

Strolling Actresses dressing in a Barn.

" Invented, Painted, Engraved, & Publish'd, by Wm Hogarth March the 25, 1738. According to Act of Parliament." 1738.

In the *first* state Flora is greasing her hair in her cap and feathers ; there are three holes in the roof, and Juno's shoe is white. The *second* state is undescribed. In the *third* Flora's cap and feathers are removed ; the roof has but one hole ; and Juno's shoe is black.

21 × 16½ in.

The Foundlings.

"W. Hogarth inv:" "F. Morellon La Cave Sculp London." [1739.]

Headpiece to a Power of Attorney for the Foundling Hospital. There is a copy at the British Museum without the writing. The *third* state is followed by the "Power of Attorney."

8⅛ × 4¼ in.

" *The Enraged Musician.*"

" Design'd, Engrav'd & Publish'd by Wm Hogarth Nov^{br} the 30th 1741. According to Act of Parliament. Price 3 Shillings." 1741.

In the *first* state, the farrier, cats, steeple, play-bill, and dog are absent. The sweep has a Grenadier's cap, and there is a doll placed under the trap of bricks. This state —of which there is a tracing in the Steevens collection at Felbrigge Park—is very rare. In the *second* state, besides the above additions, the farrier's horse is white ; in the *third* state it is *black*. The figure of the Milkmaid was engraved separately in 1824 (February 10) by B. Smith. Samuel Ireland gives an etching of what he professes to be the first design for this print at p. 115, vol. ii. of his *Graphic Illustrations.*

15¼ × 13⅛ in.

"*Martin Folkes, Esq.*"

"Wm Hogarth Pinx^t et Sculp^t"   1742.

"In early impressions, the name of W. Hogarth, etc., is not inscribed" (*Hogarth Illustrated*, iii. 342). At the British Museum there are a touched proof with MS. title, an impression before the letters, an impression with "Martin Folkes Esqr;" only, and the state described above. J. Faber also engraved this in mezzotint in 1742 with "W Hogarth pinx^t 1741. J Faber fecit 1742."

8⅞ × 11 in.

"*The Mystery of Masonry brought to Light by ye Gormagons.*"

"Hogarth inv : et Scul[p]."   [1742.]

"Done from ye Original, Painted at Pekin by Matachauter, Grav'd by Ho-ge, and sold by ye Printsellers of London Paris & Rome." There is a reference table below the Print. The *first* state is without the artist's name, the *second* has it; the *third* has in addition, "London, Printed for Robt Sayer, Map & Printseller, at No. 53 in Fleet Street."

13½ × 8½ in.

"*The Charmers of the Age.*"

[Hogarth.]   [1742.]

Ridicules Desnoyers the Dancing-Master and Signora Barberini. The original print was in the Strawberry Hill Collection. There is a modern copy by R^d. Livesay, published by M^rs. Hogarth and dated March 1, 1782, of which there are three states in the British Museum.

9⅛ × 6⅛ in.

"*Dr. Benjamin Hoadly, Lord Bishop of Winchester.*"

"W. Hogarth, Pinx."   "B. Baron, Sculp."

[1743.]

Sherlock engraved a small oval from this picture in 1759.

11¼ × 13⅞ in.

Characters and Caricaturas.

"W. Hogarth Fecit 1743." [1743.]

Under the design is :—"*For a farthar* (*sic*) *Explanation of the Difference Betwixt* Character & Caricatura *See ye Preface to* Jo^h Andrews." This was the Subscription Ticket for *Marriage A-la-Mode* ; and bears the following receipt :— "Rec^d of Half a Guinea being the first Payment for Six Prints Called MARRIAGE A LA MODE which I Promise to deliver when finish'd on Receiving half a Guinea more. N.B. The price will be one Guinea and an half after the time of Subscribing." "On this print," says Ireland, "*Hogarth* makes the following remark. 'Being perpetually plagued, from the mistakes made among the illiterate, by the similitude in the sound of the words *character* and *caricatura*, I ten years ago endeavoured to explain the distinction by the above print ; and as I was then publishing *Marriage A-la-Mode*, wherein were characters of high life ; I introduced the great number of faces there delineated, (none of which are exaggerated) varied at random, to prevent if possible, personal application when the prints should come out:

"*We neither this nor that Sir Fopling call,*
He's knight o' th' shire, and represents you all."

This, however, did not prevent a likeness being found for each head, for a general character will always bear some resemblance to a particular one'" (*Hogarth Illustrated*, iii. 343).

8 × 8¼ in.

"*The Battle of the Pictures.*"

[Hogarth] 1745.

This was the ticket for the auction of the "Rake's Progress," etc. in 1745 (see pp. 83-5). Above the design is engraved, "*The Bearer hereof is Entitled (if he thinks proper,) to be a Bidder for* Mr. Hogarth's Pictures, *which are to be Sold on the Last day of this Month*" (i.e. February, 1745). See pp. 84-5, and p. 238.

7⅞ × 6⅛ in.

"*Marriage A-la-Mode.*"

Scotin, Baron, Ravenet *ut infra.*   1745.

PLATE I. [The Contract]. "Engraved by G. Scotin" "Invented Painted & Published by Wm Hogarth" "According to Act of Parliament April 1st 1745." In the *second* state a shadow is thrown on the building seen out of window, and on the light parts of the two dogs. In the *third* state all the shadows are strengthened.

PLATE II. [The Breakfast Scene]. "Engraved by B. Baron" "Invented Painted & Published by Wm Hogarth" "According to Act of Parliament April 1st 1745." The *first* state is without the lock of hair on the lady's forehead, or with it, added in Indian ink. In the *second* state, the lock is engraved, and the shadows on the carpet are strengthened.

PLATE III. [The Scene with the Quack]. "Engraved by B. Baron" "Invented Painted & Published by Wm Hogarth" "According to Act of Parliament April 1st 1745." In the *second* state the bow under the nobleman's chin is enlarged, and the shadow on the sole of his right shoe darkened. The girl's cloak and woman's apron are also darker.

PLATE IV. [The Toilet Scene]. "Engraved by S. Ravenet" "Invented Painted & Published by Wm Hogarth" "According to Act of Parliament April 1st 1745." In the *second* state, the front of the curtains of the bed is cross-hatched ; in the *third*, the faces of the Countess and the singer are essentially altered, and the curtains, frames, etc., are also darkened.

PLATE V. [The Death of the Earl]. "Engraved by R. F. Ravenet"[1] "Invented Painted and Published by Wm Hogarth" "According to Act of Parliament April 1st 1745." In the *second* state, says Ireland (*Hogarth Illustrated*, iii. 344), "all the lights, figures on the tapestry, *etc.* are kept down, and the whole print

---

[1] Probably the writing-engraver's mistake. Ravenet's Christian names were François-Simon.

brought to a more still and sombre hue. Woman's eye, eyebrow, and neck strengthened : nostril made wider. Counsellor's leg and thigh intersected with black lines, instead of the delicate marks and dots first inserted. *Third* state ; bears marks of a coarser *burin* than that of Ravenet."

PLATE VI. [The Death of the Countess]. "Engraved by G. Scotin." "Invented Painted & Published by W^m. Hogarth " "According to Act of Parliament April 1st 1745." In the *second* state, says Ireland (*ut supra*, 345), "the whole of the print [is] rendered less brilliant, but more in harmony. Drapery of the dying woman improved." In the *third* state the shadows were strengthened.

Bowles, Sayer and Wilkinson issued cheap copies of the six prints without engraver's name, and with four lines of verse below each. In June 4, 1795—Aug. 1, 1800, the series was engraved in mezzotint for Messrs. Boydell from the original pictures by Richard Earlom. Large woodcuts of the series were issued with the *Weekly Times* and the *London Journal circa* 1847-1850.

17¼ × 13⅞ in.

Portrait of Archbishop Herring.

"William Hogarth Pinx^t" "C. Mosley sculp. according to Act of Parliam^t 1745." "Price 1^s"

1745.

Heading to a speech made by the Archbishop at York, 24 Sep^t. 1745. J. B. Nichols (*Anecdotes*, 331) speaks of a *second* state, "the head only, cut out of the large print, with the words 'Dr Herring, Lord Archbishop of Canterbury' engraved round the frame."

8¼ × 6 in.

Mask and Palette.

[Hogarth.]   [1745.]

Subscription Ticket to "Garrick in the Character of

Richard the Third." Livesay published a copy of it in 1781. (*Genuine Works*, iii. 137). The copy in the British Museum was given by Mrs. Hogarth to S. Ireland, Feby. 1781.

$4\frac{1}{2}$ × 4 in.

" *Taste in High Life.*"

"Painted by Mr. Hogarth." " Published May 24th. According to Act of Parliament." "Sold by Mr. Jarvis in Bedford Court Covent Garden. Price 6*d*. [1746.]

There is another impression which has "Invented & Painted by Wm Hogarth" only. From an Advertisement in the *General Advertiser*, this print was published in May, 1746. In 1798 the picture was copied in stipple for Boydell by Samuel Phillips ($17\frac{1}{4}$ × $14\frac{1}{8}$ in.). The *first* state of this latter is without inscription; the *second* is dated "May 1, 1798"; the third "March 1, 1808."

$10\frac{3}{8}$ × $7\frac{3}{4}$ in.

⁎ *Mr. Garrick in the Character of Richard the* 3^d."

"Painted by Wm Hogarth." "Engrav'd by Wm Hogarth & C. Grignion." "Publish'd according to Act of Parliam^t June 20th. 1746."

1746.

Under the title is—"Shakespear. Act 5. Scene 7." The British Museum has a copy of the unfinished plate. There is also a mezzotint by A. Miller, Dublin, 1746.

20 × $15\frac{1}{4}$ in.

" *Simon Lord Lovat.*"

"Drawn from the Life and Etch'd in Aquafortis by Willm Hogarth." "Publish'd according to Act of Parliament August 25th 1746." 1746.

The *second* state is marked in the left hand corner, "price

1 Shilling." The head and bust was copied in the *Gentle-man's Magazine* for December, 1746, by T. Jefferys. It was also reproduced as a watch paper, with a Calendar.

8¾ × 13⅛ in.

"*Lovat's Ghost on Pilgrimage.*"

[Hogarth ?]   " Publish'd according to Act of Parliament June 15ᵗʰ 1747."   1747.

A Mezzotint. Underneath are six lines beginning, " Disguis'd thro' Life, a Layman at yᵉ Block." A copy by S. Ireland, who asserts that Hogarth assured Dr. Webster of St. Albans it was his own design, faces p. 147 of *Graphic Illustrations*, i. A copy was also published May 1, 1788, by Molton & Co., No. 132, Pall Mall.

12⅞ × 7⅛ in.

Industry and Idleness.

" Design'd & Engrav'd by Wᵐ Hogarth. Publish'd according to Act of Parliament 30 Sep. 1747."   1747.

PLATE I. [The Fellow 'Prentices at their Looms]. In the *first* state the inscription " Plate I " does not occur.

PLATE II. [" The Industrious 'Prentice performing the Duty of a Christian."] "*Second* state : Shadows on the organ, *etc.*, deeper."

PLATE III. [" The Idle 'Prentice at Play in the Church Yard, during Divine Service."] " *Second* state : Lines stronger."

PLATE IV. [" The Industrious 'Prentice a Favourite, and entrusted by his Master."] *Second* state : Mr. West's coat cuff and porter's apron darkened.

PLATE V. [" The Idle 'Prentice turn'd away, and sent to Sea."] *Second* state : " Tender lines in the offing worn out ; broader lines in the faces."

PLATE VI. [" The Industrious 'Prentice out of his Time, & Married to his Master's Daughter."] *First* state : *Goodchild and West*, instead of *West and Goodchild* to which the sign was afterwards altered, in the *second* state. There is a *third* state with further variations.

PLATE VII. ["The Idle 'Prentice return'd from Sea, & in a Garret with a common Prostitute."] *Second* state: The bottom of the coverlid is cross hatched, and the man's hair is black. There are other variations.

PLATE VIII. ["The Industrious 'Prentice grown rich, & Sheriff of London."] "*Second* state. Shadows strengthened."

Plate IX. ["The Idle 'Prentice betray'd by his Whore, & taken in a Night Cellar with his Accomplice."] *Second* state: Woman's face altered; print darkened.

PLATE X. ["The Industrious 'Prentice Alderman of London, the Idle one brought before him, & Impeach'd by his Accomplice."] "*Second* state. Shadows heightened."

PLATE XI. ["The Idle 'Prentice Executed at Tyburn."] "*Second* state. Shadows on the parson's face, pigeon, *etc.* stronger."

PLATE XII. ["The Industrious 'Prentice Lord-Mayor of London."] *Second* state: Coachman's coat darkened; tapestry under Prince and Princess cross-hatched, etc.

Lavater reproduced some of the figures in this series for his *Physiognomy*, 1807. The fat citizen in a tie-wig in Plate VIII., says John Ireland, was copied by Bartolozzi. He also states that there are "tolerably correct copies of the same size." The original sketches (in pen and india ink) were sold at the Strawberry Hill sale in 1842, the purchaser being Mr. H. P. Standly.

v. s.

Head-piece to " The Jacobite's Journal."

[Hogarth ?]   1747.

This headpiece (a wood-cut) was prefixed to Henry Fielding's *Jacobite's Journal*, Nos. 1 to 12, after which, being worn out, it was discarded. The first number is dated Dec. 5, 1747. It was copied by Richard Livesay

(Nov. 27 : 1781); and also in vol. i. p. 149, of S. Ireland's
Graphic Illustrations, 1794. Walpole, and after him H.
P. Standly, had the alleged original sketch in red chalk
for this design.

7½ × 4½ in.

The Stage Coach ; or, Country Inn Yard.

" Price one Shilling " " Design'd and Engrav'd
by W. Hogarth." " Publish'd According to Act
of Parliament. 1747." 1747.

In the *first* state the flag in the background is without the
words "No old Baby"; in the *second* state, the words
appear; in the *third*, they have been obliterated. In the *third*
state the front of the bar is also much darkened. There
is a copy of this print by I. June, entitled "A Country Inn
Yard at the Time of an Election."

11⅝ × 8 in.

" Jacobus Gibbs, Architectus 1747."

" Willm Hogarth delin " " B. Baron Sculp " 1747.

There is a copy of this in the British Museum with architectural back-ground, and the addition of "Architectus,
A.M. and F.R.S." It was engraved, partly in mezzotint
and partly in line by J. M'Ardell, without date, and with
the title " Jacobus Gibbs, Architectus, A.M. and F.R.S."

7⅓ × 10⅛ in.

Hymen and Cupid.

[Hogarth] [1748].

This was the ticket for the Masque of *Alfred*. It was
afterwards intended to be used as the subscription ticket
for the print of " Sigismunda." '£2 *2s* ' is usually written
on the earliest impressions (*Hogarth Illustrated*, iii. 349).

" O the Roast Beef of Old England, &c."

" Painted by W. Hogarth " " Engrav'd by C.

Mosley & W. Hogarth." "Publish'd according
to Act of Parliament March 6th 1749."   1749

In the *second* state the whole of the shadow in the foreground is considerably darkened. . It was copied by J.
June and others. Robert Sayer published a reduction as
a heading to a Cantata by Theodosius Forrest entitled
The Roast Beef of Old England. (See also " *Bibliography,*"
under 1759.)

17¼ × 13½ in.

" *Mr. Hogarth.*"
" Publish'd according to Act of Parliament by R.
Sayer opposite Fetter Lane. Sep^t 29, 1749."

[1749.]

A watch-paper head of Hogarth from *Calais Gate.*

" *Captain Thomas Coram.*"
"Willm Hogarth Pinx^t." " Ja^s McArdell Fecit."

1749.

A three-quarters mezzotint. The *first* state (in the British
Museum) is before the writing; the *second* is as above.
A *third* was published by Laurie and Whittle in 1794. A
full-length copy (13⅜ × 20 in.) was engraved, Dec. 1, 1796,
by W. Nutter, in stipple, and published by R. Cribb of
No. 288, Holborn.

10 × 12⅛ in.

" *John Palmer* 1749."
" W Hogarth Pinx " " B. Baron Sculp."   1749.

This is a little circular portrait under a view of Ecton
Church, Northamptonshire.

2 in. diam.

" *Gulielmus Hogarth.*"
" Se ipse Pinxit et Sculpsit 1749."   1749.

The *first* state is without the writing, and the words " The

Line of Beauty" on the palette. This portrait (says J. B. Nichols, 227) was also mezzotinted by C. Spooner, 1749. In 1795 (June 4), Benjamin Smith engraved it for the Boydells. In this impression the three books are lettered respectively "Shakespeare," "Swift," and "Milton's Paradise Lost;" while the Palette is inscribed—"The Line of Beauty and Grace. W. H. 1745." Besides the copies in the ordinary collections (See "Introductory Note" to this Catalogue), it was engraved by T. Chambers, and then by B. P. Gibbon, for Walpole's *Anecdotes of Painting ;* by Barlow for *Hogarth Illustrated* (1791); by W. Edwards (1829) for the *Family Library ;* by I. Mills for the *Wonderful Magazine* (1808), and by Audinet (May 1, 1794) for Harrison & Co.

10¼ × 13¼ in.

Arms, Bagpipes, etc.
[Hogarth.] [1750.]

Subscription Ticket to the "March to Finchley," with the following form of Receipt :—

"Rec'd of 7ˢ: 6ᵈ : being the whole Payment for a Print Representing a March to Finchly in the year 1746 [*sic*] which I promise to deliver when finish'd on sight hereof. N.B. Each print will be half a Guinea after the Subscription is over."

7¼ × 6¼ in.

"A Representation of the March of the Guards towards Scotland in the Year, 1745."
" Engrav'd by Luke Sullivan." 1750.

Commonly called 'The March to Finchley.' There are several states of this plate. The *first* (in the British Museum) is the etching ; the *second*, the finished plate, is without writing ; the *third* has the following inscription :— "Painted by Willᵐ Hogarth & Publish'd Decᵇʳ 30. 1750. According to Act of Parliament." "A Representation of the March of the Guards towards Scotland, in the year

T

1745." "To His Majesty the King of Prusia, an Encourager of Arts and Sciences! This Plate is most humbly Dedicated." "Engrav'd by Luke Sullivan." In the *fourth* state, the beginning of this inscription is varied :—"Painted, & Publish'd by Willm Hogarth Dec^{br} 30. 1750," etc.; in the *fifth* the date is altered to Dec^{br} 31st (the 30th December having been a Sunday); in the *sixth*, the spelling of "Prussia" is corrected, and the words "Retouched and Improved by Wm Hogarth, republish'd June 12th 1761," are added. The *seventh* and *eighth* states were further worked on. There are three contemporary copies of this print. The figure of the Pie-man was also engraved separately in 1824 (Feb. 10) by Benjamin Smith.

21¼ × 16¼ in.

Archbishop Herring.

"Willm Hogarth Pinxit." "B Baron sculp^t" "Publish'd according to Act of Parliam^t 1750, for S. Austen Bookseller in Newgate Street."

1750.

At the British Museum are impressions of the unfinished print; the print without the letters; and the print as above with arms and title.

11⅛ × 13⅞ in.

"*Beer Street.*"

"Design'd by W. Hogarth" "Publish'd according to Act of Parliament Feb. 1. 1751." Price 1^s."

1751.

There are three quatrains under the plate beginning "Beer, happy Produce of our Isle." In the *first* state, the blacksmith is lifting a Frenchman by the waist-belt; in the *second*, he flourishes a shoulder of mutton, and a pair of figures etc. are added. A copy was issued by Sayer and Bowles.

11¾ × 14 in.

THE FOUR STAGES OF CRUELTY. (Plate III.)
From J. Bell's Woodcut.

"Gin Lane."

"Design'd by W. Hogarth." "Publish'd according to Act of Parliament Feb. 1, 1751. Price 1ˢ.

1751.

The three quatrains begin "Gin cursed Fiend, with Fury fraught." In the earlier impressions, the face of the falling child is plump and white; in the later ones it is wizened and much darkened. A copy was issued by Sayer and Bowles.

11¼ × 14 in.

The Four Stages of Cruelty.

"Design'd by W. Hogarth" "Published according to Act of Parliament Feb. 1. 1751." "Price 1ˢ"

1751.

The price of those on common paper was 1s.; on superior paper 1s. 6d. Under each plate are three quatrains, probably by the Rev. James Townley. The *second* states have the shadows strengthened. There are woodcut copies of Plates 3 and 4 by J. Bell. They deviate from the coppers in certain particulars.

11¼ × 14 in.

"Paul before Felix."

"Design'd and scratch'd in the true Dutch taste by Wᵐ Hogarth." "Publish'd According to Act of Parliament May 1ˢᵗ 1751." 1751.

Given as a receipt for "Paul before Felix," and "Moses brought to Pharaoh's Daughter" with this inscription,—" Recᵈ 5ˢ. being the First Payment for two Prints, one Moses brought to Pharoahs Daughter, the other Paul before Felix which I promise to Deliver when finish'd on the payment of 5 shillings more. N.B. Each Print will be 7ˢ 6ᵈ after the subscription is over." In the *second* state the publication line runs "Design'd & Etch'd in the rediculous manner of Rembrant, by Wᵐ Hogarth" and a diminutive imp is sawing through the leg of St. Paul's stool. The early impressions are stained with bistre, and have Hogarth's palette seal.

13¼ × 9¼.

" *Paul before Felix* " (1).

" Engraved from the Original Painting in Lincoln's Inn Hall, Painted by Wm Hogarth." "and Publish'd by him Feby the 5th 1752."

1752.

Over the above is the text, "And as he reasoned of righteousness, temperance and Judgment to come, Felix trembled" (See next plate).   In the *second* state, a quotation from Dr. Joseph Warton's *Essay on Pope* is engraved at the bottom corners, and the publication line is altered to "Engraved by Wm Hogarth from his Original Painting in Lincoln's Inn Hall & Publish'd as the Act directs, Feb. 5. 1752 "; in the *third* state, the quotation from Warton is omitted. (As to this, see *Genuine Works*, i. 207-13 ; and Warton's *Essay*, 2nd ed. 1762, p. 119 n.)

20 × 15 in.

Paul before Felix (2).

" From the original Painting in Lincoln's Inn Hall, Painted by Wm Hogarth." " Published Feby the 5th 1752." " Engrav'd by Luke Sullivan."   1752.

There is the same text in this as in the preceding plate ; but there are fewer figures.   In the *second* state, the same quotation from Warton as in the foregoing plate is engraved at the bottom corners, and the engraver's name and date of publication are omitted.   In the *third* state, the quotation is omitted.

19¼ × 15 in.

Moses brought to Pharaoh's daughter.

" From the Original Painting in the Foundling

Hospital, Engraved by Willm Hogarth & Luke Sullivan." " Published Feb. 5 1752 according to Act of Parliament." " W. Hogarth pinx^t."

1752.

The *second* state has the same quotation from Dr. Warton as the Paul before Felix (1) and (2) ; in the *third* state, this was omitted. " W Hogarth pinx^t," and " Published according to," etc. were also effaced, and their place supplied by " Published as the Act directs Feb^ry 5, 1752." In the British Museum there is an impression before the writing.

19¾ × 15 in.

Columbus breaking the Egg.
[Hogarth]   [1752.]
Subscription ticket for the *Analysis of Beauty*. The *first* state has the following form of receipt,—" Rec^d
of   five Shillings being the first Payment for a Short Tract in Quarto call'd the Analysis of Beauty ; wherein Forms are consider'd in a new light, to which will be added two Explanatory Prints Serious and Comical, Engraved on large Copper Plates fit to frame for Furniture." N.B. The Price will be rais'd after the Subscription is over. In the *second* state this was burnished off, the plate reduced, and " Design'd & Etch'd by Wm Hogarth Decem 1. 1753 " substituted.

7 × 5⅝ in.

Two Plates to " The Analysis of Beauty."
" Designed, Engraved, and Publish'd by Wm Hogarth, March 5th 1753, according to Act of Parliament."   1753.

In Plate 1 (A Statuary's Yard) the *first* state is distinguished by the words " Et tu Brute" upon the pedestal of Quin in the character of Brutus ; in the *second* state, this inscription is erased. In Plate 2 (A Country Dance), there is a vacant chair under the picture of Henry VIII.; in the *second* state, a sleeping figure occupies the chair, and the chief pair of dancers is considerably altered.

19¼ × 14¼ in.

Frontispiece to " Kirby's Perspective."
" W. Hogarth inv. et delin." " L. Sullivan sculp."

1753.

This was the frontispiece to Joshua Kirby's edition of D'. Brook Taylor's Method of Perspective, 1753. At the top is the word " Frontispiece," and under the plate—" *Whoever makes a* DESIGN *without the Knowledge of* PERSPECTIVE *will be liable to such Absurdities as are shewn in this* Frontispiece." S. Ireland gives a copy of the original drawing for this at p. 134, vol. ii. of his *Graphic Illustrations*, while at p. 158 of vol. i. he reproduces an oil-sketch which he calls the " first thought."

6¾ × 8$\frac{1}{16}$ in.

Crowns, Mitres, Maces, etc.
" Design'd, Etch'd & Publish'd, as the Act directs, by Wm Hogarth, March 20th 1754." 1754.

Subscription ticket to the Election series. It had originally been prepared in 1736 as a head-piece to an inscription expressing the artist's gratitude to the legislature for passing the Act 8 Geo. II. cap. 13. The receipt added at the foot varies in different cases. In the *first* state, it is for " 5'," being part payment for " An Election Entertainment "; in the *second*, " One guinea " for the first payments for the set of four; in the *third*, " 15 " for the first payments for " The Polling," " Canvassing for Votes," and " Chairing the Members."

7¼ × 8¼ in.

Four Prints of an Election.
Hogarth and others (*v. infra*). 1755-8.

PLATE I. (" An Election Entertainment "). " Painted and

the Whole Engraved by Wm Hogarth." "Published
24th Feb^{ry} 1755, as the Act directed." The *first* state
(in the British Museum) is without the writing above
and below. The *second* state, besides the title and
publication line, is inscribed "To the Right Honourable
Henry Fox, &c. &c. &c." In the *third* state, "and
the——" on the flag outside the window is removed,
and a cobweb introduced in the angle of the case-
ment. In the *fourth* state, "the whole" in the publication line is scratched over; and, among other
variations, the fat woman's right arm hangs down
instead of being bent under her apron, seven lemons
near the punch tub in the three previous states are removed; and "Pro Patria" replaces "For our Country"
in the butcher's cap. In the *fifth* state, "the whole"
is restored; in the *sixth* state it is erased once more.
In the *seventh*, it is again effaced.

PLATE II. ("Canvassing for Votes"). "Painted by W.
Hogarth. Engrav'd by C. Grignion." "Published
20th Feb^{ry} 1757. As the Act directs." The *first* state
is without the writing. The *second* state, besides the
title and publication line, is dedicated to Sir Charles
Hanbury Williams. In the *third* state, the lion's teeth
are removed. In the British Museum are three impressions of the plate in progress.

PLATE III. ("The Polling"). "Engrav'd by W. Hogarth
& Le Cave." "Published 20 Feb^{ry} 1758. As the
Act directs." The *first* state is without the writing;
the *second* state, besides the title and publication line,
is dedicated to Sir Edward Walpole. In the *third*
state, the words "Milicia Bill" appear on the coat of
the maimed elector.

PLATE IV. ("Chairing the Members"). "Engrav'd by
W. Hogarth & F. Aviline." "Published 1st Jan^{ry} 1758
as the Act directs.'" It is dedicated to the Honourable
George Hay. In the *second* state, the word "indintur"
[indenture] is written on the scroll hanging out of the
attorney's window.

21¼ × 15¼ in.

The Invasion (Two Plates).

" Design'd and Etch'd by˙ Wm Hogarth " " Publish'd according to Act of Parliament March 8th, 1756." 1756.

> In the early impressions the words "France" and "England" are omitted ; " Plate 1st " and " Plate 2nd " being the only titles. Under each design are twelve lines by David Garrick.
>
> 14¾ × 11½ and 14¼ × 11½ in.

Mr. John Pine.

[Mᶜ‘Ardell.] [*c.* 1756.]

> A mezzotint. The *first* state has no inscription ; below the *second* is—" Mr Pine, Done from an Original Picture painted by Mr Hogarth, in Imitation of Rembrant, By J^s Mᶜ‘Ardell." "sold at the Golden Head the Corner of Southampton Str^t, Cov^t Garden." " Price 2^s " The *third* state is darkened and the "sold," etc., omitted. There is also a head of Pine with " Hogarth pinx^t " and " London" "printed for Geo. Pulley at Rembrandt's head, the corner of Bride Court, Fleet Street," and there is a small copy entitled *Le Bourgmestre Syx, ami de Rembrant.*
>
> 8¾ × 11⅛ in.

Hogarth painting the Comic Muse.

[Hogarth.] 1758.

> In the *second* state at the British Museum, the inscription runs "Wm Hogarth Sergeant Painter to His Majesty. The Face Engrav'd by Wm Hogarth and Publish'd as the Act directs." The *third* state omits "and," and adds after " directs"—" March 29 1758." The *fourth* state omits "The Face Engrav'd by Wm Hogarth." In the *fifth*, "Serjeant Painter " is scratched through, Comedy has the face and mask marked with black, and on the pillar is written, "Comedy 1764." The *sixth* state has nothing but "William Hogarth. 1764." The head in this print

was copied in 1782 by Edner for A. Crayen's translation of Nichols's *Anecdotes*, 1783 (see p. 211); also for Jeffrey of Pall Mall.

13½ × 14⅝ in.

" *The Bench*."

"Design'd & Engrav'd by W. Hogarth" "Publish'd as the Act directs, 4 Sep. 1758." 1758.

Under the design (in addition to "The Bench") is written "Of the different meaning of the Words Character, Cara-catura, and Outrè in Painting and Drawing. Addressed to the Honb^le Coll. T—s—d." On a separate copper is a long explanatory inscription. In the *second* state, the word "Character" appears over the design, and "Addressed," etc. is left out. In the *third* state "Character" is effaced, as is also the King's Arms on the wall, the place of the latter being supplied by eight caricatured heads, and after the word Drawing is added—"This Plate would have been better explain'd had the Author lived a Week longer." A later state omits this, and adds at the end of the explana-tory inscription: "The unfinish'd Groupe of Heads in the upper part of this Print was added by the Author in Octr. 1764: & was intended as a further Illustration of what is here said concerning Character Caracatura & Outrè, He worked upon it the Day before his Death which happened the 26th of that Month."

7¾ × 6⅝ in.

The Cockpit.

"Design'd and Engrav'd by Willm Hogarth" "Publish'd according to Act of Parliament Nov. 5th 1759." 1759.

There is but one state of this print. At the bottom of the design, on an upright oval medallion or token, is a crowing cock; on the ground of the medallion are the words "Royal Sport." The medallion is entitled "Pit Ticket."

14⅝ × 11¾ in.

Frontispiece to " Tristram Shandy," vol. ii.
   "W Hogarth invᵗ." "S. Ravenet Sculpᵗ."

[1759.]

"Vol. 2. page 128." Over the left-hand top-corner is "Frontispiece Vol. 1." A hat and clock are introduced in the *second* state. There is a copy by the same Engraver. Heath and Grignion also reproduced the design.

3⅛ × 5¾ in.

Frontispiece to Joshua Kirby's " Perspective of Archi-tecture."
   "Wᵐ Hogarth, July 1760." "Wᵐ Woollett, sculp." 1760.

Over the design is " Frontispiece." This was also engraved by C. Grignion in 1793; and Samuel Ireland gives a copy of the original design at p. 140, vol. ii. of his *Graphic Illustrations.*

15 × 9 in.

" Huggins."
   " Hogarth pinxᵗ." " Major sculpᵗ " [1760.]

This circular plate was engraved for a translation of Dante which never got beyond the proposal stage. In the *first* state there is no writing, no bust of Ariosto, or inscription " Dante"; in the *second* these are added.

2¾ in. diam.

Frontispiece to " Tristram Shandy," vol. iv.
   " W. Hogarth invᵗ." " F. Ravanet [sic] sculp."

[1761.]

Over the right-hand top corner is " Vol. iv. page 112" There is a copy of this by John Ryland.

3⅛ × 5⅛.

Frontispiece to the Catalogue of Pictures exhibited in Spring Gardens, 1761.

"W. Hogarth inv⁺ et del."   "C Grignion sculp."
Published according to Act of Parliament May
7, 1761."   1761.

> The *second* state has the motto :—"*Et spes & ratio Studiorum in Cæsare tantum.*" JUV. There was another print from this design by the same engraver.
>
> 5¾ × 6⅞ in.

*Tailpiece to the Catalogue of Pictures exhibited in Spring Gardens,*1761.

"W. Hogarth inv⁺ et del."   [1761.]

> The second state has the motto, "*Esse quid hoc dicam ?— vivis quod Fama negatur*"—MART." and the inscription "W. Hogarth inv⁺ C. Grignion sculp. Publish'd according to Act of Parliament, May 7, 1761." The word "Obit," thrice repeated in the *first* state, is altered to "Obiit."
>
> 5¼ × 4½ in.

"*The five orders of Perriwigs as they were worn at the late Coronation, measured Architectonically.*"

[Hogarth.]   1761.

> There is no engraver's name ; and the publication line is "Publish'd as the Act directs Oct⁺ 15, 1761 by W: Hogarth." In the middle of the plate is the notice :— "Least the Beauty of these Capitels [*sic*] should chiefly depend, as usual, on the delicacy of the Engraving, the Author hath Etched them with his own hand." In the *second* state, the second " e " in the word "Advertisement," omitted in the *first* state, is added on the back of one of the figures (the Countess of Northumberland).
>
> 8¼ × 10¼ in.

Time Smoking a Picture.

[Hogarth.]   1761.

> Subscription Ticket for *Sigismunda*.   Upon the upper
> part of the picture frame is a Greek motto ; below the
> design the words—
>
>> "To Nature and your Self appeal,
>> Nor learn of others, what to feel.   Anon :"
>
> Under a broken statue to the right is
>
>> " —As Statues moulder into Worth.   P : W :"
>
> The *first* state is without the word "Crates" prefixed to
> the Greek motto.   The following form of receipt was used
> for *Sigismunda*.   "1761.   Rec^d   of
> half a Guinea being the whole Payment for a Print of
> Sigismonda mourning over the Heart of Guiscardo her
> murder'd Husband, wch I promise to deliver, when finish'd.
> N.B : the price will be 15^s after the Subscription is over."
> 6¼ × 8⅜ in.

*" Credulity,   Superstition,   and   Fanaticism.   A
    Medley."*

" Design'd   and   Engrav'd   by   W^m   Hogarth."
" Published   as   the   Act   directs   March   y^e   15th
1762."   1762.

> Under the title is—" Believe not every Spirit ; but try the
> Spirits whether they are of God : because many false
> Prophets are gone out into the World.   1. John. Ch. 4. V.
> 1."   The title, etc. is on a separate copper.
> 12½ × 14½ in.

" *The Times Plate I.*"

" Designed   &   Engraved   by   W   Hogarth "
" Published   as   the   Act   Directs   Sep^r   7   1762 "

                                                1762.

> In the *first* state, Pitt, afterwards Earl of Chatham, on stilts,
> and in the character of Henry VIII., is blowing up the

flames; in the *second*, the plate has slight variations; in the *third*, a direct portrait of Pitt is substituted for the figure of Henry VIII.

11¼ × 8¼ in.

" *The Farmer's Return.*"
" Wᵐ Hogarth delin." " James Basire. sculp."
1762.

Frontispiece to Garrick's *The Farmer's Return from London.* An Interlude. London: J. & R. Tonson, 1762. There is an impression in the British Museum without the writing. A copy of a somewhat different sketch by Hogarth of Garrick in this piece is given by S. Ireland at p. 171 of vol. i. of his *Graphic Illustrations.*

6 × 7 in.

" *T. Morell, S.T. P.—S.S.A.*"
" W. Hogarth. del," " James Basire, Sculp."
[1762.]

In the later impressions " Thesaurus " and " Ætat 60 " are added. There is an impression without the writing in the British Museum.

5⅞ × 7⅝ in.

" *Henry Fielding, Ætatis XLVIII.*"
" Wᵐ Hogarth delin." " James Basire sculp."
1762.

The *first* state is without frame or ornaments. The print was prepared as a frontispiece to the edition of Fielding's works issued in June, 1762.

Oval. 2⅞ × 3¼ in.

" *John Wilkes, Esqʳ* "
" Drawn from the Life and Etch'd in Aquafortis by Willᵐ Hogarth." " Price 1 Shilling."

" Publish'd according to Act of Parliament
May y⁰ 16.   1763."   1763.

In the later impressions the face was retouched.   There
are many pirated copies of this design.   Hogarth's original
sketch (see note to p. 174) was copied by S. Ireland in vol.
i. of the *Graphic Illustrations*, p. 176.

8⅝ × 12¼ in.

" *The Bruiser, C. Churchill,*" *etc.*

" Design'd and Engraved by Wᵐ Hogarth
Price 1ˢ."   " Publish'd according to Act of
Parliament August 1, 1763."   1763.

The full inscription is—" The Bruiser, C. Churchill (once
the Revᵈ !) in the Character of a Russian Hercules, Regaling himself after having Kill'd the Monster Caricatura that
so Sorely Gall'd his Virtuous friend, the Heaven born
Wilkes.

> " But he had a Club this Dragon to Drub,
> Or he had ne'er don't I warrant ye :"

In the *first* state, " *Lye* 1 " and " *Lye* 5 " on the club are
white, the inscription reads " a *Modern* Hercules," and the
price is 1*s.*   In the *second* state the white knots are shaded,
and " Russian " is substituted for " Modern."   In the *third*
state stronger lines have been drawn across the inscription
on the book marked " A New way to Pay Old Debts," &c.
In the *fourth* state a picture is placed before the palette in
which the figure of Hogarth wears a white hat, and the
price is raised to 1*s.* 6*d.*   In the *fifth* state " N.B." (*i.e.*
North Briton) appears on the club, Hogarth's hat is made
black, and " Dragon of Wantley" is added after the
motto.

10¼ × 13⅛ in.

" *The Weighing House* "

[Engraved by L. Sullivan.]   1763.

Frontispiece to *Physiognomy ; Being a Sketch only of a larger
Work on the same Plan, etc.*   " By the Editor of the

History and Antiquities of Wheatfield in Suffolk" [*i.e.* The
Rev. John Clubbe]. London : Dodsley, 1763. The book
is dedicated to Hogarth. A smaller copy was engraved
by W. W. Ryland for Clubbe's Works.

7⅛ × 8¼ in.

A Witch on a Broomstick.
[Hogarth.]   [1763 ?]

Engraved for a pamphlet against the Hutchinsonians by
Dr. Gregory Sharpe ; but not published. A copy faces
p. 175 of *Graphic Illustrations*, i.

3¼ × 5¼ in.

" *The Bathos, or Manner of Sinking, in Sublime Paintings, inscribed to the Dealers in Dark Pictures.*"
"Design'd and Engrav'd by Wm Hogarth."
" Publishd according to Act of Parliam^t March
3^d 1764."   1764.

There are two medallions below the design. That to the
left, a circle, contains a pyramidal shell with the inscription,
" The Conic Form in wch the Goddess of Beauty was wor-
ship^d by the Ancients at Paphos in ye Island of Cyprus"
(See p. 178)." The other, to the right, an oval, contains a
cone encircled by the line of Beauty. After the sub-title
is a Latin Cross referring to the following engraved note,
"See the manner of disgracing ye most Serious Subjects, in
many celebrated Old Pictures, by introducing Low, absurd,
obscene & often prophane Circumstances into them.'
There are other inscriptions on the plate, and over it is
engraved " Tail Piece."

12¼ × 10¼ in.

" *Satan, Sin, and Death.*"
[Hogarth.]   Engraved by C. Townley.   [1767.]

From *Paradise Lost*, Bk. 2, "and intended (says J. B.

Nichols, *Anecdotes*, 1833, p. 272) to have been published April 16, 1767; but, when a few copies were printed, the plate was destroyed." Five impressions only were known when Nichols wrote. It was etched by T. Rowlandson, "from a Painting in Chiaro Scuro by R. Livesay," and engraved by J. Ogborne, June 1, 1792; and by S. Ireland (*Graphic Illustrations*, i. 178.)

21 × 17 in.

" *The Good Samaritan.* "

" Willm. Hogarth pinxit." "Ravenet & Delatre sculpserunt." " Published, Feby 24th. 1772 by John Boydell Engraver, in Cheapside London."

1772.

Under the design is a smaller one headed "John Boydell excudit;" and the plate is said to be "Engraved from the Original Picture; Painted by William Hogarth Esqr on the Stair Case in St Bartholomew's Hospital."

21 × 16 in.

" *The Pool of Bethesda.* "

" Willm Hogarth pinxit." "Ravenet & Picot sculpserunt." " Published Feby 24th. 1772 by John Boydell Engraver, in Cheapside London."

1772.

Under the design is a smaller one headed "John Boydell excudit;" and the plate is stated to be "Engraved from the Original Picture; Painted by William Hogarth Esq. on the Stair Case in St Bartholomew's Hospital."

21 × 16 in.

" *The Politician.* "

" Willm Hogarth Inv^t " " Etch'd by J : K : Sherwin." " Pub^d as the Act directs by Jane Hogarth, 1775." 1775.

This is said to be "Etch'd from an Original Sketch of

Wm Hogarth's, in the Possession of M^r. [Theodosius] Forrest." The early impressions have "31 October" inserted with a pen. There are also two in the British Museum without the writing, and with the hilt of the sword coming through the coat. The print was copied by J. Mills for *Hogarth Illustrated*, iii. 274.

10$\frac{1}{4}$ × 13 in.

A View of M^r. Ranby's House at Chiswick.
" Publish'd as the Act directs by Jane Hogarth at the Golden-head Leicester Fields 1st May, 1781."   1781.

There is a copy in the British Museum without the writing, but with the manuscript title, "A View of M^r. Ranby the Surgeon's house. Taken from Hogarth's window at Chiswick." It is there dated 1748.

5$\frac{3}{4}$ × 3$\frac{1}{4}$ in.

Four Heads from the Hampton Court Cartoons.
[Hogarth.]   1781.

These were issued by Mrs Hogarth, May 14, 1781. According to Walpole, Sir James Thornhill meant to publish an account of the Cartoons, and an inscription on this plate says,—"As the present plate was found among others belonging to the late Mr Hogarth, it is not impossible but that it might have been engraved by him for his father-in-law Sr James's intended publication." There is an impression before the writing in the British Museum.

13$\frac{3}{4}$ × 8$\frac{1}{4}$ in.

" *Tho. Pellet M.D* ".
" Willm Hogarth Pinx^t." " Chas Hall Sculp."
" Pub^d June 1st 1781 by I. Thane Rupert Street Hay Market."   1781.

3$\frac{1}{4}$ × 4$\frac{1}{4}$ in. (Oval.)

U

" Wm Bullock the Comedian."

" W Hogarth pinx^t " " Chas Hall Sculp." Pub^d
June 1st 1781 by I. Thane Rupert Street, Hay
Market."   1781.

> "From the Original Picture in the Possession of John
> Thane."
>
> 3½ × 4¼ in.

" Hogarth."

" Charles Townley fecit " " Price 5 Shillings "
" Published according to Act of Parliament,
June 1781 and Sold by C. Townley, Arlington
Street, Piccadilly."   1781.

> An oval mezzotint.   Under the name is, "From an
> Original Portrait begun by Weltdon, And finished by Him-
> self " [*i.e.* Hogarth].   Late in the Possession of the Rev^d
> Mr Townley."   The *second* state is without " Price 5
> Shillings," and with Hogarth's name and " Charles Town-
> ley fecit " in larger script.
>
> 10⅞ × 11½ in.

Nine Prints for " Hogarth's Tour."

" R^d Livesay Fecit."   " Publish'd as the Act
directs Novr 27th, 1781, by R^d Livesay at
Mrs Hogarths Leicester Fields."

> The prints are (1) "Frontispiece," (2) "A View from
> Rochester Bridge," (3) "Upnor Castle," (4) "Breakfasting,
> &c.," (5) "The Embarcation," (6) The Town of Queen-
> borough," (7) "The Monument of a Spanish Embasador, in
> Minster Church, in the Island of Shepey," (8) "Monument
> of the Lord Shorland in Minster Church," and (9) "Tale-
> Piece.   Nos. (2) and (7) are designed by Scott ; No. (5) by
> Scott and Hogarth ; the rest are by Hogarth.   They were
> issued by Livesay with the text (see p. 36) in 1782.   As

regards the "Frontispiece" and "Tailpiece" Livesay says,
"The frontispiece of this work (M‍ʳ SOMEBODY) was designed by Hogarth, as emblematical of their journey, *viz.*
that it was a short tour by land and water, backwards
and forwards, without head or tail." "The tail-piece
(M‍ʳ NOBODY) [is] of the same whimsical nature with the
first ; the whole being intended as a burlesque on historical
writers recording a series of insignificant events entirely
uninteresting to the reader." J. B. Nichols ("Anecdotes,"
p. 343) gives the following variations : *First* state : plates
printed in outline, and afterwards coloured in imitation of
the original drawings ; descriptions filled in with a pen.
Second state : plates tinted, but descriptions written in.
Third state : writing in open hair lines. *Fourth* state :
letters filled up.

v. s.

"*Mr. Ben : Read.*"

"Hogarth Delin‍ᵗ" "R‍ᵈ Livesay Fecit." "Publish'd, Nov‍ʳ 27, 1781, by R‍ᵈ Livesay at
M‍ʳˢ : Hogarths, Leicester Fields." 1781.

Under the name is the sub-title, "A Member of Hogarth's
Club at the Bedford Arms Tavern. Drawn by Him about
the Year 1757." In the *first* state the writing is in open
hair lines.

10⅛ × 11 in.

"*Mr. Gabriel Hunt.*"

"Hogarth Delin‍ᵗ" "R‍ᵈ Livesay Fecit." "Publish'd, Nov‍ʳ 27 ; 1781, by R‍ᵈ Livesay, at
M‍ʳˢ Hogarths Leicester Fields."

Under the name is the sub-title, "A Member of Hogarth's
Club at the Bedford Arms Tavern. Drawn by Him about
the Year 1733." In the *first* state the writing is in open
hair lines.

7⅝ × 10¾ in.

"Armes for the Foundling Hospital." Wm *Hogarth*
    Inv^t : 1747."

" Publish'd, Decr 22 ; 1781, by R^d Livesay, at
    Mrs Hogarth's Leicester Fields."

> This is said to be "Engraved from the Original, in the
> Collection of the Earl of Exeter." There is an impression
> at the British Museum with the date " July 31, 1781."
> 6 × 6 in.

Lord Melcombe and Ld Winchilsea.

"W. Hogarth del^t," "F. Bartolozzi Sculp^t" "Publish'd Dec 22 ; 1781 by R^d Livesay at
Mrs Hogarth's Leicester Fields."   1781.

> An impression faces p. 150 of *Genuine Works,* iii.
> 7¼ × 6 in.

Shrimp Girl.

" W. Hogarth pinx." " F. Bartolozzi sculp."
" Engravd from an Original Sketch in Oil
by Hogarth, in the possession of Mrs Hogarth "
" Published Dec. 24, 1781, by R. Livesay."

> Impressions later than that described above have the title
> "Shrimps !" " Publish'd March 25th ; 1782 by Jane
> Hogarth & R^d Livesay Leicester Fields."
> 6⅝ × 8¼ in.

Parson's Head.

" Hogarth Delin^t " " Livesay Fecit." [1781 ?]

> Supposed to have been intended for one of the series of
> " The Happy Marriage," p. 110. It is also given in
> *Genuine Works,* iii. 158.
> 3⅝ in. diam.

The Match-maker and *Old Maid* (Two Plates).
Hogarth Delin^t" Livesay Fecit" [1781 ?]

> Figures from the first design for the *Rake's Progress.* Also
> given in *Genuine Works*, iii. 140, with the publication line
> —"Publish'd by J. Nichols and Co. Oct. 1. 1816." The
> two figures were combined in one plate by J. Mills for
> *Hogarth Illustrated*, iii. 276, and "Published March
> 1798."
>
> 4¼ × 5¾ in.

Head of Solsull.
" Hogarth del^t" "S. I. fec^t 1781" Publish'd
March 1st 1786, by W. Dickenson, N° 158,
New Bond S^t" 1781.

> " Solsull a maker of Punches for ye Engravers from a Sketch
> by Hogarth in the possession of Sam. Ireland." The
> *second* state is without these eleven words (J. B. Nichols,
> *Anecdotes*, 343).

" *Debates on Palmistry.*"
[Hogarth.] Etched by Joseph Haynes. 1782.

> *First* state, before the writing; *second* state, lettered "A
> Consultation of Physicians;" *third* state, "Debates on
> Palmistry."
>
> 13⅞ × 10¼ in.

" *The Staymaker.*"
[Hogarth.] Etched by Joseph Haynes.
1782.

> The first state is the proof before the writing.
>
> 13⅞ × 10¾ in.

Taylor and Death.
" Hogarth Delin^t" " R^d Livesay Fecit " " Pub-

lish'd March 1 1782 by R^d Livesay at
Mrs Hogarth's Leicester Fields London.

1782.

Taylor is buried at Deptford. Two sketches from the
collection of Mr. Morrison. There is also an epitaph by
Hogarth published with the same date. In the *first* state,
the letters are in hair lines. There are reduced copies in
Genuine Works, iii. 160.

14¼ × 10 in.

" *The Right Honb^le Ja^s Caulfield Earl of Charle-
mount,*" etc.

" From an original Portrait by Hogarth in the
possession of Mr Samuel Ireland etched by
Jos^h Haynes Pupil to the late Mr Mortimer."
" Pub^d as the Act directs. Mar. 19th 1782 "

1782.

There is a proof before the writing in the British Museum.
6¼ × 7¾ in.

" *The Right Honble Henry Fox, Lord Holland.*"

" From an original Portrait in Oil by Hogarth, in
the Possession of Mr, Saml. Ireland, etched by
J. Haynes, Pupil to the late M^r. Mortimer."
" Pub^d as the Act directs Mar. 19th, 1782."

1782

There is a proof before the writing in the British Museum.
6¼ × 7¾ in.

" *Hogarth's Crest.*"

" Hogarth Pinx^t." " R. L. Fec^t." " Publish'd

April 23^d; 1782, by R^d. Livesay at M^{rs}. Hogarth's, Leicester Fields." 1782.

See p. 178.

9¼ × 12¼ in.

" *Eta Beta PY.*" (*Invitation Card.*)

"Published as the Act directs, August 1st, 1782.

1782.

This, says Nichols, *Biographical Anecdotes*, 1782, p. 328, was engraved by J. Cary. See also page 56 of the same work, in the title-page of which it first appeared, being also reproduced in the edition of 1785. The "Mr. King" invited to the "Mitre" in Fleet Street was Dr. Arnold King, who selected the texts which garnish the Apprentice Series.

3¼ × 2½ in.

" *Hudibras and Sidrophel.*"

"Painted by W. Hogarth" [?]. Engraved by Thom. Gaugain." 1782.

The publication line is—"Published Octr 1st 1782 by T. Gaugain, No. 4 Little Compton Street Soho London." The print is in colours.

13⅜ × 11 in.

' *Orator Henley christening a Child.*"

"Hogarth pinx^t." "S. Ireland fecit." "Publish'd March 1, 1786, by W. Dickenson, No. 158, New Bond S^t." 1785.

"Etch'd by Saml Ireland from an Original Sketch in Oil in his possession by Hogarth;" and dedicated to Francis Grose, the antiquary. A smaller copy by Jane Ireland was also etched for vol. i. of the *Graphic Illustrations*, p. 135.

10⅝ × 12 in

" *W^m. Hogarth.*"

" Hogarth pinx^t." " Published March 1st, 1786,
by W. Dickenson, No. 158, New Bond Street."
" Etchd by Saml Ireland from an Original Portrait in oil by Hogarth in his possession."

[1786 ?]

After the name comes, " died Octr 26th 1764. Aged 67."
A smaller copy of this portrait by the same engraver faces
p. 1, vol. i., of S. Ireland's *Graphic Illustrations*, 1794.
7 × 7⅞ in.

" *Sr James Thornhill.*"

" Hogarth pinx^t." " S. I. fecit.   1786.
" Publish'd March 1st, 1786, by W. Dickenson,
No. 158, New Bond Street.

" Etch'd by S. Ireland from a portrait in oil the same size
in his possession." " By Hogarth." The same etching,
cut down, faces p. 86 of *Graphic Illustrations*, i.
6⅞ × 7⅝ in.

Miss Rich [?]

" Painted by William Hogarth." " Engraved by
Martha Knight." " London, Pub^d March 1,
1786, by Martha Knight, Brompton."   1786.

Miss Rich was the daughter of Rich, the comedian. Some
impressions have—" From an Original Sketch in the Collection of Mrs. Hogarth." That lady, it should be added,
was wont to speak of it " as a study from a Charity-girl of
St. Martin's parish." (*Genuine Works*, iii. 171*.) In 1877
this sketch was beautifully mezzotinted by the late Samuel
Cousins.
Oval, 3½ × 4½ in.

A Landscape.

" Hogarth pinx^t." " S. Ireland fecit."

"Publish'd March 1st, 1786, by W. Dickenson,
N°. 158, New Bond S^t."   1786.

"Etch'd by Saml Ireland, from an original Picture in his
possession said to be the only Landscape ever painted by
Hogarth."

10⅞ × 7½ in.

" *A Shepherd Boy.*"
" Hogarth del^t."   "Sam. Ireland fecit."
" Publish'd March 1st, 1786, by W. Dickenson,
N°. 158, New Bond S^t."   1786.

" From an original Sketch by Hogarth in the Collection of
Sam. Ireland," being a copy of a chalk sketch of a figure
designed for George Lambert.

8 × 6⅛ in.

" *Theodore Gardelle.*"
"S. Ireland, fecit."   "Published April 1, 1786."
                                            1786.

The sketch was by Mr. Richards; it was only "touch'd
on" by Hogarth. The *first* state has a long account of
this murderer. In the *second*, which was published May 1,
1788, by Molton and Co., 132, Pall Mall, there is a short
inscription; in the third there is no letterpress. An impression faces p. 172 of *Graphic Illustrations*, i.

2⅝ × 3⅞ in.

" *Jack in an Office or Peter Necessary, etc.*"
" Hogarth del^t."   "Saml Ireland fecit."
" London Publish'd April 1st, 1786 by W. Dickin-
son, N°. 158, New Bond Street."   "Price 6^d."
                                            1786.

8¼ × 7¼ in.

Head of Diana.

[Hogarth.] 1786.

" Publish'd April 1ˢᵗ 1786 by W. Dickenson, Nº 158 New Bond Street."

" Etch'd by Samˡ Ireland from an Original Portrait in oil in his possession by Hogarth." There is also an impression in *Graphic Illustrations*, i. 170.

5½ × 6¼ in.

A Black Girl.

[Hogarth.] " Publish'd April 1, 1786, by W. Dickenson, Nº. 158, New Bond Sᵗ. 1786.

" Etch'd by Sam. Ireland from an original Sketch in Oil in his possession by Hogarth." There is also an impression by S. Ireland in *Graphic Illustrations*, i. 169.

5¼ × 6¼ in.

Gamble's Book Plate.

[Hogarth.] 1786.

" London, published April 1ˢᵗ, 1786, by W. Dickinson, Nº. 158, New Bond Sᵗ.

Copied in *Graphic Illustrations*, i. 7*, and in *Genuine Works*, ii. 20.

2⅛ × 2⅝ in.

" *Characters who frequented Button's Coffee-house about the year* 1730."

" Hogarth delᵗ " " S Ireland fecit " [1786.]

" Published April 1ˢᵗ 1786, by W Dickenson, Nº. 158, New Bond Street."

Four plates containing portraits of Daniel Button, Addison, Folkes, Arbuthnot, Count Viviani, Garth, Pope, etc. Impressions face pp. 25, 31, 34, and 38 of *Graphic Illustrations*, i.

v. s.

"*Jenny Cameron.*"

"Hogarth Pinx'." "Published as the Act directs
by J. Clarke, No. 291, Strand, February 8th,
1788." 1788.

5⅜ × 7⅛ in., oval.

"*Justice Welch.*"

[W. Hogarth pinx'.] "S. I. sculp." 1788.
"London, Publish'd May 1st. 1788, by Molton &
C°. 132, Pall Mall."

"From an Original Sketch by Hogarth in the Collection
of Sam'. Ireland 1781. The portrait was began and
finish'd within an hour by which a Considerable bet was
Won." Another impression faces p. 155 of *Graphic Illustrations*, i.

4 × 3¼ in.

Ticket for Milward's Benefit.

"Etch'd by S. Ireland from a very scarce Print
by Hogarth in his Collection."
"London. Publish'd 1st May, 1788, by Molton
and Co., 132 Pall Mall."

Another impression faces p. 98 of *Graphic Illustrations*, i.
4 × 3⅛ in.

Fat Man upset like a Turtle.

"Hogarth Delin'." "Livesay Fecit." "Published
Oct^r, 1788, by Thos: King; New Broad Street."
1788.

An impression faces p. 159 of *Genuine Works*, iii.
8¼ × 5¼ in.

"*The Times Plate II*" [unfinished]

"Designed & Engraved by W. Hogarth." "Publish'd May 29; 1790, by J & J. Boydell, Cheapside, & at the Shakespeare Gallery Pall Mall London."   1790

> The *first* state is said by J. B. Nichols, *Anecdotes*, 341, to be before the usual writing, and with the line of publication only, in hair lines. There is one without any writing in the British Museum. The publication of *North Briton*, N°. 17, was the proximate cause of this plate. The central effigy represents George III., *à la* Ramsay, whose angular method is typified by the stiff folds of the drapery and by the plumb line. Bute regulates the distribution of the stream which issues from the base of the statue, but a special and particular cascade falls from Aquarius upon a laurel labelled "Culloden." In front Fox is tumbling away the Dutch horticulture of previous reigns, but his efforts are embarrassed by a roller marked £1,000,000,000 (? National Debt). To the left Parliament, among whose ranks Pitt's long gun and gouty legs are conspicuous, are firing volleys at the dove of peace ; while to the right Wilkes and the Cock Lane Ghost forlornly occupy the pillory. Behind these, "Dr. Cant, Man Midwife" (Archbishop Secker) is confirming two adults, and up the façade of the Society of Arts is being slowly hoisted a palette inscribed "Premium." Hospitals and other buildings are rising in the background. These are the chief features of the design ; but many of its allusions, unexplained at the date of issue, remain obscure.
>
> 11⅝ × 9¼ in.

"*Beggar's Opera, Act III.*"

"Painted by Wm Hogarth." "Engraved by Wm Blake." "From the original Picture, in the Collection of his Grace the Duke of Leeds." "Publish'd July 1st 1790, by J. & J. Boydell,

Cheapside, & at the Shakspeare Gallery Pall
Mall London." 1790

Under the title is, "When my hero in Court appears, &c."
The states are thus given in J. B. Nichols (*Anecdotes*, 323)
First state, etching; *second*, finished proof before writing;
third, open letters; *fourth*, letters filled up.

21¼ × 15¾ in.

Drunken Party.

[Hogarth.]   Cheesman sculpt. 1790
Published Oct. 1, 1790, by E. Walker, No. 7,
Cornhill.

16 × 13 in.

Four small Prints of Lord Lovat's Trial.

"Published Aug' 1 1791 by W Birch, Hampstead
Heath " 1791

From sketches belonging to Horace Walpole.
v. s.

Two Soldiers fighting.

" Publish'd Oct 1, 1791, by W. Birch, Hampstead
Heath from a Drawing by Hogarth." 1791

3¼ × 2¼ in.

" Conversation"

"Published Oct 1, 1791, by W. Birch, Hampstead
Heath." 1791

" From a drawing by Hogarth."
3½ × 2¼ in.

" *The Indian Emperor, or the Conquest of Mexico ;
    Act 4, Scene 4.*"

" Painted by Wm Hogarth."   " Engrav'd by Robt
    Dodd."   1792
" Publish'd Jan' 1. 1792, by J. & J. Boydell,
Cheapside, & at the Shakspeare Gallery Pall
Mall."

> " As performed in the year 1731, at Mr. Conduit's, Master
> of the Mint, before the Duke of Cumberland &c." " From
> the original Picture in the Collection of Lord Holland."
> The company are children,—" Cortez " being Lord Lemp-
> ster ; " Cydaria," Lady Caroline Lenox ; " Almeria," Lady
> Sophia Fermor ; and " Alibeck," Miss Conduit, afterwards
> Lady Lymington. Among the audience are the Duke of
> Cumberland, the Princesses Mary and Louisa, Lady Delo-
> raine, her daughters, the Duke and Duchess of Richmond,
> the Earl of Pomfret, the Duke of Montague, Tom Hill
> (or Captain Poyntz) and (on the stage) Dr. Desaguliers. In
> *Hogarth Illustrated*, ii, 331, is a key-plate to this print.
>   21 × 16 in.

" *Pisces, One of the Signs in the Zodiac.*"
" W. Hogarth Sculp^t circa annum 1730."   [1792.]

> Impressions from nine quadrille fish engraved on by
> Hogarth.   Three others, obtained from Mary Lewis, were
> published by J. Ireland as " A Tail-piece " to vol. iii. of
> *Hogarth Illustrated*, 377, which he thus explains :—" To
> enter into the spirit of the last article, the reader must be
> informed that *Hogarth* never played at cards ; and that
> while his wife and a party of friends were so employed, he
> occasionally took the quadrille fish, and cut upon them
> scales, fins, heads, *etc.* so as to give them some degree of
> character."

" *Sigismunda* " (N° 1).
" Hogarth Pinx^t " " Dunkarton Sculp^t " " London,

Published Feb 1ˢᵗ 1793, by T. B. Freeman & Cᵒ Strand, & Sold by Dickenson, New Bond Street, & Walker, Cornhill." 1793

Underneath the name is, " The original Picture in Oil [*i.e.* the original sketch] by the late Mʳ Wᵐ Hogarth, and the Drawing from which this Print is made of the same size are both in the Collection of Mʳ Samˡ Ireland, of Norfolk Street, who purchased them of Mʳˢ Hogarth in 1781. The Drawing was made by Mʳ Edwᵈ Edwards, Associate of the Royal Academy, & finished in April 1764 under the inspection of Mʳ Hogarth, from whose pencil it received its last finishing touches about six months before his death. From this Drawing Mʳ Basire, the Engraver, began a Print but the death of Mʳ. Hogarth prevented its being finished." Basire's outline was issued May 5, 1790. There are three states of Dunkarton's print :—the *first* being the unfinished etching ; the *second*, the same with the dress more finished ; the *third*, the finished print.

14⅝ × 13⅓ in.

" *Sealing the Sepulchre.*"
" W. Hogarth pinxᵗ " " I. Jenner del. et fecit."
1794
" London. Publish'd Jan 1. 1794, by A Molteno, . . Nᵒ 76, Sᵗ James's Street."

A mezzotint from the Altar Piece of St. Mary Redcliffe, Bristol. Nichols (*Anecdotes*, 1833) dates this 1790.

20 × 21 in.

" *The Resurrection of Christ.*"
" W. Hogarth pinxᵗ." " I. Jenner del. et fecit."
1794
" London. Publish'd Jan 1. 1794 by A. Molteno, . . . Nᵒ 76 Sᵗ James's Street."

A mezzotint from the Altar Piece of St. Mary Redcliffe,

Bristol. The picture was also engraved by C. Grignion, March 1798, for vol. iii. of *Hogarth Illustrated* with the title of "The Sepulchre." Nichols (*Anecdotes*, 1833,) dates this 1790.

20½ × 21 in.

Hardy's Shop Card.
[Hogarth ?]   [1794.]

A Goldsmith's card in Callot's style,—copy of which faces p. 3 of *Graphic Illustrations*, i.

2⅝ × 2 in.

Ellis Gamble's Shop Card.
[Hogarth.] "A. M. Ireland sculp."   [1794.]

See p. 16, and *Graphic Illustrations*, i. 8.

5¾ × 7¼ in.

Shop Bill for "Mary & Ann Hogarth."
[Hogarth ?]   [1794.]

A copy marked "W Hogarth del⟙." and "J. I sc." faces p. 15 of *Graphic Illustrations*, i. There is an impression of the original bill in the British Museum.

4⅛ × 3⅝ in.

A Ticket for the School of Tiverton, Devonshire.
"W. Hogarth scul."   [1794.]

Copied in *Graphic Illustrations*, i. 18 by "A. M. I[reland]." There is one of the original tickets in the British Museum.

6 × 4¼ in.

A Ticket for the Benefit of Spiller the Player.
[Hogarth.] "S. I[reland] sc."   [1794.]

Copied in *Graphic Illustrations*, i. 62 and in *Genuine Works*, ii. 69.

5¼ × 4 in.

Two Prints for Paradise Lost. (Books i. and iii.)
  "Wm Hogarth In^v. et Sculp^t." [1794.]

> There are copies by Jane Ireland at pp. 79 and 82 of
> *Graphic Illustrations,* i.
> 3 × 5⅓ in.

Ticket for James Figg.
  "Will. Hogarth f^t." [1794.]

> With Inscription. A copy by A. M. I[reland] faces p. 89
> of *Graphic Illustrations,* i.
> 4¼ × 6¾ in.

The Discovery.
  [Hogarth ?]

> " *Qui color albus erat, nunc est contrarius albo.*" A Copy by
> S. Ireland faces p. 112 of *Graphic Illustrations,* i.
> 7¼ × 6 in.

Character and Caricatura.
  "Hogarth fecit 1758" "Jane Ireland fc."
  [1794.]

> Copy of a pen-and-ink sketch made for Mr. Townley which
> appears in *Graphic Illustrations,* i. 167.

"*Sketches from Pen & Ink Drawings.*"
  [Hogarth ?] "J. I. fecit." [1794.]

> Faces p. 114 of *Graphic Illustrations,* i. One of the
> sketches is entitled "hearing void of attention."
> v. s.

"*Sigismonda*" (No. 2).
  "Painted by Willm Hogarth." "Engraved by
  Benjn Smith." "Published June 4, 1795, by J.

& J. Boydell, at N° 90, Cheapside ; & at the Shakespeare Gallery Pall-Mall."   1795.

"From the Original Picture, in the Collection of Aldⁿ Boydell." Underneath the title are eight lines from Hogarth's *Epistle to a Friend* (see p. 160 n.).

16¼ × 12⅞ in.

" *Enthusiasm Delineated* "

"W. Hogarth, inv^t." "I. Mills sculp^t" "Published Novr 12th 1795 by John Ireland, N° 3 Poets Corner, Palace Yard, Westminster."

1795.

Under the design are various explanatory notes "copied from Hogarth's hand-writing beneath the Original Print," as to which, see p. 165. Above it is engraved—"Hogarth's First Thought for The Medley. Copied from a very curious Print designed and engraved by Hogarth, of which there are only two Impressions, both of them in the possession of John Ireland—March 15th 1796 ☞ After taking the above Impressions, Hogarth changed the point of his Satire from the superstitious absurdities of popery, and ridiculous personification delineated by ancient Painters, to the popular credulities of his own day, erased or essentially altered every Figure except two, and on the same piece of copper, engraved the plate now in the possession of Messrs. Boydell, entitled 'Credulity, Superstition and Fanaticism, a Medley.'" Beyond the artist's and engraver's names and "Published by J. Ireland Novr 12th 1795," the *first* state has no writing; the *second* is that described above; in the *third*, the writing is put in neatly by the writing engraver. The design was also reduced by I. Mills for *Hogarth Illustrated*, iii., where it faces p. 233. In the same volume, there is a plate by Mills of "References to the Figures in Hogarth's Enthusiasm Delineated."

12¼ × 14 in.

Sketches of Quin and Garrick.

[Hogarth.] " Published 12th May, 1797, by Robert Laurie & James Whittle, N° 53 Fleet Street, London." An impression faces p. 280 of *Genuine Works*, ii. 1797.

From a Drawing belonging to Mr. Stevenson of Norwich.
13¼ × 9⅝ in.

" *Mrs. Hogarth.*"

" Hogarth pinx^t." " Ryder dir^t " " Pub^d for S. Ireland, June 1, 1797." 1797.

Faces p. 4 of *Graphic Illustrations*, ii.
4⅞ × 6¼ in.

" *Lavinia Fenton, afterwards Dutchess of Bolton.*"

" Hogarth pinx^t." " C. Apostool sculp^t." " Pub^d. for S. Ireland June 1, 1797." 1797.

Faces p. 49 of *Graphic Illustrations*, ii. There is a proof before letters in the British Museum. It was also engraved by Cook, May 1, 1807 (*Genuine Works*, ii. *287).
4¼ × 5⅛ in.

" *Painters Room.*"

" Hogarth pinx^t." " Ryder dir^t." " Pub^d for S. Ireland June 1 1797."

Faces p. 97 of *Graphic Illustrations*, ii.
4⅛ × 5¾ in.

" *Ill Effects of Masquerades.*"

" Hogarth pinx^t." " Le Cœur sculp." " Pub^d for S. Ireland June 1, 1797 " 1797.

Faces p. 98 of *Graphic Illustrations*, ii.
5½ × 4½ in.

"*Heidegger*"

"W. H. Delin."   "I. M[ills] sc."   "Published
by John Ireland Dec' 1797"   1797.
Represents Heidegger in a rage (see *Hogarth Illustrated*,
iii. 323, where it first appeared).
5⅛ × 3⅞ in.

"*Variety*"

"Published March 1798, for John Ireland Poets
Corner, Palace Yard, Westminster."   1798.
A serpentine candlestick which forms the vignette to the
title-page of vol. iii. of *Hogarth Illustrated*.

"*Le Basir* [*Baiser*] *Rendu*."

"W. H. del"
A woodcut, with the reference "Vide Fontaine's Tales,
p. 131," which occurs at p. xxi of *Hogarth Illustrated*,
iii.

"*The Vase*"

"W. Hogarth delin'"   "I Mills sculp'"   "Published March 1798"   1798.
Faces p. 147 of *Hogarth Illustrated*, iii.

"*Square & Round Heads*"

"W. Hogarth. Inv'"   "I : Mills. Sculp'"   "Published March 1798."   1798.
Faces p. 153 of *Hogarth Illustrated*, iii.
3¼ × 5¼ in.

"*The Savoyard Girl*."

"W. Hogarth pinx'."   "G. Sherlock sculp'."   "Published as the Act directs by G. Sherlock, March
13, 1799."   1799.
"From the Original of the same size in the possession of
S. Edwards, Esq., Beaufort Buildings, Strand."
13¼ × 17¼ in.

" *Lady Thornhill*"

" Hogarth pinx^t." " Le Cœur sc^t." " Pub^d. for S. Ireland May 1, 1799." 1799.

Faces p. 12 of *Graphic Illustrations*, ii.

4⅞ × 6¾ in.

" *M^r Ja^s.* [John] *Thornhill*."

" Hogarth pinx^t." " Whesell sc^t " " Pub for S. Ireland May 1, 1799." 1799.

Faces p. 14 of *Graphic Illustrations*, ii.

4¼ × 5⅜ in.

" *Concert Ticket*."

" W. Hogarth Inv." [?] " Jane I[reland] sculp."

" Pub. for S. Ireland May 1, 1799." 1799.

" Mary's Chappel " " Five at Night " Faces p. 43 of *Graphic Illustrations*, ii.

5¼ × 4⅞ in.

" *Design for a Shop Bill*."

" Hogarth pinx^t " " Merigot sculp^t "

" Pub. for S. Ireland May 1. 1799" 1799.

Faces p. 44 of *Graphic Illustrations*, ii.

6⅛ × 5⅛ in.

Two Sides of a " *Sign for a Paviour*."

" Hogarth pinx^t " " J. I. sc^t " " Pub. for S Ireland May 1. 1799" 1799.

Face pp. 46 and 47 of *Graphic Illustrations*, ii.

4¼ × 4¼ in.

" *Rosamond's Pond*."

" Hogarth Pinx^t." " Merigot Sc^t." " Pub^d. for S. Ireland, May 1, 1799." 1799.

Faces p. 57 of *Graphic Illustrations*, ii.

6¼ × 4¼ in.

" Tho[s] Rich Esq[r]. and family "
  " Hogarth del[t] "   " T Ryder sc[t] "   " Pub. for
  S. Ireland May 1, 1799."   1799.

> Faces p. 62 of *Graphic Illustrations*, ii.
> 5⅜ × 4¼ in.

" Gov[r] Rogers & family "
  " Hogarth pinx[t] "   " Skelton sculp[t] "   " Published
  for S. Ireland May 1. 1799."   1799.

> Faces p. 65 of *Graphic Illustrations*, ii.
> 5¼ × 4⅛ in.

*" Garden Scene at Cowley the residence of the late
  Tho[s] Rich Esq[r]."*
  " Hogarth pinx[t] "   " Skelton sculp[t] "   " Pub. for
  S. Ireland May 1. 1799"   1799.

> Faces p. 68 of *Graphic Illustrations*, ii.
> 5¼ × 4⅜ in.

" Scene in a Hay-field "
  " Hogarth del[t] "   " Brome sc[t] "   " Pub for
  S. Ireland May 1 1799 "   1799.

> Faces p. 71 of *Graphic Illustrations*, ii., and copied again
> by T. Cook in *Genuine Works*, iii. 101.
> 6 × 4¼ in.

" Falstaff examining his recruits."
  " Hogarth pinx[t]."   " Ryder sc."   " Pub. for
  S Ireland, May 1. 1799 "   1799.

> Faces p. 72 of *Graphic Illustrations*, ii., and is dedicated to
> Mrs. Garrick (who owned the picture).
> 5¼ × 4½ in.

"*John Dennis the Critic*"

" Hogarth del'." " Pub. for S. Ireland May 1.
1799 " 1799.

Faces p. 78 in *Graphic Illustrations*, ii. Over the head is
written, " M^r. D——s ÿ Critick," in Hogarth's handwriting
(says Ireland).
$3\frac{3}{8} \times 4\frac{1}{4}$ in.

" *Sleeping Shepherd.*"

" Hogarth del^t " " J. I sc^t " " Pub. for
S. Ireland May 1, 1799." 1799.

Faces p. 94 of *Graphic Illustrations*, ii.
7×5 in.

Female Curiosity.

" Hogarth pinx^t " " T. Ryder sculp^t "
" Pub. for S. Ireland May 1, 1799." 1799.

Faces p. 96 of *Graphic Illustrations*, ii.
$5\frac{1}{4} \times 4\frac{1}{4}$ in.

" *Auction of Pictures, etc.*"

" Hogarth pinx^t " " Le Cœur sc^t."
" Pub. for S. Ireland, May 1, 1799." 1799.

Faces p. 101 of *Graphic Illustrations*, ii.
$7\frac{1}{8} \times 5$ in.

" *Lady Pembroke* "

" Hogarth pinx^t " " T. Ryder fc^t " " Pub for
S. Ireland May 1, 1799." 1799.

Faces p. 102 of *Graphic Illustrations*, ii.
$4 \times 4\frac{7}{8}$ in.

" *Hazard Table*"
" Hogarth del᭄ "   " Le Cœur sc."
" Pub. for S. Ireland May 1. 1799."   1799.
> "from ỹ original drawing."   A copy faces p. 104 of
> *Graphic Illustrations*, ii.
>
> 6¼ × 4¼ in.

" *Conversation in the manner of Van Dyck.*"
" Hogarth pinxᵗ."   " Barlow sculpᵗ."
" Pub. for S. Ireland May 1, 1799."   1799.
> Faces p. 108 of *Graphic Illustrations*, ii.
>
> 5¼ × 4¼ in.

" *Scene at a Banking house in* 1745."
" Hogarth pinxᵗ "   " Barlow sculpᵗ "   " Pub. for
S. Ireland May 1, 1799."   1799.
> Faces p. 117 of *Graphic Illustrations*, ii.
>
> 3¾ × 4½ in.

" *Broughton & Slack*"
" Hogarth pinxᵗ"   " Pub. for S. Ireland May 1.
1799 "   1799.
> Faces p. 120 of *Graphic Illustrations*, ii.

" *Happy Marriage.*"
" Hogarth pinxᵗ"   " T Ryder sculpᵗ "
" Pub. for S. Ireland May 1. 1799 "   1799.
> Four plates facing pp. 125, 127, 128, and 130 of *Graphic
> Illustrations*, ii.
>
> 6 × 4¾ in.

" *George ỹ II. his Queen, & family.*"
" Hogarth pinxᵗ."   " Ryder dirᵗ."
" Pub. for S. Ireland May 1. 1799."   1799.
> Faces 137 of *Graphic Illustrations*, ii
>
> 5¼ × 4⅝ in.

" *Mary Stuart, Queen of Scotland.*"
"W. Hogarth Pinx" "F. Bartolozzi R.A.
Sculp." "Published Jany 12th, 1803 by A Mol-
teno, Printseller, to Her Royal Highness the
Dutchess of York, 29, Pall Mall, London."

1803.

4¼ × 5¼ in.

*Bambridge on Trial for Murder by a Committee of
the House of Commons.*
[T. Cook after Hogarth.] 1803.

Under the title is, " Engraved by T. Cook from an
Original Painting by Wm Hogarth in the Possession of M^r
Ray," with the publication line " Published June 1st 1803,
by G. and J. Robinson, Paternoster Row, London."

20⅛ × 15¼ in.

The House of Commons.
" Engraved by A. Fogg, Historical Engraver
to his Royal Highness Prince Wm Frederick"
" London Published Novr. 1, 1803, by E. Harding, N° 100, Pall Mall." 1803.

" From an original Picture painted by Hogarth, and Sir
James Thornhill, in the Collection of Earl Onslow."

14¼ × 17¼ in.

"*Royal Masquerade Somerset House.*"
" Hogarth pinx " " T Cook Sc." 1804.

" Engraved by T. Cook from an Original Picture painted
by William Hogarth in the collection of Roger Palmer,
Esqr." Other impressions have " Published by Thos Cook
Engraver & Printer No 11 Hay Market Oct. 21, 1805."

20¼ × 15½ in.

" *The Modern Orpheus* "

" Design'd by W. Hogarth." [?] " Etch'd by
D Smith " " Publish'd as the Act directs by
Machell Stace Augt 24, 1807."   1807.

" From an Original Sketch, in the possession of the Marquis
of Bute." An impression faces p. 138 of *Genuine Works*, iii.
7¼ × 5¼ in.

"*Joseph Porter Esqr. of Mortlake.*"

" Hogarth pinx^t. " " T Cook sculp^t." " Published
by Longman, Hurst, Rees, & Orme, March 1st
1809."   1809.

In Nichols and Steevens's *Genuine Works*, ii. * 287, where
this appears, it is stated to be "From a Drawing taken from
the Original Picture in 1807."
3 1/16^3 × 4 in.

A Night Scene.

" Hogarth pinx."   " T. Cook sculp."   1809.

Published by Longman, etc., Oct. 1st, 1809: "From an
original Sketch communicated by Messrs Boydell." Faces
p. * 288 of *Genuine Works*, ii.
8 × 5 in.

" *A Musical Study* "

" Hogarth pinx."   " T. Cook sc."   " Published by
Longman, Hurst, Rees & Orme, Nov. 1st. 1809."
1809.

In Nichols and Steevens's *Genuine Works*, ii. * 288, where
this appears, it is said to be "from an original Painting in
the possession of Mr Nichols."
4⅛ × 5⅛ in.

" *The Painter's Room* "

" Hogarth pinx." " T. Cook sc." " Published by

Longman, Hurst, Rees & Orme, Nov. 1ˢᵗ.
1809."　　　　　　　　　　　　　　　1809.

In Nichols and Steevens's *Genuine Works*, ii. *288, where
this appears, it is said to be "From an Original Painting
in the possession of Mʳ Nichols."

5$\frac{7}{8}$ × 4$\frac{1}{2}$ in.

" *The Fire-Eater* "
" Hogarth delᵗ "　　" D. B. Pyet sculpᵗ "
" London Published as the Act directs by Robert
Scholey, 46 Paternoster Row."　　　　　1810.

First published in Clerk's *Hogarth*, ii. 69.

4$\frac{3}{5}$ × 3$\frac{1}{4}$ in.

The Bruiser, and Giants in Guildhall.
" Copied from Hogarth's original Sketches by J.
Mills."
" Published by J. Nichols & Cº. March. 1. 1817."
　　　　　　　　　　　　　　　　　　　1817.

Faces p. 163 of *Genuine Works*, iii.

4$\frac{7}{8}$ × 7$\frac{7}{8}$ in.

" 4 *Logger heads or B——e Triumphant* "
" W. Hogarth, delᵗ "　　" W. J. White, Scᵗ "
" Pubᵈ by W. J. White April 1, 1818."　　1818.

2 × 2$\frac{1}{4}$ in.

" *James Thompson* (sic), *Author of the Seasons.*"
" Executed in lithography by M. Gauci, Esqʳ,
from an Original Picture painted by W. Hogarth.
Published by the proprietor, Janʸ 1820, at the
Gothic Hall, Pall Mall."　　　　　　　1820.

There is another issue of this, dated May, in which the
face looks to the left instead of to the right.

"John Gay."

" Executed in lithography by M. Gauci, from the
original Picture painted by Hogarth. Published
by the Proprietor, 1820, at the Gothic Hall,
Pall Mall "   1820.

> There is another issue of this, dated June, which is larger,
> and without background.

Plates for Don Quixote.

[Hogarth.]   1822.

> Six plates of these, said to have been prepared for Lord
> Carteret's Spanish edition of 1738, were published in *Ho-
> garth's Works* by Baldwin and Cradock, 1822.   John
> Ireland (*Hogarth Illustrated*, iii. 301-319, 372) issued small
> copies of them, with two others. See also J. B. Nichols,
> *Anecdotes*, 1833, 203-8, 329. These prints are to be found
> in three states at the British Museum.
> $6\frac{1}{8} \times 8\frac{7}{8}$ in.

Handel.

" Engraved by C. Turner." " London. Published
April 4, 1821, by (*sic*) for the Proprietor, by C.
Turner, 50 Warren S^t, Fitzroy Square."

1821.

> " From an Original Painting by Hogarth." It is dedicated
> by the engraver " To The Noblemen, Directors & Patrons,
> of The Antient Music."
> $11\frac{7}{8} \times 14\frac{7}{8}$ in.

Feeding Poultry.

" Hogarth fecit." " Reading sc."

[1821.]

> Copy of an impression from a snuff-box lid.

The Lady's last Stake; or, Picquet; or, Virtue in Danger.

Hogarth. Engraved by Cheesman. Published May 8, 1825, by Hurst, Robinson and Co.

1825.

There is a proof before the writing in the British Museum. See also p. 158 n.

23¼ × 18⅑ in.

" Garrick in the Green Room."

" Painted by Hogarth." "Engraved in mezzotinto by Wm. Ward, Jan 1, 1829." 1829.

"From the original of the same size (23 in. by 19) by Hogarth, in the possession of the publisher, J. W. Southgate" (J. B. Nichols, *Anecdotes*, p. 314).

23 × 19 in.

Portraits of a Society of Artists that existed about 1730.

[Hogarth.] "Etched by Rich⁴ Sawyer."

"London. Published May 1, 1829, by W. B. Tiffin, 3 Hay Market." 1829.

Engraved from an original sketch in oil in the possession of the publisher. Contains portraits of Rysbrack, Gibbons, Laroon, Kent, Dahl, Vanderbank, and others.

13⅛ × 11¼ in.

" Chelsea Pensioners "

[Hogarth.] " Wᵐ. Jaˢ. Smith sculpᵗ." [1829 ?]

" From the Original Drawing by Hogarth."

" *View in S'. James's Park showing Rosamond's Pond* "

"W. Hogarth pinx :." " F. Ross lith :." "London. Published for the Proprietor, Dec'. 25th 1840, by W. & G. Smith, 24 Lisle Street, Leicester Square " 1840.

> " From the original Picture by William Hogarth, in the Collection of Henry Ralph Willett, Esq', of Merly House in the County of Dorset."
>
> 17½ × 11¼ in.

" *John Broughton, Prize Fighter.* "

"W. Hogarth." " F. Ross." " London. Published for the Proprietor March 25th. 1842, by W. and G. Smith, 24 Lisle Street, Leicester Square." 1842.

> " From the Original Picture (of the same size) by William Hogarth. In the Collection of Henry Ralph Willett, Esqre of Merly House, in the County of Dorset."
>
> 11¾ × 16¼ in.

" *Garrick and his Wife.* "

"W. Hogarth, Pinx'." " H. Bourne, Sculp'."

1855.

> " From the Picture in the Royal Collection." Appeared in the *Art Journal* for February, 1855.
>
> 7¼ × 9¾ in.

PRINTS OF UNCERTAIN DATE.

"*Abraham buys a Field of Ephron y* *Hittite for a Burying-place. Gen.* 23. 10."
  [Hogarth.]
    3⅓ × 5⅕ in.

Abraham, Agar, & Ishmael.
  " W. Hogarth F*."
    Underneath is "Genesis, Ch. 21. Verse II," and the Text.
    A Frontispiece to a Tract. A copy faces p. 106 of *Genuine
    Works*, iii.
      3¼ × 6 in.

Lord Aylmer's Coat of Arms.
  [Hogarth ?]

Ayala Arms, with Terms of the Four Seasons.
  [Hogarth ?]

Beggar Girl.
  [Hogarth.]

Bust of Belinda, etc.
    Impression from plate.

" The R': Honb^{le}: Gustavus Lord Visc^t Boyne, Baron of Stackallen [sic] etc. etc."

"W. Hogarth pinx."   " Ford fecit."

" Publish'd and Sold by Mich. Ford, Painter and Print Seller on Cork Hill."   " Price 5s. 5d."

> This is a whole-length mezzotint.   There is another with the inscription "W^m. Hogarth Pinxit."   "Andrew Miller fecit."   "price 2s. 8½d.   There is a small copy in *Graphic Illustrations*, i. 133.
>
> 13⅞ × 19½ in.

Mrs. Butler; or, Goldsmith's Hostess.

[Hogarth.]

> There is a print of this before letters in the British Museum.
>
> 5¼ × 6¼ in.

The Calves' Head Club.

[Hogarth.]

> Two plates. (1)   The true Effigies, &c., and (2) The Four Healths.

Chudleigh Arms.

> From plate.

Country Dance.

" W. Hogarth inven. & sculp."

" Printed for I. Johnson, Musical Instrument Maker, at ye Harp and Crown in Cheapside, London."

> 7¼ × 3 in.

The Crying Child, in the "Analysis of Beauty."

[Hogarth.]   [W. J. White sculp.]

> "From a Drawing in the Possession of M^r. Sheepshanks."
>
> 4¾ × 5 in.

"Sir Francis Dashwood Worshipping Venus."
[Hogarth.] [Platt sc.]

> There is a print of this before letters in the British Museum.
> $8\frac{1}{4}$ × 12 in.

Sir Robert Fagg and the Gipsey.
[Hogarth ?]

> $7\frac{1}{4}$ × 6 in.

A Flower Girl.
[Hogarth.]

> From a snuff-box lid.

De la Fontaine's Shopbill.
"W. Hogarth F^t."

> A Goldsmith's shop. Underneath the design is " Peter De
> la Fontaine Goldsmith At the Golden Cup in Litchfield
> Street Soho. Makes, & Sells all Sorts of Gold & Silver
> Plate, Swords, Rings, Jewells &c, at ye lowest prices." A
> Copy faces p. 102 of *Genuine Works*, iii.

Four Elements.
[Hogarth ?]

> Figures of Vulcan, Juno, Tellus, and Neptune.

A Ticket for a Burial; or Funeral Ticket.
[Hogarth ?]

The Gin Drinkers.
[Hogarth.]

The Great Seal of England.
[Hogarth ?]

> Said to have been engraved during Hogarth's apprentice-
> ship. There is a copy by S. Ireland. (See J. B. Nichols,
> *Anecdotes*, 1833, p. 295).

Griffin and Flag.
>> Crest, from plate.

Harrison's Tobacco Paper.
> [Hogarth ?]

Arms of John Holland, herald painter.
> [Hogarth ?]   A book-plate.

Mrs. Holt's Shop Bill.
> [Hogarth ?]
>> There is a copy by M. Ireland in *Graphic Illustrations*, i. 17.

Impression from a Tankard belonging to the Clare Market Artists Club.
> [Hogarth.]

Inside of an Opera House.
> [Hogarth ?]
>> A prison scene.

Kendal Arms.
>> (See p. 18).

Six Plates for King's " Pantheon."
> [Hogarth ?]
>> There are two states of these at the British Museum.

Lacroix's Shop Bill.
> [Hogarth ?]
>> A tobacconist's Bill.   The second state has a label at top.

Arms of Count Lippe Schauenberg.

Lumber Troop Arms.

> See J. B. Nichols, *Anecdotes*, 1833, 299.

Ticket for the London Infirmary.
[Hogarth.] "T. Ramsey Sculp^t. Lombard Street."

> With the Duke of Richmond's Arms as President and motto from Matt. xxv. v. 40. Certificates of attendance at Lecture in Surgery and Anatomy. The same plate with the background altered to the London Hospital was also used as a Certificate of Attendance to the Practice of Surgery.
>
> $9\frac{1}{4} \times 13\frac{1}{2}$ in.

Ticket for the London Infirmary.
" W. Hogarth inv." " C. Grignion sculp."

> Motto from Matt. xxv. v. 40.
>
> $9 \times 6\frac{1}{4}$ in.

Benefit Ticket for Laguerre.
" W. Hogarth Inv^t."

George Lambert's Book-plate.
[Hogarth ?]

> There is a copy in *Graphic Illustrations*, i. 115.

Lee's Shop Bill.
[Hogarth ?]

> A Tobacconist's Bill, copied at p. 12 of " Graphic Illustrations," i. and based on a *Midnight Modern Conversation*.
>
> $4 \times 3\frac{1}{8}$ in.

"*Daniel Lock Esqr.*"
　"Willm Hogarth Pinx^t.　"J. McArdell Fecit."
　"Price 1^s. 6."

> Lock was Architect of the Foundling. The *second* state
> has no price.
> 9⅞ × 11¼ in.

Arms of Paul de la Marie.

Marriage for Love.
　[Hogarth.]

> From a drawing belonging to Mr. Willett.
> 8½ × 6¼ in.

Dr. Cromwell Mortimer.
　[Hogarth.]　"Rigou sculp."

> With four lines from Pope. Dr. Mortimer was Secretary
> to the Royal Society.

Orator Henley.
　[Hogarth.]

The Oratory (*i.e.,* *Henley's*).
　[Hogarth ?]

Page Turner Arms.
　[Hogarth ?]

The Prevailing Candidate; or the Election carried
　by Bribery and the Devil.
　[Hogarth ?]

A Procession of Painters to the throne of Bacchus.
[Hogarth ?]

Radnor Arms.
[Hogarth ?]

Rape of the Smock. "W. H. Fecit."

Rutter Arms.

The Scotch Congregation.
[Hogarth?]

"*A Sea Officer* [Sir A. Schomberg]."
  "Wᵐ. Hogarth pinxit"   "C. Townley scᵗ"
  "Publish'd as the Act directs, by J. Flight, N°.
  400, Strand."

> "The Original Painted by William Hogarth Esq., in possession of Sir Alexander Schomberg Knight."
> 11 × 13 in.

Study of a Gentleman sitting in his Library.
[Hogarth ?]
  7½ × 5⅛ in.

Tatton Arms.

Tavern Bill for John Shaw, Ram Inn, Cirencester.
  "W. Hogarth fᵗ"

> A copy faces p. 102 of *Genuine Works*, iii. There is an impression of the original in the British Museum.
> 4¼ × 5½ in.

"*Tragedy and Comedy.*"

Two plates without writing.   There are also reduced copies,
3 × 5⅛ in.
8¼ × 14 in.

"*A Turk's Head.*"

Shop Bill for John Barker, Goldsmith, Lombard Street.
Copied in *Genuine Works*, iii. 102.
3⅞ × 2¼ in.

[*⁎* Copious as is the foregoing list, it is possible that there
may have been inadvertent omissions.   There have, however,
been some omissions of set purpose.   Such are the tickets
(Fielding's, Walker's, etc.), suspected to be forgeries by Powell
(J. B. Nichols, *Anecdotes*, 1833, p. 300), together with sundry
doubtful or unimportant shop-bills, and certain coats-of-arms.   It
has also been thought unnecessary to include two or three designs,
the grossness of which neither the ingenuity of the artist nor the
coarse taste of his time can reasonably be held to excuse.]

Received   *of*
5 Shillings being the first Payment for two large Prints
one representing Moses brought to Pharoahs Daughter:
the other St Paul before Felix, wch I Promise to deliver
when finish'd, on Receiving 5 Shillings more.

N.B. They will be Seven and Six Pence ?
each Print, after the time of Subscribing

BOYS PEEPING AT NATURE.

From Hogarth's Engraving.

A CATALOGUE OF PAINTINGS

BY, OR ATTRIBUTED TO,

HOGARTH.

[*** Hogarth's best-known works in oil are all in public and private galleries, or in the hands of well-known collectors. A large number are here added from Exhibition Catalogues and other sources ; but although some of them have been confidently ascribed to Hogarth, it is not impossible that they may have been wrongly attributed to his brush. In doubtful cases of this kind, only the personal inspection of experts could decide with certainty, as the traditional origin is often extremely well supported.]

Twelve Pictures of Hudibras.   1726 ?

    J. B. Nichols (*Anecdotes*, 1833, 349) enumerates four series of paintings connected with this subject :—

    (1) A set, since sold in November, 1872, at the death of Mrs. Sawbridge, the owner of East Haddon Hall, Northamptonshire, and supposed to have been painted by Hogarth subsequent to the issue of the large series of prints (p. 25).

    (2) A set belonging to John Ireland, and believed by him to be Hogarth's originals ; but thought by others to be by Heemskirk. These, in 1833, belonged to Mr. Twining.

    (3) A set on panel, belonging in 1833 to Mr. J. Britton,

bought by him at Southgate's as Hogarth's, but pronounced by Sir T. Lawrence to be by Vandergucht.

(4) A set belonging in 1816 to Mr. W. Davies, bookseller
in the Strand, and attributed to Lepipre, the illus-
trator of the *Hudibras* of 1710 referred to at p. 24,
under whom Hogarth is said to have studied.

The existence of so many sets is curious ; but as
the proprietor of East Haddon in 1726 was the
William Ward to whom Hogarth dedicated the
larger *Hudibras* series (p. 25), it is probable that
the East Haddon pictures were painted from the
prints by commission (cf. on this question a very
interesting article in the "Art Journal" for Sept.
1874).   Nichols adds (p. vii.) that Mr. H. R. Willett
had a painting corresponding to plate v.

The Wanstead Assembly. 1728.

Painted for Lord Castlemaine. Belonged in 1814-22 to Mr.
W. Long Wellesley.   Exhibited in 1875 by Mr. W. Carpenter (35 × 26¼ in.).

Scene in the "Beggar's Opera." 1728-9.

Belongs to Mr. Louis Huth (22 × 19 in.).

(Another.)

Belongs to the Duke of Leeds (29 × 24 in.).

(Another.)

Belongs to Mr. John Murray (28¼ × 22 in.).   There are
records of other versions.

Committee of the House of Commons examining Bam-bridge. 1729.

Painted for Sir Archibald Grant, of Monymusk ; and now
in the possession of the Earl of Carlisle (28 × 21 in.).
Horace Walpole also had an oil-sketch of this, which was
given to him by Hogarth.   It was sold in 1842 at his
sale for £8 5s. to Mr. T. S. Forman, M.P.

Governor Rogers and Family.   1729.

 Belonged to S. Ireland; bought at his sale in 1801 by Mr. Vernon.

Mr. Woodbridge and Captain Holland?   1729.

 Belonged to Lord Gwydir; in 1833 to General Phipps. (J. B. Nichols, *Anecdotes*, 1833, 374, where it is said to be inscribed "W. Hogarth pinx. 1729.")

Henry VIII. and Ann Boleyn.   c. 1729.

 Formerly in Vauxhall Gardens.

The Wollaston Family.   1730.

 Belongs to Mr. Frederick Wollaston (49 × 39¼ in.)

The Politician.   1730.

 Given by Hogarth to Theodosius Forrest. Bought by Count Woronzow at Mr. G. Watson Taylor's sale in 1832.

The House of Commons.   1730 ?

 By Hogarth and Sir James Thornhill. Now in the possession of the Earl of Onslow.

The Rich Family.   1728-31*

 "A family piece, consisting of four figures, for Mr. Rich, 1728" (Hogarth MS.). Belonged to Mr. Vernon; afterwards to Mr. John Jackson, R.A. (1817).

The Wood Family.   1728-31.*

 "Family of four figures,—Mr. Wood, 1728" (Hogarth MS.).

The Cock Family.   1728-31.*

 "A conversation of six figures,—Mr. Cock, Nov. 1728" (Hogarth MS.). This, in 1833, was in the possession of Mr. Abraham Langford, of Highgate (23 × 19 in.).

---

 * All these occur in a list by Hogarth of pictures remaining unfinished on the 1st January, 1731 (*Hogarth Illustrated*, iii., 23).

Lord Castlemaine and Family.   1729-31.*
> " An assembly of twenty-five figures, for Lord Castlemaine,
> August 28, 1729 " [Hogarth MS.].   Belonged in 1817 to
> Mr. Gwennap.

The Jones Family.   1730-31.*
> A family of five figures,—Mr. Jones, March, 1730 "
> (Hogarth MS.).

Mr. Kirkam (?)   1730-1.*
> "Single figure,—Mr. Kirkham, April 18, 1730 " (Hogarth
> MS.).

The Vernon Family.   1730-1.*
> "Family of nine,—Mr. Vernon, Feb. 27, 1730 " (Hogarth
> MS.).

Sir Robert Pye.   1730-1.*
> " Single figure,—Sir Robert Pye, Nov. 18, 1730 " (Hogarth
> MS.).   Belonged in 1833 to the Earl of Suffolk, at Charlton
> near Malmesbury.   It is dated at back " 1731."

Before and *After* (1).   1730-1.*
> " Two little pictures, called Before and After, for Mr·
> Thomson Dec. 7, 1730 " (Hogarth MS.).   These after-
> wards belonged to Lord Besborough.   In 1833 they were in
> the possession of Mr. H. R. Willett.   There is an oil sketch
> of " Before " in the Royal Collection.

Before and *After* (2).   1730.
> A different design.   Belonged in 1879 to Mr. Locker
> Lampson ; now the property of the Duke of Hamilton
> (17½ × 12¼ in.).

Mr. Sarmond (?)   1731.*
> "A head, for Mr. Sarmond, Jan. 12, 1730-31."

> * All these occur in a list by Hogarth of pictures remaining
> unfinished on the 1st January, 1731 (*Hogarth Illustrated*, iii., 23).

A Harlot's Progress (six pictures).   1731.

See pp. 41-50. Five were burnt at Fonthill in 1755; the sixth (Picture 2), which once belonged to Lord Charlemont now belongs to the Earl of Wemyss. Lord Rosebery has also two scenes which had formed part of the Novar Collection. There are copies by J. Collett. (See also J. B. Nichols, *Anecdotes*, 1833, 353 n.)

Scene in the "Indian Emperor; or, Conquest of Mexico."   1731.

Formerly belonged to the Earl of Upper Ossory; now at Holland House.

Southwark Fair.   1733.

Exhibited in 1885 by the Trustees of the Duke of Newcastle (59 × 47½ in.).

Sarah Malcolm (1).   1733.

Belonged to Horace Walpole; afterwards to Mr. J. H. Anderdon. (17 × 20½ in.).

Sarah Malcolm (2).

A full-length. Belonged in 1793 to Josiah Boydell; in 1833 to the Earl of Mulgrave.

A Modern Midnight Conversation.   1733.

There are several copies of this. One (48 × 36 in.) was exhibited at Richmond by Mr. H. C. Bohn in 1881. It had belonged to Lord Chesterfield (*Athenæum*, Aug. 13). Another (35 × 29 in.) was shewn at the Guelph Exhibition in 1891 by Mrs Morrison of Basildon. There is also a version at Lord Leconfield's, at Petworth. See also letter from Mr. J. Wade in *Athenæum* for Sep. 24, 1881, as to another apparent version (33 × 26 in.).

A Rake's Progress (eight pictures). 1735.

See pp. 51-57. Belonged to Alderman Beckford; then to Col. Fullerton; now in the Soane Museum. Mrs. Hogarth had an oil sketch of the sixth picture; and Sir Clare Ford exhibited in 1888 a version (29 × 24 in.) of the "Tavern Scene" (III.), which had been painted for his great-great-grandfather, Mr. Benjamin Booth.

The Distressed Poet. 1735.

See p. 79. Given by the artist to Mrs. Draper, the Queen's midwife, at whose death it was bought for £5 5s. by a solicitor named Ward. Lord Grosvenor bought it at Ward's death for 14 guineas. It is now in the collection of the Duke of Westminster (29¼ × 21¼ in.).

The Western Family. c. 1735.

Belonged in 1833 to Lord Western.

The Pool of Bethesda. 1736.

Belongs to St. Bartholomew's Hospital (20 ft. 3 in. × 13 ft. 8 in.).

The Good Samaritan. 1736.

Belongs to St. Bartholomew's Hospital (16 ft. 9 in. × 13 ft. 8 in.).

The Sleeping Congregation. 1736.

See p. 68. Belonged to Sir Edward Walpole; afterwards to J. Follett, Esq. of the Temple; sold in 1807 for £20 9s. with Mr. Jackson's collection, and then by Mr. Woolner R. A. in 1875 to Messrs. Agnew for £94 10s. Exhibited in 1888 by Mr. R. Rankin (17½ × 21¼ in.).

The Strolling Actresses. 1738.

See p. 73. Belonged to Mr. Wood, of Littleton, where it was burnt in 1874.

Four Times of the Day.　　　　　　　　　1738.

See pp. 71-3. "Night" and "Morning" belong to the
Hursley Park Trustees. They are at present in the keeping of Lady Heathcote. "Noon" and "Evening" originally belonged to the Duke of Ancaster ; in 1833 they were
in possession of Lord Gwydir (24 × 29 in.). A sketch for
"Morning," purporting to have been given by Hogarth to
his friend Mr. Birch, was sold in 1827.

Captain Coram.　　　　　　　　　　　1739.

See. p. 76. In the Foundling Hospital.

Benjamin Hoadly, M.D.　　　　　　　　1740.

This, signed and dated, was for sale at Messrs. Colnaghi's in
March, 1891. It is now in the National Gallery of Ireland.

Monamy showing a Picture.　　　　　*c.* 1740.

Belonged to Mr. Thomas Walker, and was presented to
Horace Walpole by Mr. Richard Bull. The Earl of
Derby, to whom it now belongs, gave 20 guineas for it
at Walpole's sale in 1842. (24 × 19 in.) The sea-piece
in the picture is by Monamy himself.

The Enraged Musician.　　　　　　　　1741.

See p. 80. An oil sketch of this belonged to S. Ireland.
In 1833 it was in the possession of Mrs. Chambers Hall
of Southampton.

Martin Folkes, Esq., President R.S.　　　1741.

Belongs to the Royal Society (24 × 29 in.).

Taste in High Life.　　　　　　　　　1742.

Painted for Miss Edwardes (see p. 82). Belonged in 1814
to Mr. Birch of Spring Gardens.

Bishop Hoadly.　　　　　　　　　　　1743.

Belonged in 1833 to Mr. Serjeant D'Oyly.

Bishop Hoadly.

> By Hogarth and Mrs. Hoadly. This is in the National
> Portrait Gallery (40 × 50 in.).

Mrs. Hoadly.   1743.

> Belonged in 1833 to Serjeant D'Oyly.

Chancellor Hoadly.   1743.

> Belonged in 1782 to Mrs. Hoadly.

Mrs. Elizabeth Hoadly.   1743.

> Wife of Dr. Benjamin Hoadly.   Exhibited in 1879 by Mr.
> Ernest Gye.

Archbishop Herring.   1745.

> Belonged in 1833 to Mr. George Stone of Lombard Street.
> Exhibited in 1876 by the Archbishop of York.   There is
> a copy at Lambeth Palace, which was exhibited at South
> Kensington in 1867 by the Archbishop of Canterbury
> (39 × 49 in.).

Marriage A-la-Mode (Six pictures).   1745.

> See p. 90. Bought of the artist by Mr. Lane of Hillingdon,
> near Uxbridge.   Bequeathed by him to Colonel Cawthorne,
> who sold them in 1797 to Mr. Angerstein, with whose
> collection they were purchased in 1824 by the nation.
> They are now in the National Gallery (35 × 27 in.)

Hogarth with Pug Dog.   1745.

> See p. 184. Bought at Mrs. Hogarth's sale in 1790 by Mr.
> Angerstein, with whose collection it was purchased by
> Parliament in 1824 (27 × 35 in.).

Garrick as Richard III.   1746.

> See p. 117. Bought of the artist by Mr. Duncombe of
> Duncombe Park, in Yorkshire.   It now belongs to his
> descendant, the Earl of Feversham (96 × 74½ in.).

Simon Fraser, Lord Lovat.   1746.

See p. 119. Purchased by the Trustees of the National Portrait Gallery in June 1866 (16 × 25¼ in.).

(Another).

Was in 1879 in possession of Mr. H. Graves of Pall Mall.

Mary Hogarth.   1746.

Bequeathed to the National Gallery in 1861 by Mr. Richard Frankum, and dated "1746" (8¼ × 11 in.).

Saint George's Hospital (with Count Solacio on horseback).   1746.

The horse is by Sartorius. Belongs to St. George's Hospital, Hyde Park.

Paul before Felix.   1748.

See p. 134. Belongs to the Honourable Society of Lincoln's Inn.

The Gate of Calais.   1749.

See p. 125. Bought from the painter by the Earl of Charlemont. Until recently, it formed part of the Bolckow collection. Messrs. Agnew purchased it in May 1891 for 2,450 guineas. It is now in the collection of the Duke of Westminster (37½ × 31 in.).

The March to Finchley.   1750.

See p. 129. In the Foundling Hospital.

Moses brought to Pharaoh's Daughter.   1752.

See p. 134. In the Foundling Hospital.

False Perspective Exemplified.   1754.

Belonged to S. Ireland.

Four Pictures of an Election.   1755.

See p. 147. Belonged to Garrick ; now in Sir John Soane's Museum.

Altar-Piece for St. Mary Redcliffe, Bristol.   1756.

See p. 154.   To the right is *The Sealing of the Sepulchre;* to the left, *The Three Maries visiting the Sepulchre;* the centre piece represents *The Ascension.*   The pictures are now in the possession of the Fine Arts Academy at Clifton.

George II. and Family.   1757?

Belonged to S. Ireland, at whose sale in 1811 it was bought by Mr. Vernon; bought again 5 April, 1821, at Gwennap's sale by Colnaghi.   Belonged in 1833 to Mr. H. R. Willett.

David Garrick and his Wife.   1757.

See p. 117.   At Mrs. Garrick's sale in 1823 this picture was bought for £75 11s. by Mr. Edward Hawke Locker of Greenwich Hospital, who sold it to George IV.   It is now in the Royal Collection at Windsor (39 × 50 in.).

Hogarth painting the Comic Muse.   1758.

Bought by Lord Camden from Mrs. Hogarth; subsequently in the Willett collection; purchased by the Trustees of the National Portrait Gallery in June, 1869 (14¼ × 15¼ in.).

The Lady's Last Stake; or Picquet; or Virtue in Danger.

See p. 158.   Bought by Lord Charlemont from the artist for £100.   It now belongs to Mr. Louis Huth (41 × 35¼ in.).

Sigismunda.   1759.

See p. 159.   Bought at Mrs. Hogarth's sale in 1790 for 56 guineas; sold in July 1807 for 400 guineas; bequeathed to the National Gallery in 1879 by Mr. J. H. Anderdon (49¼ × 39 in.).   An oil sketch of *Sigismunda,* belonging to S. Ireland, was sold at Christie's in 1797 for £5 5s. (See *Sigismunda* (1) and (2) in the "Catalogue of Prints," pp. 302 and 305.)

William Hogarth.   1761 ?

(See p. 185).   With a pipe.   Belonged in 1825 to the Duke
of Bedford.   At the back of the picture is,—" This
portrait of Mr Hogarth was made me a present of by him
in friendly return for a Tobacco Box I gave him.   S^m
Graves, Chiswick, 29th Decr. 1761."

PAINTINGS OF UNCERTAIN DATE.

An Auction of Pictures.
> Bought of Mr. W. B. Tiffin by Francis Douce, the antiquary, to whom it belonged in 1833.

The Dance in the " Analysis of Beauty."
> Bought by Mr. Vernon at S. Ireland's sale. In 1833 it belonged to Mr. W. B. Tiffin of the Strand.

Dr. Arnold of Ashby Lodge.
> In the Fitzwilliam Museum at Cambridge (27 × 35 in.).

Miss Arnold of Ashby Lodge.
> In the Fitzwilliam Museum at Cambridge (27 × 35 in.).

Ashby Lodge, in Leicestershire.
> In the Fitzwilliam Museum at Cambridge (47 × 32 in.).

A View of Bethlehem Hospital.
> Exhibited 1814; in the possession of Mr. Jones.

The Betts Family.
> Belonged to Mr. Matthew Raper, of Wimpole Street.

Lord Bolingbroke.
> Sold at Gwennap's sale, 5 April, 1821.

Boy with a Kite.

> Belongs to the Duke of Westminster ($11\frac{1}{2}$ × 14 in.)

Viscount Boyne.

> Belonged to Mr. Bellamy, Mr. Thomas Dimsdale, and in 1833 to Mr. Woodburn. Exhibited in 1891 by Mr. M. H. Colnaghi (14 × $20\frac{1}{4}$ in.). Mr. Willett had also a repetition of it. A little picture containing among others a portrait of Lord Boyne, and said to be by Hogarth, was exhibited at South Kensington in 1867.

A Breakfast Piece.

> Represents the Strode Family. Belonged in 1833 to Mr William Finch, and now in the National Gallery (36 × 34 in.)

Mr. Bridgeman, the Gardener?

> Sold at Gwennap's sale, 5 April, 1821.

Mr. Bullock the Comedian.

> Belonged in 1833 to Mr. Charles Mathews, to whom it was presented by Mr. H. R. Willett.

A Butcher's Shop (with Slack fighting).

> Belonged in 1833 to the Marquis of Exeter.

Mrs. Butler; or, Goldsmith's Hostess.

> Belonged to Mr. Robert Graves; now in the possession of Mr. Henry Graves of Pall Mall.

Lady Byron.

> At Lowther Castle (Earl of Lonsdale's), where are also portraits of Miss and Master Byron.

Outskirts of a Camp.

> A study sold at Gwennap's sale, 5 April, 1821.

Elizabeth Canning.

> Belonged in 1833 to the Earl of Mulgrave.

Lord Charlemont.

Belonged to S. Ireland. Sold at Gwennap's sale, 5 April, 1821.

Clare Market.

Belonged to Mr. Browning, formerly of King's College, Cambridge.

The Coffee-House Politicians.

Belonged in 1827 to Rev. Mr. Williams of Hendon.

Thomas Combes of Dorsetshire.

A Conversation.

"Another of two [figures],—Mr. Cooper" (Hogarth MS.)

Captain Coram.

Exhibited in 1891 by the Duke of Sutherland (27½ × 35 in.)

The Country in the Olden Time.

Belonged in 1879 to Mr. Ayscough Fawkes.

The Earl of Coventry and his wife (Maria Gunning).

Exhibited in 1891 by the Earl of Coventry (29 × 48 in.).

Falstaff examining his Recruits.

This was bought by Garrick at Lord Exeter's sale in 1777 At Mrs. Garrick's death it passed to Mr. Cord. It was recently in the Bolckow Collection, which was dispersed in May, 1891 (23 × 19¼ in.).

Mrs. Charlton the younger.

Exhibited in 1888 by Mrs. Edgar (28 × 30 in.).

The Duke of Cumberland, K.G., when a Boy.

Belonged to Mr. W. J. Broderip, with whose collection it was sold in 1859. Exhibited in 1888 by Sir Charles Tennant, Bart. (13¼ × 17½ in.).

Danae.

Bought of Hogarth by the Duke of Ancaster for £63 (Hogarth MS.). See also Walpole's *Anecdotes.*

Sir Francis Dashwood worshipping Venus.

In 1833 this was in the room of the Dilettanti Society at the Thatched House Tavern.

Debates on Palmistry.

A Sketch. Belonged to S. Ireland; then to Sir G. Beaumont.

M^rs^*. Desauliers* (Wife of Maj. Gen. Desaguliers).

Exhibited in 1891 by Mr. W. G. Cartwright (27 × 27 in. circular).

Head of Diana.

Belonged in 1794 to S. Ireland.

The Devonshire Family.

Exhibited in 1891 by tho Duke of Devonshire (49¼ × 39¼ in.).

William 5th Duke of Devonshire.

Exhibited in 1878 by Lord Chesham (24 × 29¼ in.).

A Drunken Party.

Belonged, in 1833, to Viscount Boyne.

Female Curiosity.

Belonged to S. Ireland.

Head of a Female Moor.

Belonged to S. Ireland; bought at his sale in 1801, by Mr. Vernon.

Lavinia Fenton as " Polly Peachum."

> Bought at Samuel Ireland's sale in 1801 by Mr. Sequier. Afterwards in the collection of Mr. George Watson. Purchased for the National Gallery from Sir Philip Miles' collection in 1884 for 800 guineas (23 × 29 in. oval).

Lavinia Fenton, Duchess of Bolton.

> Exhibited in 1888 by Mr. C. Brinsley Marley (19¼ × 23½ in.).

A Village Fête.

> Belonged, in 1833, to Mr. James West of Bryanston Square.

Figg, the prize-fighter.

> Belonged to S. Ireland ; bought in 1801 by Mr. Vernon.

Florizel and Perdita.

> Belonged in 1833 to Mr. H. R. Willett.

The Fountaine Family.

> Exhibited in 1880 by Mr. A. C. Fountaine (23 × 18 in.).

Garrick in the Green Room.

> Exhibited in 1880 by Mr. Samuel Addington (24 × 18 in.).

Mrs Garrick.

> Exhibited in 1891 by Dr. Edward Hamilton (11¼ × 13½ in.).

Garrick's Villa.

John Gay.

> Bought at Gwennap's sale, 5 April 1821 by Mr. Sinclair.

Gentleman unknown.

> Belonged in 1833 to Mr. J. B. Nichols.

James Gibbs, Architect.

> Belongs to the Church of St. Martin's-in-the-Fields.

Girl with a Cage.

Belonged to Mr. G. Watson Taylor, sold at his sale in 1832 (12 × 15 in.).

The Graham Family.

Belonged in 1804-14 to " M' Graham of Chelsea ; " subsequently to Mr. Seguier and Mr. G. Watson Taylor. Now in the possession of the Earl of Normanton (71 × 63½ in.).

Hagar and Ishmael.

Bought at S. Ireland's sale in 1801 by Mr. Cummings.

Honble. J. Hamilton.

Exhibited in 1875 by the Earl of Abercorn (24 × 29 in.).

Hammond, Hogarth, etc.

A Conversation. At Stisted Hall, Essex, in 1833.

Handel.

Belonged in 1833 to Mr. Peacock of Marylebone Street (17¼ × 21 in.).

The Happy Marriage.

Bought at Mrs. Garrick's sale in 1832 by Mr. T. S. Forman (34 × 25 in.).

Sir C. Hawkins.

Belongs to the Royal College of Surgeons.

Sir George Hay, LL.D. 1760.

Sold, in 1823, at Mrs. Garrick's sale, to Mr. Dawkins Pennant.

Scene in a Hayfield.

Part of a landscape by Lambert. Belonged in 1833 to Mr. A. Langford of Highgate.

William Hogarth.

    Exhibited in 1891 by the Honble. Mrs. Maxwell Scott
(24 × 30 in. oval).

Mrs Hogarth.

    Belonged to Mr. H. R. Willett ; exhibited in 1888 by Mr.
H. Bingham Mildmay (27¼ × 35 in.).

Mary and Ann Hogarth.

    These belonged to J. B. Nichols, and are now in the
possession of Mr. R. C. Nichols of 6 Essex Place, Hyde
Park.

Ann Hogarth.

    Exhibited in 1891 by Miss Reid (24 × 30 in.).

Hogarth's five Servants.

    These belonged in 1817 to Mr. William Collins of Greenwich.

Lord Holland.

    Belonged to Mr. S. Ireland. Exhibited in 1891 by the
Earl of Ilchester (19 × 23½ in.).

Bishop Hooper.

    In Christ Church Hall, Oxford.

W. Huggins, Esq.

J. Jacobson, Esq.

    Sold in 1832 at Mr. G. Watson Taylor's sale.

The Jeffreys Family.

    Belonged in 1833 to the Rev. Mr. Jeffreys of Barnes.

William Jones, Esq.

    Father of Sir W. Jones, the Orientalist. Exhibited in 1882
by the Earl of Macclesfield (39 × 49 in.).

A Lady at a Tea-Table.

Exhibited in 1888 by Mr. John Cleland (25 × 30 in.).

A Lady Unknown.

Belonged to John Ireland ; in 1833 the property of Mr. J. B. Nichols.

Portrait of a Lady.

Exhibited in 1877 by Mr. J. B. Gibson Craig (37 × 48 in.).

Portrait of a Lady.

Exhibited in 1888 by Mr. S. N. Castle (28½ × 34½ in.).

Sir Charles Kemeys-Tynte, Bart.

Exhibited in 1888 by Colonel Kemeys-Tynte (39½ × 49 in.).

Mr. George Lambert.

Belonged in 1782 to S. Ireland.

A Landscape.

Exhibited in 1882 by the Rev. F. K. Harford (10½ × 7¼ in.). See *Notes and Queries* for 28 Jan. 1882.

The Laughing Audience.

Belonged in 1814 to R. B. Sheridan ; subsequently to Mr. G. Watson Taylor. Sold in 1848 at Mr. Richard Sanderson's sale. An original oil-sketch (16 × 19¼ in.) of the beau and orange-girl for this picture belonged in 1879 to Mr. W. S. Harvey of Stockwell.

Mrs Mary Lewis.

Daniel Lock, Esq ; F.S.A.

Belonged to Mr. Bellotti ; in 1832 the property of Mr. Peacock of Mary-le-bone Street.

George, 2nd Earl of Macclesfield.

Exhibited in 1882 by the Earl of Macclesfield (39 × 49 in.).

A View of the Mall, St. James's Park.

In the Royal Collection (50 × 40 in.).

Mr Samuel Martin.

Left by Hogarth in his will to Mr. Martin.

Mary, Queen of Scots.

Originally a portrait of Mrs. Cholmondeley.   Belonged to
Mr. Edwards of Beaufort Buildings.

Masquerade at Somerset House.

Belonged to Mr. Palmer, then to his sister, Mrs. Palmer.

Ill Effects of Masquerades.

Belonged to Mr. Peacock of Mary-le-bone Street (15 × 12 in.)

The Matthias Family.

Belonged in 1817 to Mr. T. J. Matthias (29 × 24 in.)

The Mayor of Garratt.

Mr Moses Mendez.

Belonged in 1817 to Mr. Coram of Lyon's Inn.

The Montague Family.

"Another [i.e. a family] of five—Duke of Montague"
(Hogarth MS.).

Mr Mossop as " Bajazet."

Belonged to Hogarth's godson, J. Richards, R.A.; then
to Mr. Robert Graves.   Bought in 1825 at Baker's sale,
by Mr. T. S. Forman, of Pall Mall.

A Musical Party.

Sold in Mr. W. Richardson's sale, 30 June, 1813.   Contains
portraits of the Duke of Bolton, Miss Fenton, etc.

Music Piece.

> Exhibited in 1888 by the Earl by Essex (29 × 24 in.).

A Musical Study.

> Belonged in 1833 to Miss Nicholls of Highbury Place. Exhibited in 1889 by Mrs. Gough Nichols (22 × 18½ in.).

Henry, Duke of Newcastle, K.G.

> Exhibited in 1888 by John Pender, Esq. (24 × 29½ in.).

Orator Henley christening a Child.

> Belonged to S. Ireland; now in the British Museum, who obtained it with the Payne Knight Collection (9½ × 13 in.).

Oysters ; or, St. James's Day.

> Belonged in 1833 to Mr. G. Weller. Includes portraits of the Duke of Wharton, Bab Selby, Spiller the player, Figg, Garth, Betterton, etc.

The Painter's Room.

> Belonged to S. Ireland.

The Painting Room.

> Belonged to Mr. Jennings of Chelsea : sold at Gwennap's sale, 1821. Represents Hogarth painting Lady Thornhill.

John Palmer, Esq.

> Belonged in 1833 to Mr. Thomas Whaley of Ecton, Northamptonshire.

Paviour's Sign (Two Designs).

> Belonged to S. Ireland, and bought at his sale in 1811 by Mr. Vernon.

Thomas Pellett, M.D.

> Bought at Gwennap's sale in 1821 by Mr. Penny.

Lady Pembroke.

Mr. Pine the Engraver.

Belonged to Mr. Ranby the Surgeon.

Miss Pine.

Belonged to John Ireland; bought at his sale by Mr. Spackman.

Portrait Group.

Includes portraits of Henry and Stephen Fox, Lord Hervey Winnington and two others. Exhibited in 1889 by the Earl of Ilchester (50½ × 33½ in.).

Joseph Porter, Esq. ; of Mortlake.   Before 1749.

Belonged in 1814 to the Marquis of Stafford.

The Porten Family.

Exhibited by Rev. Thos. Burningham (39 × 49 in.).

Mr. Prior, the Poet.

Belonged in 1833 to Mr. J. B. Nichols.   Probably a book-seller's sign.

James Quin, the Actor.

Belonged in 1817 to Mr. Gwennap; afterwards to Charles Mathews. Exhibited in 1885 by the Marquis Townsend (24 × 29 in.).

Miss Ray (or Reay).

Belonged to Mr. Munro, at whose sale in 1867 it passed to Mr. Addington. It now belongs to Mr F. B. Henson (21½ × 29½ in.).

Michael Rysbrack, the Sculptor.

Exhibited in 1888 by Mr. Edward Draper (24 × 28¼ in.).

Miss Rich.

Belonged to Mr. John Heywood; in 1867 in possession of Mr. J. Heywood Hawkins (14 × 16 in.).

Mr. Rich, Mr. Cock, etc.
Belonged in 1833 to Mr. Langford of Highgate (23 × 18 in).

Samuel Richardson.
Exhibited in 1889 by Sir John Neeld, Bart. (7 × 9 in.).

Satan, Sin and Death.
Belonged to Mrs. Garrick; bought at her sale in 1823 by Mr. J. S. Forman of Pall Mall.

Mrs. Salter of the Charter House.
Belonged to S. Ireland; brought at his sale by Mr. Vernon.

Our Saviour.
Belonged to Theodosius Forrest; in 1784 to his executor Mr. Peter Coxe.

The Savoyard Girl.
Sold at Mr. G. Watson Taylor's sale in 1832.

Scene in Goodman Fields Theatre.
Belonged in 1833 to Mr. Peacock of Mary-le-bone Street (22¼ × 14¼ in.)

Scene in the Suspicious Husband.
Belonged in 1782 to Mrs. Hoadly.

The Shrimp Girl.
Sold at Mrs. Hogarth's sale in April 1790, and again in 1832 at the sale of the collection of Mr. George Watson Taylor. It was purchased for the National Gallery from Sir Philip Miles's collection in 1884 (20 × 25 in.).

View in St. James's Park; or, Rosamond's Pond.
Belonged to S. Ireland; afterwards to Messrs. Gwennap, Colnaghi, and Willett. Now in the possession of Louisa Lady Ashburton (60¼ × 39¼ in.).

Captain Sir A. Schomberg.

> Exhibited in 1891 by General G. A. Schomberg.

The Sewell Family.

> Belonged to Dr. Clarke the Traveller (22¼ × 19½ in.).

Sleeping Child.

> Belonged, in 1782, to Dr. Lort.

View of Spencer House.

> Exhibited in 1889 by Earl Spencer (50 × 31 in.).

A Statuary's Shop.

> Belonged, in 1833, to Mr. Edward Rudge.

The Staymaker.

> Belonged to S. Ireland; in 1833 to Mr. W. B. Tiffin of the Strand.

Death of Sir Philip Sidney.

> Bought at Gwennap's sale in 1821 by Mr. Penny.

A Society of Artists.

> Belonged to the Boydells; afterwards to Hurst, Robinson & Co.; then to Mr. W. B. Tiffin of the Strand. In 1833 it belonged to Mr. Chambers Hall of Southampton.

Thomson the Poet.

> Belonged, in 1832, to Mr. C. Rossi.

Thomson the Poet (another).

> Belonged, in 1821, to Mr. Sinclair.

Sir James Thornhill.

Lady Thornhill.

> Belongs to Lord St. Oswald.

Mr John Thornhill.

The Thornhill Family (1).
Belonged to Mr. J. Andrews; bought at his sale by Mr. Donovan (27 × 22 in.).

The Thornhill Family (2).
Exhibited in 1889 by Mrs. Wollaston (36 × 29 in.).

The Vane Family.
Belonged, in 1882, to Lord Harry Vane, Bart. (29 × 24 in.).

View of the Treasury Garden.
Sold at Gwennap's sale in 1821.

View in a Village near London.
Belonged in 1817 to Mr. Davies of the Strand.

Sir Edward Walpole.
Belonged to his brother, Horace Walpole.

Horace Walpole.
Exhibited in 1891 by Mr. H. Spencer Walpole (27¼ × 35 in.)

Wanstead Family Group.
Belonged, in 1822, to Mr. W. Long Wellesley.

Mr Justice Welch.
Belonged to Mr. G. M. Stainforth of Berkeley Square.

Mr Western of Clare Hall.
Belonged to the Rev. W. Cole of Milton.

The Misses Weston.
Exhibited in 1891 by Mr. Horace A. Helyer (50 × 40 in.).

Mr Windham.

Belonged to S. Ireland ; bought at his sale, in 1801, by Mr. Vernon.

Mrs Woffington.

Belonged to Mr. Addington ; now in the possession of Mr. F. B. Henson (28 × 36 in.).

Mrs. Woffington.

Belongs to the Marquis of Lansdowne (23¼ × 27¼ in.).

Mrs Woffington.

Exhibited in 1888 by Sir Charles Tennant, Bart. (24¼ × 29½ in.).

ADDENDA.

Mrs Clive.

Belongs to Lord St. Oswald.

Broughton the Prize-fighter.

Exhibited in 1867 by Mr. Willett L. Adye (12 × 17½ in.). There is a version at Lowther Castle.

Captain Lord George Graham.

Exhibited in 1891 by the Duke of Montrose.

Street Scene in a French Town.

Belongs to Mr. John Reid (54 × 42 in.).

INDEX.

[N.B.— Titles of Books are in *inverted commas*; titles of Prints and Pictures in *italics*.]

A A

CHISWICK PRESS : —C. WHITTINGHAM AND CO., TOOKS COURT, CHANCERY LANE.

www.ingramcontent.com/pod-product-compliance
Lightning Source LLC
Chambersburg PA
CBHW031046110726
47900CB00003B/829